THE CASE
~ OF THE ~
MISSING
COBRAS
~ A NOVEL ~

KATHY KAYE

The Case of the Missing Cobras

Library of Congress Catalog Card Number: 2010911094

ISBN 1453725067
ISBN 13 9781453725061

Acknowledgments

I am indebted to many individuals who gave their time and expertise, and otherwise provided crucial background information, during the writing of this book. Foremost is my brother-in-law, Chris Mohrman, a conservation police officer for the state of Illinois, who described several encounters with exotic snakes—and snake collectors—not all of which went well. Some of Chris's stories have made their way into this book.

I also wish to thank Frank Slavens, former curator of reptiles at Woodland Park Zoo in Seattle, who spent hours on the telephone answering questions about snake habitat and behavior, specifically about the king cobra.

Also gracious with his time was Ken Goddard, a novelist himself and director of the U.S. Fish and Wildlife Service's state-of-the-art forensics lab in Ashland, Oregon. Over the course of a morning, Ken gave me an insider's view of Fish and Wildlife's CSI operations, including an unfortunately well-stocked evidence room.

Countless friends, family members, co-workers, and physicians I've worked with over the years also deserve mention for their interest and support, as do members of my stellar writing group, The Woodshed Writers Guild. This group includes Rick Paul, Maurice Robkin, Dave Wilma, T. S. Loomis, and Janet Wittig, who critically reviewed the novel in its entirety, several times. To Heidi Hough in Chicago and Dr. Jacob Heller in Seattle, a special thank-you for your expert reviews of chapter 1; to Noel Lakey, who provided fascinating information about the name and image of the cobra used by the U.S. military; to my sister, Maggie, and members of my extended family, including Diane, Liz, Travis, and

Jessica, thank you for *your* expert reviews; to Phyllis, Camille, Lees, Susan, Mary, Debora, Marta, Maureen, Marilyn, Vicki, Holly, Melissa, and many others, thank you for your support.

I also would like to acknowledge the officers and special agents in understaffed wildlife law enforcement departments who work tirelessly on behalf of animals, for our benefit. Any gaffes in their work procedures and undercover operations are strictly my own.

Kathy Kaye
Shoreline,Washington

To my parents, Barbara and Edward Kaye.
And to Nancy, for your many years of encouragement and support.

THE CASE

~ OF THE ~

MISSING
COBRAS

I

Dennis Walker rose slowly to avoid startling the cobra. He stepped forward, snake sticks in hand, their prongs covered in cotton rags to lessen trauma to the reptile.

Too close.

The sixteen-foot-long snake swung away from the baseboard, forming an S curve with its upper body. It faced him dead-on, its tongue darting in and out. Walker stopped, bringing one of the sticks in front of his shin.

And waited.

The snake maintained its position.

Walker waited some more.

Finally, he opened the stick's prongs and again moved toward the cobra, closing the distance to within five feet.

The snake lifted its head and eyed him squarely.

Walker stopped once more, puzzled. He'd been giving this snake a routine checkup every six months for ten years. And the reptile knew him. He closed the prongs and rested the tip on his shoe. He'd have to wait until the cobra assumed a less aggressive position.

He glanced over at the untouched scotch and soda on his desk, taking on water from the ice cubes, his third drink of the evening.

Or was it the fourth?

He looked back at the cobra.

How long is this gonna take?

Walker glanced at the clock—11:22 p.m.

He looked around the room, taking in the framed newspaper articles about himself and his collection that filled one wall. All around him snake eyes watched from the hundred-plus terrariums that held the most venomous species in the world.

He heard a bedroom door close softly at one end of the hallway; his twelve-year-old son, Nick, finally going to bed. He'd never get him up in the morning. Apparently, his admonition about getting an early start for Denver had gone unheeded, lost in preteen concerns of music and girls.

Walker fingered his cell phone in his breast pocket and looked back at the snake. *Concentrate*, he reminded himself. *Don't make the same mistake twice.*

The cobra remained in place, its head and neck swaying slightly.

No hood. Good sign.

He met the snake's eyes. And held its gaze.

An old-timer once told him never to look a cobra in the eye, but to focus elsewhere on its body. The hypnotic gaze locks you into a trance, he said, and the swaying relaxes frightened prey. Humans included.

Walker didn't believe any of that.

He yawned, realizing how tired he was. But he knew the snake could hold its position for hours.

Suddenly, the cobra lowered itself and moved back to the safety of the wall, its body sliding slightly on the white linoleum floor. Walker gave it time to recover. Then slowly, carefully, he moved closer, and in one practiced move placed a stick behind its head.

Swiftly, the back end of the snake spun around toward his legs. Walker met it with the sole of his shoe and clamped down softly in this oft-rehearsed dance. He placed the other stick over the snake's slender three-inch girth in the middle of its body. He felt pressure on the sticks as the cobra tried to raise its head.

"Easy, easy."

Walker began the inspection, scanning the snake's black-hued back for signs of parasites.

"Now the hard part."

He waited until he felt less resistance and then repositioned one stick further down its back. Alternating between firm and loose grips, he turned the snake over and quickly looked at the reptile's underside, then turned it over again, a difficult maneuver for one person.

"We're done."

But Walker felt more resistance and maintained his hold because of it. "Flipping" the snake always made it angry, and this part—the waiting—was his least favorite ritual. He wondered if he should call out for his son to help him get the snake back in its terrarium.

"Nick!"

No response.

He's got those damn earphones in again.

"NICK!"

The snake moved under him. He'd have to wait. Another glance at the clock: eleven thirty p.m.

Walker eased his grip on the stick at the snake's midsection. The reptile maintained its position, not moving at all when he released the stick entirely.

He was breaking every rule in the book.

Walker secured his grip on the stick holding the cobra's head, then inched closer to it to maintain better balance.

So far, so good.

Leaning one stick against the wall, he crouched down and placed his hand firmly behind the cobra's head. And removed the second stick.

Suddenly, the back end of the snake reared around, slapping him sideways to the floor, his hold on the head lost. He felt his cell phone spin out of his pocket and it slid across the floor like a hockey puck.

The cobra, contorted and angry, rose up six feet over him, the hood extended, the throaty hiss unmistakable, the hit from the fangs like a ninety-mile-an-hour fastball meeting its mark, in this case the underside of his left arm, raised involuntarily to protect his face.

"No! No!" He clawed at the snake's head but it held on, delivering ten cc's of venom into flesh and veins.

"NO!" He pounded on the snake's four-inch head with his fist. The cobra shook its upper body to fend off the attack. Walker's arm moved back and forth like a rag doll.

"NIIICK!"

In eight seconds, drained of toxin, the snake relaxed its upper jaw. Walker pulled his arm free. The cobra lowered itself to the floor and moved in a wide arc to the distant wall.

He sat up, dazed, holding his arm where the snake had hit, the toxin beginning to work its way through his system.

"Christ!"

A metallic taste filled his mouth.

Get the cell phone!

Walker looked around the room. He saw his phone lying upside down opposite the snake. His stomach churning, he crawled slowly toward it. But a new sensation registered. He screamed in pain and scratched at the ring on his left hand, the gold band disappearing under a fold of swelling flesh. He squeezed his finger until the pain deadened.

He reached out for the phone, his fingers a mass of bloated skin, the ring finger a purple beacon. *No pain now*, he thought. He knew his body would shut down the extremities first.

He sat up. Nausea swept through him.

He lay down instead and punched in 911 with the nail on his little finger.

Sheila Sands answered the first call of her evening shift at the Pima County call center.

"Nine-one-one."

"Snake bite. King...cobra,"Walker mumbled. He felt cold.

"Where?"

"On the arm."

"No! Your address."

He answered slowly. "Fourteen ten Upper Ridge Drive." His tongue felt thick.

"How long ago?"

He heard the words, but his mouth wouldn't form a response.

"Where is the snake?" she asked instead.

"In...the...room." He noticed blurring at the edges of his vision.

"Hang on. Paramedics are on the way."

"Six...feet. Two...twenty," he said.

"What?" Sands asked.

"For...anti...venin."

"Can you get out of the room?" Sands asked.

No answer.

"Hello? Can you get out of the room?"

"Yeah." Walker tried to straighten his right leg, the paralysis beginning. "No," he corrected himself.

Rick Parsons was about to down the last of his hamburger when the call came in.

"Damn!" he said to the rookie paramedic seated next to him. "I thought this was going to be a slow night."

"Parsons," he answered.

"Snake bite. King cobra. Man's in bad shape."

"Uh-oh." He glanced at his young partner, Derek Bryant, drinking a large Coke.

Derek nodded, not sure of the problem but wanting to please the man who would be training him for the next six weeks.

"Where?"

"Fourteen ten Upper Ridge Drive. And the snake's in the room. Be careful."

"Wait a minute," Parsons said. "I've been to that house. He's got a ton of snakes."

Derek's eyes widened.

"In containers," Parsons added.

"Well, one of 'em is out. And the man's bad. He can't talk," Sands said.

"We're on our way."

Parsons threw his food on the floor and turned on the siren. He swung the ambulance out of the parking lot.

"I got a feeling about this one," Parsons said, maneuvering into the left lane of traffic. He glanced at his partner. "Derek! Go in the back and check on the antivenins."

Derek jumped up.

"*Not* rattlesnake!" he yelled.

Derek made his way to the back of the truck. He struggled to maintain balance as Parsons swung the vehicle around traffic, the siren deafening. He opened a metal container that held vials of off-white liquid, each cushioned in its own padded enclosure. He held up a vial of antivenin and read the contents. *Micrurus fulvius*. He counted out loud.

"We've got twenty vials," he said, over the sound of the siren.

"That's all?"

"Yes."

"Okay. Come back up here."

Derek made his way to the front. He plopped down in his seat, his meal beginning to sour in his stomach.

Parsons looked at his watch. Way past closing for the zoo, but he gave the order anyway.

"Call the zoo. Ask for the herpetologist and ask about cobra antivenins."

Derek did as he was told, his finger shaking slightly as he speed dialed the number. "There's no answer."

Parsons swung the ambulance around a corner, almost clipping a car's front bumper. He thought about calling Poison Control, but knew that only the zoo, with its resident king cobra, had the needed antivenin.

They would go to plan B. That is, they would use what they had.

"What do we need to think about with a cobra bite?" Parsons asked, weaving through more traffic and running a red light, deciding to educate his young charge and go through the steps for himself at the same time.

"Well...breathing."

"Right. But how are we going to *treat* it? What do we *do*?"

"Um...first, check for a pulse. Possibly use antihistamine."

"Right."

"Hydrate with saline."

"Right."

"Maybe an antibiotic."

"No. He'll get that at the hospital. What else?"

"We have to start the antivenin."

"Right. How many?"

"Um, a lot. We probably don't have enough."

"Correct," Parsons answered, turning into a subdivision and gunning the van up the steep incline to Walker's house.

"You know what else about those antivenins in back?" Derek added.

"What?"

"They're expired."

Parsons turned off the siren and screeched to a halt in Walker's driveway. He jumped out and hurried to the back of the van. Moving quickly, he reached for a headset and dialed the number for Tucson General's Emergency Department. He grabbed two metal emergency kits—one holding the antivenins—a sharps container, and collapsible poles for saline bags and anything else they would be using. Slamming the door, he took off past his flat-footed partner, handing him one of the containers as he swept by.

"Derek, I want you to step up and do everything I tell you." Parsons race-walked to the front door.

Derek fell in next to him, the edge of the metal kit hitting him in the back of the leg.

"Why are we bringing the antivenin if we can't use it?" Derrick asked.

"Because we don't know that we can't use it."

"Oh."

Parsons adjusted the mouthpiece on the headset. "If my gut is right, this guy is not going to be pretty," he added.

"Tucson General," a woman's voice answered.

He pounded on the front door and then answered. "Toni, it's Rick Parsons." Through a window he peered into the darkened living room. A dim light was visible down a hallway.

"Hey, Rick. What's up?"

"I'm in a situation," Parsons began. He pounded harder on the door. A porch light came on across the street. "Is there an attending I can talk to?"

"I can give you Bertrand. It's slow tonight," Toni said, referring to the head of the emergency department.

"Great. Put him on."

"What about the snake?" Derek asked, standing behind him.

"We're not going to worry about the snake," Parsons answered. "If we leave it alone it won't bother us."

Derek paused before responding. "But it's a cobra."

"Yes. It is. Stand back. We're breaking the window," Parsons said.

He smashed the edge of the metal container against the window. Nothing. He tried again, this time with success. Broken glass crashed down onto the window frame and the plants in front of them.

"Wow!" Derek exclaimed.

"We hardly *ever* do this," Parsons reminded him.

He removed two pieces of jagged glass from the window casing and scoped out the floor.

Nothing.

He turned to Derek. "Follow behind me. And don't bump into anything. We'll probably see the snake when we go into the room," he added. "*Don't* look at it. We're here to work on the man."

Parsons stepped gingerly into the living room. Broken glass crunched underfoot. The stench of vomit hit his nostrils.

Derek waited, then entered behind him, coughing suddenly.

"Bertrand!" the head of emergency barked into the phone.

Parsons walked carefully to the edge of the room, and then quickened his pace toward the light emanating from under a closed door.

"Derek, get behind me!" Parsons ordered.

Derek obliged, moving to his right.

"This is BERTRAND!" the doctor repeated gruffly.

"Dr. Bertrand, Rick Parsons with Pima County Paramedics," he said softly. "I'm in a house." Parsons slowly opened the door. "A man has been bitten by a king cobra." He looked at the floor to his right. Nothing. "Our coral antivenin is expired." He looked to his left. "The zoo isn't answering."

No snake. He saw Walker's outstretched legs, swollen grotesquely, his upper body hidden from view by rows of terrariums.

"Well, what do you have?" Bertrand asked.

Derek entered the room behind Parsons. "Oh, man!" he exclaimed.

Parsons walked further into the room.

"This is not good," Derek whined.

Parsons stopped.

"WHAT DO YOU HAVE, PARSONS?"

Parsons regained his composure. "Sir, we have a very bad situation. I'm sure it's a grade IV envenomation. We have massive edema, including the face. There's vomit everywhere."

"*Don't give me that shit!*" Bertrand yelled. "Tell me if he's got a pulse!"

"I don't know where the snake is."

"It's probably in a closet!"

Parsons looked around the room, doorless, save for the one they had entered.

"GET A PULSE!"

"Derek!" Parsons yelled. "Get a pulse! Clear the airway!"

Derek kneeled in vomit next to Walker's right side. He bent down close to his face, fumes from the stomach contents permeating his nose and mouth. With two fingers he reached deep into Walker's throat. "It's clear!"

Parsons knelt across from Derek and searched with him for a pulse on Walker's swollen neck. "I can't find the carotid," he said.

"He's breathing! Barely," Derek said, his head close to Walker's nose.

"He's breathing," Parsons said into the mouthpiece.

"You're sure?" Bertrand asked.

"You're sure?" Parsons repeated the question to Derek.

"Yes," Derek responded.

"We're sure," Parsons said, eyeing his partner.

"How old is the antivenin?" Bertrand asked.

"Derek! How old is the antivenin?"

"Four months past. Twenty vials."

Parsons repeated the figures.

"Use them," Bertrand said. "Where was he bitten?"

"We don't know," Parsons answered.

"WELL…LOOK!"

"Derek! Find the fang marks."

He did as he was told. "I think here, on the forearm." Derek picked up Walker's swollen left arm, noting the purple ring finger.

"On the forearm! Left arm!" Parsons repeated to Bertrand.

"Start a line in the opposite arm!"

"Derek! Start a line in the other arm!"

Derek sat back, befuddled, all of Walker's veins inaccessible. "Where?"

"Can't find the veins, sir!" Parsons heard new instructions. "In the leg, Derek! Either leg!"

Derek pushed up Walker's now leg-hugging pants.

"Put it in the saphenous vein," Parsons added.

"Give a bolus of two hundred cc's saline!" Bertrand ordered. "Use a five-bore needle. Get the antivenins hydrated and start another line! *Don't* shake the antivenin! *Before* using them, give one gram of Solu-Medrol, IV push. NOW! Have epinephrine, prednisone, and Benadryl ready for anaphylaxis."

Parsons repeated the instructions to Derek, who dug around in his case for the drugs.

"Get HemoC and take readings," Bertrand instructed, meaning the laboratory on a card that gives blood values.

Parsons reached in his case, pulled out the card, and ripped off the covering. He pricked one of Walker's swollen fingertips and put a blood sample on the front of the card. The readings came up instantly.

Parsons told Bertrand, "BUN is sixty milligrams/dl… creatinine three-point-five milligrams/dl…potassium six-point-five milligrams/dl. Sodium is one twenty-six."

"All are off. No surprise," Bertrand said. "A king can kill twenty people. He's probably got enough venom in him for a small party. You're going to use all twenty vials, and even *that* may not be enough. Are the first five ready?"

Parsons glanced at Derek, ready to go. "Yes."

"Begin the antivenin in the second line. Do it *quickly*," Bertrand barked. "Do *not* follow SOP."

Derek stopped when he heard the instructions. Parsons, irritated at Derek's hesitation, pointed repeatedly at the line for him to begin.

Bertrand continued, "Give me vitals every thirty seconds."

"Got it," Parsons responded. He placed a blood pressure cuff around Walker's swollen right arm and waited for the reading. He glanced at Derek, still kneeling in vomit, but seemingly oblivious to it, intent on administering the antivenin.

He's doing a good job.

"Tell me what you're doing," Bertrand said.

"We've got the antivenin started—"

"Pulse and blood pressure?" Bertrand interrupted.

Parsons placed two fingers behind the knee and pressed on the popliteal artery. "Pulse is weak," he answered. "Blood pressure is eighty over sixty." Parsons looked at Derek, but didn't say anything.

Suddenly, Walker's face and neck became flushed. They heard secretions in the man's throat.

"Uh-oh," Derek said.

Parsons relayed the symptoms to Bertrand.

"Stop the antivenin! Turn him on his side! Suction the airway! Start epinephrine! Get the steroid! Get Benadryl ready! Have an ET tube ready!"

Both men did as they were told, not talking, working furiously on Walker.

Parsons saw Walker's chest heaving. "He's having more trouble, sir!"

"Give ten milligrams more epinephrine! *Now!*" Bertrand barked.

Parsons repeated the instructions to Derek.

"But…," Derek said, and stopped, sitting upright. He watched his partner, silently.

"HAVE YOU PUT IT IN?" Bertrand asked.

"We'll blow out his heart!" Parsons whined.

"YOU…DON'T…HAVE…A…CHOICE."

Parsons forced the mouthpiece to the top of his head. "We're putting in ten milligrams."

"That's too much," Derek responded.

"HAVE YOU DONE WHAT I ASKED?"

Parsons recovered the mouthpiece. "I'm about to."

"STEP ON IT!"

Parsons filled a syringe with the synthetic, adrenaline-like fluid. He held it up.

"TELL ME WHAT YOU'RE DOING!" Bertrand yelled.

Derek watched as Parsons hesitated, then filled the syringe two-thirds full with the fluid.

"It's going in," Parsons said, giving the liquid intramuscularly in Walker's leg. "Derek, hold his head."

Derek placed both hands under Walker's head.

Suddenly, involuntarily, Walker turned toward Parsons, a thin brown line of iris visible under swollen eyelids.

"Yes!" Derek exclaimed.

Walker's head fell to the side.

"What's going on?" Bertrand asked.

"Movement. Now, nothing," Parsons responded.

"CPR!" Derek yelled.

Parsons grabbed his arm. "Wait."

"Is there a pulse?" Bertrand asked.

"Check the pulse," Parsons ordered.

Derek eased Walker's head back to the floor. He placed two fingers on his swollen neck where he thought the carotid artery would be and pressed down. Then shook his head.

Parsons watched Walker's chest. No movement. He placed two fingers on the popiteal artery again and pressed down.

"No pulse, sir."

"Start CPR," Bertrand barked.

They worked feverishly over Walker's body for ten minutes, trading off chest compressions after five minutes each.

"I think we've lost him," Parsons said into the mouthpiece.

"Keep going ten more minutes," Bertrand said. "I'll wait."

They did as they were told.

"Nothing, sir," Parsons said after the allotted time.

"All right. Unhook everything," Bertrand said. "You did everything you could, Parsons. Good job."

He heard a click as Bertrand hung up.

Parsons sat back on his heels. Derek looked at Walker's puffy, bluish-tinged face, the lips swollen and off-colored, the eyelids drooping from ptosis. They sat in silence for a few moments, both drenched in sweat from the CPR maneuvers. An air conditioner hummed continuously behind them.

"He looked at me," Parsons said finally.

Derek said nothing.

"It's always creepy when that happens. The person knows you're working on them. With his face that bad...and the type of snake...I bet his vocal chords were paralyzed."

They fell back into silence. Derek looked up at the rows of terrariums that extended around the room, some lit with ultraviolet light. In one corner, a long rectangular bin, its glass roof up, sat alone, away from the others. Empty.

"Where's the snake?" Derek asked.

"I don't know. But we've got to get going," Parsons said, throwing empty vials into his emergency kit. "Start undoing the lines. I'll call the police and animal control."

Derek responded, slowly pulling out one, then the remaining line. He eyed the floor around him.

"You don't have to be that careful," Parsons said. "It's not like he's gonna notice."

"Right." Derek quickened his movements, removing the sharps from the end of the lines and putting them into the orange biohazard container. "Should we call somebody?"

"Animal control can get rid of the shit in this room," Parsons said, taking in the terrariums around them. "Stinking snakes."

"What about family?" Derek asked.

"I think the guy lives alone." He closed his kit and took one last look at Walker's bloated body.

"Are we gonna cover the body or anything?" Derek asked.

Parsons thought about that. "I'll go out to the truck and get a blanket." He stood and stretched his legs. "This is what happens when you have snakes, man," he said to Walker's body. "Let that be a lesson," he added, pointing at Derek.

"Yeah." Derek closed the lid on the sharps container.

Parsons started for the door. "You snakes are all going to hell," he said to the room. He was about to exit when he detected movement to his right, on top of a terrarium.

Parsons froze. Three feet of cobra emerged from the highest container and came between him and the door. Three more feet eased down. The snake balanced in a six-foot U-shape in front of Parsons's face, then lowered itself to the floor.

Derek sat motionless. "Goddamn."

The cobra coiled into a loose figure-eight formation near the door.

"Move back," Derek said.

Parsons remained planted in place. "Call the police," he said evenly. Finally, he moved back toward the wall, bumping into a terrarium. He heard a low hiss near his left ear.

"Call now," Parsons said in a low monotone.

Derek grabbed the cell phone near Walker's body.

"Tell them to hurry."

2

Jim Sheridan fingered the sweat-stained basketball and looked for someone to pass to. In front of him, Ray Desmond, a close friend and co-worker—and a member of the defense—waved his hands.

"Give it up, you sissy! You got no game!"

Sheridan knew he could breeze past Des so he didn't worry about the catcalls. Instead, he dribbled in place, faked a move to his right and bounced a pass to his teammate Jimmy Sloan, who moved center court to receive it, then quickly and effortlessly made a two-point shot.

It wasn't what they had practiced. But it worked.

Fourteen children sitting in the stands, the offspring of the players, clapped or booed loudly, depending on team affiliation.

Des walked over to longtime friend Randy Pruitt, a Maryland state police officer, and ribbed him affectionately. "Man! What ya doing? You're asleep at the wheel!"

"I know," Pruitt answered, sweating profusely.

A cell phone ringing somewhere in the stands interrupted them. The men instinctively looked to the children, who busily searched backpacks and pockets for phones. Jason, Sheridan's son, raised his hand, and the game ground to a halt.

"No way," Sheridan groaned. *I'm still on vacation.*

Des picked up the loose ball and followed him off the court. "It's gotta be Egan," he said. Their boss, Samuel Egan, was head of Special Operations at the U.S. Fish and Wildlife Service.

Sheridan took the phone from his son, rubbing his head affectionately. He glanced at the number and nodded at Des.

"Sheridan," he answered, sweating in the August heat.

Des stood by, wicking beads of sweat from his forehead. He looked out over the wide expanse of parkland that separated them from their cars. Players were retrieving belongings and children, and making their way across the lawn. Several turned and waved, and he returned the gesture.

He bounced the ball on a dirt spot in front of the stands and looked again at his partner, who now had his back to Des. How many years had they been meeting for these games? he wondered. About thirteen, he surmised. It was when he had first met Sheridan in Ops: he from the military, the first black man in covert work for "fish and feathers," and Sheridan from state law conservation. In their special agent roles they had quickly become buddies, though different in every way: personality, appearance, political affiliations, even the way they conversed. He was the talker. Sheridan was not.

Des stopped bouncing the ball and looked at Jason, who was balancing a baseball mitt on his tanned legs and waiting for his father to finish. He eased his compact frame into the second row of the stands next to the kid. "How ya doing?"

"Good," Jason replied.

"Enjoy your vacation?"

"Yep."

A man of few words, just like his father, Des thought. He placed the ball between his feet. "See many games?"

"Yeah."

"Which ones?"

"Orioles."

"Who's your favorite player?"

"Actually, I have several."

And a serious one, too.

Sheridan turned toward Des. "I'll tell him. We'll be in soon." He ended the call and handed his phone back to his son. "We're meeting Egan at the office."

"Why?"

"Some problem." Sheridan picked up a towel and wiped his face.

"A *wildlife* problem?" Des asked.

Sheridan nodded. "Something to do with Thailand…a State Department request."

Des thought that through. "This couldn't wait till Monday?"

"Apparently not. Egan's leaving for vacation." He looked at his watch. "In an hour." He saw the look of disappointment on his son's face.

Des responded with all the enthusiasm of the overworked federal employee he was. "Wow."

Realizing he hadn't fully explained the reason for Egan's call, Sheridan added, "Thailand is missing some cobras."

Des stared at him without responding.

"*King* cobras," Sheridan added.

"This isn't Chameleon all over again, is it?" Des asked.

"I hope not." Sheridan picked up his old gym bag and motioned for them to follow. "I'll meet your there."

"Right." Des gathered his things and they walked to their cars.

Sheridan maneuvered the SUV north for the quick drive to headquarters in Arlington, Virginia. He glanced at his eight-year-old son who sat silently staring out the window, his profile now so much like his mother's. He wondered how their divorce was going to sit with him. More importantly, he wondered if this unscheduled trip to the office would derail their afternoon plans.

As if reading his mind, Jason turned to him. "Are we still going to the game?"

"Absolutely!" Sheridan answered, turning up the air-conditioning. "This shouldn't take long. We'll go home, have lunch and get ready. Okay?"

"Okay," Jason answered, and resumed staring out the window.

They drove on in silence, passing Reagan National Airport. Sheridan replayed the conversation with Egan: Thailand was reporting a sudden, catastrophic drop in its population of king cobras, which it considered a national icon, much like the bald eagle in the United States.

There were no carcasses, no environmental triggers, no known disease.

Nothing.

But the problem went further. Thailand blamed the U.S. and its legions of exotic snake collectors who wanted only the rarest of species. And those legions were growing. Wildlife smuggling was now a billion-dollar industry, sandwiched between the drug trade and human smuggling.

But king cobras? Only an experienced collector had one. The snakes were large, at eighteen feet when full grown. And they were deadly.

Sheridan passed Arlington National Cemetery. He looked in his rearview mirror and saw Des behind him.

Operation Chameleon had come to mind for him as well. It had been their most notorious case, which brought a federal grand jury indictment against a Florida reptile dealer and three associates in Asia for wildlife smuggling, conspiracy, and money laundering. The international case spanned three continents and had taken five years to crack. But the op, which he had been in charge of, had been an embarrassment for them. The biggest perpetrator had gotten away.

Sheridan turned onto 10th Street and then Fairfax Drive, and pulled into his usual space at the building that housed several governmental law enforcement divisions, including Fish and Wildlife.

A country doesn't just lose a native species, he thought, turning off his SUV. In his experience, a sudden population drop was almost *always* the result of an environmental event.

Collectors had nothing to do with it.

He saw Des drive by and park two spaces away.

Egan had said something else: the U.S. secretary of state would be in Thailand in two weeks. And she didn't want to talk about snakes.

Jason jumped out of the car and over a row of low-lying bushes as the men approached their place of work. They walked in—the cool air a welcome respite—and took the elevator to the fifth floor. Co-workers were at their computers, those few who had chosen to spend a beautiful—albeit hot and humid—Saturday morning at the office.

The three turned a corner and walked down a hallway to Egan's office.

Jason took a seat in the outer foyer and the two men took their respective places in front of Egan's desk. And his empty chair.

Sheridan saw a folder on the perennially clean desktop and recognized the State Department seal on the front of it.

Finally, Egan entered and sat down. "Thanks for coming in."

Sheridan and Des nodded at him. Sheridan, in his sweaty basketball clothes, took in Egan's perfectly groomed, casual appearance: wrinkle-free, light blue polo shirt, pressed jeans, boat shoes. All for the soon-to-commence vacation at the in-laws' in Maine. He looked like he was returning from rather than leaving for his annual two-week hiatus.

Egan got right to the point, addressing Sheridan. "Tell me again what's on your plate."

Sheridan sat up, visualizing the files left on his desk almost two weeks ago. He felt his vacation state of mind slipping away.

"There's the eagle problem in Wyoming, the report on threatened species…"

Egan nodded in agreement.

"CoP Eighteen in October," Sheridan continued, meaning the International Conference of Parties to CITES, an international wildlife consortium. "The Western Regional in November—"

"Move everything off," Egan interrupted. "Pass the eagle problem to Vicki. And put a priority on that." He turned to Des. "Can you help Sheridan with this?"

Des shifted in his chair. "Sure."

"I don't want to spend a lot of time on it."

A quick in and out.

"Do what you can and write a report for me to take to Donohue," he said, referring to the head of law enforcement.

"You know this is an old story," Sheridan told him. "Snakes are taken for collections."

"It's more than that," Egan said. "Their numbers are down. In fact, they're negative. Villagers rarely see them."

Sheridan found that hard to believe. The snakes were elusive, hiding in rice paddies or coming out at night to hunt. "Collectors are an easy target. Not that I'm defending them."

Egan looked at his watch.

"You know the State Department doesn't care," Des added, meaning the agency's involvement in wildlife issues.

Sheridan nodded in agreement.

"They do when the situation reflects unfavorably on us," Egan responded. "Which is what we've got. Start with Ashland." The Service's state-of-the-art wildlife forensics lab in Ashland, Oregon, kept track of animal counts and other pending issues worldwide. "See if anything's come up."

Sheridan and Des sat silently.

Egan continued, "I need to impress upon you that the State Department does indeed care. The secretary will be in Thailand and this whole thing has caused an uproar over there."

"Any chance we can get those two positions filled?" Sheridan ventured.

Egan stared at him with a look that said, "You're kidding, right?" He pulled a file out from under the State Department folder and handed both to him. "A new recruit is coming in while I'm gone. Johnny Lee. That's the only person I can give you."

Des leaned over and perused the contents, then looked up. "Johnny's a woman?"

"Yes," Egan said. "One of four at the top of her class." He hesitated. "Is that a problem?"

"No...but...she doesn't know anything," Des said.

"Neither would anyone else just coming out," Egan countered, in reference to the law enforcement training school in Georgia. "Give her something to do. Acquaint her with collectors, the ones around here, and K. C., on the off chance she hasn't heard of him."

"Most snake collectors are men," Sheridan added.

"Not all."

"Right," Sheridan answered.

Egan retrieved his briefcase and rose from his chair. "See you in two weeks. You're in change, Sher." Egan exited, leaving his two deputies sitting in his office.

Des turned to his buddy and smiled. "Welcome *back!*"

3

"Just dumb luck, don't you think?"

The reporter from *Dateline*—young, blonde Cameron Phillips—had just asked K. C. Sawyer a question about his name. "Kenneth Charles: King Cobra."

So far, the queries were run-of-the-mill, just as he expected. *Every interview is a new interview*, he reminded himself. Across from him, sitting on his couch, Cameron glanced down at notes splayed out on his coffee table. He came to the not-so-startling realization that he was twice her age.

She looked up suddenly. "People say you look like the actor Sean Penn, but with gray hair. Do you agree with that?"

"Yes. I'm flattered."

She reached for his best-selling book, held it out for the camera, and read the title: *A Cobra in My Pocket and Other Tales from Thirty Years in the Snake Business*.

"How was this picture taken?" She pointed to the small cobra, hood flared, sticking its head up from what looked like the pocket of a lab coat, albeit a *black* lab coat.

"Through the magic of PhotoShop."

"So, you've never had a cobra in your pocket?"

"Are you kidding?"

He heard laughter beyond the camera lights and looked at the dark outlines of people—so many of them—standing behind her in his spacious living room. Off to the right he made out the silhouette of Mark Reeves, his closest friend, leaning against the wall, his usual spot in these situations. Just last month he'd leaned against that wall three different times for three different interviews, all on the same topic—himself and the world's fascination with venomous reptiles.

Cameron asked, "Why the title, then?"

"I don't know...ask the marketing department."

The group laughed again. He wondered if his remarks would make the cut.

She changed the subject. "You've become synonymous with snake collecting, cobras specifically. You seem to revere these snakes."

K. C. nodded in agreement.

"But they are endangered species, are they not?"

"No, they are not." He paused. "My view about having cobras in collections is well-known."

Cameron continued, "You are a spokesman for a line of reptile vitamins and another product."

"A mist," K. C. responded. "It's sprayed on reptiles in captivity, a common thing to do."

"And you make millions from this."

K. C. laughed. "I make nowhere near that. But yes, I make a living from it."

She pressed on, "So, with your business concerns, your TV show, your position as a well-known collector and best-selling author, plus your on-again, off-again embattlements with wildlife agents, you would not be in a position to help the government crack down on collectors then, would you?"

"Of course I would. *Illegal* collectors."

"Have you been bitten?" Cameron asked, suddenly changing the subject.

"Yes."

"But you are the primo handler."

"Reptiles are unpredictable. But that doesn't mean they're stupid."

"So they're smart?"

"Actually, they are. Lizards have the highest brain-size index in relation to their body."

"What about snakes?"

"They're in the middle. But the king cobra is highly evolved."

"Do they have parental instincts?"

Not so run-of-the-mill.

"Male alligators have been known to care for their young. I know of only one snake that does and that's the king cobra. And its instinct is to move away once the young are born."

"Why is that?"

"Because it's in the family known as snake eaters."

Her expression told him that his point hit the mark. "Can we see your collection?"

"Sure."

K. C. motioned Cameron and a cameraman in and then followed. Inside, cool air engulfed them. The scent of a cleaning product filled the air, along with something else—the faint odor of musk.

K. C. closed the door. "This is my snake room," he explained, holding out his hand to indicate the room at large. It was a rectangular space formed by two adjoining rooms. Overhead, dimmed ceiling lights shone down on terrariums, stacked three high and placed in a semicircle. Each was covered with a glass top and had ultraviolet lighting. The semicircle was broken only by a long terrarium at the opposite end of the room where his friend Reeves stood. Classical music played softly in the background.

"I can't believe I'm in the same room with a cobra," the reporter said.

"Use the plural," K. C. corrected. "They're all around you."

"Where would you like us to be?" Cameron asked.

"You can walk with me as we take the tour. I'd like the cameraman to stay by the door."

"Okay." Cameron looked down at her notes. "I need you to show me a common cobra, the least common one, and of course the king cobra."

"Okay. First," K. C. began, "let me explain that everything in here, from the lighting and temperature to the heat and light sources in the terrariums, is computer controlled. The temperature right now is about sixty degrees. It will go up one or two degrees, then down to fifty-eight degrees at night. I've provided a safe, secure, and pleasant environment for these animals, from the diorama inside each terrarium to the classical music you hear. Even the sand for the Egyptian cobras is from Egypt."

K. C. pointed to his left. "Let's begin over here."

They walked to the first terrarium and Cameron bent down, taking in a brown-and-white-striped snake, about five feet long, lying motionless inside.

"What's this one?" she asked.

"That's a Thai spitting cobra."

"It's so beautiful."

"Yes. It's one of the most colorful. I wear protective glasses when I take it out."

"Would it hit you, really?"

"A perfect bull's eye." K. C. thought she might become unhinged at that, but she continued.

"Does the venom blind you?"

"Temporarily. In the wild, that's enough time for the snake to move away. Or forward."

"I see." Cameron stood up. "What do you do, exactly, when you *take a snake out*?"

"Usually I'm cleaning its terrarium," K. C. said, as they moved on. "It also gives me time to check it for parasites or other problems. When I do that, I put the snake in a holding bin with a secure top. It's quite stressful to the reptile to handle it."

"You don't let it walk around, then?"

K. C. laughed. "No, it doesn't 'walk around.' I only let the king cobra walk around."

They stopped in front of the next terrarium. Inside, behind the snake, was a Middle Eastern scene, right down to perfectly scaled pyramids in the background.

"This is the Asp that bit Cleopatra," K. C. said. "It's full grown at about six feet. It's one of my oldest snakes."

Cameron bent down again and looked at the light gray-brown cobra staring back at her. "So it's deadly?"

"Its venom is pretty potent, yes."

She turned back to him. "Is it endangered?"

K. C. thought for a moment. "I believe this one is on a CITES list."

"And that is…?" She waited for him to explain.

"CITES is a consortium of countries—governments—that have agreed to certain regulations about their natural resources. *Endangered* is a U.S. term. This is not an endangered snake."

"So, how would one get a snake like this?"

"It depends." It was a question he expected. "If the snake is on the CITES Appendix I list, it's against international code to own it. I've had this snake for many years, before any of the cobras appeared on any lists."

She paused, and K. C. thought she would ask the question he was waiting for: But where did you get this one?

She didn't. Instead, they walked on, passing an empty terrarium.

"What happened here?" Cameron asked.

"That's where my Russian cobra used to be," K. C. explained. "It died not too long ago."

"It's from Russia…really?"

"Old Russia, yes. Not a spectacular snake, actually," he added. "It's dark, almost black in color. Its appeal is its rarity and that it lives so far north."

They were now almost next to Reeves, waiting for them near the king cobra.

"Let me ask you," Cameron said, "why would I want to own poisonous snakes?"

"Because you are a collector and they hold appeal," K. C. answered. "It's that simple."

They had stopped next to Reeves, but Cameron, her eyes on K. C., continued.

"You once made the remark in an interview that *hot* collectors, a word that refers to poisonous snakes—"

"*Venomous* snakes is the correct term," K. C. interjected. "But continue."

"These collectors are saving the species the way zoos are saving elephants. A lot of people, wildlife experts in particular, thought that comparison was way off base."

"And I answered by saying that I didn't understand why. We're talking about environmentally challenged animals. But elephants are cute in a way that snakes are not. Zoos come to snake collectors to help fill out their exhibits. That's a known fact. So I think there is a bit of hypocrisy going on."

"What about endangered species? You have some in your collection."

She must have forgotten. "I have no endangered species."

"How did you get the snakes you have?"

"I bought them."

"From where?"

"Reputable sources."

"Who?"

"People who owned the snakes and wanted to get rid of them. And from breeders."

"Breeders in the U.S.?"

"Yes."

"Wouldn't breeding an endangered species be a crime?"

The woman does not have a brain.

"No. The crime is taking an endangered species out of its environment."

"So, the government sanctions the breeding of an endangered species?"

"I don't know whether it's sanctioned or not," K. C. answered, keeping his tone of voice level. "But it's not criminal. The U.S. government and I disagree on many things. And one is making criminals out of people who are not criminals."

"How have you helped change that perception?"

"My philosophy is one of education, understanding, tolerance...the things I talk about in my book."

Enough.

K. C. changed the subject. "Let's look at this." He pointed to the snake before them. "This is a full-grown, eighteen-foot king cobra that I've had for twenty-two years. It's Appendix II-listed now, meaning it can be bought and sold with restrictions."

Cameron looked down at the slender, brownish-black cobra with a tint of green, folded over on itself several times. She turned back to K. C., unimpressed.

"*That's* a king cobra?" she asked.

"Yes."

"But...it's not even *pretty*."

Women! They want ten colors in shoes. And snakes.

"Its appeal is its size. And it's deadly."

"I think I expected..."—she turned back toward the brown and white spitting cobra—"something more regal to go with its reputation."

"If I were to put this snake on the floor and it were to rise up, it would tower over you and meet me eye to eye," K. C. explained.

"And I'm six feet tall." He added, "You don't have many places to go when this snake rises up to say hello."

"And it's quite…venomous?" Cameron asked.

"One bite can kill twenty men."

"Will you take it out for us?"

4

From the comfort of his air-conditioned truck, Leland Chang—international animal broker, albeit one without an office, address, or business card—surveyed the work of the ten men in front of him, their backbreaking movements reflected in the gray lenses of his designer sunglasses. They had been hacking away at the jungle for more than four hours. Finally, the clearing they had set out to create lay in front of them.

Chang wondered if the Thai boys with the snakes would find them, their only landmark being the stream and this small clearing carved into the middle of the jungle. He pushed up the sleeves on his starched white shirt and looked at his watch.

"Not bad for a morning's work," his driver and go-to man in Bangkok said. Through their network of snake buyers based around the country, they had gotten the word out to the young snake catchers in this part of Thailand to be here, and had transported the workers to this remote spot to fashion a "storefront."

Chang stepped out of the truck without answering. The men were sitting down, taking a much-needed break out of the sun. He walked into the middle of the clearing, surrounded on all sides by the oppressive jungle. The driver came up beside him and Chang nodded in agreement.

"Yes, they did a good job." Chang pointed to the back of the truck. "Get the tent up. And the tables."

The driver barked instructions at three men who had just settled into their break.

When the open-sided tent had been assembled and the tables arranged, Chang retrieved his briefcase. He set it on a table and opened it. Inside was Thai currency—three hundred thousand dollars in stacks of hundreds. He paid above-market rates— literally, the open-market rates of Thailand—for the king cobras he purchased.

His offer: eight thousand dollars a snake, three thousand dollars more than the Europeans paid for the same reptiles. It was simple economics: pay more, get more.

He closed the briefcase. And looked up.

Two young boys had emerged from the brush, struggling with a long rectangular box.

His first customers.

Chang could see that they were drenched in sweat from their journey, and no doubt were carrying a full-grown king cobra.

Two of the workers ran over to help them and set the box on a table.

Chang walked over to it and bent down. He removed his sunglasses, revealing piercing blue eyes, and peered inside the small screened front of the box. He took in the snake, folded over on itself several times. The young boys stood at his side, and Chang smiled at them.

He would pay them big money, but first he wanted their assurance that they would keep the business they were about to transact a private matter.

"We won't be in this place again," he said to them in their native Thai language.

They nodded and Chang counted out eight thousand dollars, easily enough for five families to live on for years. He put the money in a plastic bag and handed it to the eldest one.

He saw the smiles on their faces and watched them disappear back into the jungle.

Other boys—the backbone of his business—were coming forward now, some with small boxes, always at least two carrying the larger containers. They had gotten word.

His cell phone rang, and he pulled it out and answered. Chang listened for a few moments and then replied, "Yes. We've got them."

He quickly scanned the tables where his driver and some of the men were bending down to look inside the boxes.

"That part doesn't matter," Chang answered in response to a question. "We'll meet our numbers." He listened again to something his caller was saying and watched as other boys were appearing now from out of the jungle. "Wait!" He added one more thing before ending the call. "Make sure a Russian cobra is on that ship."

5

K. C. unlatched the lid of the terrarium and, with Reeves's help, pushed it back. Instantly, the head of the king cobra popped up and turned from side to side, eyeing all in the room. The two men remained next to it, giving the reptile plenty of time to scope out its surroundings.

Cameron, the reporter from *Dateline*, stood next to the cameraman now and watched, transfixed, as K. C. began.

"You'll notice that the head is about the size of a squirrel's head," K. C. said. "That makes it easy to grab, easier than a juvenile venomous snake." He moved his hand to the back of the snake's neck and grabbed it from behind. "That's why I strongly advise collectors to have only full-grown snakes. The babies can really inflict some damage."

On cue, Reeves reached in and grabbed the last third of the snake's body, and together they moved it onto the floor.

"You'll notice that the floor has no pattern," K. C. continued, as he reached for a snake stick leaning against the terrarium. He moved the stick behind his hand and then removed his hand from the snake's head. "With a venomous snake, you always want to know where it is."

"Wouldn't size dictate where it was?" Cameron asked.

K. C. glanced over at her and back at the snake. "You'd be surprised."

The cobra had curled its long body into several S shapes.

"We'll give the snake a bit more time, then we'll let it go. One has to have patience. You're on its time when it's out like this."

"What can you tell us about venomous snakes while we're waiting?" Cameron asked.

Without taking his eye off the reptile, K. C. responded. "We know that they are the most advanced of the species. Boas are the most primitive. The venomous ones came later in the evolutionary chain."

"How so?" Cameron asked.

"We can only speculate that when the dinosaurs died off and predators became smaller and quicker, venom evolved as an effective weapon. It sort of leveled the playing field. This then makes venomous snakes a later, more advanced group."

"Does this one have its fangs?"

"Yes, all my snakes do." He spoke to Reeves. "We'll let him go now."

K. C. eased the stick off the snake's head and stepped back. Released of its hold, the snake moved its head from side to side again, its tongue testing the air.

"How much does it weigh?" Cameron asked.

"About seventy-five pounds," K. C. answered, moving into the center of the room. He crouched down, five feet away from the snake, and put his hand out, palm up. The cobra moved toward him.

He heard Cameron gasp.

The snake's tongue touched K. C.'s fingertips.

"The king cobra recognizes its handlers and comes to know their movements and patterns. With its eyes, it will follow its owner out of a room, and turn its head to look around someone who might be blocking its view. I came up to speed pretty quickly on this snake—its intelligence, how docile it is. It's only grouped with cobras because it can flare out its neck the way they do." He added, "It's even kept as a pet in Thailand."

"Really?" Cameron asked, somewhat amazed.

"Yes."

"Let's say that *I* want a snake like this as a pet," Cameron inquired. "How would I get one?"

K. C. stood up slowly and walked a few steps to the sink to wash his hands. The cobra remained in the middle of the floor and turned its head in its owner's direction.

She's not going to let it go.

"You could go online and find a store that would sell it to you."

"And where would the store get it?" Cameron asked.

"They would import it. The store would need a federal import/export license."

"And the snake would be sent...how?"

"Hopefully, in the most humane way possible, and right after eating. It would be put in a thick cotton bag, maybe double bagged—Customs likes that—and hung on a rack in a plane so it's off the floor. After passing inspection it would go on to the store, and the store would contact you."

"Would I need a license?"

"Most definitely." He turned his back for the first time as he reached for a paper towel, then turned to look at Cameron. "Do you live in New York City?"

"Yes."

"You'd have to check the city, county, and state laws and ordinances. New York is quite strict."

"But not everyone goes to the trouble of doing that."

"No, not everyone does," he answered, throwing the paper towel away.

This interview is over.

He leaned against the sink and looked down at his snake, all eighteen feet of it looped in an abstract pattern in the middle of the floor. He had already moved on, thinking through his list for the drive north to the Reptile Show in a few days.

He looked up at Cameron. "Anything else?"

6

Sheridan drove into the church parking lot, the usual transfer spot for Jason. He saw Joanna, his soon-to-be-ex-wife, standing near her car, arms folded in front of her, a stern look on her face.

Or was that just her usual demeanor of late?

He felt Jason tense up next to him as he pulled into the space near hers. Sheridan glanced at the clock on the dash: eight a.m. *Right on time.*

Jason jumped out and grabbed his belongings, including bags of new clothes and baseball souvenirs.

"Hi, Mom!"

Sheridan walked over and kissed Joanna lightly on the cheek. She remained planted in place, barely acknowledging him.

Must be the magnitude of the day.

She grabbed Jason's backpack as he passed by. "Let me see that." She rooted around inside and pulled out an inhaler he used for his asthma.

Empty.

She sighed heavily. "Get in the car, Jase." And turned back to Sheridan.

Here it comes.

"This is what I mean." She held up the empty inhaler. "This is a perfect example of your lack of communication. If you had called, I could have had this filled this morning. Or, heaven forbid, *yesterday!*"

Sheridan saw Jason in the front seat of Joanna's car. He glanced at his father, and then quickly looked away.

Joanna ranted on. "I don't have time this morning. I'm leaving work early. You *do* remember what we're doing this afternoon?"

Sheridan nodded slowly and then answered, "There was a miscommunication about the inhaler."

She shook her head and got in her car. Sheridan watched her pull out and drive away, leaving him standing there.

Yes, thank you. The vacation was great.

Back in his car, he maneuvered his way through the morning commute, grateful for the twenty-minute drive to Arlington that would help him defuse yet another encounter with Joanna. And give him time to think.

Sheridan got onto I-395. With some difficulty, he pushed this latest encounter to the side and instead ran through his to-do list for the day: a hundred e-mails; Thailand; the meeting with Des and the new recruit, Johnny Lee.

And at three p.m. exactly, his divorce.

Do I not communicate effectively?

People at work said he didn't let them in on his thinking until he had everything figured out. He didn't know about that. He watched for nuances, details. He talked when he had something to say. It wasn't that he was afraid to be wrong, like someone once said in a stinging management evaluation. He was self-contained.

That was who he was. He wasn't Des, his smooth-talking partner.

Sheridan, on his usual route, passed the wide expanse of Arlington National Cemetery again and, after a short time, exited for Fish and Wildlife. Des's car was already there.

What went wrong in our seventeen-year marriage?

He had been asking that question for some time now.

Sheridan grabbed his briefcase and exited, locking the SUV with a click of the remote. He walked into headquarters, the cool air always a relief. He turned left and headed toward the cafeteria. Perusing his pastry choices, he picked out a chocolate muffin, poured a large coffee, and made his way to the checkout. He saw Sabrina, his usual cashier, and smiled.

"How was your vacation, Mr. Sheridan?"

"Great, Sabrina." *Someone* cared. He put down his coffee and muffin and dug through his wallet for a five-dollar bill.

"They always go fast," she said, ringing up his order and readying his change. "Go anywhere special?"

"Nope, just stayed close to home."

"How's your boy?" she inquired.

"Growing! And a baseball fanatic. How 'bout yours?" It was their usual banter, a closeness brought about through the similar ages of their children. He couldn't remember how or when they had started talking about them.

"Oh, the same. But I can't keep up with his sports. There's too many." She changed the subject. "You're not the first one here."

"Oh?" he responded, knowing full well that Des was upstairs.

"Des beat you by five minutes. And Lindsay is in," she added, referring to the department's computer expert.

She was always on top of things, eavesdropping on conversations when no one thought she was listening. A perfect candidate for surveillance work.

"Thanks for the heads-up."

"You have a nice day now."

He walked down the long corridor to the elevators. *Time to get into this day.*

Exiting on his floor, he saw support staff already at work and they greeted him as he passed by. His co-worker, Lindsay, turned a corner and almost bumped into him.

"Hey, man. Welcome back." And kept walking.

Sheridan stopped. *Unusual*, he thought, since he and Lindsay usually talked sports every day. He shrugged it off, entered his small office, and sat down at his desk, noting the two stacks of folders right where he had left them. He reached over and turned on his computer. Before he had the top off the coffee, Kim Allerton, the intern working with Egan, came in, two yellow Post-it notes in hand.

"Hello, Kim."

"Hi, Mr. Sheridan. Nice vacation?" she asked.

"Yes. Hard to be back."

Sheridan took in her young face. She looked all of sixteen, belying the fact that she would be a senior at Georgetown in a month.

She smiled and looked down at her notes. "Mr. Egan wanted me to remind you that the International Reptile Show is here next week." She waited for him to acknowledge that.

"Yes, right," Sheridan said.

"And," she added, reading from the second note, "he wants you to go to a meeting for him on Friday, at Interior. Three thirty p.m. They'll want an update on Thailand."

"Okay." Sheridan held out his hand and she passed him the notes. Kim, an office favorite, had—over the summer months—mastered the ins and outs of their small world. Luckily for them, she had agreed to stay on part-time. *In ten years she'll probably be running the place*, he thought. "Thanks." He stuck the notes on his calendar and she left.

He'd forgotten about the show, one of the world's largest. That meant they would be in Maryland, in the jurisdiction of Daniel Stone, their former co-worker.

He'd deal with that later.

Sheridan opened his e-mail. The new messages filled the screen and, no doubt, beyond. He scrolled to the bottom to begin at the beginning. Quickly glossing over the ones that could wait, Sheridan clicked on the ones of import. There were several from

Marshall Sullivan, aka "Marsh," in Wyoming, regarding the eagle situation that he would be passing to Vicki.

He stopped for a moment to think about Vicki, then thought better of it.

In the two e-mails he opened, Marsh was telling him that nothing had changed. The birds were missing. And by that he meant the whole bird, which was unusual. Eagles were taken for feathers, leaving carcasses behind. They were at a loss for motive.

He scrolled up the screen. Vicki, the department's bird expert, like her father and grandfather before her, was the obvious choice to take this on.

Des poked his head in. "Hey."

Sheridan looked up.

"Johnny will be here at ten a.m. She's in HR right now."

Sheridan glanced at his watch: 9:20 a.m.

"I'll bring her in," Des added.

"Okay."

Des left and he went back to his e-mail. Getting through all of them would be impossible. He scrolled back toward the top to see if there was anything more from Egan about Thailand.

Nothing.

He decided to spend the rest of his time getting organized about the cobra situation. He reached for his coffee, but sensed someone else at his doorway. He turned and saw Vicki.

"Hey," he said, their usual department greeting.

"Hi." She entered and came up to his desk, and leaned against a corner. She smiled, her deep brown eyes boring into him.

"Did you get my e-mail?" she asked.

He turned back to the computer screen. "Um…not yet. What did it say?"

"I'm inviting you for dinner. Tonight."

"Oh." He felt uncomfortable…her perfume…*too close*.

"Thought you might need a reprieve after cooking for two weeks," Vicki added.

He laughed.

"Maybe I should say a reprieve from hamburgers and hot dogs."

"That's more like it." He looked away. *So much to do*.

"You can let me know...see how your day goes." She moved to leave.

Sheridan nodded in agreement. "Before you go," he said, fishing around in one of his piles, "Egan wants me to give you a case."

"The eagles," she said.

"He mentioned it, then?" He handed her a file.

"Yes," she answered, taking it, "but none of the details."

"I'll forward Marsh's e-mails. Still no carcasses. And no motive."

Vicki had her head down and was thumbing through the file he had given her. He allowed himself that moment. Vicki's short black hair perfectly framed the face he knew well.

"Thanks for taking this on," he added. "Something else has come up."

"Thailand," she said casually, still going through the file.

He was surprised she knew. But then, in their office, there were no secrets.

"A lot happened while I was gone," he said.

She nodded in agreement, finally looking at him. "Unusual for August. How's Jason?"

"Good." He felt a pang of sadness talking about his son. "We went to games, card shows, movies."

"Sounds like fun." There was an awkward pause. Vicki held up the file. "I'll get started. Let me know later about dinner." And she left.

Sheridan got up and closed his door. Vicki and the dinner invitation not withstanding, he needed time on Thailand. He went back to his computer and opened TESS, the Service's database that brought up lists of threatened and endangered species.

The fact that a foreign government would request help from the United States, tapping its resources for wildlife protection and recovery, wasn't unusual. The U.S. helped most countries enforce wildlife laws, often working in tandem with special units set up within international agencies like INTERPOL and the World Wildlife Federation. And as a member of CITES, the Convention on International Trade in Endangered Species, the U.S. was part of a collective attempt by nations to stem the worldwide trade in vanishing plants and animals. Coupled with the Endangered Species Act of 1973, some of those vanishing populations had recovered. Birds, plants, and other animals had even moved off the list.

But that didn't mean they were no longer taken.

He scrolled down TESS's long list of national and international flora and fauna. Just as he thought, no cobras were listed. Sheridan opened the CITES Web site and clicked on "Appendices" that opened three comprehensive lists of endangered and imperiled species. He scanned to the bottom, to SERPENTES, and found what he was looking for. Over half of the world's cobras were listed on Appendix II, which meant strict enforcement for importing or exporting the snakes. He scrolled to the bottom and saw *Ophiophagus hannah*, the king cobra.

Sheridan stared at the screen and reached for his coffee.

He was of the opinion—shared by many of his cohorts— that an animal went on the U.S. endangered list long after its population had been depleted. CITES gave an accurate decline *while it was happening.* Yet not even CITES had caught up with the situation in Thailand, which would have moved the king cobra to Appendix I status: *near extinction.*

What does this mean for Thailand?

It meant no one was looking.

He continued staring at the screen. His remarks to Egan notwithstanding, Thailand was not completely wrong in blaming collectors, who continued to siphon off the world's most exotic animals. That had been proven during Operation Chameleon. They were collectors, after all. He understood the mentality of moving up the ranks and the thrill in possessing something so coveted.

He took the top off his muffin and broke it into small pieces, then ate each one methodically. To a seasoned collector, the king cobra was the equivalent of a rare, mint-condition baseball card.

And about as expensive.

He looked at the clock. He'd do more research later. He went back to e-mail and shot off a message to Isaac Harris, at INTER-POL's International Wildlife Working Group in Germany, and a former associate on Chameleon.

> Isaac—
> Have you heard about the situation in Thailand with the disappearance of king cobras? I'm researching it on this end. Let me know if you have anything.
> Thanks.
> Sheridan

He pecked at the rest of his muffin, then picked up the phone and called Fish and Wildlife's forensics lab in Ashland, Oregon, which held the largest collection of animal evidence anywhere in the world. After a few moments he was connected to Jerry Terrelli, the lab's director, a former Special Ops guy. They talked about the weather, baseball, and the usual cuts in the annual budget. Sheridan filled him in on the cobra situation.

"What would cause a sudden loss of a native population, if you are assuming no disease, no habitat destruction, and no extreme weather event?" Sheridan asked.

"The food source moved," Jerry said immediately, "or poaching. But we haven't seen poaching on the scale you're talking about. There's been a *slight* uptick in smaller cobra skins for belts and boots. We're seeing garments *with the head of the snake still attached*, if you can imagine that."

No, he really couldn't.

"Our source says it's a symbol of wealth in Asia."

"I see," Sheridan said. He glanced at his watch. "Tell you what…give me a call if you hear anything, even if you think it's nothing."

Jerry promised he would, and after more exchanges about their respective cases, Sheridan thanked him and hung up.

Des and Johnny would be in his office in five minutes. He dashed off a quick e-mail to Des, hoping he would read what he had in mind for Johnny before the meeting. Then he picked up the phone and made one more call, to DC's National Zoo.

7

Arlington, Virginia
Monday morning

Sheridan heard the knock at his door, right on time.

"Come in!"

He turned to see Des with a young and quite beautiful Asian woman standing next to him. Sheridan stood up, motioning them in.

"Sher, this is Johnny Lee," Des said, introducing them.

Johnny held out her hand and Sheridan took it, getting a firm handshake in return.

"Sit down," Sheridan said, moving his half-eaten muffin to a back credenza.

They settled into the two chairs in front of Sheridan's desk. Des cranked his back and put his feet up.

"We're very informal here," Des remarked.

Johnny smiled and seemed to relax somewhat.

"Did you meet everyone and get the lay of the land?" Sheridan asked.

"Yes. Everyone's been very helpful," she said, clearly and concisely.

"Great." Sheridan opened her file and began reading. "You have impressive credentials. Highest-ranking woman at school... great conditioning...gets along with people."

Johnny nodded.

"You'll be using all those qualities. And more."

She nodded again in understanding.

"I don't know how much you know about some of our cases," Sheridan began.

"We studied a few at Glynco," she answered, referring to the Law Enforcement Training Center she had just left.

"Chameleon?" Des asked.

"Yes."

Des laughed. "Did they go over our mistakes?"

"Just that one person got away. Two were sentenced."

"Correct," Sheridan said. He got to the point. "We want you to work with us on something."

Sheridan took in her perfectly coifed, shoulder-length dark hair, light makeup, simple blue blouse, and dark pants. She sat ramrod straight and maintained eye contact, completely composed.

"The prime minister of Thailand contacted our State Department about a disappearance in their population of king cobras. The snake is revered in their country and the loss is enough that the prime minister is worried about it. And is blaming collectors. U.S. collectors."

"It's a large snake," Johnny said.

Sheridan nodded. He was sure she could recite all the facts and figures about endangered species and wildlife poaching.

"Most collectors won't own one," he added. He took a sip of his cold coffee. "Our charge is to find out what's going on"— he remembered Egan's admonition—"as quickly as we can." He reached for files and handed them to her. "While we sort out what we have"—he glanced at Des—"I want you to become familiar with a group of collectors here."

She opened the file on top.

"During Chameleon, we started following what we call the 'Beltway group.' Collectors are buyers and that's what we're interested in: how they buy and sell."

"Where *do* they get them?" Johnny asked.

"We don't know...still don't know." Sheridan pointed at the files. "There's a brief profile in there of a *hot* collector taken from my notes. Just FYI."

Johnny closed the file to concentrate on what Sheridan was saying.

"Everyone in those files has exotic reptiles, cobras specifically," Sheridan went on. "And some of them have local infractions. One is an owner of a reptile store in Alexandria, not a bright light. He advertised the sale of a protected species and paid a fine."

Des jumped in, following Sheridan's lead. "Sometimes they meet at Exotic Reptiles—that's the reptile store. You should get familiar with it. They also meet in their apartments. Their addresses are all there."

Sheridan said, "I want you to learn everything you can about collecting snakes." He handed her a copy of K. C.'s new book.

"I've heard of him," she said, taking it from him.

"Everybody's heard of him," Des replied.

Sheridan told her, "Your only task right now is to get involved with these people." He nodded toward the files. "Find out if there are any new collectors in their group. New collectors get trained in the ways and means of obtaining snakes." He paused. "Get to know those *ways and means*."

Johnny looked up at him. "So I'm going undercover?"

Sheridan paused again. "In a way, yes. Des will fill you in. Those men aren't charged with anything. We're just keeping an eye on them." He added, "I want you to do something else."

Johnny held his gaze.

"Do you have a fear of snakes?"

"I...don't have much experience with them," Johnny answered.

He sensed a problem. "Could you handle a snake, a *modified* venomous snake, without fangs?"

"I don't know."

"But you could if you were trained."

"I believe I could."

He wasn't sure how much he could press. Sheridan glanced at Des, who seemed surprised at the line of questioning. *He didn't get the e-mail.*

Johnny fidgeted in her chair, the first sign of a chink in her composure, but nodded. "Yes, I could handle a snake."

He handed her a piece of paper. "Good. You have an appointment tomorrow at two p.m. with Michael Trainor. He's the head herpetologist at the National Zoo."

She took the paper from him and set it on top of the files.

"He's going to set you up with some snakes." Sheridan watched for a reaction. He got none. "It will give you credibility."

"I'll have them at home, then," she said matter-of-factly.

"Yes." He looked for another chink, but she had recovered. *Good for you.*

"They'll be in terrariums," Sheridan added. "They won't have fangs. Most likely, you'll never touch one." He looked over at Des and then continued. "Remember this: when you work with us, you never work alone. You can come to us with anything. Des will be your mentor on this case and beyond. He's going to walk you through what you need to know. Don't do *anything* without running it by him first."

She nodded again.

Sheridan pointed to the files on her lap. "You're going to be our eyes and ears with these guys."

"Okay."

Sheridan stood up and she followed. He stuck out his hand and she took it once again.

"Remember to pass everything by Des," he said.

"I will."

"I'll introduce you to the rest of the staff in just a sec," Des said, rising. He held the door open for her and she left. Des hesitated and then closed the door.

Sheridan sat down and leaned back in his chair. "You didn't get my e-mail."

"No, but it all sounds…plausible. No fluffy, four-legged creatures for her."

"Yeah." Sheridan rubbed his face. "She'll do okay."

"Do you know who she is?" Des asked, suddenly changing the subject.

Sheridan met him with a blank stare.

Des waited, watching his partner. "Think San Francisco… Chinatown…*Leland Chang*."

Sheridan looked stunned. "No way."

"I started putting two and two together—her name, age, SF—it all adds up."

Sheridan sat for a moment. "We have to be sure."

Des nodded. "I'll get more information from her."

"If it's true, we'll have to find a time to talk to her," Sheridan added.

"Or we say nothing at all."

8

The captain of the *Southern Breeze*, his view impeded by driving rain, struggled to control his thirty-five-foot fishing trawler as he brought it close to the stern of the container ship less than twenty feet from his bow.

"I thought he was gonna stop!"

"I didn't know!" the thin, nervous Asian man standing at his side replied.

"Yeah, well, I don't know either. And I'm not doing this again," the captain added, "or I'm upping my take."

A deckhand from the front of the boat entered the cramped quarters, slamming the door, puddles forming immediately at his feet. "He must be late! He's really moving."

The captain eyed the temperature gauges for his overworked engines and inched his boat closer to the large vessel.

Finally, the container ship slowed.

"It's about time."

The fishing boat caught up quickly and moved halfway down the length of the ship's port side.

"He's got twenty minutes," the captain said to no one in particular.

Outside again, the deckhand looked up at three stories of solid steel and containers that formed an impermeable wall next to them. Vaguely, he saw boxes stacked on the upper deck that seemed to reach to the sky. "He's gonna climb down that?"

Three stories below the main deck, Deng Nyugen stretched his legs inside a forty-foot container. He felt the ship slow and knew it was time to move. Stuffing his belongings into a small backpack, he placed it on top of one of the eight rectangular boxes, four on either side, which had framed his sleeping area during the journey.

After eleven days at sea, one too many because of the unexpected storm, all his supplies were gone—water, food, anti-nausea pills, which, in a moment of weakness, he had shared with his unlikely companions huddled in the opposite corner, last-minute stowaways he had agreed to let into his small living quarters.

He felt the queasiness in his stomach returning, and for a moment leaned his head against the cool back side of the container. He placed his hands on his thighs and breathed out slowly. He heard retching in the corner and groaning, and then heard one of the men moving. The pills had worn off for them, too.

Why had he ever thought being a "runner" was glamorous? He knew he would never do this again. He would go back to catching snakes and selling them in the market. He didn't care that this one trip would allow him to live for two years or longer without working. He wanted no part of it.

Deng stood slowly, feeling his way up along the wall of the container. As he rose to full height, his watch—given to him by the men who bought the snakes—gave its familiar beep. He knew the time without looking. The watch beeped every twelve hours.

He took out his flashlight and focused the beam on the boxes, and then on the two men in the opposite corner, who winced involuntarily at the intruding light.

"You cannot stay in here," he said to them in their native Thai. "Once I open this door, you have to get out."

"No! Too sick!" one responded.

"You will be caught," he reminded them.

"Where will we go?"

"Anywhere on board. They won't find you. But if you stay here, you will be caught."

One of the men waved him away, and he gave up trying to convince them otherwise.

Deng directed the light on the side of the container and found the outline of the door, large enough for a slender man to squeeze through. Moving quickly, he took ropes out of his backpack and tied two of the boxes together, then did the same for the remaining six, bundling them in pairs. He aimed the flashlight once more on the two men, who stared back at him blankly.

"Good-bye."

"Can we go with you?"

"No. There is only room for me." He pointed to the boxes. "And the snakes."

The men's eyes widened. "Snakes? Not medicinals?"

Deng ignored them and pressed forcefully on the side of the container. Feeling a portion give way, he caught the side of it and brought it inside. Diffused light from the upper deck outlined the small opening. Deng began lowering the boxes to the floor of the ship.

"Why so many?" one man in the corner asked.

"Not so many," Deng answered, lowering the last pair. Without looking back, he waved to the men and then climbed down the side of the container, and two more below it, to the floor. He felt rain on his head. A good sign: deckhands might stay inside.

Deng looked around in the semidarkness. He listened, but heard only the creaking of containers and a fan blowing in a distant wall. Quickly, he pushed the boxes further into the shadows. This was the time they had planned on, to move when the crew changed watch. Now the hard part. He looked up at the five flights of stairs that led to the main landing. He would make the trip twice.

Slowly, he tipped two roped-together boxes on end, the contents of each sliding to the bottom. He knew the snakes—a juvenile king cobra in each, save for one, a rare Russian cobra— would be angry beyond belief. Maneuvering himself into arm- holes made of ropes, he hoisted the pair onto his back. He picked up two more and walked toward the stairs. And began his climb.

He knew this ship inside and out, courtesy of his brother, who had told him: If you hear voices, get to the nearest landing. Move back against the wall and remain still. If you hear move- ment on the stairs, stop and wait. They may be going up or down only one flight. And they won't expect you to be there. But if they are very close and see you, drop the boxes and run. Save yourself.

And not get paid! Deng thought, climbing quietly. He wouldn't do that.

He reached the upper deck and, seeing no one there, moved against the wall of the tall deckhouse, his view of the side of the ship blocked by containers. Glancing left and right, Deng saw the only alley to the ship's port side, right under the gaze of the cap- tain in the deckhouse.

His arms felt numb from the weight of his load. He shifted the boxes and moved slowly away from the wall. He looked above him at the wide windows in the deckhouse and saw two men engaged in conversation, their backs turned away from the front of the boat. He quickly ran to the alley and walked as fast as he could through the canyon of containers. Finally, Deng reached the end of the row. Just thirty feet away, his rescue boat waited below.

He emerged into the open and, glancing once more at the deckhouse, quickly scurried under the curved side of the vessel. His arms aching, he placed the boxes against the side of the ship, then swung the others off his back and stacked them next to the first two.

Engines idling, the captain of the *Southern Breeze* worked to keep the boat from hitting the side of the ship. "He's got ten minutes!"

Saying nothing, the Asian man joined the deckhand outside to watch for Deng's signal.

Deng retraced his steps, making his way back to the bottom of the ship. It was when he was unstrapping the second load from his back, near the first four boxes, that he heard them coming down the stairs of the deckhouse.

He guessed there were two. They were loud. And laughing.

And not at all aware of him, he decided. But he would have to move fast. With his view of them blocked by containers, he would need to rely on sound alone.

Deftly, he jumped up and grabbed the railing two feet above his head. He held on with one hand, retrieving the flashlight from his pocket with the other. He shone it over the side of the ship and blinked twice. Since he couldn't see them, he could only surmise that they were following the plan and watching for him.

He waited, suspended in air, and gave the signal again.

"There!" The Asian man on the *Southern Breeze* pointed to the light. The two men moved closer to the bow of their boat. Suddenly, two rectangular boxes came into view and began their lengthy descent. When they were within reach and swung onto the deck, the Asian man pulled on the rope, a signal to Deng that his long journey was almost at an end.

Deng heard the voices again, much closer. They had to be in the alley of containers and coming toward him! Frantically, he roped together two more boxes and quickly lowered them over the side, the wait excruciatingly long. Finally, a tug. And slack on the line. He pulled up the rope. No time!

He roped together the remaining four boxes, tying them quickly. He lifted them up, over his head, toward the railing. But one was loose! It began sliding toward him. He couldn't stop it.

The wayward box wiggled free and crashed onto the deck, its wood splintering in four directions. He saw a snake's squatty body slide across the wet deck, then stop.

Deng quickened the speed of the contraband making its way down the side of the ship. He looked back and saw the Russian cobra drawing into itself defensively.

Where are the men?

He felt slack on the line and pulled up the rope.

Deng turned back to the snake. It was moving away over splintered wood to the underside of a container. He grabbed for the tail but missed, and the snake disappeared from view.

He heard the men near the end of the row, fifty feet away.

Deng checked the rope secured to the railing. He quickly donned gloves and, with the other end of the rope tied around his waist, jumped up and over the side of the ship.

9

Chang drove his black sedan down the busy main street. Next to him, motorbikes jostled for position as he made his way through them. It was late in the day, yet the stalls were still crowded with people buying food and homemade wares. At the end of the road, he passed the covered area where snakes had been sold, the place now bare as it had been for months.

Chang turned left off the main road and came to a weather-beaten garage on a side street. He stopped in front and saw a face pop up in a window. The door opened immediately and he drove in, and it closed behind him.

He pulled a few paces into the garage and got out, nodding to workers who were building crates nearby. Before heading to his office, he paused in front of a terrarium and looked in on the reptile lying inside. Not quite full grown, the king cobra nonetheless filled out all of its glass-walled enclosure. At its age this prized catch could expect to be around for two decades or longer. Multiply this one by the number he had given his client and he would easily meet the figure he had determined.

A worker on a forklift came by and Chang got out of the way. He watched him take the terrarium and head off to another part of the garage. As it disappeared around a stack of newly made crates, Chang turned and headed for his office.

He himself had never handled a king cobra, he thought, reaching in his back pocket for his list of things to do. The snake made him think about the people working for him who did.

Cobras were a native resource and revenue stream for them. It was one thing for the developed world to talk about saving a natural resource. It was quite another to be in the third world making a living day-to-day.

Chang entered his makeshift office situated behind partially collapsed cardboard boxes. Discarded yellowed paper bulged from several on the bottom. It was an arrangement he disliked intensely, but one that would do for the short time he would be in the city.

He looked at his watch. Ever aware of time, Chang sat down at his computer, set on a plank of wood laid across several crates. He turned it on, bringing up a map with forty-four checkpoints for cobras that had been set up throughout Thailand. He had been to all of them, supervising the work and harassing the men to work faster.

Chang perused the map for a short time and then opened an Excel file. Thai communities filled the screen: Mae Sai, Wiang Kaen, Thoena, and Pa Daet in the north...Nong Phok, At Samat, Phanom Phrai, and Suwannaphum in the northeast.

And on and on.

They would have their populations within a week and then they would leave. Phase seven—Malaysia, and phase eight—Sumatra, would commence soon thereafter.

His vast empire of king cobras was taking shape, the numbers adding up. He glanced at his list again, the plane reservation not yet made for the hastily called meeting next week. He made a mental note to do so, then crumpled the list and threw it toward an empty box.

And missed. That would not do. Chang got up and retrieved it, and set it purposefully in the bottom of the box.

He tapped his breast pocket and felt a pack of cigarettes, the one vice he allowed himself. He moved to a window, knowing how the smell of smoke bothered the snakes.

10

Sheridan glanced at his watch and quickly got up from his desk. The divorce proceedings were set to begin at the courthouse in thirty minutes. He passed Kim's desk and got her attention.

"Kim."

She looked up.

"I'm gone for the rest of the day."

"Okay," she answered.

Almost to the door, he stopped by to see Vicki and found her engrossed in something online.

"Hey," he said, poking his head in.

She turned to face him.

"I may drop by to see Stone," he began, mentioning their former co-worker but not the reason for his middle-of-the-day departure, which, if office gossip was working as well as he knew it did, she would already be privy to. He looked for a reaction at the mention of Stone's name, but there was none. Not that her lack of response distilled any thoughts he had that they had once been together. "About dinner…"

"Don't worry about it," she said quickly, adding, "I'll be at Hugo's, then home." Hugo's was the popular after-work bar that drew in mostly government employees. "You can call me."

"Okay."

"Good luck," she said, before he headed out.

* * *

Miami, Florida

First the reporter, now the marketing people were driving him crazy.

The young man with short, red-tipped hair, a "branding wiz" from Netterman's Vitamins for Reptiles, stood in the middle of K. C.'s snake room. He reached into a box, pulled out a T-shirt and snapped it open.

K. C. took in the front of the black shirt with a four-color cobra, hood raised, on the left breast. He had to admit he liked it.

"Look at this," the rep said, turning the shirt around. On the back, below the slogan All the World's Cobras, were all the world's cobras in various poses, all in color.

The rep reached into the box again, pulled out a black hat with a king cobra dead center and threw it to K. C. Then he took out a small cobra flashlight and key ring. He pressed the button. A light emanated from the open mouth. "Only six ninety-nine."

"Great."

The pain I go through for American commerce.

"By the way," the rep said, "the T-shirt comes in blue, black, and white, and with long sleeves. They've already been shipped to the show."

"Okay." K. C. looked past the young man to his desk, where a week's worth of mail and his ever-growing to-do list waited.

Sensing that his time was up, the rep hastily packed up the box and made for the door. "I'll see you in DC."

K. C. set aside items he would attend to later and went on to e-mail. He looked for last-minute messages from friends and his literary agent, who was hosting a reception in his honor the night before the International Reptile Show opened. Seeing nothing, he decided to answer a few of the many queries from fans that came in every day.

Dave in Dallas was at the top of the list.

> *Hi K. C. — My full-grown copperhead got out in the house and I can't find it anywhere. I've searched all the obvious places. Can you tell me other areas to look? It's been three days and my wife is going to kill me.*

> Dave — You'd be amazed where snakes end up. Start thinking like a snake and you'll find its hiding places: file cabinets, dresser drawers, pots, pans, clothes dryers, etc. Finding a loose snake is difficult and a venomous one doubly dangerous. I'm assuming you've looked in heater vents, the clothes hamper, under the couch. Be careful if you move a piece of furniture. This snake can jump. Here's what I suggest:
> Put a substance—dirt, flour, cornmeal—on the floor near doorways before you go to bed. The snake will come out at night to look for food and will leave a trail, even telling you what direction it's going. That's a start. Get a snake-handling friend to help you. Good luck.

Robbi from Spokane wrote in with a kid-level question.

> *K. C., I just learned that snakes hiss, so are they related to cats?*

> Robbi — When you hear a cat hiss, you're hearing the cobra, only the cobra's hiss is deeper, louder, throatier. Some people say that the great cats developed the hiss to sound like snakes so

that predators would go away. But no, they're
not related.

Another kid, he presumed. Logan from Long Island:
Do snakes sneeze?

Hi, Logan —Yes. They also yawn and cough.

K. C. opened one more e-mail, from Jason in
Reno:
*I have a long green viper in a terrarium that is too
small for it. Can I let it loose in the room so it can
stretch out while I clean its terrarium?*

Some people shouldn't be parents, K. C. thought.
No, Jason. You cannot let it loose in the room.
Think of your own safety and that of the snake.
Get yourself a large Rubbermaid trash container,
the one with the handles that snap over the lid,
and put the snake in that. Poke *small* holes in the
lid first for ventilation. And get yourself a larger
terrarium. *Right away*. Do you sleep in a bed
that's too short for you?

He struck the last sentence and sent the message.

Caring for snakes took simple common sense, yet people
didn't seem to realize that. He decided to make a point to cover
the basics of snake collecting in all his talks from now on. It would
be a way to tie in his book.

K. C. sat back and stretched, taking in the wall in front of
him. Across the whole of it were rows of local, state, and federal licenses, newspaper clippings of himself with schoolchildren,
along with photos of him receiving awards or posing with politi-

cians and professional athletes. These in turn were surrounded by plaques—too many to count—from various herpetological associations, national wildlife groups, the local TV affiliate that ran his nationally syndicated *Snake Show*, and other interested parties that liked the stance he took on species preservation.

Off to the far right was a photo of himself and his ex-wife on their wedding day. His personal life, admittedly, had taken a different route than that of his business ventures.

He saw the plaque from Netterman's Pharmaceuticals, Inc., the world's largest maker of reptilian supplements, which had recognized his ongoing good works in the community at large. With the explosion in exotic animal collecting, the small company had moved out of commercial markets and into retail trade with astonishing success, enriching him along the way. But a millionaire? He chuckled at the thought of the reporter's comment.

Not!

He sat upright, the list for the trip north beckoning. At the top: Reeves would arrive in the morning with the air-conditioned truck. It would take most of a day to move and position all twenty-two snakes into specially equipped crates for the trip to Baltimore's Convention Center. While he was away, a zoology student who occasionally helped him would come in and feed the other snakes. Thinking of that, he rose and opened the medicine cabinet and checked his supply of antivenins.

All there. All up-to-date.

He glanced at his USDA license that granted him permission to have exotic animals, which would need to be with him at all times.

He was thinking through what else needed to be done when he heard a knock at his back door. He walked to a window and parted the blinds, and saw a man with boxes standing on his small back porch.

II

Alexandria, Virginia
Monday afternoon

Sheridan sat behind the wheel of his SUV watching his ex-wife and her attorney in the parking lot of the courthouse. The lawyer, his jacket draped over one arm, was rolling up his shirt sleeves—a useless gesture, Sheridan thought, in the August heat. Joanna stood by, briefcase in hand, looking cool and crisp as ever.

The anger she had shown earlier in the day, in another parking lot, had dissipated, gone as well during their hour-long divorce proceeding. This new reality fit her better, he decided.

The attorney shook Joanna's hand and turned toward his car. Seeing Sheridan, she walked over to him. He lowered the window as she approached.

"So…" She let the rest of the thought go.

He nodded and looked away.

"Jason wants to spend the weekend with you again, if that's all right."

He looked back at her. "Sure."

"The usual time?" she asked.

"That's fine."

"He has a lot of games."

"Not a problem."

She glanced at her watch. "I'm gonna go."

"Okay."

She stepped back and held his gaze. He raised a hand in a gesture of good-bye, then closed the window as she turned toward her car. When she was gone, he exited onto a two-way street.

Easing into traffic, he headed...where? Seventeen years of marriage. Gone.

He wondered how Des, divorced six years, had come to terms with it. He realized he didn't know. They had never talked about it.

Sheridan pulled up to a stoplight. Since it was a day for unpleasantness, he decided to make good on a visit to Daniel Stone at the Maryland Department of Natural Resources, fifty minutes away in Annapolis.

Their former co-worker, Stone, had been an undercover specialist with Sheridan and Des, but had never been one for fieldwork, which always seemed odd to the two longtime agents. More an administrative type, he disdained getting his hands dirty and had been the lone dissenting voice on almost everything the department did.

During Operation Chameleon, when the department sought to identify and shut down the source in Europe—the source being the point at which illegally taken, protected reptiles came in for dissemination around the world—Stone took the opposite tack. True, they didn't know *exactly* where the source was. They had guessed, with the help of European agents, that it was in the Netherlands. Others had placed it in Germany, where earlier infractions had taken place.

Stone lobbied for them to focus on the U.S., instead of "running around the world chasing shadows." Shut down the collectors here, he had said, and traffic will stop. The department had chosen to stay with its original plan.

That mistake had proven Stone right.

Sheridan left the highway and pulled into the Department of Natural Resources on Taylor Avenue. After announcing his unscheduled visit, he took a seat in the reception area. Soon enough, Stone appeared.

"Sher!" he said, extending a hand, his cuff links reflecting the glare from the fluorescent lights above.

Sheridan, dressed in dark casual slacks and a tan short-sleeved shirt, would never get over this most unlikely looking wildlife specialist outfitted like a corporate VP.

"How goes it?" Stone asked.

"Good," Sheridan answered, rising. "Nice to see you." He sensed Stone's congeniality would end soon.

"Come on back." Stone retraced his steps and Sheridan followed. They walked by cubicles not unlike his own to Stone's impeccable office. Sheridan wondered what position he was gunning for. Knowing his outsized ambitions, it was probably the governor's seat.

Stone motioned to a chair in front of his desk and Sheridan sat down.

"What's up?" Stone asked, sitting down and leaning back in his chair. He ran his fingers down the length of his tie, flipping the end out toward his guest.

"We'll be in your jurisdiction Saturday when the reptile show opens."

"Okay." Stone shrugged. "That's not unusual. Unless it's unusual."

Sheridan paused for a moment, getting his thoughts together. "We have a situation in Thailand. A loss of cobras."

"Where again?" Stone asked.

"Thailand," Sheridan repeated. "We're working on the case."

"The case being…" Stone waited, allowing Sheridan to fill in the blanks.

"A precipitous drop in king cobras."

"They probably moved to find rats."

"No, no one is seeing *any* king cobras."

Stone thought that through without saying anything.

"We're just at the beginning," Sheridan continued. "We'll be here talking to K. C."

"He'll enjoy that," Stone responded.

"I'll get information out to the regions," Sheridan offered, meaning Fish and Wildlife's usual chain of dissemination. "But I wanted to tell you in person."

"I appreciate that."

An awkward pause settled over them.

"How are you organizing this?" Stone inquired.

Sheridan half expected his question, their brief encounter being way too civil. "We've got Isaac involved, we're looking at the collectors, and we're keeping an eye on K. C. for the moment."

Stone harrumphed under his breath, a not unexpected response, but then moved on. "Well, let me know how we can help."

"I will."

Stone ran a hand through his blond hair, pushing it back, a vanity Sheridan had always disliked. Then he sat forward, looking at something on his desk. It was as if Sheridan were no longer there.

"What's going on in Maryland?" Sheridan offered.

Stone looked up at him. "Pretty quiet...shoreline issues, habitat disputes." He shrugged as if uninterested.

"You'll be at the show, then?" Sheridan asked.

"Oh, yeah."

More silence. *Perhaps this was a mistake.*

"Well." Sheridan stood to leave, the visit as short as he thought it would be. Stone rose without saying anything and the two men walked down the hallway to the front door.

Stone looked back over his shoulder. "How's Vicki?"

Sheridan's stomach lurched. "Not sure."

They reached the reception area.

"Well, say hello to her. She always had a *big* heart." Stone laughed at his private joke. "I'll wait to hear from Region five," he added, holding the door open for Sheridan. "And I'll see you Saturday."

12

K. C. opened his back door and let the stranger with seven boxes inside. After some halting English, K. C. began to understand what his visitor was attempting to say.

"What do you mean, the Russian is gone?"

"It get loose. On ship!"

"Do you realize that is a thirty-thousand-dollar snake?"

The man said nothing.

K. C. shook his head in disgust. The loss meant a hole for the exhibit in Maryland. What was he going to tell *The Today Show*, which was interviewing him live Monday morning? He'd have to borrow a Russian, he decided. He made a mental note to call the National Zoo. With the show opening Saturday, it was another detail he didn't have time for.

He eyeballed the man in front of him, who appeared nervous, shifting position whenever K. C. looked at him. *This is a different man*, K. C. thought, *older than most who deliver the snakes*.

"What's your name?" K. C. asked.

"Deng."

K. C. didn't know if that was true or not. He glanced at the boxes on the floor. "What else do you have?"

"Six small king cobras. And one Thai spitter," Deng said.

"I'll take all of them."

Deng stacked the boxes on top of one another.

"One hundred twenty-eight thousand, right?" K. C. asked.

Deng nodded in agreement.

"These snakes are clean, right? No diseases?"

"Oh yes! Very clean. They arrive yesterday."

"How long on the ship?"

"Eleven days."

So, twelve days in a box. Hungry and mad, K. C. reasoned. He moved toward his snake room. "Come with me."

Deng followed, sans boxes.

K. C. stopped and pointed to them. "Bring those with you."

"Yes!" Deng backpedaled, retrieving two of the containers.

They walked into the coolness of the room.

"Put them on the floor."

Deng put them down and left to get the others.

"We're going to check each one," K. C. said, when all had been assembled. He reached for protective glasses and two snake sticks, then slowly and gently, with his foot, slid one of the boxes into the center of the floor. "Stand by the door."

Deng did as he was told.

K. C. gingerly maneuvered the end of a stick toward one of two half-moon-shaped locks on the outside of the box. He unlocked the first latch, then the second, and eased the top back. Instantly, the head of a young, brown-and-white-striped spitting cobra sprang up, its hood flared. It looked steadily at K. C.

K. C. waited. The hood finally resolved and the snake moved partially out of the box, its head on the floor, tongue moving in and out. K. C. moved closer and, hooking on to it, brought the rest of the snake onto the floor. It slid slightly and then curled into itself protectively. He guessed it was three feet long. It would grow a few more feet in length and two inches more in girth. And live to be twenty, if it was lucky. He quickly eyeballed the reptile for lesions and parasites. Nothing so far.

Moving with practiced ease, K. C. positioned one snake stick behind the crown and another midway down the snake's back and flipped it over, gently setting it down. The snake struggled as K. C. checked its underside. He flipped it back and released it. The snake coiled again defensively.

K. C. waited a short time, then moved toward it, mindful that if it spit, the venom would hit squarely on his glasses where one pupil was. He quickly positioned the snake stick behind the reptile's head and stooped down to pick it up. He let the stick drop to the floor and, holding the snake securely, placed it in a terrarium next to the large king cobra.

With Deng motionless near the door, K. C. repeated the exercise with the remaining snakes. Satisfied that they were clean, he put each into its own terrarium. Then he went to a container across the room and took out mice, one for each snake, and dropped them inside.

K. C. watched as the spitter's mouse froze in place, seemingly aware now of its new surroundings. And its fate. The spitter rose up, swaying slightly. Then, without warning, it struck down on the mouse's spine and rose again. Soon, the mouse's head flew back and its legs went into a spasm. As if in slow motion, the mouse rolled on its side, its legs becoming rigid. K. C. could see that its breathing was slowing. The snake struck again and held on, then slowly began the process of ingesting its meal. Most people, he knew, sided with the mouse in this unequal battle. But it was simply nature doing its work.

K. C. turned to Deng. "Let's go out here."

They walked back to the main part of the house. Deng stood by while K. C. unlocked a drawer and took out a tan-colored envelope. Without saying anything, he handed it to him.

When his visitor had left, K. C. went back to the snake room to check on his new charges.

All were lying quietly, a distinct bulge visible in the upper third of their bodies.

He leaned over and looked in on one of the snakes. "You guys have made a long journey. And you are finally home."

Thinking again of his lost Russian cobra, he picked up his cell phone and made a call.

13

Leland Chang felt his phone vibrate but declined to answer it, focusing instead on the two executives sitting across from him. They were in an airport lounge and he was waiting while they discussed the financial details he had just proposed.

A woman's voice came from the overhead speakers, announcing in several languages gate changes for recent arrivals and departures. A soothing voice, one that could put him to sleep. He realized how tired he was. Airport lounges were his home away from home these days. Yet he was never in one long enough to catch up to local time.

The drink in front of him remained untouched, while the men across from him were on their third. *Perhaps they are celebrating*, he thought. *As they should*. He was about to make them, and himself, very wealthy indeed.

He eyed one of the men, who gulped down the last of his liquid. He spoke louder than the other, the alcohol loosening who-knew-what inside his brain. *He shouldn't imbibe*, Chang thought. For *himself*, drink took him out of the realm in which he liked to do business: organized, calculated, in control. This man had none of those qualities.

While they conversed, Chang scanned the people walking by as well as those ensconced at nearby tables. He had become adept at knowing where all the players in the room were. A sudden disappearance in tight situations was a trait he had perfected since a close call with U.S. wildlife agents five years previously.

Finally, the men at his table turned back to him. One of them buttoned his double-breasted business suit jacket and began.

"I think it's a reasonable offer and one that we can agree to. You are assuring absolute discretion, are you not?"

"It will not be a problem," Chang assured him. "I have every avenue covered."

"We cannot risk having this become an international event, for obvious reasons," the other man insisted, above the voice of his partner.

"You have my assurances that your names will never be made public," Chang answered.

The man in the double-breasted suit leaned forward and stuck out his hand, and Chang responded in kind.

His inebriated partner also leaned forward and raised his empty glass. "Let's celebrate!"

* * *

Arlington, Virginia

Sheridan pulled into the parking lot of Hugo's Grill, a hangout for government staffers that was two blocks from the Arlington office. He glanced at his watch: 5:10 p.m. If anyone showed up it wouldn't be for awhile. He clicked the car doors locked behind him and walked into the bar. He saw one person nursing a beer and watching TV. Off to the side, a few government workers he recognized were standing at a table and he nodded at them. Two or three couples filled booths.

"Surviving the heat?" Stan the bartender asked, placing a coaster in front of him as Sheridan sat down.

"Barely," Sheridan answered. "I'll have the usual"

While Stan poured him a beer, Sheridan surveyed the rest of the room in the mirror behind the bar. He'd been in here when it was standing room only, for retirements, birthdays, the successful completion of an op. Something about its décor was comforting and homey, and it attracted people like himself: government types, those who had a lot of years in the system.

People who knew how things worked.

Stan put the beer in front of him and he took a long sip. He looked up at the TV. Early news was on, with the volume muted.

"When are the Orioles on?"

"Starts at seven."

"New York?"

"That would be correct," Stan answered, then changed the subject. "Speaking of New York...what did that '52 Mantle go for?" He meant the mint-condition Topps baseball card Sheridan had mentioned often.

"Hasn't sold yet," Sheridan responded.

Stan shook his head. "I saw that card once."

"Yeah, I know."

"It's like that Ichiro that went for twelve thousand dollars," Stan said.

"Unbelievable," Sheridan said. A man at the end of the bar smiled at them in agreement.

Stan left to wait on other patrons and Sheridan's thoughts returned to the day's events: Joanna...Johnny...Stone. He felt a presence over his left shoulder and turned to see Des.

"Hey, man. You're early," Sheridan said.

"Yeah." Des plopped down on the stool next to him. "Time to bring Monday to a close. How'd it go?"

"What you'd expect," Sheridan answered. "He's a viper. No pun intended."

"I meant with Joanna."

"Oh."

Des motioned for a beer and Stan acknowledged it.

"How I thought it would," Sheridan answered.

Des asked, "Is she with someone?"

It was as personal as he'd ever been about Sheridan's now ex-wife. "Yeah. Jason's mentioned him." He wondered why Des was being so straightforward now, when they had never broached the subject before.

Stan placed a glass of beer in front of Des. More government staffers came in and took seats around them.

Des played with the edge of his coaster, avoiding Sheridan's gaze in the mirror. "You've gone your separate ways," he said finally. "Time to move on. That's all I can tell you."

It was more than he had ever said.

"I thought about keeping it together," Sheridan offered.

"That's because you're a good guy," Des replied, clinking his beer glass to Sheridan's. "Someone *else* is interested in you."

Sheridan didn't say anything.

"What do you think?"

"I don't know."

"She could be good for you right now."

"There's a lot going on."

"So? She could help you through this," Des replied, Vicki's name going unmentioned. He changed the subject. "How's Stone?"

"Same." Sheridan ordered another beer.

"He knows we'll be around?" Des asked.

"Yep."

This time Sheridan moved on to another subject. "About Johnny...you're sure about her? Lee is a common name."

Des nodded that he was. "I'll find out the year her father died. That'll nail it."

"She'll have access to files."

"We never said anything."

"Right." Sheridan shook his head. "So she went into law enforcement to find the man who killed her father."

"That's my take on it," Des said.

"So, what do you think of her?" Sheridan asked.

Des shrugged. "Got some determination."

"Yeah, that's what I think." Sheridan took a long draw on his beer. "But I wonder if she'll stay."

"I think so. I have a feeling this one will work out," Des added, a reference to other young staffers they had taken on over the years, some the sons and daughters of government employees, who had eventually left. Or been asked to leave. "I'm meeting her tomorrow."

"Good."

"What's the news on Thailand?" Des asked.

"I need to talk to Ashland again," Sheridan responded. "My hunch is that the loss is endemic to the species."

They heard laughter at one of the tables. Sheridan turned to see Vicki, Kim the intern, and a woman from another department settling in.

Vicki walked up to them. "Hi, guys."

"Hello," Des said, turning toward her.

Stan took her order for three light beers.

"That's not beer," Des kidded, glancing at Sheridan.

"You say that every time," she reminded him, hitting him in the knee. She turned to Sheridan. "How'd it go?"

He didn't know which part of his day she was referring to. But he had an idea. "It went alright."

"We're having a birthday drink with Kristy, then I'll be home," she said to Sheridan. Stan placed three beers on the bar. "The offer still stands." She gathered the drinks and walked back to her table.

"You've got nothing to lose," Des reminded him.

14

Sheridan parked in the driveway of Vicki's small house.

"It's just a simple pasta dinner," she said, as he walked in.

Sheridan took in the aroma of tomato sauce and garlic. "It smells great," he said, handing her a bottle of red wine and following her into the kitchen.

"I've got wine open over there," Vicki said, setting the new bottle on the counter. "Or there's beer in the fridge."

"Think I'll stick with beer," he said opening, the refrigerator door. She turned her attention back to the stove.

"What, no light stuff?" he kidded, looking inside. Sheridan pulled out a microbrew, opened it, and leaned back against the counter. She turned and smiled at him.

"So how was *your* day?" he asked, nervous about being there. And sure it showed.

She glanced at him again over her shoulder. "All right, for the start of the week. How was the...you know..."

Vicki hesitated, but this time he knew what she was referring to. "It'll take time to get used to," he replied. "In some ways, I'm already used to it."

Vicki nodded in understanding.

He wanted to move beyond this, knowing that discussions about work would be more comfortable. Yet he knew her inquiry was one of genuine interest. Vicki didn't play games. *He* seemed to be the one having difficulty coming to terms with their history, one night three years ago while at an out-of-town meeting. That night had created awkwardness and tension for him ever since, perhaps because it had signaled the end of his marriage.

She stirred the sauce and then turned down the heat. "How's Stone?"

She is simply inquiring about an ex-employee. "Same as he ever was."

"So, a pain in the ass."

He laughed. "Yeah."

Vicki maneuvered a strand of thin spaghetti out of boiling water and sampled it. With her back to him, Sheridan took in her finely sculpted body, none of it hidden by her T-shirt and tight shorts. Lost in his thoughts, it startled him when she turned suddenly.

Vicki smiled slowly. "Want to sit down?"

"No. I'm good," he replied.

"What I mean is, we're ready." She pointed to the table in the dining room. "You can toss the salad."

"All right." He walked into the dining room and placed his beer on the table, then thought the better of it and poured the contents into a glass. Leaning into the kitchen, he set the empty container on the counter. Then he stirred the oil and vinegar dressing, poured it over the salad, and tossed.

She walked up behind him, steaming plates of spaghetti balanced in both hands.

"You sit here," she said, placing one plate in front of him."

She walked around the table until she was across from him and sat down. He served salad for both of them.

"This looks great, Vicki," he said, and started in. He looked across at her and smiled.

"I'm glad you came," she answered, taking a sip of her wine.

He devoured the meal, two servings, and then helped himself to the rest of the garlic bread. They talked about Jason, the weather, the Thailand case. Nothing was mentioned again about the divorce. Later, sitting in her living room, watching the end of the Orioles' game, she brought up work again.

"I'm flying to Wyoming next week," she said.

"They've got something, finally?" he asked, in reference to the eagle case she was now in charge of.

"Not really. It's about the same, actually: a lack of evidence." She got up to adjust the air conditioner, then walked back to the couch and sat down.

"Have you checked with Alaska?" Sheridan asked. It was the most populous eagle state.

"There isn't a problem in Alaska. Marsh said it's only Wyoming where they aren't seeing eagles."

"That's just odd," Sheridan said.

"I know." Vicki hesitated before continuing. "There's something else I want to tell you."

Sheridan waited for her to continue, taking in her finely chiseled features.

"I'm applying for a job out there."

The news hit him like a lightning bolt, both the revelation and his reaction.

"I didn't know that."

"I want to get back in the field and work on cases like this. I don't want to be in the office."

That wasn't a surprise. "I know what you mean."

"I *know* you know what I mean."

"Is there an opening?" he asked.

"Yes."

Sheridan looked at her and realized she was serious. "I think you should do it." He stared at the bookcase against the wall and then back at her. He wasn't sure what else to say. "It's where your history is," he said finally, referencing her father's and grandfather's work at Fish and Wildlife. A response without emotion— and not at all how he felt.

She nodded, then asked suddenly, "What are you gonna do?"

He thought of his workload. "I've got the thing with—"

"That's not what I mean." Vicki picked up the remote and muted the game. "You, personally."

"I don't know," he said, meeting her gaze.

"You're divorced."

"Yes."

"Now what?"

"I don't know." He looked back at the TV. Someone was running around the bases. Fast. "Jason's here. That will be a deciding factor."

"What about moving out West?" she asked, referring to a yearning he had voiced to her years earlier.

"It's only a thought right now."

She got up a second time and closed the blinds. He watched her move from window to window. If Vicki had ever been an option for him it was one that was quickly slipping away.

He wasn't sure what to do.

At the door, he thanked her for the meal and the company, her revelation about her plans still very much with him. In the hallway's semidarkness, she moved closer to him and placed her hand lightly on his hip. He leaned over and kissed her on the cheek, lingering there for a moment, the closeness to her almost unbearable. He had to proceed slowly, he thought. If at all.

She turned her head toward him and he felt her breath on his cheek.

He knew what she was suggesting, but decided to leave. "I've gotta go."

"Why?"

Vicki reached up and wrapped her arms around his neck. And pressed into him. Without thinking, he responded in kind, engulfing her, kissing her deeply.

"Come with me," she whispered.

He allowed himself to be led. They passed through the hallway of her small house and into her bedroom. Fully aroused, he let his passion take over. He brought her close and kissed her long and hard. Sheridan heard her moan. She took his head in her hands and kissed him deeply, taking control, driving him crazy.

In the darkness of her bedroom, Sheridan lay on his back and stared up at the ceiling, the many pieces of his day replaying in his mind. Next to him, Vicki slept soundly, her hand on his chest. He placed his hand gently on top of hers and felt sleep coming on. But before drifting off he saw a disturbing scene, vestiges of an old op—a San Francisco case—and one that visited him only in his most tired and unguarded moments.

15

Washington, DC
Tuesday morning

Johnny sat at her computer in her sparsely furnished apartment not far from the Capitol building. She scrolled through Web pages for the National Zoo, clicking on the Reptile Discovery Center and bringing up the full-color image of the building. She clicked on its residents and read through the holdings, which included a king cobra.

Glancing away from the screen for a moment, she took in the four walls of her small apartment. Her heart began beating rapidly as she tried to imagine having terrariums filled with snakes in the place where she lived. For a moment, she regretted what she was getting into.

And just what is it I'm getting into?

Realistically, she did not believe Sheridan and Des would put her in a position beyond what she was capable of handling. And yet...

Putting the thought out of her mind, she turned back to the screen and printed pages for the Reptile Center. Then she reached for the file titled "Collectors" that Sheridan had given her. She opened it and began reading the brief summary of the individuals who collected venomous snakes.

Profile
Single. White. Male. Middle class. High school grad. Some college. Age: 19–28. And 38–55. Marriage—the new wife—made many of them give up the hobby. Divorce brought them back. Note by Sheridan: They knew that

collectors started much earlier, but to have *hots*, you had
to have money. Most lived in California and Florida. Then
Texas and Arizona. Florida had the most stringent laws.

Collections

Most started with local venomous varieties: rattlers, cop-
perheads, cottonmouths. In a few states, collecting these
types wasn't against the law. However, transporting them
to another state was. It depended on what state the snake
was moved from and what state it entered. Sheridan note:
For the international varieties, a surprising number collected mambas from Africa, snakes that both chase and
attack humans. Some favored the South American varieties: bushmaster and Fer de Lance, both considered
extremely dangerous. Others liked Asian reptiles: the
smaller cobras and the large Russell's viper, which was
considered deadly, with no antivenin for it in the U.S.

She read Sheridan's hand-scribbled notes in the margins.
USDA placed the number of hot collectors in the U.S. at fourteen
thousand, based on the number of permits it granted. The underground zoo, which she knew was a network of exotic snake collectors, swelled the ranks to forty-two thousand, three times as
many. It was a one-billion-dollar industry in the U.S., just above
smuggling in humans.

All of which she knew.

She read the last category.

Collecting cobras

Collectors graduated to cobras, which were considered
the top rung of snake collecting, much later. Most hot
snake collectors will never own a cobra.

Sheridan had underlined this last sentence.

She thought about that as she moved on to the "Beltway collectors" files. Johnny opened the file on Paul St. John, owner
of the Exotic Reptiles store in Alexandria. Soon she would be

among them. And because they had cobras, she reminded herself, they were an elite group.

She glanced at the police photo of St. John, taken when he had attempted to sell a rare Appendix I-listed juvenile rock python, not a venomous variety but an extremely threatened one in its Indian habitat. In the picture, he appeared frumpy and over-weight, with stringy dark hair that hung down over his forehead. Maybe in his late twenties. His expression was one of resignation, and like he carried the weight of the world on his shoulders. Now he had a police record. She noted that the snake had been confis-cated and he had paid a $5,500 fine.

Johnny glanced at the clock. Her meeting with Michael Trainor, the herpetologist, was scheduled for later that afternoon. She opened the next file, for Adam Hunter, and immediately saw a dark, handsome young man staring back at her. If she hadn't known better, she might have thought he was a grad student at one of DC's elite universities. Instead, he too had a police record, with infractions going back to his early teens.

He doesn't look the part.

Without reading further, she placed Adam's file on top of her keyboard and quickly perused another one, for Warren Anderson, a PhD candidate in biochemistry at the time. He looked like an All-American blond surfer type to her.

These were the men she was going to get to know.

Shifting gears, she moved the files to the side and wrote a quick e-mail to her mother in San Francisco, letting her know how she was. She flirted briefly with the idea of sending Brian, a love left in California, an e-mail. But she decided against it and turned off the computer.

Reaching for Adam's file again, she sat back and reread the information, taking in the photo, making assumptions about who he was, what he liked. He no doubt held himself in high regard, she surmised, working the world to fit his place in it.

He had found a way to make money and he wasn't going to let that go. He would always be a felon.

Johnny stood up suddenly and went into the bathroom, taking Adam's file with her. She had an idea about how could she enter his world and make herself *believable*. She put the file on top of a shelf and opened it so that his photo was looking back at her.

Johnny stood in front of the mirror contemplating her next move. Her mind made up, she picked up scissors and began cutting her long black hair, the strands falling silently around her feet. She chopped at it indiscriminately until she had the edgier look she was aiming for. Then she put on black mascara, all the while glancing at Adam's photo. Liking the way that looked, she walked into her bedroom and fished around for pierced earrings on her dresser, and put them on. She stood back, arms folded in front of her, and inspected her appearance in the mirror.

Not bad.

But not wanting to scare the herpetologist, whom she assumed was a white middle-aged man like Sheridan, she removed the mascara and carefully put the earrings in her jewelry case. Then she returned to the bathroom and took a quick shower.

16

Sheridan lay awake, listening to the silence. Soon, he heard a faint swooshing sound as Vicki's central air-conditioning ratcheted up. She stirred beside him and opened her eyes.

"Hi," she said sleepily. "You look awake."

"I am," he replied.

She inched closer. "What are you thinking about?"

"Oh...work...Jason." He put his arm around her shoulders and drew her close to him, feeling the warmth of her body.

"And us?" she asked.

He smiled. "That, too."

He kissed her hair, her forehead. They lay together, lost in thought. He tried to push aside his concerns, but they stayed with him. Suddenly, Vicki rolled onto her elbow and looked at him.

"I want to ask you something," she said, the sleepiness gone.

He didn't say anything.

"Will you come with me if I move to Wyoming?" Her thoughts poured out, leaving him little time to answer. "I'd have a job. And a place to live."

"What would I do?" he said finally.

"Hire yourself out. Wyoming would hire you in a minute."

"I have a mortgage...Jason...a new case."

"The case will end," she answered. "You can sell your house. And live with me." She remained above him and held his gaze. "It would be a tremendous experience for Jason," she went on. "He'd discover a whole new world."

"He has friends here. And his sports."

"He'll make new friends. He's young. Would your wife agree to it?"

"I doubt it," he answered, noting Vicki still had referred to Joanna as his wife.

She waited for him to continue, but he left the thought hanging.

"You told me three years ago you wanted to go back in the field," Vicki said.

"That's the plan."

"And if that plan includes me, this is a start."

He put his hand behind his head and looked past her, to the wall across from the bed. He saw picture frames that he knew held photos of her famous grandfather. And her father. And herself. Three generations spanning the Service's existence. He looked back at her, at her exquisite face, her hair tousled from a night of lovemaking.

"I'm not dismissing it out of hand," he said finally. "I want us to be together. You have to believe me on that."

Vicki looked down, at nothing in particular, then back at him. Not wanting to press the point further, she said simply, "Okay." She kissed him and asked, "Will you do something else?"

"What?"

"Will you be my date this Saturday? You and Jason? It's my parents' annual get-together."

"Sure."

"Good. Then it's a date."

* * *

Washington, DC

Johnny walked through the grounds of the National Zoo until she came to the Reptile Discovery Center. Early for her appointment, she sat on a bench under a tree to gather her thoughts.

And calm her anxiety.

It wasn't that she especially *disliked* snakes. She just didn't have much experience with them. She wasn't completely squeamish like a lot of women were. She had grown up in a city, after all, and had rarely seen them. What she didn't like was the surprise factor: walking in a field, for example, and looking down and seeing one. Her heart always jumped in those situations.

She glanced at the papers in her hand. She had read about snakes online, cobras in particular. She knew about their endangered habitat, their loss in population, why their neck swelled out to form a hood. It was a defensive measure and a sign of aggression. She was surprised to learn that *all* snakes could flare out their neck ribs if they chose to do so. Only the cobras did it regularly.

Who would have known?

Suddenly, her heart started pounding again. Panicked, she stood up. *What if one got out? What if it got behind the refrigerator? What if…?*

Johnny turned and walked away. In an effort to quell her thoughts, she took out her phone and called a classmate from the Glynco training center now working in Customs at Dulles International Airport.

"Steffy, it's Johnny," she said after her friend answered.

"Hey. Are you okay? You don't sound good."

"I'm all right," Johnny replied, gaining some composure. She walked around the corner of the building. "I'm at the zoo. I'm meeting a herpetologist."

"Why?"

"I'll tell you later." She looked at her watch. "How are you?"

Steffy laughed. "I'm okay. You wouldn't believe what comes through here." She paused before continuing. "I'm not convinced you're all right."

Johnny exhaled loudly. "Really, I'm good. Talking to you is helping. Want to have dinner Friday?"

"Sure."

"I changed my hair. You'll notice." Johnny looked at her watch. "I gotta go."

Steffy laughed a second time. "Okay. Call me later."

Johnny put her phone away and walked back toward the reptile house, the time for her meeting at hand. She looked up and read a date above the doorway—1954—then entered and walked down a ramp into the darkened facility.

On this weekday in August, only a few family groups were inside, touring the exhibits. She noticed the scent of reptile musk and wondered if a similar smell would permeate her apartment. Suddenly, she felt her heart beating rapidly again.

Johnny stopped in front of an exhibit and saw a monocled cobra partially hidden behind a rock, and took in the distinctive marking on the back of its neck.

Her eye caught someone moving toward her from the opposite end of the room, a short, stocky balding man with a big smile. He was dressed in a brown shirt and pants, and she assumed he was Michael Trainor, the man she was supposed to meet.

He came closer and closed the space between them to two feet. Instinctively, Johnny stepped back.

"Exactly the response I wanted!" He stuck out his hand. "Mike Trainor. That little exercise illustrates an animal's comfort zone, humans included. You'll want to remember that when you're dealing with venomous snakes. Grant them eight feet at a minimum." Before she could respond, he turned abruptly and signaled with a raised hand. "Follow me."

17

Miami, Florida
Tuesday afternoon

K. C. and Reeves rolled the large king cobra terrarium out of the snake room and down the hallway to the back door. They eased it onto the ramp that led out of the house, then onto another long ramp in the driveway.

"I'll push from behind," K. C. said.

Reeves walked up the side of the ramp and positioned himself at the top of the cart. They pushed and pulled in unison and rolled the heavy cart into the depths of the cushioned, air-conditioned truck. Positioned next to two monocled cobras and secured tightly to the side of the truck, the king and twenty-two other cobras were now in place. Reeves put the ramp back in the truck and closed the door.

K. C. jumped down and mopped his forehead. He looked at his watch. "That took six hours. It doesn't get any easier."

Reeves wiped his face on the sleeve of his shirt. "Think I'll go home and get ready. Meet you back here in what...two hours?"

"Sounds good," K. C. said.

K. C. stood under the shower, the steady stream pelting his face and chest. He slicked water off his head, then stepped out and dried quickly. Placing a towel around his waist, he ran a comb through his hair and walked into his bedroom. He picked out clothes for the drive, his usual black jeans and T-shirt, then other clothes for his time in DC. He packed them and closed the suitcase.

K. C. knew Reeves would arrive shortly with everything set: coffee, food, music, maps. Always dependable, his good friend never failed him. Their arrangement was now twenty years on from the time K. C. had taken him in after a particularly messy stretch that included drunken blackouts and a second divorce. He had propped Reeves up with odd jobs and errands. As good fortune shined on him, K. C. simply hired his friend permanently as his right-hand man, an arrangement that was convenient for both of them.

K. C. walked down the hallway to his snake room. He entered and surveyed the partially empty quarters. Piles of dust sat where the king cobra terrarium had been.

This is the last time I'm doing this.

"It doesn't make sense," he said to himself, "to cause these animals so much stress, all for a little prime time."

He walked over to a smaller terrarium that would stay behind and straightened the ultraviolet light he had bumped while moving.

Perhaps the snakes have nothing to do with it, he thought. *Perhaps the stress is all my own.*

He went to the wall that held his state and federal licenses. He took down his USDA permit that doubled as a passport, allowing him to travel throughout the U.S. without obtaining individual state permits for exotic animals.

And wouldn't that be a royal pain in the ass, he thought, wiping dust from the top of the frame, having some hyper-caffeinated cop pulling them over and demanding they get those state permits *right now* before moving *one more foot*.

He heard his back door open and Reeves calling out. "I've got the route set."

"Great. I'll be right there."

18

Sheridan closed the last of his e-mails, then began more research on the Web.

How many have to be missing before you notice?

For his present case, he determined that Thailand was missing *some* of its snakes in areas where they were usually seen, and not the grand majority the prime minister's office would have them believe.

Important to know, of course, was the total count of king cobras in the country. No one could provide an exact figure. Every wild animal's population was a guesstimate, including that of these revered creatures.

He entered the Web site for the International Union for the Conservation of Nature (IUCN) or simply IUC, as he and his colleagues referred to it. The group, based in Switzerland, had as its mission to "influence, encourage, and assist societies throughout the world to conserve the integrity and diversity of nature." It worked closely with UNESCO and World Heritage sites to meet its goals of conservation, biodiversity, and sustainability.

But, as he had learned throughout the years with all things governmental—U.S. governmental, that is—the Department of the Interior didn't give the group much credence. It was too European, too *green*, for the staid U.S. political types.

Sheridan himself thought the work IUC did was exemplary. And so did most of the people he worked with, especially when it came to the organization's wild.cu.com Web pages, where it kept track of animal populations, species by species, country by country. It was the best place to go to for an updated list of threatened species area by area.

He clicked on background papers, then on a link for king cobras. A map of the world popped up with the king cobra's range throughout India and Asia highlighted, including Thailand, Malaysia, Indonesia, China, and the Philippines. Off to the side was a brief history about the snake. He scanned the information, noting a population in the world of 253,322—a statistic, he knew, which had a high margin of error.

Sheridan reached for his coffee. Every five years, IUC epidemiologists fanned out across the globe to do animal counts, just like Fish and Wildlife did in the U.S. It appeared that the group was set to do another one next year.

He put his cup down, and came back to his initial thought about the problem: no one, except Thailand itself, was watching the snakes' disappearance within its borders.

And in the world at large, *who cared?*

No one wanted to deal with snakes, especially big venomous ones.

He clicked on the link for Thailand. A detailed map appeared, with dark red spots in outlying rural and jungle areas indicating concentrations of kings. The largest cities—Bangkok and Nonthaburi, as well as Chiang Mai in the north—had lightly shaded areas, evidence of king cobra populations even within these metropolitan areas, and almost always due to the snake following its food source: rats. The total number of king cobras in Thailand was listed at 43,073.

He clicked on Provinces, which brought up a listing of king cobra populations area by area throughout Thailand. Not surprisingly, distribution was higher in the north, northeast, and central provinces, and away from the beaches and tourists in the south.

Was the disappearance because the food source had moved, as Terelli in Ashland had suggested? If that were the case, they wouldn't know where the snakes had gone for a year *after* the IUC survey. Sheridan thought about that, then picked up the phone and called Ashland. After the usual pleasantries with Terelli again, he started in.

"I'm still on that Thailand case," Sheridan explained.

"Oh, yeah?" Terelli answered a question posed by someone in his office, then came back on the line. "You know, after you and I talked I called our source in Asia. But he hasn't seen anything."

"Really."

"So here's what I think," Terelli offered. "Someone will flood the market soon with skins or meat. We're ready for the first indication of that. We just have to wait."

"We don't have time to wait," Sheridan responded.

"Says who?"

"The State Department."

Sheridan heard him laugh—not that he blamed him, being, as they always were, at the beck and call of every federal everyone.

"Do you want to talk to Mel?" Terelli asked. Mel was the agency's brilliant yet difficult biostatistician.

"Do I have to?"

"Might help. Might be able to offer something."

Sheridan hesitated. None of his previous encounters with the man had been pleasant. He didn't know why Terelli kept him on.

"All right," Sheridan said finally.

"Hang on."

Sheridan waited while he was transferred. After a short time, Mel came on with a brief introduction of his last name.

"Simpson."

"Mel, Sheridan here. I want to ask—"

"Terelli told me," Simpson interrupted.

Sheridan got right to the point. "IUC figures show about forty-four thousand king cobras in Thailand. Let's say, arbitrarily, that forty percent, or roughly seventeen thousand, go missing. Is that a number you'd notice, do you think?"

"Hard to say. Are you talking about one area of the country or the whole country? If you're talking about one area, you'd notice way before seventeen thousand. If it's the whole country, you wouldn't notice. Not for awhile."

"I see."

"What *exactly* are you trying to determine?" Mel asked.

Sheridan hesitated. "I'm trying to get a handle on numbers," he answered, thinking through the likely scenarios again for the disappearance. He knew an environmental event or a virus would have left carcasses. Poaching to the extent that a population drops significantly is difficult, impossible in jungle communities. The Thai people would not take the snake for consumption. What was left? "Would an entire population move to follow a food source?" Sheridan asked finally.

"Over time, yes. Acutely? No," Mel answered.

Sheridan started to say something else, but Simpson preempted him.

"Global warming is here. The snakes have gone deeper into the jungle."

"But *no one* has seen them."

"You can't say that!" Mel countered. "They're hard to track." He paused, and then added, "They gotta be *somewhere*."

Sheridan realized he had gotten all he was going to get from the man. He thanked him for his input and hung up.

Searching for the State Department file on his desk, he found it and the name of the contact inside. He turned back to his computer and composed a quick e-mail. Given Thailand's priority status, he expected an answer in short order.

Sheridan thought again about his less-than-satisfying conversation, knowing there was someone who would give him an explanation he could work with, even though the subject matter was outside of his expertise. That person was his stepbrother, a professor of economics and a math wiz at the University of Chicago.

They hadn't talked in almost a year.

Nevertheless, Sheridan searched through his Rolodex and found his stepbrother's telephone number. He picked up the phone and called him.

What exactly are you trying to determine?

Sheridan got voice mail. Instead of leaving a long-winded message, he hung up.

Why don't I have his e-mail address?

He brought up the Web site for the University of Chicago and searched through the faculty listing for his stepbrother's name.

Out of the corner of his eye, he caught movement in his office and saw Vicki enter and close his door.

Sheridan turned and smiled at her. "Hey."

"Hey to you," she answered softly. "I have something for you."

He laughed.

Vicki crossed her arms. "Come here."

On cue, Sheridan got up and walked over to her.

"We're not supposed to do this," she said, putting her arms around his waist and drawing him closer.

"I know," he added, immersed in her presence. He kissed her warm lips and embraced her, losing track of cobras and his stepbrother for the moment.

She pulled back. "How's your case?"

Surprised, he stared down at her. "You're asking about my case?"

"Uh-huh."

"Why?"

"Because I'm here to tell you about mine."

"Had me fooled." He kissed the top of her head and then returned to his desk.

"Marsh called," she began, in regard to the eagle case.

"What'd he say?"

"There are no problems with eagles anywhere else in the country."

"How did he arrive at that?" Sheridan asked.

"He contacted everyone he knows—Alaska to Tennessee."

"Not a bad idea," Sheridan remarked, making a mental note to write Isaac in Germany again. "What else?"

"Not much, except that he's following up on some well-known takers. He's calling me every day. I'm working on this and nothing else."

"Good. That's what Egan wanted," Sheridan answered.

Vicki looked at her watch. "I've got to run. Later?"

"Yeah." He hesitated, wanting her to linger.

She winked at him as she left, running into Des at the door.

"Hey, Vick!" Des said, as she passed by. He came into Sheridan's office and gave his buddy a sly smile.

Sheridan pointed a finger at him. "Don't you say anything."

Des held up both hands to indicate that nothing would be said. "I'm off to meet Johnny. Just wanted you to know."

"Good. Do me favor, when you get a chance?" Sheridan asked, changing the subject.

"What?"

"Call Matt at NOAA," Sheridan said. "Ask about climate change, anything that's happened abruptly in the past twelve months. I couldn't find anything. But that may be because I don't think there's anything to find."

"Okay."

Sheridan thought for a moment. "While you're at it, call Trainor after Johnny's visit. Ask him about reptile extinctions—if there were any and what the causes were."

"Got it."

19

Johnny followed Michael Trainor through the Reptile House past exhibits where snakes of various stripes lay quietly. A bright green, nonvenomous tree snake, its slender body wrapped around a branch, stared back at her.

Trainor stopped at a well-camouflaged door across from the empty king cobra exhibit. "The king is being looked at in the back," he said, as if reading her mind. "I'll show you once we're inside."

He inserted a key and opened the door into the brightly lit "back office" of the reptile house. Blinking against the light, Johnny followed him in.

"So, you're working with Sher and Des?" he asked, as they passed a table where two people her age were holding a large turtle. An older man—a veterinarian, she guessed—was shining a beam of light in its eye.

"Yes," she answered, as they walked down a corridor past the back side of the exhibits.

"I like those guys," Trainor said. "You'll learn a lot from them."

They entered a large room at the end of the corridor. Johnny took in the surroundings. There were more bright lights above. A large map of the world covered one wall. At the end of the room four men stood around a table with sides on it.

"They're giving the king cobra a checkup," Trainor explained. He indicated again for her to follow.

They came up behind the men. Johnny noted an amazing amount of coils on the table, and then realized they belonged to one snake. One of the men turned to look at her and Trainor signaled for him to come over.

"Johnny, this is Jeff," Trainor said. "It's his snakes you're going to have."

Jeff stuck out his hand. "Nice to meet you."

"Same here," Johnny said. She thought it odd that, since he had exotic snakes, he wasn't in Sheridan's files. She asked him about the men whose files she had.

"Yeah," Jeff answered. They moved away from the table and into yet another room, where Johnny saw terrariums and a smaller, four-sided table. "I know them. I'd keep away from them."

"Why?" she asked.

"They're not…um…good to hang with," he replied, "if you know what I mean."

"I'm not sure what you mean," she said.

He shrugged.

Trainor interrupted them, getting to the point. "In case you're wondering, we're not setting you up with a king cobra. It's the most docile snake here but it's too big. We're giving you defanged smaller cobras, ones that will give you *cachet*."

She nodded.

"Of the ones we have," Trainor said, as he walked in front of the terrariums and pointed them out, "you're getting a monocled, an African, a Russian—that one is quite rare, by the way—and an Indian cobra."

Jeff interjected, "Those guys will be impressed that you have a Russian."

"Where did I get it?" Johnny asked, wondering how she would explain its presence.

"You'll have to talk to your bosses about that," Trainor answered. "Step over here. I'm going to show you what you need to have. Then I'll show you what you need to know." He pointed to a desk. "These are the accoutrements snake handlers use," he said, pointing to snake sticks of various lengths, hide boxes, cages with small mice, books, magazines, vitamins, and a bottle with liquid inside and a spray top. "If I think of something else I'll let you know. Jeff will show you how to take a snake out. It would be best if you didn't handle one. But you need to know how none-theless."

Jeff grabbed a short snake stick and walked back to the first terrarium. He stood on a step stool. "I picked out the smallest ones I have. They're defanged." He turned to her. "I don't defang snakes. These are rescued ones."

Trainor interrupted. "They're defanged, but they still have teeth. If you're bitten, that's a puncture would. Wash it off, then get yourself to the ER."

Johnny nodded that she understood.

"Snakes carry salmonella," Trainor added.

Jeff lifted the lid on the Russian cobra's terrarium. The dark-colored snake stirred slightly. He put the snake stick behind its head. Instinctively, the reptile coiled defensively. With his other hand, Jeff grabbed the back of the snake's head, then removed the stick and picked up its body, and brought it out. He stepped down. Johnny moved back to give him room, lots of room, her heart beating rapidly again.

"You always want to know where the head is," Jeff explained. "Keep it out in front of you. You can hold the snake's body close to you. He positioned the three-foot snake's body under his arm. "It's more comfortable for you that way."

She watched the snake's tongue flick in and out.

"Go ahead and touch it," Trainor said.

Johnny hesitated, and then stepped forward. "It looks so... serious."

"They all look that way," Trainor said.

She put her hand behind Jeff's near the back of the reptile's head, where the neck flared out to form the hood. She felt a slight undulation under her fingers. The snake felt cool and dry, the neck taught, seemingly like the rest of the body.

"I thought the neck would be loose because of the hood," she commented.

"The ribs flare when the snake wants them to," Trainer told her. "Otherwise, he's in standard mode."

"I see," she said.

"I'll show you how to put it down," Jeff said. "Make sure your longer snake stick is close by." He leaned down and rested the snake on the floor. Holding the head firmly, he let go of the body, which instantly arched toward the head. He stepped lightly on the reptile's back to keep its motion from dislodging his hand. He put the longer snake stick on the neck. "You don't have to keep the stick on the snake. You can let go after a time." Slowly, he moved the stick away. The snake remained where it was.

Trainor said, "You should take out the Russian if you're going to take out anything. It's more sluggish than the others. Try to avoid taking out the African asp, which is quicker and will rise up."

"Did you see all the steps?" Jeff asked.

Johnny folded her arms defensively in front of her. "Yes."

"I'll put this one away and go through it all again, okay?" he asked, without looking at her.

"That would be helpful."

"Always keep your focus on the head of the snake," Trainor reiterated. "Don't look away, answer the phone, or get distracted by people talking to you. Again, we don't really *want* you to take these snakes out."

"Watch while I put the snake back," Jeff said. "Then you can try."

"When you let go of the head, does it ever turn and...you know...go after you?" she asked nervously.

"No," Trainor said. "Not normally. The snake is interested in protecting its body. If you come straight toward it, it will coil first. Remember that when you are around venomous snakes, you are on their terms. *Give them time to recover with everything that you do.*"

20

Des sat behind a newspaper and looked up as the female server placed a steaming cappuccino in front of him. She left, only to be replaced by a young woman he was sure he didn't know.

"Holy…!" he exclaimed, finally seeing Johnny in her new incarnation that included a tight, short-sleeved black T-shirt and jeans, and pierced earrings of various sizes. "Amazing." He took in her short spiked hair as she sat down, keeping his eyes level with hers, not wanting to gaze at her small waist or her partially exposed midriff.

"I figured black is a primary color with this group," she offered, as Des looked for the young woman he had last seen only twenty-four hours earlier.

"You figured right." He put the paper aside. "How'd it go?"

"Okay. I got to hold a snake." She smiled.

A sense of accomplishment.

"Do you know that scales are just fingernails?" She held up her hands, the black-painted nails part of her new persona.

"No. I never thought about it," Des remarked.

"Trainor likes you guys," she added.

Des smiled. "Yeah. He's a character."

"My snakes come tomorrow."

She's really into this.

"Good," he replied. "Did you read the files?"

"Yes," Johnny answered. "I'm going to Exotic Reptiles later."

"We need to get your story right before you begin."

"Okay."

The server came back and took Johnny's order for a latte. Des listened and nodded periodically as she explained her rationale for the short hair and grunge-infused look. When she finished, he started in about getting her cover established before she met the Beltway collectors.

"I need to know the personal side of you," Des said. He sat back as Johnny began, knowing full well the details of the most important event in her life.

"Well, my father owned a grocery store in San Francisco. He did okay, like most people there. He also…" She hesitated and looked away.

He knew it would be coming, just not so soon. Instead of saying anything, he waited for her to continue.

"Sorry," Johnny said.

"It's all right."

"He had a side business. Many Asian medicinals are illegal to bring into this country," Johnny continued. "But people relied on my father. He had everything and that business supported his grocery. And his family."

"What happened?" Des asked.

"The supplier who brought him…the medicines… started asking for more money. And my father paid it. Up to a point."

She looked away again. Des waited, and as he did so he took in her profile, of a classically beautiful Asian woman. He dropped his eyes as she came back to the conversation.

"Eventually, he couldn't pay more," she continued. "Or didn't want to. The supplier cut him off. My father threatened to go the police."

Des nodded.

"But I knew he would never get the police involved. He would want to work things out himself." Johnny hesitated. "Then…"—she paused again, her eyes filling with tears—"his supplier killed him." She added softly, "He would not have gone to the police."

Do I tell her who that supplier is? Do I go even further and tell her how two young special agents itching to look good bumbled a case that cost her father his life?

The server interrupted them momentarily, placing a latte in front of Johnny.

"When did this happen?" Des asked.

"It was September eighteenth, at five p.m., twenty years ago," she answered matter-of-factly, without looking at him.

As I thought.

He watched her pick up the cup and take a hesitant sip of the hot beverage.

"Did you witness the shooting?" Des asked, somewhat tentatively, knowing how she would respond.

"Yes."

He looked down. "I'm really sorry." And he was. Des changed the subject. "What kind of medicinals did your father have?"

"Everything. Bear gall...tiger testicles...snake parts."

"So you *do* have a history with snakes," Des replied, trying to lift the cloud that hung over their conversation.

"Not really." She smiled at a long-forgotten memory, then continued. "A friend in middle school...her father was a snake collector. She and her sister—there were no brothers—got involved in it with him. They would bring boas to school."

Des sat up, a credible alias for her beginning to form.

"I think we've got your cover," he offered. "And it won't take much doing on your part, which is perfect. Are you still in touch with your friend?"

Johnny shook her head.

"Good. But it doesn't matter. You'll be in the DC area only."

He signaled the server for another cappuccino, then dove into the particulars about the identity she was to assume. "You are going to take on your friend's persona only as far as her last name and family history, specifically about the snakes. Can you do that?"

Johnny nodded that she could.

Des's countenance changed abruptly. "You know that you are a woman in a man's world with these collectors. You'll have to talk a good game."

"I know."

"When you are with them, I want you to stay focused on the situation you're in. Don't let your mind wander."

"Okay."

He thought about something and added, "In my day, we went into the *great out there* on our wits. In a way, you still do."

"So use common sense," Johnny offered.

"*Sixth* sense," he corrected. "I want you to call me after every contact. If I don't hear from you, I'll assume something went wrong."

"All right."

"Remember: not every situation will play by the book."

21

Alexandria,Virginia
Tuesday afternoon

Paul St. John, owner of Exotic Reptiles, flipped the sign from Closed to Open as he perused items in his vast window display, a microcosm of what he had in his store: T-shirts, books, food items, snake key chains, bottle openers. Anything that had anything to do with snakes—minus the live creatures—was in view.

He ran his fingers over the cover of one of the books. It looked like Patrick had missed dusting the display. And he hadn't changed the paperbacks. He'd get after him when he came in, he decided, adjusting the packages of food and vitamins so they angled in toward the T-shirts. If Patrick was going to work for him, he'd have to do what he was told and not fool around on the computer.

St. John, a heavy-set man of twenty-seven, had been collecting snakes all his life. Like many collectors, he had begun in his preteen years with garter snakes, lots of them, then moved on to purchases at pet stores, like the milk snakes—starter snakes, he told his customers—that he sold in his own shop.

He remembered how excited he was when he bought his first exotic snake. He had saved all his money to get it, a Sinaloan milk snake—*Lampropeltis triangulum sinaloae*—its Latin name. It had been the biggest day of his life.

Unlike now, he thought, pushing up his thick, dark-framed glasses as he walked to the back of the store. Now he was a hard-pressed business owner, barely able to buy the varieties he had on display. Collecting as a hobby was vastly different from selling to make a living.

St. John noticed an ultraviolet light flickering in the rear of the store. It was probably causing the snakes back there some grief. Even he wasn't going to work all day in that compromised lighting.

Exotic Reptiles operated at just above break-even. Eight years ago, when he decided to be on his own rather than sitting in a classroom at the local junior college, two relatives and two snake-handling buddies had given him start-up money for the store. It was enough to sign a six-month lease and go into business.

His shop sat in the corner of a strip mall and faced a courtyard. He would have preferred a street-side location, facing out on the mall's immense parking lot, but he couldn't afford that. And his hand-lettered sign looked amateurish compared to the more expensive neon and professionally painted signs other merchants had. But it didn't matter. He didn't talk to them anyway. Or rather, they didn't talk to him.

Snake people were a close-knit community. They were willing to share their knowledge about one of nature's most misunderstood creatures, but the general public didn't want to hear it. Mostly, people left them alone.

He looked up again at the flickering light and decided to fix it.

He passed a display of reptile mist and vitamins hawked by a lifelike image of K. C. Sawyer, who smiled out at him, his steely green eyes catching St. John's. His right hand, palm up, jutted out from the display, as if he were handing the customer something. That something was usually a jar of vitamins, but the display jar was gone and someone had put an empty candy wrapper in its place. St. John removed the wrapper and filled the empty spot with a new jar.

"Nice angle you got for yourself," he said to the cardboard K. C. "You get a couple of cobras, get on TV, write a book, and now you're living the high life."

It wasn't right for one man to make so much money, he thought. He had a mind to remove the sign and kick K. C. out of the store, but that would be self-defeating. He did, after all, make a good profit on the products. And that profit kept the lights on.

St. John walked over to the cash register, situated halfway into the store so he could watch all four corners of his business. He pushed back a curtain where he kept his supplies and took out a stepladder and a fluorescent tube. He placed the ladder under the offending light and removed the plastic cover. Flies and dirt lined the bottom of it. Probably hadn't been cleaned since the last tenant. St. John removed the long tube and carefully brought it to rest on the top of a display case.

K. C. was probably counting his money right now, even as he was changing this light, St. John thought. What did he know about working twelve-hour days? With the expenses he had, he couldn't afford even one cobra, and K. C. had more than India.

He maneuvered the new tube into place and the light hummed on.

He'd have to change his attitude, he decided, especially since K. C. would be making a special appearance at his store in a few days, courtesy of Netterman's Food and Vitamins. He'd have to think more like a marketing man. Like a business owner, he decided. Every amateur herpetologist who came in the store idolized K. C. And they'd be descending on his store soon for his appearance. The book rep had already called to make sure he had enough copies of K. C.'s book and to ensure that there would be a table and chair set up for signings.

He had to hand it to Patrick. It was because of him that K. C. was visiting. All he did was send him an e-mail: "Come for a special appearance! We'd love to have you!"

And the great man had said yes! Imagine that. St. John, a nobody, was going to host the best-known snake collector in the world. He had thought Patrick was an accident waiting to happen, but that move was brilliant. *He's got a career ahead of him in P.R.*, he decided.

But there was much to do. He had to think about refreshments, extra chairs, and preparing a fact sheet. And what should be on sale while people were in the store. Plus, he needed a new and bigger ad for the paper, due today. He'd work on it later.

He swiped the flies and dirt onto the floor and replaced the cover.

St. John stared at the young gray-banded king snake—*Lampropelitis mexicana thayeri*—in terrarium #1 at the front of the store. The terrariums were numbered 1 through 35, nonvenomous to venomous, banded kings to rocky mountain rattlers. Lining the wall on the other side were the lizards. And live food: mice, small rats, and crickets.

The snake stared back.

Looks good, St. John thought.

He took the top off the terrarium.

The snake coiled.

He opted not to use a snake stick, and instead moved his hand into the cage in front of the snake's face, decidedly the *wrong* way to approach it. He moved his hand slowly to the side and around the back of the reptile's head. He'd been bitten before doing just this maneuver, and right now risked being bitten on the underside of his arm. Undeterred, he kept going. He grabbed it from behind and brought it out. The snake remained tightly coiled, the tongue darting in and out.

Supporting its body, St. John looked it over as best he could. Top to bottom. And underneath, on the belly, where the unsavory pests liked to live. Everything checked out. He placed it back in its terrarium and moved to the next one, a tan-and-reddish-brown-patterned corn snake (*Elaphe guttata*). He'd do this with every snake, right up to terrarium #25, the beginning of his venomous varieties. He'd checked those yesterday before the store opened, handling them only with a snake stick.

This checking out of the snake, from head to "toe," was an exercise recommended by K. C., so St. John reluctantly gave him credit for that. K. C. advised that it be an isolated event, separate from other snake chores, like cleaning and feeding. You did one thing at a time. Especially with venomous varieties. And you didn't rush. He had to admit it was good advice.

St. John handed the customer his bag of vitamins and thanked him for coming in.

He glanced at his watch: 4:01 p.m. He hadn't done anything for K. C.'s visit.

"Hey, there." He felt a tap on his right shoulder and turned to see no one.

"Hello, Patrick," he said, realizing he had been caught yet again in one of his assistant's juvenile pranks. He turned to see five-foot-ten, sandy-haired Patrick Gonzales, a handsome young man of twenty with a perpetual smile and boundless teenage energy.

"I'm early," he said, looking at his watch. "By two minutes."

"No, you're a minute late," St. John answered, glancing at the clock across from him.

Patrick must have come in the back entrance for his four to seven p.m. shift, which he worked three days a week. Plus all day Saturday. And other days when he thought he could miss his junior college courses. Patrick told him once that his dream was to have his own reptile shop. And that wish might become reality, St. John had come to realize, because his knowledge of snakes was impressive. It was the reason he had hired him. Nonetheless, he needed to pay attention to what he had been asked to do.

"Come over here," St. John said, changing the subject. Patrick walked with him to the front of the store.

"See this in here?" He pointed to the books in the display. "I want these dusted. And rearranged. And change the paperbacks. When you're done, go outside and look at the display like you're walking by. Make sure it looks good."

"Okay!" Patrick hoisted himself over the small wooden barricade into the display.

"You don't have a dust rag."

"Right!" He jumped back out.

St. John thought about the things he'd like to say, but refrained. He found it difficult to believe that he was beginning to sound like a parent.

"And when you're done with this I've got work I want you to do on the computer."

"For K. C.'s visit?"

"Yes."

"All right!"

22

On the road
Tuesday evening

K. C. extended his legs within the confines of the truck's cab and stretched. They were somewhere along Interstate 95 in South Carolina.

"We've got a ways to go," Reeves said from behind the wheel, anticipating what was about to be asked.

K. C. bent down and picked up a thermos near his feet. "More coffee?"

"Sure."

He unscrewed the lid and poured a hot cup for his friend, who took it and cradled it carefully in his lap.

"What do you think happened to Walker?" Reeves asked, in regard to their good friend in Arizona who had died from the bite of his king cobra.

K. C. thought for a moment. "Got careless." He took a sip of his coffee. "Odd. He had all the experience in the world. As much as I have." K. C. paused. "He was hitting the drink a bit."

Reeves looked over at his friend and nodded in agreement, knowing what that was about. He sipped his coffee. "He wanted to meet us in DC. I spoke to him a week before he died. I think he wanted to unload his snakes."

K. C. looked out at the headlight-brightened road in front of him. "Well, it happens. You reach a point where it's too much."

"We'll never know," Reeves added. He changed the subject. "What are we doing first, in DC?"

"We'll go to the hotel, get situated, and then take the snakes to the convention center. We've got to pick up the Russian at the National Zoo."

"I'll do that," Reeves offered.

"There's the cocktail party Saturday night."

Reeves nodded.

K. C. reached for an index card in his breast pocket. Retrieving his reading glasses, he read from it. "I have a talk and signing at Exotic Reptiles in Virginia." He thought for a moment. "It's been a long time since I've been in a reptile store."

"When are you doing that?" Reeves asked.

"Sunday." He put the card back in his pocket. "When you're picking up the Russian, how 'bout stopping by that store and scoping things out?"

"Sure."

Of course you will, Reeves. I can count on you.

K. C. lay his head back, lulled by the sound of the truck's wheels on the pavement. He thought again of his agenda for the week. There was the show, of course, where thousands would come to see his snakes and be in the same room with something as dangerous as a cobra. He wondered what the stage looked like. His publisher had arranged for elaborate lighting and sets to complement the snakes. All to sell the book.

He began nodding off. He couldn't remember the name of the man who had written to him to give a talk at the reptile store. He was sure the store was small and cramped, and he hoped the air-conditioning worked. He thought again about his missing Russian cobra, and the fact that Chang hadn't called him back.

* * *

Alexandria, Virginia

Sheridan flipped the steak on the grill, then plopped it onto a plate and walked inside.

"That smells good," Jason, said, already seated at the table.

Sheridan cut the sizzling meat in half and gave Jason his share. Sitting down, he reached for his napkin and noticed something small near his plate, wrapped in brightly colored paper.

"What's this?"

Jason busied himself with his knife and fork. "I don't know."

"You do too."

Jason smiled suddenly. "Happy birthday!"

"Can I open it?"

"Yeah!"

Sheridan carefully unwrapped the paper. Dave McNally, former pitcher for the Orioles, stared back at him from inside a plastic card case.

"Do you know him?" Jason asked.

"Of course! He was a twenty-one-game winner in '71. And this is a PSA 8," he said of the card's rating. "This cost you money."

Jason beamed.

"Thanks, Jase." Sheridan leaned over and kissed his son on the forehead. "Now I've got almost all the '71 pitchers. All I need is that other guy...what's his name..."

"Pat Dobson!" Jason shouted.

"Right!" The two continued to talk baseball throughout dinner, Sheridan filling his son in again on the amazing stable of pitchers the Orioles had from the early 1970s, four of whom were twenty-game winners in one season.

When he had finished, Jason got up and retrieved two cupcakes he had hidden in his bedroom.

"I don't have a candle," he said, placing one on Sheridan's plate.

"It's okay. They look great. Did you make them?"

"No. I can't cook."

"I can't either," Sheridan remarked.

Sheridan grabbed another beer and they ate their cupcakes in silence. He looked at his son, who was smoothing icing from the cupcake's wrapper onto his finger.

"Do you understand why your mother and I are not together?" Sheridan asked.

Jason swallowed and then replied. "Yes. It's over and you've moved on."

Sheridan was taken aback by his son's matter-of-fact answer. He wondered if he had gotten this information from friends. Or figured it out on his own.

"Actually, I'm not sure why these things happen, Jase, but they do."

"It's okay. I've already had this talk with Mom." He finished the cupcake and folded the wrapper into a tiny square, then let it go.

Sheridan realized that Joanna was further along on this topic than he was.

"Nothing between you and me will change."

"I know," Jason said, watching his creation unfold.

This was old news. "Do any of your friends have snakes?" Sheridan asked, changing the subject.

"No. That's weird."

"Really? You don't think it's cool?"

"No."

"Does *anyone* you know have snakes?"

"Yeah."

"Who?"

"This guy, Ryan. He brought them to school."

"I bet people liked that."

"Sort of," Jason answered. "He had a cool boa constrictor."

"Really."

"It's his father's."

"What's his last name?"

"Berry."

The name didn't ring a bell. "Do you know who K. C. Sawyer is?"

Jason nodded that he did.

"I may be seeing him this weekend." Sheridan changed the subject again. "Where's that schedule of your games?"

After committing Jason's baseball games to his calendar and before heading to bed, Sheridan logged on to his work e-mail. He saw a reply from the State Department and opened it. It was a brief answer to his earlier query:

> *We've heard nothing from Thailand that anything*
> *has changed.*

That'll go over well with Interior, Sheridan thought, considering the upcoming meeting.

He scrolled down and saw a message from Isaac and opened it.

> *David is in Thailand and will look around for us.*

Good. David Shelton, a London-based member of INTER-POL's wildlife group whom he had met at CITES meetings, was very capable. Finally, they'd have a firsthand account. Perhaps some answers.

As he was about to turn off his computer a new message popped up, one from his stepbrother, the only person he knew who addressed him by his first name.

> *Jim, great to hear from you. I'm coming to DC.*
> *Let's meet and catch up.*

23

Alexandria, Virginia
Wednesday morning

Johnny parked the car in a far space of the mall's massive parking lot and walked the added distance to Exotic Reptiles. Doing so gave her time to concentrate on her new last name, Mellman, the moniker of her middle-school friend. While she relished the thrill of assuming a new identity, like being in a school play, she couldn't take this too far from her real self, as Des had instructed. Only the last name and her friend's family story would be hers. Everything else—her own personality, likes, and dislikes—were to remain the same.

She approached the stores fronting the big parking lot. Not seeing Exotic Reptiles, Johnny looked down a corridor leading into a triangular courtyard, finally seeing the hand-painted sign above, in the back. She spiked up her dark hair as she got closer and walked in. A bell on the door announced her entrance as she took in the now familiar scent of reptiles. She saw no one, just rows and rows of terrariums that lined the walls all the way to the back of the store.

She walked down an aisle, viewing the snakes inside. Halfway into the store she came upon a life-sized cutout of K. C. Sawyer, his deep green eyes staring at her. She took the bottle of vitamins he appeared to be handing her and read the label, not seeing a large man approaching her from behind.

"Can I help you?" St. John asked.

Startled, she turned and recognized St. John instantly.

"Hi," she said, putting the vitamins back on K. C.'s outstretched palm.

"Hi," he answered.

"I'm just looking around," she added.

"Okay. I'm in the back if you need anything."

She smiled and then jumped in. "I'm a collector. I have several cobras from my father."

St. John's eyes lit up. "You have cobras?"

"Yes, and I'm wondering about these vitamins…if they're worth it."

St. John shrugged. "I don't use them but I know people who do." He stared at the likeness of K. C. "Sometimes I think people buy them just because he tells them to."

Johnny smiled. "Yeah. He's got quite a gig going."

"No kidding! So, what kind of cobras?" St. John asked.

"Small ones."

"Like what?"

"A Russian, a monocled—"

"You've got a Russian?" St. John interrupted.

"Yeah. Like I said, it was my father's."

"Man, I'd like to see that."

Johnny picked up the vitamins again and looked at the back label, then up at St. John. "Well, that can be arranged."

"Really? Can…some other people come? They'd be interested." He didn't wait for her to answer. "That's not a snake most collectors have. We have a group here with cobras. They all have kings."

"Wow."

"Yeah." He looked at K. C.'s likeness and turned back to Johnny. "I'd forget the vitamins. You feed them mice, right?"

"Yes." She changed the subject. "Do you have any cobras here?"

St. John shook his head. "Too expensive…too many hoops to jump through to get them."

Johnny nodded.

St. John seemed to be scrutinizing her appearance. "I haven't seen you before."

Johnny felt her stomach tighten. As she answered, she concentrated on moving the discomfort out of her diaphragm, down her legs and into her shoes, a technique she had learned long ago for public speaking.

"I just moved here. My sister and I inherited the snakes when my father died. We have experience with them so we decided to keep them."

"That's cool. You should meet our group."

"I'd like that."

"We meet on Wednesdays. Tonight, actually. Want to come?"

"I can do that," Johnny answered, setting the vitamins once again on the outstretched hand and concentrating on the feeling in her toes.

St. John nodded in approval. "What's your name?"

24

The request from Isaac: search out snake sellers, inquire about king cobras.

Reptiles weren't David Shelton's specialty. His expertise resided with Asia's ever-dwindling tiger population. But he wouldn't refuse a request from a good friend. With that in mind, he made his way to snake alley, an area of Bangkok he had only passing knowledge of.

At six feet four inches in height, Shelton towered over the vendors in Bangkok's busy marketplace, now teeming with activity. As he walked through the throng, tourists in front of him stopped suddenly to pick up items on tables or listen to townspeople hawking their wares, and he bumped into several of them, apologizing before moving on.

Shelton bypassed the fish vendors and headed straight for "the alley." Here, in a half-block area behind the tables selling counterfeit CDs and DVDs, reptiles—dead and alive—were sold for food. And restaurants lining the alley served up their snake-based specialties. In this part of Bangkok, one could find any exotic snake species one was looking for, including cobras.

Passing a lone stand with snake skins for sale and another with wallets made out of the same, Shelton came upon men selling live reptiles in covered baskets. He got one's attention and pointed to a basket. The man picked it up and brought it to a table. Slowly, he removed the lid. Shelton watched as a juvenile monocled cobra started to make its way up the side.

Shelton shook his head and in the native Thai dialect asked for a king cobra, extending his arms wide to indicate the snake he was looking for.

The vendor shook his head, explaining that there were none.

"Where are they?" Shelton asked.

The man pointed to his right, indicating the end of the market, but added that no kings were being sold there.

"Why not?"

"The man bought them all," the vendor explained.

"What man?"

"The man who buys from the boys."

"What does he look like?" Shelton asked.

The vendor shook his head again. "Don't know. He bought them all."

The vendor carefully closed the lid on the basket and then rejoined his companions.

Shelton left and continued on through the marketplace until he came to the end of it. Ahead was a small town square, a park, which held a large gazebo-like structure. He assumed it was in this area where the snakes were sold, since no other place in the market sold snakes.

He walked over to the covered area, the ceiling above protecting well-used wooden tables inside. But there were no seats. And no people. He looked down at the dirt "floor" where strands of grass were beginning to pop through.

Shelton looked at his watch and then took out his cell phone. He saw a black Mercedes drive by as he left a message for Isaac.

"David here," he began. "Nothing so far. Think I'll contact Jik after all."

* * *

Ty watched the Mercedes slowly wind its way through the busy street and turn a corner. Where did that man with the blue eyes go with all those snakes, he wondered, the ones he bought from boys like himself?

He decided to find out.

Ty rose from the park and followed the Mercedes's path around a corner and down a side street. Ahead of him he saw the car disappear into a garage.

He crossed the street and came up to the building. Standing on his toes he peered in a window. Inside, men were moving crates and stacking them next to other crates, which seemed to fill one side of the garage. The man with the blue eyes was bending down, looking into a terrarium, and a man on a forklift was coming toward him.

Afraid that he would be seen, Ty left the window and walked around to the back of the building. There were more garage doors here and they were open. Trucks had backed in and workers were moving crates into them. He passed in front of the vehicles and kept going, the workers too busy to acknowledge him. He was on the far side of the building now, but the windows on this side were out of reach.

Ty walked by the front where he had seen the car enter, and took his position again at the window. He stood up to peer inside, but quickly leaned back as the window opened outward. Soon, cigarette smoke drifted out and upward, disappearing above him.

Ty waited until the window closed. Finally, he peered inside again. He saw terrariums again and saw one a lone snake in each. He looked to his right and saw a truck leaving the warehouse, heading down the road leading out of town. Someone would be getting a shipment of crates, he decided.

Crates with snakes.

25

Des moved files on pending cases to the side and reached for a pad of paper. He pushed his chair back and assumed his favorite work mode, with feet propped up against the edge of the desk.

He began writing down thoughts about cobras, going through a reporter's familiar repertoire of questions: the *who, what, where, and when* of the case.

In passing, he and Sheridan had discussed three scenarios for the reptiles' disappearance: they died, they moved, or they were taken. If he could also answer *how*, it might solve the puzzle, he reasoned. And then he and his partner Carole could get away for a few days.

But Des jotted down another question, one that had stayed with him since the meeting with Egan: *Why?*

Fish and Wildlife's files were riddled with reports about taking animals for personal gain. But why would someone do that with one of the world's most dangerous species?

And where would you put them?

He sat forward and reached for his phone, calling Matt—one of their fellow Saturday morning basketball buddies—at the National Oceanic and Atmospheric Administration (NOAA).

Matt was an expert in international weather patterns and tended to ramble on about his work, caught up as he was with the popular topic. Des put him on speaker phone and resumed his favorite position.

"Matt, Des here."

"Hey, man. You playing Saturday?"

"No, we've got the reptile show," Des answered.

"Ah, right. What's up?"

Des filled him in on the cobra situation and proceeded with questions. "Do you know of any climatic events that might affect movement of a species in Asia, to the extent that the species is suddenly dropping out of sight?"

Des waited while, it seemed, Matt thought this through. "Not off the top of my head. We *are* starting to see birds, fish, and some mammals extend their ranges northward, like marlin near Puget Sound, strange as that sounds."

"Hmm."

"But a species won't completely leave its habitat all at once," Matt continued. "You'd have stragglers. Having said that, some butterflies in Europe *are* leaving en masse."

"Really," Des responded.

"The earth is warming," he explained. "They're searching for a latitude that's comfortable. Did you know…"

Here we go.

"…that the dinosaurs lived in one of the hottest climates on earth? And right after a Permian frost."

"Wow."

Matt continued, "But are we going to see alligators in England again?"

Alligators in England?

"No," Matt answered, "we won't."

Des realized he needed to bone up on his paleoclimatology.

Matt went on. "Take Hurricane Andrew or Katrina. Were those aberrations, as everyone thought, or the beginning of a trend, as we now believe?" Matt paused, coming back to Des's query. "When was the disappearance noticed?"

"Um…I think only recently."

"Well, most likely you would have seen an early indication of what you now have, a few of the species being seen in an area where they haven't been seen before."

"They haven't been seen at all," Des said.

"I see."

Des wrote down notes for Sheridan, but he had a gut feeling that they could cross climate off his list as a factor in the cobras' disappearance. He picked up the phone and called Mike Trainor at the National Zoo.

"Mike, it's Des."

"Hey, how're doing?" the zoo's herpetologist inquired.

"Good."

"How's the rookie?" Trainor asked.

"She's okay. Making her way. Thanks for your help."

"Not a problem. Don't mind doing it."

"Listen, Sheridan and I are still working on that Thailand case...missing king cobras."

"Right," Trainor said.

"Sheridan wanted me to ask you about reptile extinctions. Might help us put things in perspective." Des heard nothing but silence. But before Trainor said anything, Des interjected, "Personally, I think we'll be ruling this out, not including it as cause."

"There wasn't anything on the scale of the dinosaurs—I'm assuming that's what you're looking for, the species being wiped out," Trainor began.

"Sort of. We're only talking about Thailand."

"That's odd," Trainor said. "Could be a virus, starting in one part of the world. But the virus would spread and you'd see deaths elsewhere."

"Then we'd have carcasses," Des replied.

"Yes. You have no carcasses?" Trainor asked.

"None."

"Hmm." Trainor seemed to mull that over for a moment, and then he continued. "There have been some recent, isolated extinctions of reptiles, mostly tortoises, on islands. And by recent I mean in the last century. Usually, when you have an isolated event it is caused by the introduction of a non-native species—cats, for example, are deadly to reptiles—or destruction of habitat, purposeful killing, or a species-specific virus. Or, as I am sure you know," Trainor added, "by taking. Those are your choices."

"Right."

"That's all I know," Trainor said.

"Okay," Des replied. "This is helpful, really."

They discussed more information about Johnny. Trainor thought she would do fine, adding that her snakes had been delivered and set up in her apartment. Des thanked him and ended the call. He glanced at his watch. He had an hour before meeting Carole for a movie and a late dinner. He went back to writing. When his cell phone rang, Des looked at the number and saw that it was the rookie herself.

He listened while Johnny described her first undercover role at Exotic Reptiles and what her plans were for the evening. When she added that no cobras were being sold at the store, Des replied, "You just told us something we didn't know." He paused. "About tonight: be careful. And remember to call me."

26

Johnny looked up at the 1950s-era apartment building on the edge of Dupont Circle, confirming the address she had scribbled on a piece of paper at Exotic Reptiles. She walked to the door, saw the name for Warren Anderson, and pushed the button. A pleasant male voice answered and buzzed her in.

The man who opened the door had darker hair and a bit more weight on him than the photo Sheridan had given her from five years ago. Thinking again of the three men in the Beltway group, she wouldn't have pegged him as a snake collector.

"You're Johnny," Warren said, extending his hand and moving aside so she could enter.

"Yes." She stepped in and saw a clean but sparsely furnished apartment. The three large white pizza boxes on the table explained the pleasant aroma. No terrariums were in sight.

"Is anyone here?" she asked.

"Not yet."

"Where are your snakes?" she asked, moving along.

He closed the door and pointed down a hallway. "In the bedroom. I have to move them out of there. My girlfriend is insisting on it." He turned toward the refrigerator. "What can I get you to drink?"

"Do you have a Coke?"

"That I have." He reached for one and handed it to her. "What do you do?"

Johnny took a long drink before answering. "I'm an office assistant at one of the agencies," she said, referring to her made-up role in the federal government.

"Which one?"

"EPA," she answered, then quickly changed the subject. "I understand you have a PhD."

"Yeah, finally. Do you want to see the snakes?"

"Sure."

"Have you met Adam yet?" Warren asked, as they walked down a hallway.

"No."

He laughed. "That guy needs to be on drugs."

"Why?"

"You'll see."

They walked to a door and Warren opened it. They stepped into a large room with a king-sized bed against one wall. Along another wall where one might have expected a dresser, book-shelves, or a television, were terrariums, twelve in all, including a large one with a king cobra in it.

Johnny walked up to the king and peered in. "How long have you had him?"

"About six years."

"My father had one, but it died. He had it a long time." She turned to him. "My sister and I inherited his snakes, mostly cobras. My father referred to them as the *lesser* cobras. He was always comparing them to this one," she said, turning back to the king.

"It's a grand snake, no doubt about it."

Johnny focused on the perfectly still reptile. *That went well.*

The doorbell rang. "Finally. We can eat!"

The two walked back to the living/dining area and Warren answered the door.

"Hey, man!" Adam, even more handsome than his photo, entered, punching Warren halfheartedly in the stomach.

Odd gesture, she thought.

Behind him were St. John and another man of Hispanic descent she didn't know.

Adam walked up to Johnny, his eyes boring into her as those in his photo had.

Lots going on behind those eyes, she thought.

Adam extended his hand. "You're Johnny."

"Yes," she answered, responding in kind. *A firm handshake*. He wasn't much taller than she was.

St. John came up to them. "Glad you made it."

"Yes, so am I," Johnny said with sincerity.

She noticed that Adam moved away from St. John. But St. John didn't seem to notice, calling Patrick over instead.

"I'm new, too," Patrick said, after St. John introduced them. "You've got a king?"

"No, my father did. It died. I have other cobras."

"Which ones?" Adam asked, standing near a table and lifting the tops on the pizza boxes.

"A monocled, an African, an Indian, and a Russian." She looked directly at him, and then asked coyly, "Or did you want the scientific names?"

Adam stopped perusing the pizzas. He looked up and held her gaze. "No. We're informal here."

"You've got a Russian? Wow." Warren placed bottles of beer on the table. "Okay, guys. Let's eat!"

They sat on an old couch and old chairs and quickly downed their meals, saying little while they ate. They drank their beers quickly as well, Johnny noted, unhappy that she had been served one and that they could see how little she was drinking.

The men soon lapsed into their familiar roles with one another. Johnny listened as they talked about their day jobs, base-ball teams, women—though with her present she guessed they were toning that down a bit—and of course snakes. St. John told them about new additions to his store, mostly nonvenomous vari-eties that young collectors started with.

As she observed them, she made mental notes on person-alities and exchanges, and came to one unmistakable conclusion: Adam ruled the group. Edgy and intense was how she would describe him, and Warren's comment about him rang true.

When they were done eating, Adam muffled a burp and sat back. He crossed his legs and balanced a beer on one knee.

And stared at her.

Johnny avoided his gaze while she finished eating.

Keep yourself present within the encounter.

She re-entered the conversation. "When are you guys going to the show?"

"Soon as it opens!" Patrick exclaimed.

"Probably Saturday," St. John answered.

Warren and Adam didn't respond. Instead, Warren inquired about K. C. "What's the word on him?"

"He's coming. His advance man"—St. John hesitated, try-ing to remember Reeves's name—"anyway, the guy called and is coming to look at the store. The talk is on for Sunday."

"Amazing," Warren said.

"We have Patrick to thank," St. John added.

Adam fiddled with the label on his beer bottle, peeling off little pieces and rolling them into balls and throwing them on the table.

"Why do you think he is such a big deal?" Adam asked St. John.

"Everybody knows him. I sell a lot of his vitamins," St. John responded.

"So? Any one of us could be doing what he's doing," Adam retorted.

"He wrote a book," St. John added.

Adam scoffed at the comment. "He didn't write a book. He has a PR firm."

Warren stepped in. "Leave him alone, Adam."

Adam went on, addressing Patrick. "You remember a package is coming tomorrow?"

"Yeah, I remember."

"You'll be home to get it?"

"What time is it coming?"

"*Tomorrow*." Adam paused, letting that sink in, then drank from his beer.

"Right," Patrick answered.

Adam swigged the last of his drink and turned to Warren. "We gonna do this thing?"

"Yep." Warren picked up the used paper plates and carried them into the kitchen. He opened a cabinet, took out something and brought it to the dining room table.

"Want to help?" Warren asked Adam.

Adam got up. "Sure."

Johnny watched the two men disappear down the hallway. In lockstep, St. John and Patrick rose and walked over to the dining room table, so she joined them. She looked down at what Warren had placed there: an empty jelly jar with a mesh lid on top held in place with a rubber band.

Alone with the two men, Johnny saw an opportunity. "Is Adam always that short with people?"

"Yeah," Patrick answered. "You get used to it. Sort of."

"Warren's gonna milk the king," St. John said, ignoring their conversation. "Did your father ever milk his snakes?"

Suddenly, her heart began pounding so loudly she was sure they could hear it. She strained to keep her voice level, realizing

that for a brief moment—which is all it takes, Des had warned—
she had left the encounter.

"No, he never did," she answered.

Warren entered the room with his back to them. Adam
brought up the rear. Both cradled coils and coils of the king cobra,
more snake even than the cobra at the zoo. The muscles in both
men's arms bulged from the weight of their load.

They carefully placed the reptile on the dining room table.
Johnny saw the glint of fluorescent green on the tips of its scales
as they briefly caught the light in the room. Warren held the
head while Adam adjusted the snake. The others moved around
the table so they had a better view of what was about to take
place.

"He's trying to rise up," Warren said, keeping both hands on
the neck and head, which was as big as his fist. "I need to give
him a bit of time. What I'm gonna do, Johnny," Warren explained,
without looking at her, "is milk the snake. I inject myself with
venom."

"Oh?" Johnny inquired. This bit of information was not on
any profile she had read.

"My blood's building up immunities," he added. "Then I sell it
to a biotech firm in Maryland."

"I see," she answered, remembering his PhD in biochemistry.
"How often do you inject yourself?"

"Once a month."

She wanted to ask more, but refrained.

"Put the glass closer to me, if you would," Warren asked, nodding to St. John.

St. John did as he was told. Warren moved the snake's mouth
toward the edge of the glass jar and pressed down.

The snake kept its mouth closed.

Adam readjusted the coils and Warren tried again. With a
slight lunge forward the snake gripped the jar. Johnny heard a

distinct "clink" as the fangs clamped on. She watched as a steady stream of clear, yellow-tinged liquid rolled down the jar's side.

"He's pissed," Warren said.

"I can feel it," Adam added.

The snake bit again. More venom spewed forth, to the other side of the glass jar.

"You inject yourself with raw venom?" Johnny asked.

"Yes," Warren answered. "He's done. Way to go," he said to the snake, stepping back. "Let's take him back."

After adjusting their load, the two men retraced their steps, leaving Johnny, St. John, and Patrick standing alone at the table again, staring at the jar.

Patrick picked it up and took the lid off.

"Hey," St. John said. "He may not want you to do that."

"He doesn't care," Patrick answered cavalierly.

He smelled the contents and then passed the jar to Johnny. When she took it, the bottom felt cool. *Of course.*

She held it up to her nose. "It doesn't smell."

"No," Patrick said.

"I thought it might smell like, you know, snakes," Johnny said.

"It's a pure substance," Adam said, reentering the room. She felt conspicuous holding the jar, and handed it to him.

"I'll show you." He dipped his finger into the liquid and tasted it. He handed the jar back to her. "You do it."

Here was her test moment, she decided. Without missing a beat, she took it and dipped her finger in the contents, then lightly touched the edge of her tongue.

"Metallic," she said finally. "Like an old can of Coke."

"Yeah, that's the proteins," Adam replied.

The evening at an end, everyone thanked Warren and left. Outside, Johnny stood alone with Adam. She wanted to ask him about the package he had mentioned earlier, but her instincts told her not to. Yet, she was aware that the sole reason she was among these men was to get just that kind of information.

"So…I'd like to see your collection," Adam said, lighting a cigarette. "It's not often you get to see a Russian." He took a long drag and blew a stream of smoke past her. "What do you think? Then we can get something to eat."

"When, were you thinking?" Johnny asked.

"Tomorrow. Give me your address and phone number."

Back in her car and driving home, Johnny called Des and left a message, adding at the end, "I know you said not to, but I went ahead and said okay. Don't worry. I know I can handle him."

27

Des picked up the message at dinner and then put his phone away. He apologized to Carole, who was sitting across from him in their neighborhood restaurant.

"Now what?" she asked.

He shook his head, trying to conceal his anger, and then explained the situation. "Our new recruit. She's bringing one of the Beltway collectors home. It isn't good."

"It's not like this guy has killed anyone, has he?" Carole asked.

Des picked up his fork and poked at his food. "No, but he's a felon. I didn't expect her to be *alone* with one. In her own place."

Carole finished the last of her dinner and reached for her wineglass, cradling it between her hands.

"I'm sure you know this is an opportunity for you," she offered.

Carole held his attention. The two often discussed their respective cases and Des willingly sought out her counsel. As a forensic accountant at the Office of Management and Budget, her sleuthing skills served him well. Carole knew the details about his present case. And about Johnny.

"Take advantage of it," she continued. "You couldn't meet this guy the way she is. You may learn more than you'd hoped for," she added, sipping her wine.

"It's her safety I'm thinking about," Des answered.

"If she's as smart as you say she is, she'll be okay."

His gut told him otherwise.

"So where are you on your case?" she asked.

Des shrugged. "We don't have anything more than we had when we started. Thailand says large numbers are missing. Sheridan thinks it's something inherent with the species."

"And you?" she asked.

He paused, thinking through his case. "I'm not sure. If Sheridan is right, then we'd have carcasses, and there are none. If they're being taken, we'd see evidence of that in the Asian markets. So far, nothing's showing up. If it's collectors, we'd be seeing live snakes. But then we're talking about thousands."

"They have to be somewhere," Carole said, declining the waiter's offer of dessert.

"Where?" Des asked.

"Well, they're *accounted* for," she answered. "In my line of work it's in parallel accounting books. It's not just money—in your case, snakes—being siphoned off. It's how it's kept track of. And it's *always* accounted for when you're dealing with large numbers. Find the books and you'll find the money—I mean the snakes."

Des finished his beer and set the glass on the table. He looked at her and nodded in agreement, but then added, "I can't get my head around someone having thousands of snakes. It doesn't make sense. They have to be kept separate from each other. King cobras are snake eaters. They would be eating one another." He shook his head. "It's a logistical nightmare."

The waiter brought the check and Des changed the subject. "We need to have Sheridan and Vicki over. Vick's leaving soon."

"Where's she going?" Carole asked.

"Wyoming."

"Really?"

"Yeah. She's working on a case there."

"And Sher's divorce?"

"Done," Des responded. "He doesn't talk much about it. So don't say anything to him." He realized he'd crossed a line as soon as the words left his mouth.

Carole put down her glass and folded her arms on the table. "You mean I'm not supposed to notice he's not with his wife of seventeen years? People we've associated with, say, *forever?*"

He couldn't tell if she was kidding or not.

She held his gaze again. He stared into her hazel eyes, her face framed by highlighted blonde hair. He knew intuitively how much she supported him, and knew he had made a mistake.

"I didn't mean to tell you what to say," he answered. "We'll have them over. You just play it the way you think is best," he added, turning his thoughts back to Johnny.

28

A box of live mice tucked under one arm, Patrick unlocked the door to his two-bedroom apartment. He switched on the lights, dropped his bag and books onto a well-used couch in the living room, and headed for the kitchen. He placed the box of mice on the counter and leafed through his mail. Seeing nothing of interest, he threw the envelopes into a recycling pile. Grabbing a bottle of beer from the refrigerator, he scooped up the mice and walked down the hallway to his bedroom, humming the last tune he'd heard on the radio.

He flipped on the lights and set the beer and mice on a worn dresser. He pulled off his clothes and threw them in a corner, emphasizing each toss with a loud hum. Then he donned a pair of running shorts, and snapped the waistband tight against his taught stomach.

Patrick walked to the window and took a long drink from his beer. A couple in the brownstone next to his sat on a couch watching TV.

He wondered if he should feed the snakes first or check his text messages. *No decision there*, he thought, walking toward the second bedroom. He would only have more messages from Adam and he didn't want to deal with him right now. He didn't know why Adam was so short with him. He barely knew him. Just because he forgot to come to one meeting…

Patrick opened the door. Cool air rushed out at him. He closed the door behind him and turned on a small halogen light,

which complemented the ultraviolet lights illuminating five terrariums, including an extra-large one against the back wall.

"Hello, kids," he said, walking into the middle of the room.
He bent down and looked at the four monocled cobras in the
tanks in front of him. "Guess what I've got?" He held up the box
of mice. "Pizza!"

He opened the box, grabbed one of the mice by the tail, and
dropped it headfirst into a terrarium. The snake turned to face its
meal. The mouse, its fate secure, moved to a corner of the tank
and froze.

Patrick fed all five snakes—the king cobra got extra por-
tions—and threw the empty box onto a table. He took another
long swig of beer and thought about a snack. It was already ten
forty-five p.m. He decided on peanut butter, for the third night
in a row.

Patrick leaned against the table, crossing his arms and legs in
front of him. The long-neck bottle dangled loosely from his hand.
He stared back at his pets that were in the process of ingesting
their meals.

He should get more respect from the group, especially since
offering to take in the new shipment. Maybe doing so would
change Adam's view of him. But he doubted it. Adam's distrust
was something he was going to have to work around.

Patrick turned off the light and walked out into the hot
hallway, closing the door behind him. *I think I'll sleep in there*, he
thought, walking toward the kitchen. *It's the coolest place I know*.

29

Bangkok, Thailand
Thursday morning

David Shelton sat at his desk sipping tea in his well-appointed hotel room. He looked at his watch, then picked up his cell phone and called his old friend and contact in the city, Jik Sim.

Sim, a police officer, had occasionally worked on conservation issues with Shelton and the international wildlife group. Shelton had learned that Sim had left the field to help his parents run their lucrative clothing shop.

"Jik. It's David," Shelton said, hearing the familiar voice. "Yes, I *am* back. Just helping out this time." They continued catching up since the last time they had seen each other two years ago. Then Shelton got to the point. "I want to ask you about the snake sellers in the market."

"What about them?" Jik asked.

"Something is going on with king cobras in Thailand. On a whim, I went to the market."

"They aren't sold in the markets," Jik said immediately.

"Why not?"

"They are not for sale."

"Is that because—"

"It's cultural," Jik answered. "They are not for consumption."

Shelton paused, thinking through his next question. "So, the market won't give me *any* information about kings, then?"

"It depends on what you are looking for," Jik replied. "All snake people know one another."

"I couldn't get anything."

Jik paused, and then continued. "Well, that's not that unusual."

Shelton thought Jik had more information. But he didn't elaborate.

"How do the sellers in the markets get their snakes?" Shelton asked.

"Some deal with the boys. Some have middlemen."

"Where do they do their transactions?"

Jik paused again. Now instinct told him that Jik was holding something back.

"It varies," Jik began. "Some are sold out in the rural communities. Some are brought to the market. It depends who's buying."

"I'm not sure I have much more than I did before." Shelton changed the subject, asking his old acquaintance, "How's the clothing business, by the way?"

"Quite good. I miss the old days, but we are doing very well."

"Great to hear, Jik. I'll stop by if—"

"*The snakes are not here.*" Jik's comment was a whisper, a last-minute add-on to their conversation.

"Sorry?"

"*They don't stay in Bangkok. They are shipped out. Don't come by.*"

Shelton heard a click. He sat for a moment, the message "call ended" running across the screen of his cell phone. He could only guess that Jik feared for his life if he said anything further. Shelton stared out the window piecing together what he had heard to what he knew, which added up to very little. Except that now he knew king cobras were indeed leaving Bangkok. How were the large snakes moved? he wondered.

Shelton rose and left, taking his wallet and cell phone. Outside, he headed back toward the market. He glanced at his watch. It was early morning. He decided to observe snake alley's inner workings to see if he could pick up something.

He entered the main market again where people were setting up for the day. Food vendors were already stationed at their woks cooking meats and vegetables, and their enticing aromas filled his senses. He passed tables not yet set up with products and entered snake alley.

No one was there.

Too early?

He didn't know.

He saw a seating area with a few tables off to the side and went over to one and sat down. At least he wouldn't be visible.

An hour passed. In that time, vendors hawking snake products—wallets, belts, vests—had set up their wares and a few had had some sales. But still no snake sellers.

He was relieved he didn't work in this part of intelligence, keeping track of exotic reptiles. It seemed like dirty work. And difficult to get information.

Another hour passed. It was ten a.m. Perhaps this was not a snake-selling day?

Shelton waited another forty-five minutes. Finally, the back end of a beat-up white pickup truck appeared on a side street that emptied into the alley. A man jumped out and lowered the tailgate. Other men appeared seemingly out of nowhere.

There was the man he had talked to two days ago, and Shelton thought he recognized the others. They were taking baskets out of the back of the truck and bringing them into the alley. They set them on the ground and went back to retrieve more. Two men set up tables and started placing the baskets on top of them.

Ready for business.

Shelton watched the driver get back in the truck and drive off. He rose, wondering how he would get to the street—and the truck—without being seen. He decided to retrace his steps out of the alley to find a side street.

Shelton hurried past the snake product vendors and looked to his left for a way to connect to the side street. He found another alley and hurried down it, past the storefronts. Above him women were hanging wet clothes out to dry. He reached a street and looked to his right. In the distance he saw the white truck proceeding slowly as people moved out of the way to let it pass.

Shelton took off after it. He saw the truck turn left and out of sight. Shelton quickened his step. He caught up to the street and saw the truck waiting to enter the road that ran past the park. He followed the truck as it made its way around the park and down another side street.

Shelton ran faster, then stopped when he saw the truck enter a garage. He watched a door come down and the truck disappear behind it.

30

A handful of cars made their way near the Hilton Baltimore, as did a few early morning runners getting in workouts before the day's humidity started its climb.

Reeves saw the entrance for their hotel and drove into the receiving area in back. Here, plenty of activity was going on, with fish and vegetable deliveries occupying the brightly lit loading dock. Leaving the air-conditioning running for the snakes, the two men got out, grabbed suitcases, and approached the back of the hotel. A few dock workers who recognized K. C. waved and hollered at him. K. C. waved back, shaking a few hands as they entered a back door.

Going in the back of a hotel was something he and Reeves had done for years. It was where K. C. felt the real people worked, and it gave him the lay of the land for the place in which he would be staying. People hustled, as they usually did on loading docks and in hotel kitchens.

This exercise was his last contact with reality before entering his celebrity "showtime" world.

The two men walked down a brightly lit hallway past harried kitchen staff preparing a rush of early morning breakfasts.

"Smells good," Reeves remarked.

"We'll settle in and then go to the Convention center," K. C. remarked.

"Sounds like a plan."

Reeves opened a door that led into an opulent, well-appointed lobby where smiling front-desk people greeted them and checked them in.

Several of the hosts stared at K. C. without saying anything, and he was sure they had been trained to treat all their guests, even the occasional celebrity, in the same way. K. C. upgraded Reeves's room to a suite and the two headed to the elevator. Upstairs, they parted company, agreeing to meet in an hour to have breakfast.

K. C. opened his door and entered his three-room accommodations, complete with floor-to-ceiling windows, courtesy of his publisher. They would have the cocktail party here and K. C. would conduct his usual business, meeting reps from Netterman's reptile food company, the T-shirt company, his book publisher, the public relations firm, and who knew whom else.

He walked into the large bedroom. Dropping his suitcase on the floor, he entered the bathroom and turned on the shower's hot water, letting it steam up the room.

Back in the bedroom, he noticed the phone light was on and he picked up the receiver. His agent had left a message: Everything was set for the cocktail party. He would meet with him an hour beforehand in his suite.

"Whatever," K. C. said, hanging up.

He undressed. Standing naked in the room, he grabbed his cell phone. Someone had left a message there, too.

He retrieved it and heard Chang's cryptic, broken transmission: *I'll see you soon.*

* * *

Arlington, Virginia

"David didn't find much in snake alley," Isaac began, during his early morning phone call to Sheridan. "He thinks our contact there knows something. But he isn't talking."

"Wonder why," Sheridan remarked.

"David will look into it," Isaac answered. "A snake seller indicated that a man there was buying king cobras. But not any longer. No one knows who he is. Or they're not saying."

"I'll bet Bangkok itself cracked down on the sale of kings," Sheridan offered. "Or, there simply are none to sell."

Isaac paused. "David will let us know."

"What about snake skins?" Sheridan asked, still trying to put two and two together. "Are you seeing any products?"

"We haven't seen anything out of the ordinary," Isaac answered, mirroring comments from Terelli in the Ashland lab.

Sheridan knew from CITES reports that skins from the Indian cobra *Naja kaothia* were considered the best "leather" for boots. And they were taken just for that reason, even while India had strict laws against the capture of its reptiles. He also knew that very few *king* cobra skins turned up as products—vests, boots, belts, wallets. They were too highly prized for that.

Or was that yesterday's thinking?

"We're seeing some new things in the Asian markets that your people may not be aware of yet," Isaac added. "Cobra gall bladders, for one."

"From which snake?" Sheridan asked.

"Can't tell. It's just labeled as such. We're also seeing cobra wine, young snakes in bottles of wine. It's big in Hong Kong and Taiwan. Obviously, that rules out the king. In south China cobras are consumed, as you know."

"But king cobras?" Sheridan asked.

Isaac hesitated. "To my knowledge, the king is not eaten."

"Things change," Sheridan said.

"I'll ask around," Isaac answered.

Sheridan stared at his list, under pressure as he was to have something for the meeting at Interior the next day. He scratched off taking the king cobra for its skin. Isaac wasn't going to find anything on that point. Tradition doesn't change that quickly, especially not in Asia.

What about taking the snake for food? Had there been a drought?

He'd have to wait to see what Des had found. Before he could turn to his computer Vicki entered and closed the door. She took a seat in front of his desk and looked at him without saying anything.

But her look said it all.

"I've accepted a job in Wyoming," she announced.

"They've already offered it?" Sheridan asked in amazement.

"Yes. They need someone right away."

"Obviously."

"I'm meeting Marsh out there next week. Things will move fast after that."

Sheridan didn't respond.

"Do you want a report on the eagles?" Vicki asked.

"Not now," he replied, the enormity of her revelation beginning to sink in.

He heard a knock at the door, and assumed it was Des and Johnny for their scheduled meeting.

Vicki glanced at the door and then turned back to Sheridan. "We'll talk about this later," she said, rising and quickly leaving.

Johnny brought the two men up-to-date on her encounters so far with the Beltway collectors.

"Adam mentioned something about a package being delivered. I couldn't get any more information, but everyone seemed to know about it, especially a new guy, Patrick, the one getting the shipment," Johnny said.

Sheridan struggled to focus on the meeting. He concentrated on Johnny—her new look something he wasn't quite sure he liked. He also thought she appeared distraught, as if she should have valuable information right from the get-go.

"Give it some time, Johnny," Sheridan said. And then, without elaborating, "We've got bigger things right now."

But Des had more to add in light of her voice-mail message the previous evening. "You need to watch what you're doing."

"I know," she answered, looking at him, seemingly not offended by his fatherly stance.

"Don't step outside the parameters we set up," he added.

"But Adam wanted to see the snakes," Johnny answered, suddenly on the defensive and knowing exactly what he was referring to.

"I mean *after* this," Des responded. "Try to meet these guys as a group."

"I don't think that'll be possible with Adam," Johnny said. "He's a loner."

"And a felon," Des retorted.

Sheraton watched the exchange without adding anything. The look on his partner's face told him Des wouldn't have brought up the issue if there hadn't been cause for concern.

"You said to call you and I'm doing that," Johnny added. "I've got Adam's confidence." She looked to Sheridan. "I know I can get information for you."

31

Baltimore, Maryland
Thursday morning

The apartment bell rang again in the three-story walkup. Upstairs, Patrick, sound asleep on his couch, never heard it. The FedEx delivery woman waited a few moments and then placed the box on the sidewalk.

She looked at her watch, wrote out a delivery notice and slapped it on the door. Wiping perspiration from her forehead, she picked up the box and walked back to her truck. Opening the passenger-side door, she placed the package on the floor, to deliver again on her way home.

* * *

Maryland suburbs

"That little shit hasn't gotten back to me."

Adam stared at his phone, his many text messages unanswered. He sat in the loft of his mother's garage, which served as his makeshift bedroom and holding area for his collection of venomous snakes. Ever since his mother had told him she didn't want snakes in the house—especially cobras that could "bite her on the foot and kill her"—he lived here, above the two old cars, in the detached two-story building.

And he liked that just fine.

There was enough room for the single bed, shoved into the corner under the eaves, and the small refrigerator that sat next to it. Plus, the improvised bathroom, closet, and old table and chairs. And two lamps.

He glanced at his phone again. Nothing. Patrick was taking his sweet time responding to his messages reminding him again about the package.

"I'm gonna kill that prick." He whipped off another message:

Patrick! Where are you?!

That was too kind.

Adam put his phone away and looked at his watch. He would be late to meet Johnny if he dicked around any longer.

He went into his closet that consisted of boxes behind a curtain. He donned dark pants and a dark denim shirt. He'd let Patrick into the group under duress because St. John liked the fact that he had a king cobra. He would have kicked him out long ago. Absent-minded Patrick. If he had his druthers, he'd end his affiliation with all of them.

Adam went to the mirror and ran a brush through his thick black hair. This Johnny, he thought. Punk-looking, but not really. Actually, she came across as quite conservative.

So why the look?

Maybe he could figure it out. He took one last look at his reflection in the mirror, smiling to himself.

No way a girl takes a taste of venom.

He grabbed his keys and left, walking quickly by the terrariums that held his full-grown, monocled cobras and his one king.

32

Bangkok, Thailand
Thursday morning

Shelton remained where he was, a good distance from where he had seen the truck enter the garage. He wanted to walk up to it but felt he couldn't, conspicuous as he knew he appeared.

Instead, he turned away, knowing who he had to see to get more information.

Shelton walked back to the main thoroughfare and hailed a taxi, not an easy task on the crowded road. Finally, a beat-up Mini pulled over and he wedged himself into the backseat.

I wonder if the driver speaks English.

It was imperative to know before he began a conversation with Isaac, so Shelton asked him. The driver looked at him in his rearview mirror and feigned confusion.

Good. Shelton quickly took out a pen and piece of paper and wrote down Jik's address.

The driver read it, nodded, then eased into traffic.

Shelton called Isaac's number, but then remembered the time. He would be asleep now. Sure enough, Isaac's voice mail came on asking him to leave a message.

"Isaac," Shelton began, watching the motorbikes and bicycles looming close to the small car. "I'm on my way to see Jik to get more information about the cobras which, I've been told, are indeed leaving Bangkok. I followed a truck today that brings snakes to the market for the sellers. It went to a warehouse. I don't know anything beyond that."

Shelton lurched forward suddenly as the driver slammed on the brakes to avoid hitting a cart crossing the road.

"I'll call you back."

33

With the Russian cobra from the National Zoo stashed safely in back, Reeves turned the truck onto the highway for the drive to Alexandria and Exotic Reptiles. Odd comment, he thought, coming from the zoo's herpetologist, that there seemed to be a run on Russian cobras. But Trainor hadn't elaborated.

Seeing his exit, he pulled off and drove the short distance to the mall where Exotic Reptiles resided. Leaving the cool air running for the snakes, he got out and locked the van.

He walked past storefronts until he saw a banner announcing K. C.'s visit, back in a cubbyhole area of smaller shops, the Netterman's Vitamins name prominently displayed. Reeves approached the store, walking gingerly on the uneven sidewalk. This part of the mall obviously was not as well tended as the stores in front.

At least the banner looks good.

The bell at the top of the door announced his entrance. He saw a figure in black at the back.

"Hello?" Reeves said.

St. John turned and walked toward him. "Can I help you?"

Reeves took in St. John's lumbering body; the man seemed to radiate heat even in air-conditioning.

"I'm Mark Reeves, K. C.'s assistant." He extended his hand.

"Wow. This is an honor," St. John replied.

"He likes things to go smoothly." Reeves looked down at a common corn snake lying motionless in a terrarium. "Is there anything you need for his talk?"

"No, we're good," St. John answered. "We'll set up chairs and have a table for signing books, over there." He motioned to a small open area in the crowded store. "And the publishing guy was already here," he added, pointing to a stack of boxes containing K. C.'s book.

"Refreshments?" Reeves asked.

"Those, too," St. John responded.

"Great. K. C. usually meets with collectors privately after his talk. Can you identify three or four who will be here?"

"That would be us—our group!" St. John answered, then remembered Adam's opinion about K. C.

Reeves reached into a pocket and pulled out a small notepad and pen as St. John began ticking off names.

"All of us have king cobras," St. John explained. "That is, except me." He looked around. "I have this store."

Reeves finished writing and put away the pad and pen. "This is helpful. Mind if I look around?"

"Not at all. Can I show you some snakes?"

"I'm not gonna be here that long."

"Okay. I'll leave you alone."

St. John shook his hand again and then returned to the back of the store. Reeves took a look at the rest of his surroundings, following St. John to the back. He stopped in front of the cardboard likeness of K. C.

Not a bad image.

He kept going, passing terrariums of venomous snakes. Then he walked down the aisle on the other side of the store.

Not enough room.

He wondered why K. C. had agreed to a talk at this store.

Probably because St. John simply asked him to.

At the front, before leaving, he made a mental note of the layout. It was not quite the place he had envisioned. He knew his boss would make the best of it.

* * *

Arlington, Virginia

The FedEx driver glanced at her watch.

Would this day never end?

She turned the truck onto a service road to make deliveries at Home Depot, her second-to-last stop. As she reached for her drink in the cup holder next to her, she noticed movement near the front of the box she had placed on the floor.

Something is chewing through!

"What the...?"

She saw a head...an eye.

It emerged from the box—*a snake!*—and came toward her, under the gas pedal!

She screamed, driving the truck erratically through traffic, running a red light and crashing into a roadside popcorn stand. Still screaming, she jumped out, crying and clawing irrationally at her hair.

34

Adam looked in on the reptile. "So that's the Russian."

Johnny stood next to him, arms crossed in front of her, as he bent over the terrarium and scoped it out.

"That snake lives the furthest north of any cobra," he added. "You probably knew that."

"Hmmm," she answered, neither confirming nor denying his remark.

"Let's milk it," he said suddenly.

Johnny felt heat rising on the back of her neck. "No."

He turned to face her. "Why not?"

"My father never did."

"So?"

"It's stressful for the snake," she replied, struggling to stay calm. She knew he knew that was true.

Adam looked back at the cobra, then at Johnny again, without responding. Finally, he agreed.

"Okay. Let's get something to eat."

She was relieved to be outside, walking in her neighborhood. Since she had made arrangements not to handle the snakes—zoo personnel stopped by at odd hours to do that—she wondered if having defanged reptiles had been a wise choice.

Knowing as she did that seasoned collectors *never* defanged their snakes, what would she have come up with if Adam had discovered the truth? More importantly, could she have thought up a believable story on the spot?

They chose a Chinese restaurant not far from her apartment and settled in. They spoke little about snakes at first. Instead, the conversation centered around jobs, college, past loves.

Throughout the meal Adam seemed like a different person, not at all like the controlling, fidgety guy she'd met at Warren's. She wondered if being around the other collectors made him that way.

She reminded herself that she was sitting with a felon, with infractions that included theft and assault of a live-in girlfriend. Did he have an inkling of who she really was?

He asked her a lot of questions, and she used the tight story line she and Des had practiced: Her father had been a collector. She and her sister inherited his snakes. She worked at the EPA.

The rest was her real self.

Then he covered his territory, mentioning mistakes he'd made in his life—though he didn't elaborate. There were things he wasn't about to repeat.

Over the course of the evening he had been—what's the word her mother would use? *Charming*. She let the situation that had occurred in her apartment slip away.

Standing outside her building, they made plans to meet for the reptile show on Sunday. He leaned forward and kissed her lightly on the cheek, and said he'd call tomorrow. She went inside to call Des, pleased that the evening had gone well.

Adam walked to his car, passing an electronics store on the way. A large-screen television in the window was replaying the evening's top news: a FedEx truck had crashed after the driver noticed a snake coming out of a box she was to deliver.

He stopped in mid-stride and stared at the television through the window.

"*Shit!*"

35

"It was a juvenile king cobra in that truck," Sheridan began, as Johnny and Des stood in his office for the hastily arranged Friday morning meeting.

"The shipment!" Johnny exclaimed. Suddenly, the information she had not been privy to seemed quite important.

"The box was sent from Germany from an address that doesn't exist," Sheridan added.

Des, standing by, said, "Sounds like the UPS package that came into Reagan a couple of years ago. Remember that? The one with the monocled cobras labeled as bracelets?"

"Similar but not the same," Sheridan said. "I called Customs this morning. Maryland is handling this." He watched Des roll his eyes at the mention of former co-worker Stone's state of business, then continued. "Stone called and asked about our case. We need to keep him in the loop—now that he's interested."

"Great," Des said.

Sheridan turned to Johnny. "Did anyone at your meeting say who the sender was?"

"No," she answered. "But I'll try to find out. All Adam said to Patrick—Patrick Gonzales—is that a package would be delivered." She looked at the two men, who waited for her to continue. "I'm meeting Adam at the reptile show on Sunday. I'll ask him about it."

"Don't ask too many questions," Sheridan warned her.

Johnny gave him a blank stare.

"Don't make him suspicious," he clarified, now sounding more like Des and worried for her safety.

"I won't," she replied.

Johnny left and Des sat down. He looked at his partner, who seemed preoccupied with staring at his desktop. "What are you thinking?"

Sheridan looked up at him. "About FedEx? Too soon to know."

"That's what I think. What else?"

"Other than Vicki leaving?"

"Oh…" Des hesitated before continuing. "You mean… permanently?"

Sheridan nodded.

"When?"

"She flies out next week to see Marsh and find a place to live."

"Wow." Des let that sink in. "Carole and I were just talking about you two, coming for dinner some evening."

"We'd like that," Sheridan responded. He paused. "We don't have an evening."

Des remained silent.

Sheridan changed the subject. "Did you get anything from Matt or Trainor?"

"Yeah. You can cross two things off your list."

"So nothing on climate or extinctions."

"Correct," Des answered, noting that his partner had moved beyond further talk about Vicki.

"So we have…nothing. Not on skins, body parts, food products," he said, ticking off scenarios from his ever-shrinking list. "Collectors are still the easy target. But I'm beginning to think the snakes have packed up and moved, like Simpson said all along," he added, in a rare display of deference to the Ashland statistician. "That still doesn't explain why we don't see them."

"You know, I began thinking about the *why* in all of this," Des said. "If someone has the snakes there has to be a reason."

"Agreed. But they're not showing up anywhere. It's as if there's a void in the world," Sheridan replied.

Des thought about that. "Is that what you're going to tell Interior?"

36

Sheridan sat at the long, polished-wood table in the spacious, high-ceilinged conference room. Huge oil paintings—big enough to walk into—of early American wilderness scenes hugged the oak-paneled walls. From above, stained-glass chandeliers cast muted light onto the tabletop, Interior's way of bringing lodge-style accoutrements into neoclassic architecture. He felt small sitting there, the way he sometimes did in nature.

Perhaps that was the intent.

The Department of the Interior, based in DC's downtown corridor, was a monstrous government entity, employing eighty thousand men and women nationwide, managing every aspect of conservation: minerals, parks, water, lands for the nation's Native American tribes, and, of course, Fish and Wildlife. Its hierarchy, difficult and complex, was one Sheridan preferred to ignore.

Every so often Egan made the trek here to brief the politically anointed about their activities on behalf of world wildlife. With both Egan and Donahue on vacation, Sheridan was left to fill in the blanks regarding Thailand, the immediacy of it timed to the secretary of state's visit there.

He looked at the assembled players, empty seats interspersed among them, the August vacation schedule visible here as well. Other than himself, it was Vince Valcone—the one who had answered his e-mail and who introduced himself as the under-secretary's manager—a few indistinguishable suits, and some top-level minions, Sheridan surmised, based on their age. It was obvious from the discarded food containers and coffee cups that they'd been here a while. He was merely a spot on their Friday-afternoon agenda.

Valcone crossed his legs and turned a page in a folder. They were seated on the same side of the table. Sheridan glanced down at Valcone's polished, tasseled loafers.

So unlike the treads of my associates.

"Mr. Sheridan, thanks for joining us," Valcone began, as the participants looked down at their agendas. "Can you bring us up-to-date on Thailand?"

"Of course."

Over the next ten minutes, Sheridan briefed the group on the situation, educating them on the species in general, the cobra's population range, its habitat, and habitat destruction. He refrained from telling them that the king was not really a cobra. He did tell them it was revered as a symbol and was often a pet in Thailand.

He saw eyebrows go up.

"It is quite docile unless threatened," Sheridan explained.

He moved on to the king cobra's Appendix II listing, just shy—in U.S. parlance—of an endangered species. The last count by the IUC was five years ago. Another would begin in January. Next, he outlined scenarios for the disappearance.

Sheridan put his hands out in front of him in a gesture of explanation. "There are several," he began. "First is the taking of the snake for its skin and body parts. In Asia, the snake's pelt is used for boots, purses, shoes, vests, belts, wallets, and hats. Using the head of a cobra on a hat or boot is common." He saw expressions of surprise around him. "Our sources in Europe and Asia say there hasn't been an increase in this activity." He started to go on, but stopped. "I should add that using a *king* cobra in this way is highly unusual."

"Why's that?" Valcone asked.

"Because of its stature in Asian culture. The Thais in particular would be upset if they saw this." He paused. "We have not seen this occurring." Sheridan continued. "Next is the taking of snakes for food. In Asia reptiles are eaten, as many of you know."

Some at the table squirmed, unattuned as they seemed to be to Asian delicacies.

"Again, nothing out of the ordinary." Sheridan summarized his brief comments. "So, king cobras' skins are not being used for products, and the snake, as far as we can determine, is not being used for food. That leaves an environmental event—none is on record—or a killing, but no carcasses have been found. Large-scale taking that depletes a population is unheard of among snakes." Sheridan remained quiet, allowing his comments to sink in.

"What are you hanging your hat on?" Valcone asked suddenly.

Sheridan looked across the table at the people waiting for him to answer. All he had was a guesstimate, one he knew intuitively was wrong. "The snakes moved to find food, a population shift that hasn't yet been recorded by international agencies. Or by Thailand."

"So it's a natural event?" Valcone asked.

"Apparently," Sheridan answered. "Except that they haven't been seen."

"They're in the jungle," one of the suits offered.

Valcone seemed to buy that and nodded in approval. "Thanks for your time. We'll ensure that the secretary is briefed."

37

The driver maneuvered the semi with one hand while he strained to read the address on the bill of lading. Circling once in the deserted warehouse district, he returned to the street he had come in on.

He stopped, turned on the overhead light and read the whole document. No other address was listed. He looked at the old warehouse he had just passed, surrounded by a dirt field and rusty, discarded oil drums. Wire mesh covered broken windows. He looked up and read the faded block letters at the top of the building—a German name he couldn't decipher, and the word *Bäckerei*, just as faded, after it.

He inched the cab forward, then stopped when he saw a police car pulling up alongside his door.

The policeman got out and came over to him.

"*Guten abend!* You know you got a back light out?"

"No, I didn't know that." The driver hesitated. "I'm doing this shift for a friend. I'll tell him."

"What're you looking for?" the officer asked.

"An address. It should be right here."

"What's the name?"

The driver looked down at the paperwork. "Leschman Graphics."

The officer stared at him for a moment. "Never heard of it. What's the load?"

The driver read from the page. "Ink." He looked up. "It's a load of ink."

The officer looked at the old warehouse and then back at the driver. Without saying anything, he walked to the back of the truck.

In his rearview mirror, the driver watched him shine his flashlight on the small twenty-foot container, then walk back to talk to him.

"Why don't you step down and we'll open this thing up."

The driver shrugged. He turned off the engine and got out.

They went to the back and jumped up on the truck bed. The driver released the hold on the container's door and swung it open. The policeman shone his flashlight on the contents: wooden crates—too many to count—black plastic covering whatever was inside each.

The officer looked at the driver, who shrugged again.

"Where did this come from?" the officer asked.

"Don't know." The driver jumped down and went back to his cab. He retrieved his paperwork and returned. The men stood shoulder to shoulder reading the document in the light of the flashlight.

"I don't see anything," the driver said.

"Doesn't that seem odd to you?"

"Yeah. I can take it back to the yard."

The officer thought for a moment. "Why don't you follow me instead?"

38

Baltimore, Maryland
Friday evening

Adam picked the lock easily, knowing how old-building owners never changed them, and entered the apartment. He stood for
a moment in the entryway and listened, hearing only the traffic
below through the open windows. Moving quickly past a littered
coffee table, he walked over and closed them.

Then he proceeded down the hallway, past the kitchen, to
the thermostat, which he inched up to ninety-five degrees, and
then to the closed door. Adam heard an air conditioner humming
peacefully inside. He opened the door and stepped in. Cool air
bathed his face. Light from the ultraviolet lamps lit the room.

Adam walked to the air conditioner and turned it off, then
moved in front of the king cobra terrarium. The big snake stared
back at him. He turned off the ultraviolet light above it and slowly
removed the cover, placing it on the floor. The snake watched but
didn't move. He performed the same maneuver with the monocled cobra terrariums nearby.

Then, without looking back, he left.

* * *

Washington, DC

Johnny made her way though the Friday night crowd at one
of Georgetown's most popular meet-and-greet places. She saw
her friend Steffy sitting at the bar, engaged in conversation with

two young men in suits, and surmised that they were government attorneys or congressional staffers of some sort.

She walked up to them and stood by, waiting for Steffy to recognize her.

Suddenly, her friend's mouth popped open. "You really did change this!" she exclaimed, putting a hand out toward Johnny's short spiky hair.

She was introduced to the two men. They were indeed attorneys and they were indeed on the make, not the evening Johnny had in mind. They parted company when Steffy's name was called for a table.

Conveniently, they were seated away from the other diners, at a corner booth where no one bothered them. When they had ordered dinner and more drinks, Steffy gave Johnny news of their classmates.

"Jordan is in Alaska, Kelly went to New Orleans, and Rosetta is at O'Hare working in Customs, like me." Suddenly, Steffy leaned forward. "So tell me, what're you working on?"

"You *know* I can't say," Johnny replied.

"But it's just you and me. And *I'm* not gonna tell anyone." She waited. "You were calling me from the zoo!" Steffy turned serious. "Is it something with the zoo?"

"No," Johnny said, dismissing the question. "Okay." She looked around before beginning. "I'm on this assignment to keep track of a group of guys called the Beltway collectors. They collect snakes."

"Really?"

Johnny nodded. "They have cobras." She paused. "Most of them do. The owner of Exotic Reptiles doesn't. He's sort of a sad guy, but nice."

"What do you do?"

"Well, I meet with them. And I have snakes at home."

"No way!"

Johnny nodded that she did.

"Cobras?"

Johnny nodded again. "That's why I was at the zoo."

"Do you touch them?" Steffy asked.

"No! I think the zoo saw that I was...awkward...and so someone stops by each week and feeds them and checks them. I have them to give me credibility with the collectors."

"Wow."

"I know how to handle them, just in case. But I haven't."

"So...who are you, undercover?" Steffy asked.

"I'm not supposed to say, but I'll tell you. I'm sort of a compilation of a friend of mine back in San Francisco," Johnny explained, "whose father had snakes. But mostly I'm myself." Suddenly, she seemed concerned. "You're not going to tell anyone, are you?"

"No, no! Don't worry!" Steffy assured her. "So you just follow around some snake collectors?"

"I'm supposed to find out where they get their cobras, which you know are Appendix II. That may or may not be related to the bigger case my bosses are working on, which is about missing *king* cobras in Thailand."

"Really?"

"Yeah."

"Are your bosses undercover?" Steffy asked.

"No. They're just under pressure!"

Their drinks were delivered and they clinked glasses. Johnny continued telling Steffy about her first week on the job, filling her in on the collectors she had met and the venom she had tasted.

"You tasted venom?" Steffy asked, astonished. "Did you drink it?"

"No! I got a little on my finger and put it on my tongue."

"Why?"

Johnny hesitated. "Because I was passed the little jar the venom had been milked into and Adam told me to. So I did. He's one of the collectors."

"He was testing you."

Johnny nodded in agreement.

Steffy scrunched up her face. "I don't think I could do that. What did it taste like?"

Johnny paused again, remembering the experience. "Like nothing. And then, after a few seconds, it had a metallic taste."

"Wow." Steffy changed the subject. "So, what's the story with your hair?"

"I changed it," Johnny explained, "because of Adam. I knew from the moment I saw his picture that he was the one I wanted to focus on. He's edgy, dangerous. I needed a look that said I was that way."

"So you like him, the guy who asked you to drink venom?" Steffy asked.

"No. It's the challenge."

"How so?"

"To make him believe in my make-believe self," Johnny answered, sipping her wine.

"And *does* he?"

"Oh, sure! He's a guy. I could get him in bed."

Steffy laughed. "And *will* you?"

"I don't know. I mean…I don't really want to be with someone who has *snakes*. That's weird!"

"And you might slip and be your real self," Steffy added.

"Hmm. I don't know," Johnny answered, wondering if that were true.

They leaned back as their steaming pasta dinners were placed in front of them. They ate in silence, devouring their food.

Finally, Steffy blurted out, "I wish I could be undercover like you are. I just stand around and look in bags or go through cargo.

Although this guy tried to bring in a suitcase full of Caribbean turtles." She gave a look that said, "How stupid is that?" Then she continued, "But you're actually *on* a case."

Johnny discounted it. "They just want to keep me busy. I'm not on *their* case." Johnny thought of something else. "Des is nice. He's the guy I report to. Sheridan is too, but he's a little preoccupied with this woman in our office leaving. They're involved," she clarified.

"Hmm," was all Steffy said.

A server removed their empty plates. Instead of moving on, they decided to stay where they were and ordered more drinks. Johnny looked around at the people, mostly her age, filling tables and standing in the crowded bar conversing and laughing.

"I need to get more information," Johnny said suddenly. "I need to get Des and Sheridan something they can use."

39

Baltimore, Maryland
Friday evening

Patrick paid the cab driver and got out. He unlocked the front door of his apartment building and stepped into the lobby, where he retrieved his mail. He saw flyers and nothing of import except a Domino's pizza ad. He threw everything away except the ad.

He ascended the stairs to his apartment and tried to organize his thoughts about what he was going to do next. One thing for sure: he didn't want to face Adam because of that shipment. There hadn't been a plan B if the snakes arrived and he wasn't there. Or sleeping, he admitted.

He opened the door to the third floor and walked down the hallway to his apartment. Was this what he wanted, to be a lackey for Adam? No, it wasn't, he decided. He put his key in the lock, feeling better already, and opened the door.

Oppressive heat!

He stepped inside.

The windows! He never closed them in summer. Did the landlord do it? He hurried over to them, but stopped.

Something on the floor moved under the couch.

Holy shit!

He inched back and stared at the spot on the worn Persian rug where he had seen the snake. Thoughts began to register. Forgetting the windows, Patrick moved with his back against his living room wall until he came to the end of it.

And turned the corner.

He stopped.

The king cobra, no more than five feet from him, rose up a third of its length, dominating the space in the hallway, backlit by the light coming through the bathroom window behind it.

It swayed and hissed. A deep, wet, throaty sound.

Patrick stepped backward. Slowly. Even if he got to the open door, the snake could strike, using all eighteen feet of its body to project itself forward. He fought to gain control of his breathing. Perspiration soaked his shirt.

He stepped backward again, then again, but his heel touched down on something. The small monocled cobra responded instantly, driving its fangs into the soft area near his ankle.

Patrick yelled and grabbed his leg, hitting the snake's head as he did so. In response, the reptile chewed deeper into the skin, delivering more venom.

He fell backward as the snake loosened its grip. He grabbed his ankle, seeing the jagged mark left by teeth and fangs. He knew he had to get help, knowing the bite of the cobra would kill him.

Patrick looked at the king cobra that remained in front of him. He thought about his cell phone deep in his pocket. He reached for it but moved in slow motion, the venom already taking effect. He lay down instead, aware of his protracted movements. He stared up at the ceiling, the periphery of his vision blurry now, his ankle throbbing with pain, his shoe tight on his foot.

He lay there for some time, his breathing quick and shallow. Then his head flopped to the side, and as he took his last breath, Patrick watched the king cobra disappear into the kitchen.

40

Sheridan sat at the bar at Hugo's waiting for Des before heading to Vicki's for a late dinner. On the TV above, the Orioles struggled to make up three runs late in the game. He signaled to Stan, then went back to thoughts about his afternoon meeting.

He didn't know what bothered him more: his position in federal bureaucracy or dealing with people he had little in common with. Valcone had been professional, running the meeting in an organized way. Still, he had felt uncomfortable. With what?

With myself. Do what Vicki's doing.

Stan ambled over. "You said another?" he asked, pointing to Sheridan's glass.

"Yeah. Great."

Stan picked up the empty glass. "So, I'm curious, did that guy sell his '52 Mantle yet?"

Sheridan nodded that he had. "Got sixty-four thousand dollars."

"You're shitting me."

Sheridan replied, "No. I'm not."

Stan laughed. "You know, if I could do *one* thing"—he held up his finger indicating the number—"I'd go back to the fifties and bring back *five* of those Mantles. I don't think I'd ever sell them."

Sheridan nodded in agreement and Stan walked off. But just as quickly he turned around.

"I take that back," Stan said. "I'd sell every one!"

Sheridan laughed. "You got that right!"

A bar regular listening to them sidled over to Sheridan.

Sheridan gave him the once-over: tie loosened and cocked at an angle, hair that needed combing, thumbprints on oversized glasses. Without question, some type of government geek.

"I've been listening to you guys talk about baseball cards," the man began. He held out his hand. "Curtis Marks."

Sheridan shook his hand. "Jim Sheridan."

"Can I buy you a beer?"

"No, I'm good, thanks," Sheridan replied, as Stan placed a fresh glass in front of him.

"You seem to know a lot about cards and I've got a ton of them. How much do you think the 'forgotten men' are worth?"

"Like who?" Sheridan replied, thinking the question odd.

"You know, second-rate second basemen…pitchers you don't remember."

"What years?"

"Mostly sixties. Couple a fifties."

"Depends on the condition," Sheridan responded. "Someone will want them to fill out collections. Bring 'em in. I'll take a look."

"I'll do that! You'll be here tomorrow?" he asked.

"No," Sheridan answered. "Next week sometime."

Des came up to them and stood by as Curtis gathered his briefcase and keys.

"Great! I'll catch you later," Curtis said, departing.

"Who's that?" Des asked, sitting down next to Sheridan.

"Some guy who has cards." Sheridan looked up at the TV. The Orioles had dropped another one. He wondered if his stepbrother still had his baseball cards.

"How'd it go at Interior?" Des asked.

Sheridan filled him in on the meeting without disclosing his discomfort. He took a long draw on his beer. "I did my part. I can hand it back to Egan." He changed the subject. "My stepbrother called. He's coming to visit."

"The one you haven't seen in awhile?" Des asked.

Sheridan nodded. "You get along with your siblings?"

"Yeah. Why?"

"I don't know. We weren't close." Then, in a way that voiced amazement, he said, "You *all* get along?" He knew Des had a large family, with get-togethers spread throughout the year.

"Well…" Des moved his hands as a beer was placed on a coaster. "There are times…" He shifted position. "We try to put those aside. Maybe it's different with a stepbrother."

Sheridan agreed. "Yeah, maybe."

"What time do you wanna meet tomorrow?" Des inquired.

"Seven a.m."

"How about eight a.m.?" Des replied, never the morning person.

"Seven thirty a.m., at the main entrance," Sheridan countered. "Maybe we'll beat Stone."

"All right. Seven thirty," Des agreed.

They watched the wrap-up of the game. When it was over, Sheridan paid for their drinks and the two walked out together.

Before parting, Des turned to him. "You don't think someone *has* all these snakes, do you?"

Sheridan lifted his head from his pillow. He glanced across Vicki to the clock on her nightstand: 2:44 a.m.

Wide awake, with too many thoughts bouncing around, he got up and went into her spare bedroom, and turned on her computer. Thinking about Des's question, he logged on to his work e-mail and shipped off a request to his associate at INTERPOL.

> *Isaac—*
> *Do me a favor:*
> *Look into places that sell mice and rats.*
> *If someone has these snakes they have to be fed.*

41

Bangkok, Thailand
Saturday afternoon

Shelton sat in a café across the street from Jik's parents' clothing plant. He had been idling around this part of Bangkok, filled with warehouses and small eateries and bars, for four hours while he waited for Jik to join him. After much cajoling during a quick phone call, Jik had agreed to do so—but only for a short time—after work.

Shelton switched from tea to Chinese beer and watched street traffic pass by the back door of the clothing plant. Jik finally appeared, crossed the street, and sat down across from him.

"Anything to eat?" Shelton offered.

"No," Jik answered abruptly.

"Okay."

Jik refused to meet him eye to eye.

"I appreciate your meeting with me. Can you tell me what you know?"

Jik hesitated. "Who will be given the information?"

"What you say will go to INTERPOL's Wildlife Group and to U.S. authorities," Shelton answered.

"The U.S. is a problem," Jik said. "They move on incomplete information."

Shelton waited for him to continue. He seemed to be thinking through how to proceed.

Then he began. "I will tell you as much as I know, but you must not say I told you."

"Isaac already knows that I've contacted you."

"I mean to anyone here."

"I'll keep your identity unknown," Shelton promised.

Jik said, "A reptile broker is obtaining king cobras and selling them to a company."

"A *company*?" Shelton asked, somewhat surprised.

"Yes."

"What company?"

"I don't know. But the man has a well-connected operation and his people pay well for the snakes."

Shelton thought for a moment. "Do you know why they are being taken?"

Jik shook his head, indicating that he did not.

"Do you know where this person is from?"

Jik hesitated. "He...doesn't really have an address."

"Okay." Shelton thought about that, and then asked, "Is it possible that he is taking enough that it is noticed?"

"Yes."

"So we are talking about something quite large," Shelton remarked.

Jik nodded in agreement.

"Do the snakes come to Bangkok for dissemination?" Shelton asked.

"Yes."

"Where are they shipped to?"

Jik looked away.

Shelton said, "I followed a truck from snake alley to a warehouse. Are the cobras there?"

Jik started to say something, then paused. "I can't talk about any warehouse."

Shelton didn't press the point. "Are the snakes shipped to the U.S.?"

Jik shook his head.

"Europe?"

Jik nodded.

"Where?"

Jik shrugged.

"Do you really not know?"

"I really do not know."

"How are they shipped?"

"In containers, by rail and ship," Jik answered.

Shelton paused again. "How is it that you know this?"

"The money being paid to the boys is very big. And to the people doing the packing and shipping. Word gets around."

Shelton considered what he had heard so far. "And you don't know *why* all of this is happening?"

"No."

Shelton noticed again the pained look, and now the slumped shoulders of the man sitting across from him.

"Jik, everything you've told me will be helpful," Shelton said, trying to reassure him. "This is an enormous operation, I think."

Suddenly, Jik squared himself, assuming the professional look Shelton had always associated with him. Jik nodded that he understood, and let whatever else he might have said go unspoken.

After saying good-bye, Shelton made his way along the now empty back road to a main street. And a taxi, he hoped. He thought about the animal trade in Asia, mostly underground operations that no one could find or trace back to anyone. Skins from reptiles were made into any number of clothing items and accessories, and the meat was not going unused. But the snakes Jik talked about were being sent away.

That was something out of the ordinary for Asia.

He rounded a corner, still looking for a main thoroughfare. Thinking again of Isaac, he took out his cell phone. But before he could make his call a white light enveloped him. Pain registered as a metal bar cracked his skull from behind. His phone slipped from his hand and was quickly picked up and pocketed.

Barely conscious, Shelton was aware of people around him and being dragged off the quiet street. After several more blows to the head, Shelton's body was placed in the back of a white van. The men quickly scattered as it drove away.

Jik walked quickly in an effort to reach his home. He had said too much and had put friends in jeopardy. *Too late now*, he thought. He felt his stomach tighten. He would have to warn them. Perhaps they could move their operation to another part of Bangkok. Or even better, outside the city.

He rounded a corner and saw three men emerge from an alley. And stop. He slowed down, looked to his left and right and then turned to run, but was quickly detained. One of the men produced a knife. Jik felt a warm sensation on his chest and looked down. He saw blood running down the front of his shirt like a faucet had been turned on. Jik lost consciousness and fell to the ground. His body was quickly placed in a bag, and then in the van alongside Shelton's. The three men jumped into the back of the white vehicle and it drove away, heading for a warehouse on the other side of Bangkok.

42

Chang handed over his passport—one of four he carried—to the agent requesting it at Dulles International Airport.

"Put your hand on the scanner, please," the Customs agent said.

Chang did as he was told, placing his palm down as the scanner took "prints" of all five fingers.

The agent looked at her computer screen and then eyed him—aka Raymond Chou—then scrutinized the passport and regarded Chang again.

"Your business here?" she asked.

"A trade meeting," Chang answered.

"How long will you be in the country?"

"A week."

He watched as she thumbed through the passport, its many stamped pages visible to both of them. She looked back at her computer, and for some time he stood there waiting.

Wondering.

He had calculated this time to be at this airport, on this day, one of the heaviest-traveling days for tourists from Asia coming into DC. Just in case, he located an escape route to his right, as he normally did for situations in which he wasn't sure of the outcome.

Finally, without comment, the agent closed the passport and handed it back to him, and Chang moved on. He placed it in his breast pocket, and joined others walking toward baggage claim, smiling to himself as he did so.

Driving up I-270, Maryland's biotech corridor, Chang looked to the left and right as buildings whizzed by. Nothing appeared different. It had been eight years since he'd been on U.S. soil. This area, around Rockville, had been the base for his dealings, when he and two others had organized the largest influx of near-extinct South American boas and Caribbean turtles for the voracious U.S. collecting market. Back then, they had managed to get a good portion of their reptiles through Baltimore, bypassing the always-watched New York Kennedy and Miami International Airports. But U.S. Fish and Wildlife agents began to suspect something when collectors in the DC area suddenly had some of these rare and prized reptiles. He had left the country; his two associates had fled to Mexico, where they were caught, and were now serving time for Lacey Act violations and money laundering, the last bringing a stiff and expensive U.S. sentence. He read years later that the feds referred to their sting as Operation Chameleon.

Back in Hong Kong, over the ensuing years, he had had time to think about what he would do next. With so much knowledge about exotic animals, it seemed a shame to waste it. That's when his present plan had come to him. He would exit the collecting market. Instead, he had found an even more lucrative business, and one that promised him great fortune.

He saw signs for Gaithersburg and realized he'd gone too far. Chang turned around and headed back, eventually exiting onto Route 95 for the trip to his Baltimore hotel. His decision to ease himself out of the exotic collecting market, he knew, was the right one. Without revealing his other plans, he would let K. C. know that he would no longer be supplying him or his vast network of collectors with snakes.

Chang looked at his watch, set on Hong Kong time. The operation in Thailand should be just about completed. Things were progressing as he had planned.

It was all about numbers.

43

Crews moved inside Baltimore's cavernous convention center, constructing last-minute display booths, hanging banners, and checking lighting for the center stage, even as people began streaming in. Vendors unpacked goods and arranged them carefully on draped tables, while exhibitors moved terrariums into view for all who would be walking by.

Sheridan stood near the entrance drinking coffee, waiting for his partner and thinking through what the morning might entail. Certainly, that was determining whether K. C. had a role in the Thailand situation. But ostracizing the planet's most well-known snake collector was something he didn't want to do.

Sheridan leaned against the wall and watched people enter. He'd have to play this carefully, asking questions that didn't alienate the man, questions that appealed to K. C.'s sense of conservation, which put them both on the same page. Although K. C. had not done so in the past, Sheridan was sure he had information to impart. They simply needed to find a way for him to share it.

He finished his drink and tossed the cup in the trash. He saw Des hurrying in, keys in one hand, a take-out coffee in the other.

"Sorry," Des said, approaching him.

"Not a problem."

"Where to first?"

"Let's just take it in," Sheridan replied, as they walked down the wide main thoroughfare of the show. He looked up. A huge banner behind the main stage welcomed them to "The 16th Annual International Reptile Show."

"About K. C.," Sheridan began, "I think I'll just mention the cobras and see what his reaction is. I don't want to alienate him."

"Good idea," Des responded.

"We may want to talk to him again later."

"Right." Des blew on his coffee, taking small sips as they walked past exhibits.

"That question you asked last night," Sheridan added, "about someone having the snakes."

"Yeah."

"I wrote Isaac and asked him to look around."

"Great. What's he been up to?" Des inquired. Isaac was their European-based cohort on the Chameleon case.

"Not sure, other than helping us."

They saw Stone talking to a woman from a local news station. The two were standing in front of a Maryland Department of Natural Resources booth. Stone, immaculately dressed in a suit and tie, gestured to a display on the front table.

"Everything about that guy is wrong," Des said.

"Let's see what's going on."

They came up to their former co-worker as he was answering a query.

"It's a problem everywhere," they heard him explain "Taking natural resources is a crime."

"Whatever," Des said under his breath.

His interview at an end, Stone motioned them over. "Nice to see you, Desmond."

"Yeah, you too," Des answered, concentrating on his coffee.

"Where's Egan?" Stone asked.

"On vacation," Sheridan answered. He got out of the way of a forklift taking boxes to the back of the hall.

"Who else is coming?"

"No one I know of," Sheridan replied.

"This is a big show," Stone said, looking around. "Everyone should be here. Where's Vicki?"

"She's busy," Sheridan said, not going into detail.

"I bet." Stone fooled with his cuff links and then laughed. "She still have those plaques on her bedroom wall——"

Des interrupted before Sheridan could respond. "Let's pay a visit to K. C. before things get started."

"He's down there," Stone said, pointing down the aisle. "Nice that you guys made it."

"He's an ass," Des reminded Sheridan as they walked away.

Sheridan remained silent. He had never questioned Vicki about Stone and she had never mentioned him. But office gossip being what it was, Stone's comment was a painful reminder of what he had long thought about the two of them being together.

They walked toward the main stage and, off to the left, an area the size of four or five displays opened up, revealing K. C.'s exhibit. Groups of people stood around talking. A large photo of the reptile collector himself, from the cover of his book, hung from a purple curtain in front. Plush carpeting ran throughout.

"You have to think that promoting *All the World's Cobras* in one place is going to be popular at a snake show," Des said, as they approached.

At the entrance they passed a box holding flyers, noting K. C.'s talk at Exotic Reptiles the following night. Sheridan took one as they walked onto the thick carpeting, to a table set up with free soft drinks, coffee, and cookies. Des parked himself by the cookies.

Smack in the middle, dominating the space, was a large terrarium holding, Sheridan surmised, a king cobra. People young and old crowded near it and walked slowly around it, counterclockwise, as if viewing a sacred object. Sentinels, dressed in identical polo shirts, stood nearby.

Sheridan watched people enthralled with the snakes. And with K. C., apparently.

He followed the crowd through the exhibit of *All the World's Cobras*, stopping in front of a terrarium holding a monocled variety. Sheridan crouched down to look at it. The reptile, once the most common snake in India, was now one step away from an Appendix I listing, on par with the United States' category for endangered species. He took in its black, brown, and white scales that he knew formed the familiar eyeglass pattern on its back when the hood was extended.

This snake, however, lay perfectly still. And stared back at him. Sheridan felt someone come up next to him and he looked up, noting the name tag.

"He's got permits for these, right?" Sheridan asked, standing up.

"Oh, yeah," Reeves responded, seemingly put off by the question.

Sheridan stood eye to eye with him, a cold, expressionless man, not unlike the creatures around them. "When is K. C. speaking?"

Reeves looked at his watch. "About an hour."

"Where is he now?" Sheridan asked.

"On the stage."

Sheridan turned and looked out the back end of the exhibit. K. C. was looking at him. Their eyes locked, neither man blinking, the first time they'd seen each other in five years. Finally, Sheridan looked away.

Des came over and offered him a cookie. Sheridan declined. "Let's go up to the stage."

They made their way through people filling the main aisle. K. C. had his back to them now, talking to a workman.

As they approached, Sheridan felt his phone vibrate and stopped. "Hang on a sec." He looked at the international number and answered.

"You found mice and rats?" Sheridan asked his colleague in Europe.

"Something else," Isaac replied. "A container was intercepted in an industrial area here. The only things out there are old buildings and distribution centers. Seems a trucker was having a hard time finding an address. What police found was a shipment of king cobras, about two hundred of them, nicely packed—professionally—in terrariums."

"No kidding," Sheridan replied.

"The shipment was traced to a company called Global Initiatives in Germany. It was sent from a false address in Thailand."

"Interesting." Sheridan shot a glance at Des.

"Global Initiatives is a private company, so there's not much to go on. I'll try to get more."

"Thanks, Isaac." Sheridan put his phone away and relayed the conversation to Des. "This may be our first lead, sparse as it is."

They walked on, up a flight of stairs, and approached K. C., who turned to face them.

Sheridan extended his hand and, after a moment, K. C. took it.

"Been a while," K. C. said, addressing both men.

"Looks like you're set up for the show," Sheridan replied, as a group of people gathered below.

"Almost there," K. C. answered. "What's up?"

Sheridan got to the point. "We want to ask you some questions about missing snakes."

K. C. folded his arms in front of him. "Cobras, no doubt."

Des chewed on his cookie as he watched the exchange unfold.

"King cobras. In Thailand," Sheridan explained. "Do you know anything about that?"

K. C. shook his head. "No."

"Villagers say they don't see them," Sheridan added.

K. C. shrugged. "I don't know what to tell you." He thought for a moment. "Disease, maybe?"

Sheridan shook his head. He folded the Exotic Reptile flyer in half, then in half again, then once more, and put it in his breast pocket as K. C. watched him.

"So, what do you *think* is going on?" K. C. asked.

"Don't know," Sheridan replied. "As you can imagine, the Thai people are quite upset."

"I imagine they are."

Sheridan eyed the man in front of him. *No matter what, this topic always begins and ends with you.*

"There was a shipment, a juvenile king cobra intercepted here," Sheridan continued. "Do you know anything about that?"

K. C. shook his head. "Having cobras isn't a crime."

"Having some of them is," Sheridan answered.

K. C. didn't respond.

Sheridan looked out from the stage at the number of exhibits and people filling the hall. He looked down and saw that the group below had gotten bigger.

"Thailand has an unusual situation, in that quite a *large* number of snakes are missing," Sheridan added, ready to end his brief line of questioning, since nothing in K. C.'s demeanor was telling him he knew anything.

"This is the first I've heard of it," K. C. replied. "Maybe it's...I don't know, habitat issues. It would have to be something big for big numbers."

"Nothing about that has been observed," Sheridan answered.

K. C. thought again. "They're sensitive to temperature. Maybe this is a seminal event. Have you looked at other species? Other snakes?"

"Yes," Des answered. "It's only the king cobra."

"That doesn't make sense," K. C. said.

Sheridan felt the man's eyes boring into him and wondered what he was thinking. He reached for a business card and handed it to K. C. "If you don't mind, call us if you hear of something."

K. C. pocketed the card without looking at it and nodded in agreement.

Des finished his cookie and wiped his hands on his pants. "You know, K. C., we're asking you about this because if someone is taking snakes, it has to be someone in the snake community doing it."

"Why do you say that?" K. C. asked.

"Because no one else would bother."

44

Coffee cup in hand, the woman in the apartment building opened her blinds and looked up at the sky. It was a maneuver she did every morning, although a bit later this morning since it was Saturday.

She took a sip of coffee and looked to her left, into her neighbor Patrick's apartment, an unconscious move she also did every day before heading back to the kitchen.

"John?" she called out in a calm voice, posed more as a question, to her husband, who was reading the newspaper.

Then, not so calmly.

"John!"

Her husband hurried into the room and joined her. Before them, crawling up and sliding down their neighbor's window—its white underbelly clearly visible to them both—was a snake. Below it, on the windowsill, was another one.

"Oh my God," John said.

The woman moved to the phone. "I'm calling the police."

* * *

Animal control pulled up behind police cars assembled outside of Patrick's brick apartment building.

"We should be outta here in a few minutes," the driver said to his partner.

"Yeah, but we got snakes," his partner responded. "Not my favorite."

The two agents jumped out and grabbed burlap bags and snake sticks from the back of their van. Behind them, a Maryland conservation officer pulled up and got out with a young black Labrador, and joined the men waiting at the door. The manager opened it for them, taking note of the crowd gathering across the street.

The men brushed by him and climbed the stairs. At the third floor they fell in behind several police officers who had gathered outside of Patrick's apartment.

"Is the owner home?" one policeman asked, as the manager huffed up alongside of him.

"I don't know. Knock and see."

Instead, the policeman yelled out past the open door. And waited. He heard the Labrador behind him straining at its leash.

"Hello!" he called out again, and then cracked the door open wider. "Shit!"

A foot and leg came into view.

He pushed the door open all the way and saw Patrick's body.

"Call an ambulance!"

The Labrador barked and struggled as the conservation officer tightened his grip on the leash.

"Keep ahold of that dog!" the first policeman admonished. He walked in and saw newspapers and pizza boxes covering an old coffee table. A framed poster on the wall tilted to the side. Next to it was a fire extinguisher. Oddly, he noted several more around the apartment.

Animal control followed him in.

"Keep the dog out there!" the cop reprimanded, as the conservation officer began to step inside.

The men carefully walked around Patrick's body. One of the animal control officers bent down and peered into Patrick's eyes.

"He be dead." He glanced at the floor. "Let's see what else we've got."

The policeman walked slowly to the windows—now void of snakes—checking out the floor first before planting his feet. He gently eased the windows up, the rush of hot fresh air an effective balm against the putrid air in the room.

He turned around and something caught his eye.

"Over there!" The policeman pointed toward the baseboard.

A small cobra moved around the corner and then down the hallway, away from them.

"Get it!" an animal control officer yelled.

His partner hurried after it, quickly positioning a snake stick behind its head and gently puting his shoe on its coiling back end. The policeman came up behind him. He looked down at the snake, the distinctive monocled marking on the back of the reptile's head visible to both.

"Damn! That's a cobra!" the policeman said. He shook his head in disbelief. "What's a cobra doing in Baltimore?"

"Hell if I know." The animal control officer carefully picked it up, put it tail first into a burlap bag, and closed it. The policeman walked into Patrick's second bedroom, the "snake" room, and made a note of the empty terrariums.

In the main room, the second animal control officer gingerly stepped around the back of the sofa and bent down to look under a table.

"Why don't you let me bring the dog in?" the conservation officer said from the doorway. "He can find what you're looking for."

"Just keep him there!" the annoyed policeman shot back, as he rejoined animal control in the living room. "We've got four empty terrariums back there, plus a *huge* one."

Noise in the third-floor hallway escalated as neighbors crowded in doorways and blocked the stairwell, straining to see what was causing the commotion.

One of the animal control officers peered behind a bookcase. "Another one!" he shouted.

The police officer reached for a fire extinguisher.

"Don't use that!" the conservation officer shouted.

"He's coming out that side! Get him! Get him!"

The snake emerged from behind the bookcase, moving frantically. The policeman pointed the hose and sprayed. The small cobra arched up and then froze as liquid carbon dioxide engulfed its mouth and eyes.

"Don't kill the snakes!" the conservation officer yelled. "Let me get them for you!"

"Will you shut up? And keep that damn dog quiet!" the policeman responded, as the dog barked uncontrollably.

"One more!" animal control called out, as he kicked at the bookcase.

The cobra came out the front toward the policeman's feet. He pointed the nozzle and sprayed. The reptile froze in mid-flight, its tail still moving. The policeman sprayed the snake's back end until the reptile was motionless. He waited while the compressed gas took effect, then sprayed it again for good measure.

"Don't waste it!" one of the policemen said from the door.

"So we've got two more?" animal control asked.

A siren wailed somewhere in the distance.

"Who knows," his partner replied. He stopped and thought about it. "Ask the manager."

Hearing their conversation, the conservation officer asked the manager how many snakes Patrick had, then turned back to the two men. "He didn't know he had *any*."

"Great," the older one replied.

"Let me bring the dog in," the conservation officer suggested again.

The animal control officers looked at each other and then at the policeman, who finally agreed.

"All right," the policeman answered. "But we can't help him if he gets bit."

The dog entered the room straining at its leash. It sniffed at Patrick's foot, then moved to the immobilized snakes by the bookcase. The Labrador approached slowly, bobbing its head, sniffing tentatively. Then it moved toward the kitchen, nose to the floor. And stopped, whining.

"What's he doing?" the policeman asked.

The dog barked.

"He doesn't want to go in," the conservation officer replied.

The Labrador took a tentative step forward and whined again.

The animal control men moved forward. "Let's see what we've got."

"Wait." The conservation officer tightened the leash on the dog. "What's that, behind the garbage can?"

The two men peered in at the layers of coils behind the blue plastic container.

"You gotta be shitting me."

"Get another can!" the older man said.

"No!" the conservation officer said.

His partner turned back to the living room, bumping into paramedics making their way in. "Why don't you wait," he said to them. "He's not going anywhere."

He grabbed a fire extinguisher off the wall and rushed back.

"On second thought," the first animal control officer said, "we're only gonna piss him off. We gotta bag him. Get the stick."

"You can't be serious!" the conservation officer replied. "It's a toothpick against"—he pointed to the garbage can—"I think it's a king cobra."

Ignoring him, the man retraced his steps to retrieve his snake stick and bag.

His partner grabbed a broom by the side of the refrigerator and motioned to his buddy as he came back to the kitchen. He took the snake stick and bag and handed him the broom.

"Go flush him out." He pointed to the left side of the can.

"But…we don't know where the head is."

"We're gonna find out."

The young man felt his heart pounding. He peered at the coils behind the can. With the broom steadied in front of him, he walked forward. He reached the snake and passed the broom over its body, lightly brushing its back.

The reptile shifted, and was still.

"Again," the first man said. "Harder."

He positioned the broom over the snake once more, then came down hard on the coils. Instantly, the head emerged from the right side of the can.

"There it is! There it is!" his partner yelled. He had the snake stick open, but the snake continued toward him.

"I can't get the head! Get it with the broom! The broom! *Quick!*" The man moved forward and swatted the snake's head to the floor.

People in the hallway crowded near the door to get a better look.

"Watch the back end!" the conservation officer yelled over the barking dog.

The king cobra's tail knocked over the garbage can, scattering its contents. A sea of coils swung forward toward the men's legs.

"Step on him! Step on him!" the conservation officer yelled.

They stepped on the coils but were unable to contain it. The conservation officer flipped the dog's leash to a policeman and hurried in. He stepped on the snake, using both feet, as the cobra bucked and struggled.

"I can't hold the head!" the animal control officer with the broom yelled. The cobra's mouth opened. "It's trying to rise up! I can't hold it!"

"Keep it steady!" the conservation officer yelled back. "Don't let go of the head!" He stood on the coils, feeling the snake's movement under his feet.

Suddenly, the snake jerked its upper body to the side and the broom flew to a corner.

"Christ!" one of the men yelled. "Look out!"

The snake began to rise. The conservation officer backed off the coils as the cobra repositioned itself.

"Get back!" he warned the animal control agents, as he walked slowly backward toward the door. But they remained in place.

The eighteen-foot king cobra rose six feet in height. The two animal control officers stared at the snake as tall as they were, and slowly moved backward.

Suddenly, the snake cocked its head back and then rushed forward, using the power of its coils to slide toward them.

"Look out!" one man yelled as they moved back into the living room. The snake, its hood splayed, emitted a loud, throaty hiss. Beads of venom dripped from its mouth onto the floor.

People in the hallway screamed and moved back.

"Get out! Close the door!"

"Where's a can!" one of the animal control officers yelled.

"There's not enough!" his partner answered.

"Let him resolve!" the conservation officer yelled, his dog barking frantically.

"I can shoot it!" one of the cops yelled.

"No! He'll strike!" the conservation officer warned.

The cop moved forward anyway and pointed his gun at the snake.

And fired.

The deafening shot hit the cobra squarely below the hood. In its moment of anguish, the reptile let out a high-pitched squeal, then—the life gone out of it—dropped to the floor and remained motionless, a pool of blood forming under it.

Silence enveloped the group. For several moments, no one moved.

The dog stopped barking. People stood still in the hallway.

After a time, the men inched forward and surrounded the snake.

"I didn't know a snake could cry out," the policeman said. He kicked lightly at the coils with his boot.

"Look at the size of that thing," an animal control officer said.

"Get a bag and let's get it out of here," his partner replied.

With the help of the conservation officer, the two men lifted the cobra into the burlap bag. People at the door gave the young animal control officer a wide berth as he dragged the bag out of the apartment.

"I'll be back for the others," he said over his shoulder.

The other shook the conservation officer's hand. "Thanks for your help, man."

The conservation officer wanted to say more, but refrained.

"Something like this," the animal control officer continued, looking back at the garbage-strewn floor, "makes me think I need a new job."

45

The garage door slid open and the white van pulled out onto the quiet street. It made its way through Bangkok's smaller side streets and alleys until it entered a dusty main road out of town, toward Nonthaburi and one of its several klongs, or canals, ancient waterways where Thai life came alive.

After thirty minutes, the driver maneuvered off to the side at a secluded rural area and backed the van's rear end close to the canal's edge. He and his passenger jumped out, lifted the van's accordion-style closure in back, and disappeared inside. They rolled two large plastic bags to the opening and pushed them off the back. The bags splashed into the murky water and quickly sank out of sight.

* * *

Adam stood with St. John and looked around the convention hall filling with people.

"Patrick's late," St. John said.

"Patrick's not coming," Adam replied. "That little prick has fucked up big-time."

"He'd better show up," St. John said. "We've got work to do for tomorrow night."

Adam looked at him without responding.

"For K. C.'s visit," St. John added.

"Don't you watch the news?" Adam inquired.

"No."

St. John wiped his brow, perspiration flowing even in air-conditioning. His faded maroon T-shirt clung to his bulging stomach. Adam wondered again how he had gotten hooked up with such a loser.

"The police confiscated the shipment," Adam explained. "*Our* first shipment."

"Oh, man!" St. John exclaimed, wiping his forehead. "How'd that happen?"

"Patrick wasn't home," Adam answered, ending the conversation about their associate. He looked at his watch. "Where's Warren?"

"He's not coming."

"Why *not*?"

"He sold his snakes."

"To *who*?" Adam asked incredulously.

"I don't know."

"I would have bought them!" Agitation rose in Adam's voice. He glanced at St. John. "Fuck this! Why didn't you buy those snakes?"

"Are you kidding? I can't afford snakes like that."

His frustration boiling over, Adam stalked off, leaving St. John standing by himself.

46

Sheridan sat in the bleachers watching Jason and his team going through drills prior to their afternoon game. Around him the distinctive sound of metal bats hitting balls filled the air. Sheridan felt his cell phone vibrate and looked at the number, seeing Des's name. When he had answered, his partner started in.

"It's a day for cobras," Des began.

Sheridan heard road noise and muffled music in the background. "How so?"

"Chris just finished at an apartment in Baltimore," Des answered. Chris, a conservation officer, was another Saturday morning basketball buddy. "The apartment of one Patrick Gonzales."

"Do we know that name?" Sheridan asked, trying to place it.

"He's part of the Beltway group, according to Johnny. He was the one who was supposed to get that package she told us about."

"Right, right."

"He's no longer with us."

"Oh?"

"Loose snakes," Des replied. "The scene doesn't jibe with a collector."

"Death by snake?"

"Could be. Chris said the place was a mess. Police took over and wouldn't let him in with his dog. When they found the snakes, they killed most of them."

"Great." Sheridan knew that common scenario. Police officers, unaccustomed as they were to dealing with reptiles, often simply shot them. Or confiscated them and left them to die, without food or water. Even animal control stepped aside if a conservation officer was on the scene, uncomfortable as they were dealing with snakes.

"I'm about to call Johnny," Des added. "I'll get back to you."

"Okay." Sheridan put his phone away and stared out at the field. Jason and his teammates were moving to the plate to take batting practice.

He had given the Beltway collectors no thought other than as a get-acquainted distraction for their rookie while he and Des worked their Thailand case. But he was beginning to think that that laissez-faire attitude had been a mistake.

There was no doubt now that activity among them was increasing. Were they connected to K. C.? he wondered. They hadn't proven that in the past. Did they have a role in the Thailand case? No. Too small, too insignificant. And yet...

A delivery had been mentioned. A king cobra showed up in a FedEx truck. The person who was to have received the shipment was now dead.

Who sent the snake? And how did the small king cobra get to Germany? Could Adam Hunter have a connection in Germany? Perhaps they are not so insignificant after all.

He wondered if Stone had made progress in tracking the FedEx shipment, since the situation had fallen in his jurisdiction. Sheridan took out his phone to call him. But suddenly, he changed his mind and called Des back instead.

"I left a message," Des said, meaning his call to Johnny.

"I'm thinking of something else," Sheridan replied. "We need more information about that FedEx package, the one from Germany."

"That would help," Des replied. "What are you thinking?"

"Someone in the Beltway group has a connection in Germany and that person, no doubt, is Adam, based on what Johnny's told us. The snake was transported from somewhere else by someone else in Europe. *That* someone else is important."

"Don't tell me you're thinking Chameleon again."

"I don't know. Possibly."

"You can't think Adam has a connection to Chang."

"We can't rule it out," Sheridan said.

"So Adam—more likely Chang—is a player in Thailand?"

"That's a jump we can't make yet," Sheridan said. "But we may have stumbled onto something. We need to keep an eye on Adam."

"Are you calling Stone?" Des asked.

"Yes," Sheridan answered. He paused for a moment. "Stone won't know Patrick was involved with the Beltway group. He was new. Let's keep that bit of information to ourselves."

"Good plan," Des replied.

"Impress upon Johnny the need for her to be careful."

"Will do."

"I'm calling Stone now."

"Have fun with that," Des said, and Sheridan ended the call.

He watched as the visiting team took the field. He put his phone down for a minute and reached for a small camera in his breast pocket as Jason came up to the plate, and took a picture.

He thought again about Patrick Gonzales. Logistically, he knew, Maryland authorities would go through their paces solving Patrick's death with the information they had. The coroner would show cause of death as respiratory failure from a neurotoxic substance, then identify that substance as venom from one of Patrick's cobras, a few of which they had in "custody." The *how* of the death would be solved. And unless a very astute investigator was involved, the *why* of venomous snakes being out of their terrariums in a hot apartment in August would go unanswered.

Maryland police, overworked and understaffed, and not wanting to deal with the issue of exotic reptiles, most likely would let it go at that.

47

"Tell me what you know," Des said. He pulled into the parking lot of a large organic grocery store near his home and turned off the engine.

"I met him only once," Johnny said. She had heard the news of Patrick's demise. "He seemed absent-minded. But to have snakes out? That's just odd."

"Do you think Adam had a hand in his death?"

Johnny took her time before answering. "I think...with him, anything's possible. The information in his file," she said, meaning the folder Sheridan had given her at their first meeting, "and the way he acted at Warren's...possibly."

"Patrick didn't get the package for the group," Des said.

"Right," Johnny replied. "Adam was very clear that Patrick be home to get it."

There was a slight pause. "Are you seeing him this weekend?" Des asked.

"Yes. A zoo person is coming by tomorrow to check the snakes. After that, I'm meeting him at the show. I'll try to get more information."

"All right. Be careful."

"I will. We're going to K. C.'s talk tomorrow night at Exotic Reptiles," she added.

"Sheridan and I will be there," Des said.

"You will?"

"Yes."

"I won't say hello," Johnny stated.

"No, don't. We'll be watching Adam. And keep your wits about you."

"I will," she said again.

Des closed his phone. He stared at the busy parking lot as cars and people with carts passed by. He didn't trust Adam. But it wasn't Adam he was worried about. It was Johnny. She was in a situation now that had more significance.

For himself and Sheridan.

Could he count on her not to do something extreme? Rookies had a tendency to overextend themselves. That he knew from experience.

Perhaps he would know more—about Adam and how Johnny interacted with him—after observing them together at the reptile store. There wasn't a lot he could do about it now. Pulling her off the "case" certainly would alert Adam to something going on.

He used his phone's Internet connection, piggybacking onto someone's Wi-Fi nearby. It was his turn to cook dinner and he was hungry. He logged on to AllRecipes.com and began searching for semi-vegetarian dishes, given his and Carole's recent decision to stop eating meat to help the animals of the earth. And themselves.

He thought about a pasta dish with vegetables. Too light.

Des typed in fish and perused the listings. He glanced at his watch. Most were too complicated for his late start, he decided.

He typed in shrimp. Pages and pages came up. He settled on a simple recipe of grilled shrimp with a pineapple-cilantro relish, couscous, and a huge salad. A dessert of light ice cream would follow, along with his favorite: cookies.

Des made a mental note of the recipe, then opened his door and got out.

Johnny was a lot like he had been at her age, he decided. Petulant. Wanting to please. And that's what made him nervous.

Feeling his stomach growl, he increased his pace toward the store.

* * *

Baltimore, Maryland

The elderly woman stood at her apartment door and peered out her peephole, her gateway to the world. She watched the young couple leaving, letting the door slam shut behind them, as it seemed everyone had today.

Why can't they close their doors softly? And why is that dog barking again?

She looked left and right, her view distorted by the glass in the tiny opening. She saw nothing clearly but the entrance to the trash bin directly across from her. Through this very peephole she'd had a partial view of the commotion that had happened earlier in the day: police, people standing around, a man dragging a bag to the stairwell.

And a dog she couldn't see that wouldn't stop barking.

She opened the door, unlocking several locks in the process. She had lived in the old brick apartment building practically since the time it was built, but in all her years she had never experienced the craziness that had happened today.

She dragged the heavy white garbage bag into the hallway and closed the door.

"Hush up," she said, in response to the incessant barking somewhere on the floor.

She reached for the door to the trash bin, but stopped. An object swayed slightly not more than three feet from her. She looked again, and recognized it for what it was: a snake rising up from the worn, patterned carpeting, the hood extended, its eyes focused directly on her.

The woman screamed uncontrollably and dropped the bag. She rushed back into her apartment and locked the locks, then looked down at the opening under the door and screamed again. Quickly, she grabbed a blanket off the couch and pressed it into the crack. Then, with great difficulty, she pushed a chair to the door and wedged the back of it under the doorknob.

She sat on her couch and cried, occasionally glancing at the door. When she felt she could do so, she picked up the phone and called the police.

"There is a snake in my hallway," she said, sniffling, to the young male who answered.

"A snake."

She waited for him to continue. He didn't.

"Yes. It's a cobra."

"A *cobra*," the man repeated.

"Yes." The woman started crying. "It tried to attack me!"

"All right. I'll send people out. Where are you now?"

"In my apartment. With the door locked."

48

K. C. looked out over the assembled crowd and saw friends and associates he hadn't seen in years, talking and laughing among themselves, the din rising as the alcohol flowed. Waiters carrying trays of hors d'oeuvres worked their way through the throng while bartenders struggled to keep up with drink orders.

Scanning the group, K. C. knew he had made the right decision. It was a perfect time to make his announcement. He glanced at his friend Reeves, the only one in the room who knew what was coming. Reeves raised his tonic and lime and K. C. nodded to him.

People he knew—and some he didn't—gathered around him. He reached for a glass of red wine on a passing tray and then felt a hand land gently on his back. He turned to see his editor, Skip.

"We're ready anytime you are," Skip said.

"Great. Let's do it."

K. C. inched toward the front and got up on a coffee table.

"Everybody!" K. C. shouted, raising his hands to silence the crowd. "Everyone! Thank you for coming!"

A guest at the back of the room raised his glass and yelled out, "K. C.!"

K. C. acknowledged him as the crowd turned to face him.

"Thank you, all of you, for being here," he said, as the noise began to die down. "First, I want to thank my publisher and Skip, here"—acknowledging his editor—"for hosting this party tonight."

People whistled. Someone yelled out, "Yeah!"

"It's been a long time since we've been together. I look out and I see people I've known for thirty years. Dean," he said, hoisting his glass. "Charlie back there," he said, pointing to the back of the room. "Jim right there from Texas, and of course my good friend Reeves," he said, acknowledging the man standing to his right. "This is what it's all about. All of you." He glanced at his agent. "Skip here said the media wanted to be part of this tonight and I said, 'Hell, no! This is for the guys!'"

A wave of cheers went up.

"Because when I'm with all of you," he yelled over them, "it's like old times!" K. C. waited before continuing. "I had a visit from the feds today."

A few boos filled the room.

"You know how unlikely it is that I welcome the feds."

People nodded, waiting for him to continue.

"They're saying king cobras are missing. There seem to be fewer and fewer of them in Thailand, a place where this snake thrives. The feds don't know what's going on." He paused. "Of course, neither do I. You know, about two thousand of us collect cobras. We've become celebrities of a sort—educators—in our communities. And there's a reason for that." He paused again. "The reason is, we're conservationists when it comes to these animals. We know the effect global warming has on them. We know the effect of habitat destruction, and ignorance, and needless killing. In our care, cobras are protected. Today, I think the feds were asking for my help. Hard to tell."

He took a quick sip of his wine, and then passed the glass to Reeves as polite laughter rose around the room.

"Whenever there's a problem with snakes, I'm the first one called—and the first one implicated. Indirectly, the feds implicate everyone in this room."

A few people grumbled. Those in front of him nodded again in agreement.

"But this time, something else is going on, something I've never heard of in my lifetime. At the show tomorrow, I'll have graphics about what loss of habitat has done to these animals. All over the world, snakes are being pushed into smaller and smaller spaces, fighting for territory instead of food. Many won't make it."

He paused. "Asia is booming. India is booming. That doesn't bode well for snakes. How do you stop progress?" he asked his rapt audience. "You know that answer as well as I: you don't. That's where we come in. Because we help these creatures survive. You know, I've spent most of my life educating people about reptiles, ever since I was a kid and brought garter snakes to school, and stood up there at the front of the classroom—just like now—like it was the most natural thing in the world. Just like many of you have done."

He knew he was about to drop a bomb.

"Over the years," he went on, "I've been fortunate—blessed, really—to be our group's unofficial spokesman. But times change."

A hushed silence descended once again. He decided to get right to the point.

"This is my last gig as a spokesman for king cobras." K. C. paused and looked around the room. "This is my last reptile show."

K. C. looked to a far corner. He saw his public relations person, his literary agent, his editor, the manager of his TV show, the rep for the vitamins he hawked, the kid who had shown him the T-shirts in his snake room—all of them, as well as countless friends, staring back at him. Speechless.

He continued, "It's time for someone else to stand at the front of the line and welcome those visits from the feds." He looked around at the faces. "Who among you is willing to step forward?"

His announcement seemed to have put a pall on the evening. He looked at his core group: Dean Berry from Maryland; Jim Hatchez from Texas; Charlie Templeton from San Francisco; Norm Reilly, recently retired, from New York; and of course Mark Reeves, all of whom had been with him for decades. None of them responded. He knew he would have to convince one of them to take his place. Already, he had an inkling of who that person would be.

He extended a hand out in front of him. "C'mon people! It wasn't my intent to bring this party to a standstill!" K. C. looked out over the crowd. "I'm gonna come talk to each one of you." He raised his glass. "Let's do what we came here to do: have a party!"

49

Vicki stood in front of the refrigerator, rooting around for something inside. Sheridan came up behind her and kissed her on the cheek as he reached in and grabbed two beers.

"You've told your parents?" he asked, referring to her impending move.

"Yes."

"I assume they're unhappy with it."

"Correct," she answered, finding the container of mixed olives and taking it to the antipasto platter she was assembling.

Jason hurried in with one of Vicki's nephews and the two quickly disappeared into the garage.

"I'm taking this to your father," Sheridan said, holding up a beer. Before leaving he kissed her again, lingering there for a moment.

"Later," she promised, returning to her Italian dish.

Sheridan walked into the dining room where the McDermott party was in full swing. He passed a table overflowing with food. Crowded around it were friends, relatives, and neighbors, all blocking his path to a room beyond.

He passed through the living room where more people had gathered, finally entering a book-lined den. Through French doors he could see the home's wisteria-covered seating area outside, and beyond that the garden and manicured lawn that seemed to extend forever. Ancient trees blocked the sight of other houses, but on the twenty-acre estate it was doubtful they would even be seen.

Vicki's father sat on a leather couch talking with his brother, whom Sheridan had met earlier in the evening. Couples in the room watched the Orioles' game, and Sheridan himself glanced at the screen before handing the beer to Vicki's father.

"Thanks, Jim."

Sheridan winced privately; he'd been unable to convince either of Vicki's parents to call him by his last name.

"I'll get back to you on that," the brother said, rising. Vicki's father motioned for Sheridan to sit next to him.

"So the Service is in full swing, I gather, saving the world's wildlife?"

"Oh, yes," Sheridan replied, settling in. "We stay busy."

"Vick said you have a case dealing with snakes?"

Sheridan nodded in agreement. "King cobras, in Thailand. They're disappearing, apparently, but we have nothing beyond that."

"Large numbers?" Vicki's father asked.

"Enough to be noticed," Sheridan replied.

"Hmm. I don't remember anything like that. Not with snakes, anyway," he replied.

Sheridan took in his brilliant blue eyes, his gray hair neatly parted and combed to the side, not a strand out of place. He was, seemingly, a man content with what he had accomplished and where he was presently.

Quite the opposite of myself.

"It sounds like some of the early cases we had with game birds," Vicki's father continued. "Remember the Heath Hens?"

"Only the reports," Sheridan responded.

"It was big bird. Big as a prairie chicken. It died out along the East Coast by the mid-1800s. Taken for food. Few people remember we had a Carolina parakeet—big as a tropical bird. But it pecked at fruit, leaving holes. Farmers shot them because of that. Soldiers found enough of them during the Civil War to feed themselves." He paused for emphasis. "They were gone by 1918. Vicki's father seemed to be thinking through something else. "When you say disappearing, are you talking about displacement?"

"Not sure of the cause," Sheridan replied.

Vicki's father paused to watch a runner stealing third, then continued, "Might be worth looking at some of those early reports in the archives. Might hold some clues."

"Not a bad idea," Sheridan said.

"You know, in my time in the Service," Vicki's father went on, "I found that cases came down to one of two things: either the animals were coming in or the animals were going out. Everything we ever worked on was a variation on those themes."

Sheridan thought about that. "I'm beginning to think we have the *going out*. But that's all we have."

Vicki entered with two plates of food and handed them to the men on the couch, winking at Sheridan as she did so.

Vicki's father noted the exchange. When she had left, he asked of Sheridan, "How does this sit with you—her leaving?"

"Not well, actually," Sheridan answered finally. "But I've encouraged her to go. She can help them out there."

"Hmm."

They sat in silence for some time as they ate dinner and watched the game. Other guests came in and stood around the television, talking among themselves, or left to refill plates and glasses.

Suddenly, Sheridan looked around the room. "I should find Vicki."

"She might be out in the painting shed," her father replied, "where her grandfather found solace."

* * *

Sheridan walked down a stone path that led away from the house. Behind him he could hear the party moving out onto the deck off the kitchen. He came up to the shed, which was more like a small house away from the big house.

The door was ajar and he entered, coming into a room filled with Vicki's grandfather's paintings. Sheridan took it all in. Behind a low-rise partition, an old icebox and stove took up one part of the room. Opposite was a twin bed, the quilt and pillows in disarray. Kids probably, he decided, from earlier in the evening.

Paintbrushes were left where, presumably, the second director of U.S. Fish and Wildlife, Jeremiah McDermott, had last placed them. A half-finished painting of an Oriole sat on an easel, an old chair positioned in front of it.

It was a comfortable space, Sheridan surmised, walking further inside, a quiet getaway for the great man.

Vicki stood near a window. Arms crossed in front of her, she turned to look at him.

Sheridan walked past the painting and saw that it was a watercolor.

"He was quite good," he remarked, complimenting the picture.

Vicki smiled. "It's not his."

Sheridan looked back at her in disbelief. "It's yours?"

She nodded.

"I didn't know you painted." *So much I don't know*.

"Guess I got the gene," she answered.

He came up to her and embraced her, feeling her familiar warmth, taking in the familiar perfume. But something nagged at him, something he couldn't shake: Stone's comment from earlier about her bedroom and the plaques on her wall. He pushed it away, but it stayed with him.

He decided to say something.

"You can't possibly believe I was with him," Vicki responded, breaking away.

Sheridan didn't reply.

"He's an ass. He's trying to get a rise out of you," Vicki continued.

He looked at her and nodded, then looked away.

Vicki moved closer. "Look at me." Gently, she took his chin and turned him toward her. "You know how I respond to you," she said softly.

She wrapped her arms around him and he pulled her close again. Emotions swelled inside of him—loss...loneliness...love?

"I'm sorry," he whispered, cradling her head against his chest, kissing her hair, her face. They stood there embracing, kissing, her warmth seeping into him. Sheridan caressed her back, feeling the curve of her spine, the top of her hips. He brought his hands around and caressed her breasts. He kissed her deeply and began unbuttoning her blouse.

She stopped him. "People could walk in."

"We'll make it quick."

"There are kids—"

"They've already been here. You got me to come down here," he added.

"Yes. I did."

Abruptly, she kissed him back, a response that delighted him.

"Over there," he said, backing them behind the low-rise partition. Vicki quickly began removing her clothes and Sheridan followed her lead. He grabbed coats on a rack and threw them down. He embraced her again, and with one hand lowered her to the floor, then lowered himself on top of her.

She caressed his back and legs as he slowly began making love to her, kissing her deeply. Her tongue found his and held him there. His urgency quickened, and he heard her breathing deepen as he moved down the length of her body, kissing her breasts, stomach, legs, the inside of her thighs. He felt her warmness, sweetness. She gently held his head and moaned softly as he rhythmically caressed her.

They had lain there for some time not saying anything. Sheridan heard noises from the deck as the party got louder. He thought they should get back to the group. But Vicki didn't seem as concerned as he was.

He looked up at the paintings that lined the walls, of wildlife and the big house and the surrounding grounds. "Did your grandfather sleep out here?" he asked.

"Sometimes. I heard that he would paint into the night and didn't want to disturb my grandmother."

"Hmm."

Silence engulfed them again before Sheridan changed the subject. "Tell me what you have on your case."

"All right." Vicki propped herself up on one elbow and gently put her hand on his chest. "Marsh thinks he has something different from what they've had in the past."

"How so?"

"There were eight thousand five hundred and sixty eagles in Wyoming last year. This year's guesstimate is under two thousand."

"That's quite a drop."

"Right. They're finding carcasses now, but not enough to make up the numbers that are missing."

"So, someone is sacrificing birds to cover up something else?"

"Very good, but Marsh doesn't think so." She added, "The carcasses have feathers missing."

"Of course," Sheridan replied. "They're valuable." He thought for a moment. "Are we talking about two different things?"

"That's what Marsh thinks. He has his eye on some takers. But a known one is in jail."

"And nothing's going on in Alaska?" Sheridan asked, repeating a question he already had an answer for.

She shook her head. "Wyoming's it."

"An out-of-the-way place with no one looking," he added, realizing what he had just said. "What else does he think?"

Vicki hesitated. "Well, he thinks there's a petty criminal out there killing birds and taking feathers to Canada and Mexico. And, for the more pressing case, he thinks either that the eagles are not coming to Wyoming—which wouldn't be possible, since we think a petty criminal is finding them—or that someone *has* them."

Sheridan stared at her. "*Has* the eagles? How? Dead or alive?"

"Who knows? Let's not rule out the impossible," she added, repeating a refrain Sheridan himself often voiced.

"Right, right." He thought about what she had just said. "What do you think?"

"I think we have to find the small-time crook."

"And the larger case?" Sheridan asked.

"I'm reserving judgment till I get there," she replied.

The remark didn't jibe with the decisive woman he knew lying next to him.

"You think someone has the birds."

"Yes," she answered.

"Wow," he responded, trying to visualize that scenario, their two cases seemingly similar.

Vicki interrupted his line of thought. "We have to talk about this," she said softly. "I leave Wednesday."

"I know."

"I want some indication from you that we will continue once I'm out West."

"I've given you my word on that," he replied.

"What I'm saying is…I want you to put action behind those words."

"Vick, you and I are going to be together. I don't know when, but it will happen." He looked into her eyes and saw the concern she was voicing. Sheridan kissed her lightly and pulled her close. "I'll finish my case, and we'll go from there."

50

Hilton Baltimore
Late Saturday evening

K. C. stood with his close friends near the door of his suite as the night's festivities came to a close. Over the course of the evening, the party had gotten back to full swing as the music played and old friends greeted old friends. As they departed, many of the invited guests had come up to him and thanked him for his contributions.

"So you think this disappearance is about habitat?" his friend Dean Berry from the Maryland suburbs asked, bringing the conversation back to the current crisis.

"I can't think of anything else," K. C. answered, getting another glass of wine from the bar and bidding more party stragglers good-bye.

"Could be a virus," offered Jim Hatchez, a former Marine from Texas, as he gulped down the last of his drink. His huge hand covered the glass so that it appeared he was drinking from his palm.

"I don't think so," K. C. replied. "Where are the carcasses? This is disruption of habitat. It's everything I've been about preaching for years."

"Well, I don't want reporters around," Hatchez said, "since… you know…I have *unregistered* varieties…" He let the rest of his sentence trail off.

"You've got permits, right?" K. C. asked.

"Not for all of them."

"Just don't transport them," K. C. stated.

"Maybe this is related to that thing back in the seventies," Norm Reilly, one of K. C.'s oldest friends, suggested. "Remember that, when there was a drop in kings?"

K. C. shook his head. "That was due to Vietnam," he answered, meaning the war and the little-publicized loss of natural resources that occurred throughout that part of the world.

K. C. changed the subject. "Dean, why don't you take the reins and lead the group? You know as much as I do."

Dean Berry let out a long, slow sigh. "I'm not sure that's a good idea, being in the shadow of the feds and all," he replied, referring to the proximity of Fish and Wildlife's national organization. "Plus, my son goes to school with the son of a federal guy."

"What's the fed's name?" K. C. asked.

"Jim Sheridan."

K. C. chuckled at the memory of his visit with him earlier. "He's the one who came to see me today."

"See what I mean?" Dean replied.

"Just think about it," K. C. responded. "Remember, we're the good guys."

"That's not what the feds think," Dean countered.

"What did you tell them?" Charlie Templeton from San Francisco asked.

"I told them what I know, which is nothing. Whether they choose to believe that or not is another matter." K. C. paused as the last of the well-wishers came up to him. When they had departed, he changed the subject once again. "Our Mr. Chang is here."

Dean seemed surprised by that. "Why?"

"Good question," K. C. answered.

"He's here to see you, then," Dean said.

"Apparently."

"You think he's got something to do with what's going on in Thailand?" Reilly asked.

K. C. didn't have to think much about that before answering. "Oh, yeah, I think he's a big part of what's going on."

* * *

Reeves left K. C. behind in the room with his friends, whom he knew only as acquaintances. It had been a long day, first at the convention center and then in his role as personal attaché to K. C.'s business interests.

The news of his boss's impending retirement had shocked all parties, as both he and K. C. had known it would. Reeves had tried to convince them that little would change. K. C. simply wanted more time at home and a bit less public exposure.

They immediately thought of their own interests, which was only natural. K. C. said he would honor all his contractual agreements and appearances, then ease away from public work. He'd still be around, they had been told.

But the business people wouldn't buy it. Snake collecting among young boys was at an all-time high. There was no one else to take his place. *He was the face.*

There would be more discussions, they had promised.

Whatever, Reeves had thought. He knew nothing was going to change.

He turned right down the hallway toward his room, instantly recognizing the figure coming toward him.

"Just the person I want to see," Chang said, sticking out his hand.

"What are you doing here?" Reeves asked.

"I'm here to see your boss."

"Why?" Reeves asked.

"There's been a change in plans," Chang replied, after taking some time to think about his response. "A change in how we'll be doing business."

"How so?"

"K. C. will be privy to that information tomorrow night." Chang took out a business card on which he'd written the number for his hotel room and handed it to Reeves. "Have him meet me in my room. I'd prefer that he come alone."

51

The snake picked up speed in the open grassland as the four men closed in, race-walking as they were to keep up with it.

"Stay with it! Stay with it!" the leader of the men yelled from the left side of the reptile. He knew the king cobra was moving for cover at the edge of the jungle and they needed to detain it before it got there.

The leader bent over suddenly, even as he maintained his pace alongside the snake, a signal to the men to be ready. Suddenly, he reached down and grabbed the back of the cobra's head. The other three responded in kind as the snake's back end hurled up in ringlets around them.

The men grabbed at the cobra's body and pushed it to the ground, stepping on its back end with all their weight. All four then crouched down and waited until the cobra had given up its fight, resigned to the men's hold.

When it was time to rise the leader nodded and, moving in unison, the men lifted the seventeen-foot-long Malaysian king cobra, taking it to the truck parked a hundred yards away.

The snake would be positioned inside its own enclosure, a wooden box crudely nailed together, joining four hundred other snake-filled wooden boxes on the old flatbed Ford.

With the snake safely secured, the leader signaled to the trucks parked behind him—five, six, seven more—all filled with precious cargo awaiting their trip to Europe.

52

Johnny watched the zoo employee take out the African cobra, hold it up to look at its underside, and then put it back in its terrarium. "We need to keep an eye on this one," he said, in regard to the snake he had just examined. "I was told he had a mite infestation a few months back."

She nodded in agreement as he continued, scoping out the others in terrariums lining one wall in her small apartment. "All the rest look good!" he exclaimed. Proclaiming his work done, Johnny showed him to the door.

When he was gone, she came back to the terrariums and slowly walked in front of them, looking down at the snakes.

She thought about the other night and her taste of venom, odd as that was, and how she had played it perfectly, not flinching at all in front of the group. But that was nothing compared to what she was about to do next.

She stopped in front of the Russian cobra. The reptile lay motionless in profile to her, with part of its body and head leaning against the glass.

She bent down to look at it.

The snake was only inches away from her. At this angle, she clearly saw how its scales fit together in an overlapping, geometric pattern all the way down its body. She looked again at the head, marveling at the cobra's ability to splay its neck ribs to form a hood, but looking normal now in its "un-hooded" form.

Johnny swallowed hard. Her heart pounded rapidly as it did when she was nervous. Instead of proceeding, she stood up in an attempt to quiet her distress.

She thought through the moves she was about to make, visualizing each segment, remembering what she had seen the zoo employee do.

Finally, she took the top off the terrarium. A slight musk odor rose to greet her. She leaned the lid against the wall as she kept her eye on the reptile.

Her problem, she had come to realize, was that she had no experience with snakes. And that equaled no credibility. Once she had *exposure* she would be fine.

Johnny moved her hands inside the terrarium. Sensing something, the reptile moved slightly. She grabbed it firmly with one hand behind the head, and then grabbed the body which had begun to coil.

Amazingly cold! And dry, she thought, as she lifted it out, the scales like the finest sandpaper.

Johnny felt the snake contract somewhat as she brought it close to her side. She kept the head in front of her as Jeff at the zoo had shown her.

She wondered if the snake knew how nervous she was. Johnny supposed that it did, guessing that animal senses were attuned to those kinds of things.

She walked around her apartment, smiling as she did so, one finger lightly caressing the snake's smooth belly. *Odd animals*, she thought. *So ancient and maligned. I've had no appreciation of them until now.* Johnny made a mental note to seek out K. C.'s exhibit, maybe learn a little more.

She was feeling more confident now, stopping in front of a window and looking out. *I am holding a venomous snake!* She decided that the steps she had just taken would be no different if the reptile had fangs, so this exercise, in her book, counted as handling a dangerous reptile.

Johnny continued on, passing her bookcases, computer, table, and chairs.

She stopped in front of a mirror. Warm early morning sunlight from the window hit the snake's back, and in response it coiled its tail around her arm.

Suddenly she froze. She looked up and saw her reflection in the mirror.

It wasn't the cobra staring back at her that was the unnerving. It was the sight and feel of its tail holding her, as if to say, "If you drop me, I'll still be with you."

Johnny felt her composure slipping away. Her hands remained frozen, but she no longer felt them.

Or the snake.

Or did she?

She wasn't sure.

Time to put him away, she said to herself. But fear had gripped her.

She concentrated on moving back to the terrarium and carefully performing the steps in reverse.

Her legs were wooden, but she forced herself to move and stood in front of the terrarium. Slowly, she lowered the cobra inside, and in a circular motion, unwrapped her arm from the snake. With it repositioned, she let go, quickly pulling back, her arms numb. She put the lid back on, but in her haste dropped one end, almost hitting the reptile.

The cobra coiled defensively and remained still.

Then all was quiet.

Johnny moved to a chair and collapsed into it, her hands shaking. She crossed her arms in front of her, hugging herself, and leaned back and closed her eyes.

Unaware of how long she had been sitting there, she finally got up and washed her hands. She dried them off, but thinking of the snake made her wash them again.

When she was finished, she walked back to the terrarium and crouched down to look in on the Russian, now partly hidden behind its hide box.

"Not your fault," she said, by way of apology. "Only my own inexperience."

Johnny thought about what she had just done. Could she do it again?

"I think so," she said out loud. She traced the outline of the snake's body on the glass with her finger. She felt bonded with it now in a way she knew no one would understand.

She decided to keep this little exercise to herself.

53

From the stage, K. C. scanned the crowd that had gathered to see his show, his last show. Standing there, looking out over a sea of heads, one thing always amazed him: the number of people fascinated with cobras.

He had decided long ago about the reason for the snakes' allure: simply being in a room with one brought Asia home, within striking distance, so to speak.

Suddenly, the stage went dark. The light show began and K. C. was bathed in purples and blues. Behind him, on three huge screens, a king cobra moved forward in its strike position, its loud hiss magnified by the surrounding stereo system.

From the side of the stage, an announcer in a tuxedo introduced K. C. The king cobra hiss was replaced by resounding, thumping music.

All to get the crowd whooping and hollering.

The crowd started clapping and chanting his name. "K. C.! K. C.!"

Showtime had begun.

K. C. stepped forward and raised his hands as images of the world's cobras flashed on the screens behind him. Over the course of his one-hour show all twenty-three varieties would have their moment of glory. All to play into the attention span of the current generation of collectors now half his age.

"Thank you!" K. C. shouted, hoping the small microphone clipped to his shirt would carry his voice to the back of the hall. "Let's get started!"

K. C. looked up and waved into a huge mirror above him that projected his image to the last rows.

Instantly, three handlers rounded the stage, each holding a monocled cobra. Behind them a map of the snake's habitat flashed on the screen, its locations digitally spelled out row upon row, tumbling down the front of the map like destinations in a European train station. All thanks to wild.cu.com that made such information available.

"I'm sure you know this variety," K. C. began, as images of snake charmers loomed behind him. "How many of you have a snake like this?"

A resounding number hollered that they did.

"Here's a tip," K. C. said, moving to one of the handlers and taking the snake from him. "Don't put him in a basket. The snake is rising up on the screen because he's angry. He's claustrophobic, as *any* animal would be in a confined space. Have some respect," he added. "The snake respects you."

Behind him, names and percentage declines in population dropped down the map of the world: Myanmar -28 percent; Thailand -26 percent; Malaysia -31 percent; India -31 percent; Indonesia -33 percent.

"This snake's habitat is disappearing," K. C. said. "Will it become extinct? I don't know. But their numbers are dropping."

He held the snake up to the mirror so the audience in back could see all five feet of it clearly. "These snakes just ate so they are a little sluggish," he explained. "We'll move on."

K. C. handed the snake back to its handler and the men moved off the stage. Three new men took their places, as images of the pyramids appeared on the screen and locations throughout Egypt tumbled down the front.

"This is the Egyptian asp, one of the fastest-moving snakes in the world," K. C. began. "These cobras haven't eaten so we're not going to put them down on the stage."

He pointed to the screen as percentage drops in population appeared: Cairo -31 percent; Al Minyā -26 percent; Asyut -22 percent; Luxor -26 percent; Aswan -34 percent.

"All the way down the Nile River…" He paused for effect. "Are you starting to see a pattern here? These snakes are disappearing right before our eyes. That's where you come in," he added. "You're an important part of conservation."

With that, a loud cheer went up.

K. C. motioned to all three men to hold up the snakes so that their images appeared in the mirror above. Then, they too moved offstage and three more appeared, each holding a brown and white Thai spitter. Each of the men wore protective glasses.

"How many of you know what snake this is?"

From the back people called out, "Thai spitter!"

"Very good. It too is experiencing loss of habitat, and loss of numbers."

The screen behind him revealed a map of Thailand and the provinces where the cobra lived.

"All of the snakes you see here have their fangs. I would encourage you not to have fangs removed. The onus is on you, then, to be careful."

The Thai spitters exited as more men joined K. C. on stage. They fanned out and began throwing T-shirts to the crowd as the drumbeat rolled on. Over the next thirty minutes, and with the help of several multimedia presentations, K. C. explained each cobra's habitat, history, and declining populations, never once failing to convey how dangerous the reptiles were. After reptile 22 had been introduced, he made the statement the crowd had been waiting for.

"I think I know which snake you came to see."

Johnny entered the convention center as a loud roar went up toward the front of the hall. She imagined it was K. C.'s show, and since she was early to meet Adam she headed in that direction down the main aisle, passing endless displays of various reptile-related items.

Who knew the snake world had so much to offer?

She came up behind the huge crowd and saw K. C. standing in the middle of the stage, with screens above and behind him showing ever-changing graphics. Men around him on the stage threw things out far and wide to the crowd below. She looked around as people jumped up to grab at what she now saw were T-shirts, fighting among themselves to get at them.

Johnny took a quick survey of the audience. Most were male, about her age. Some were older. They seemed edgy, energized, in tune with the low rumble of drumbeat that was part of the show. Lots of them wore black. And there were plenty of tattoos. On the periphery were parents, but few women, with mostly young boys on shoulders of fathers to get a better look.

Their mentor on stage seemed to be fanning the flames, stoking the fire in all of them, she thought.

"Let's talk about the main attraction," she heard K. C. say.

K. C. looked out over his audience, which he now had in the palm of his hand.

Would he miss this? Of course.

Would he change his mind? Not a chance.

He strolled far to his right to deliver the educational part of his show, which he loved.

"You know, when we talk about snakes, we're talking about an ancient species that was here with the dinosaurs." He moved back to his left along the very front of the stage. "You know what the oldest snake is, right?"

He gestured toward the back.

People yelled out, "Boas!"

"Right, boas. What's the oldest venomous snake?" he asked.

No one answered.

"We don't know," K. C. answered. "Venom seemed to evolve all at once. And how did that happen?" K. C. asked, as four men appeared behind him supporting a full-grown king cobra.

The graphics above changed again to images of the king cobra in its environment, then to a map of the world with digital locations tumbling down the front of the screen, from Myanmar to China and points in between. The drumbeat got louder.

"Well, what happened to us?" K. C. asked. "We got more intelligent," he answered. "We got better at being human. Snakes in the snake world did the same thing. Venom evolved after the dinosaurs. Prey got smaller and faster. Striking and injecting venom became a quicker means of stopping a meal than constriction. And the snake could hit and move back, out of the way of danger. Remember, with less foliage around after Jurassic, snakes were pretty much out in the open. That's a theory, of course. And it's not a bad one."

K. C. moved back to the men, alongside the huge snake. The drumbeat permeated the hall and people in the audience began whooping and hollering.

"Ladies and gentlemen, I present the king cobra!"

A current of electricity seemed to run through them, connecting them to the man on the stage, Johnny thought, as she scanned the crowd again. She looked for security staff in the event some of them got out of hand, which seemed very likely. But she didn't see any. They were probably as engaged with the show as the audience was.

She wondered what K. C. would do next.

K. C. moved to the side as the men gently placed the king cobra down on the stage. And let it go.

He moved to the front again. "Normally I tell people, 'Never turn your back on a venomous snake,' especially when you're in this kind of proximity."

K. C. moved to his right.

The snake followed.

"A lot of people—not this group," he said, gesturing to the audience, "don't realize that king cobras are docile—kept as pets in places like Thailand. "They get to know their owners."

K. C. stopped suddenly and turned toward the snake. He crouched down and put his hand out toward the reptile. The snake came toward him and touched its nose to his outstretched fingers. He stopped short of moving his hand over the plane of its head to pet it.

The crowd that had been so energized before was strangely quiet.

K. C. stood up. "These are intelligent animals. I know you know that. And it's our job to protect them."

He looked out over his audience. "I'm going to need a volunteer!" K. C. scanned the front rows and pointed to a boy about ten years old. "You! C'mon up here!"

The young man hurried to the stairs, where he was met by one of the four snake handlers, all of whom had returned to the stage.

"What's your name?" K. C. asked as he walked over to greet the volunteer.

"Jeremy."

"And where are you from?"

"Silver Springs."

"Okay, Jeremy," K. C. said, leading him behind the reptile to a place near its tail while the other men stood in a row next to him behind the cobra. "Even though this snake is docile, I want you to be careful and stand right here...because as you know, this is the largest venomous snake in the world. Right?"

"Right!"

A few people clapped and whistled, but most of the crowd remained silent.

"You might also know that the king is not a cobra at all, but a snake eater from the *Ophiophagus hannah* family. We don't know why this snake has a hood like the cobras, but it does. We don't know why it's as big as it is. It just is."

Jeremy nodded in agreement but stood nervously, fidgeting a bit next to the men.

"We're going to take this snake back to its terrarium. Jeremy, have you ever touched a king cobra?"

Jeremy shook his head that he hadn't.

"You just follow what the men are doing," K. C. reassured him, as he moved to the front of the snake. K. C. crouched down and slowly placed two fingers behind its head. With his other hand he supported the body, and then all five helpers, with Jeremy a few seconds off, lifted the snake for the audience to see.

"By the way," K. C. added, as they began to move in unison offstage, "this snake's name is Hobey. It's one of my oldest cobras at twenty-two years. And it's never once risen up on me."

People clapped as the men disappeared for a few minutes. When K. C. returned with Jeremy, he thanked him for his assistance, then turned to the audience and thanked them for their attention.

A slow cheer went up around her, and even Johnny began clapping along with the crowd. He certainly had a way about him that made you want to go along with everything he said.

And that snake! It followed him!

Odd that it was the one that had her two bosses wrapped up in their present case.

She looked again at the well-known snake collector, so sure of himself and his message.

Johnny didn't find that he was a felon like the collectors she was studying, as Des had once mentioned. Rather, he appeared to be an ally, repeating what Fish and Wildlife itself was preaching about endangered populations.

The show over, K. C. reminded people to remain conservationists in everything they did.

Did that mean harboring exotic reptiles? She guessed that's what he meant.

Johnny glanced at her watch and saw that she had a few minutes before meeting Adam. She looked around, wondering if he had gotten here early to take in K. C.'s show.

On stage, the man himself was exiting to loud cheers. She didn't know why Sheridan and Des thought he was a target once again, as he had been during Operation Chameleon. If anything, from the reading she'd done at Glynco, they were the ones who had made a mistake.

54

Oriole players fanned out across the field to take their positions for the fourth inning. Sheridan, sitting with Jason near third base, felt his cell phone vibrate and answered it.

"David found something," Isaac began, not bothering to introduce himself. "He has word that king cobras are leaving Thailand. He doesn't know where they're going. Just that they're not staying."

"That's huge, Isaac," Sheridan responded, as he signaled for a soft drink for Jason and a beer for himself.

"Something else," Isaac continued. "You know that shipment of cobras I told you about in Germany? The trucker who couldn't find an address?"

"Yeah."

"The company is Schauffmann Trucking. It's a subsidiary of Global Initiatives."

"Really." Sheridan remembered the name from Isaac's previous call. He started putting the pieces together. "So, the company the snakes were sent to owns the trucking firm?"

"Apparently so."

Sheridan heard noises in the background. "Where are you?"

"I'm at the yard looking at the container," Isaac answered. "I'll get back to you."

"Okay. Thanks."

Sheridan put his phone away and watched the players. Earlier in the week, he'd done research on Global Initiatives, finding only that it was as Isaac had indicated, a private company based in Frankfurt, with its beginnings in the tool and die industry. Two world wars—and the lucrative government contracts that followed—allowed it to expand into larger metal works.

But it wasn't a behemoth, like ThyssenKrupp.

Still, not the type of background that lent itself to trade in exotic species, he thought.

The visiting team was coming up to bat, the player readying himself at the plate. Sheridan noted the home team, in position, ready to go. As he did so, he put together a mental diagram of what he had in his case.

Using the infield as his diagram, he started at first base. Here he put the Beltway collectors: Adam, St. John, and the rest. He still didn't believe they were accessories in international crime. But then, there was that FedEx shipment...

At home plate he put K. C. Sheridan thought about his interactions with him so far. Not much to go on. He appeared to be telling the truth when he said he knew nothing about the missing cobras. With Operation Chameleon a sore point in their past— Sheridan himself had been responsible for K. C. being implicated in that case—the man was being as civil as could be expected.

In front of him, at third base, he placed Global Initiatives, Germany, the trucking line, and all his unanswered questions about snakes sent throughout Europe. Obviously, something was going on there.

He moved to second base and put Op Chameleon there. It was their last large reptile case involving snakes, also based in Europe.

In the center, on the pitching mound, he included themselves, Fish and Wildlife, and also the missing cobras.

All the players. All in position.

The Oriole pitcher walked the first batter, interrupting his internal diagram.

He went back to Isaac's revelation about snakes being shipped out of Bangkok.

Who's organizing it?

He looked around the infield. At shortstop, a position without a base, he drew an imaginary box and then envisioned a line between home plate and short: K. C. and an entity in Bangkok.

Not a given.

Sheridan looked up as the Oriole right fielder caught a high, easy fly ball. He made a mental note to get his musings on paper when he was back in the office.

"Dad!" Jason admonished, pointing to a popcorn vendor passing them by.

Sheridan committed his diagram to memory and motioned to the vendor.

* * *

Baltimore Convention Center

Johnny stood inside the door, the agreed-upon meeting place, as she waited for Adam. He was ten minutes late, and she wondered if he remembered, since they hadn't talked since Friday. She was still revved up from K. C.'s show—in a way she hadn't expected—and taken by his message, not just about *having* snakes, but how doing so contributed to world conservation.

Not something Fish and Wildlife would buy into, she decided. Not from him, anyway.

She'd learned at Glynco how much the Service disliked big-time collectors and TV spokesmen for wild animals. As they gained in popularity, so did collections of exotic species, making their world—the world of Fish and Wildlife—a nightmare.

Johnny and her classmates had been taught that most infractions involving exotic species were handled at the state level. But if a case involved an international incident, that was when federal law enforcement stepped in. Like her two bosses.

Still, there had been some pretty odd cases over the years. Since most of her colleagues were with state Fish and Wildlife groups, they spent quite a bit of time on them, like the early ones involving birds, buffalo, beavers—anything that flew or walked on four legs, it seemed.

It was all fair *game* back then, she had realized, in a world that was all about poaching.

And poaching was all about money.

She got out of the way as people exited, again noticing that they were all young males, similar to the Beltway group she was involved with. Johnny crossed her arms and leaned against the door. She wondered if Adam suspected her.

But then she dismissed the thought. It was simply too soon to tell, and so far, everything seemed to be going according to plan, the plan being getting to know the players within their group. Instead, she thought about other things. She should call Steffy again. She should call her mother. Thinking of her mother made her think about her father, which brought her back to that fateful night long ago. She replayed the familiar scene: a streetlight, her father standing in the middle of the road, Johnny and her mother on the curb, then her father—in slow motion now—turning away from them to confront a figure nearby. Then a loud noise.

There was something else: the man who had pulled the trigger. His eyes had met hers.

Johnny looked down at the floor. It was about this time that she went from sadness to anger because she couldn't remember anything more about what had happened. And, the man who shot her father had never been caught.

She needed to get her mind off this.

Other thoughts crept in: her experience earlier with the snake, the conversation yesterday with Des, how she rarely saw Sheridan.

Finally, she saw Adam approaching and opened the door for him.

He kissed her on the cheek and she caught a whiff of after-shave.

"Sorry. Traffic," he said.

He seemed a bit agitated. Preoccupied. "You missed the show," she responded.

"K. C.?" he asked. "He's got nothing to say."

"I'm not so sure," Johnny replied, as they began walking into the exhibit area. "There were a lot of people here."

"So?"

She didn't like this new demeanor, afraid that he might get away from her.

"Why don't you like him?" she asked, as they passed exhibits and crowds of people, and approached the main stage, which was now empty.

"Because *I* can do what he's doing," Adam responded, stopping in the middle of the aisle. "*I'm* building a collection."

She gazed at him without replying, hoping he would continue.

Adam waved toward the stage. "He built his reputation on little people. *I can do that.*"

"He's been doing this for years," Johnny replied.

"And it's time for someone new!" Adam retorted. "He's old."

She approached the next question cautiously.

"What happened to Patrick?" she asked. "I saw something on the news."

"He fucked up big-time. He's not going to do it again."

"But he's dead."

Above them, workmen came onto the stage and began taking down the huge screens.

"Look," Adam continued. "I don't want to be with these people. I've dumped St. John. Warren's out of the picture."

"What do you mean?"

"I don't know." He seemed even more agitated. "Warren said something about the girlfriend. He got rid of his snakes." He looked at her. "I get close and then"—he snapped his fingers—"it's gone."

Johnny wasn't following his confusing monologue. She pressed on. "But...Patrick had all of his snakes out."

"He made mistakes. Why do you keep asking about him?"

Johnny cut the conversation short and began moving away from the stage.

"Let's look at terrariums," she suggested. She saw a women's restroom and excused herself to take advantage of it. "Wait for me here. I'll be right back."

Adam watched her leave. He stuck his hands in his back pockets.

No way a woman tastes venom.

No way this woman is real.

Johnny went into a stall and took out her cell phone to call Des, but decided to stand there for a moment instead. An uneasy feeling washed over her, a feeling that something was not quite right with how Adam perceived her. In short, he was slipping away. And she needed to do something to bring him back.

She called Des. When he answered, she said, "I can't seem to get any information from him. I'm afraid to ask him again about Patrick."

"Then don't," Des responded quickly. "He may say something when you least expect it. The best you can do is listen."

"Okay."

"You're still going to the store tonight?" Des asked.

"I think so," Johnny replied. "Adam doesn't seem to like K. C."

"Why?"

Johnny let out an exasperated sound. "I don't know... jealousy."

"I see," Des replied. "Well, call me later."

"I will. I'll talk him into going."

55

This is the most important day of my life, St. John decided, looking out over his freshly washed floor and dusted shelves. *Today is the day the snake-collecting world comes to my store.*

Beyond his front door, he saw that a line that had formed outside. People were waiting patiently in the heat for a chance to be close to K. C. If a lot more showed up, he surmised, they'd have to continue standing out there and looking in at the goings-on through the window.

Common sense got the better of him. He walked to the door, unlocked it, and held it open for the patient crowd. Once over the threshold, people hurried in and took seats near the small stage set up near terrariums. A young man he had hired on the spot yesterday unfolded chairs and rushed to keep up with them.

St. John glanced at his new assistant, hoping it would light a fire under him. Instead, the man fumbled with the chairs, finally offering them for people to deal with themselves. He wasn't sure that Patrick—poor deceased Patrick—would have done any better.

St. John went over to two empty card tables set up in a corner. It was thirty minutes before showtime and his mother still hadn't shown up with the refreshments. But that was the least of his worries. He looked at his watch. *How did I get behind the eight ball again?*

St. John wiped his brow on his shirtsleeve and began unpacking boxes of books. People milled about, looking in on the snakes, picking up K. C.'s book as he was placing it on the tables.

They probably think I'm a nobody here, he thought. While he unpacked, he added up figures in his head. *If I sell twenty vitamins, twenty mists, and a couple of snakes and books, I'll break even for the month. Without that, another rent payment goes on the credit card—a maxed-out card*, he thought. His imagination got the best of him. *What if I sell double that amount?*

St. John heard a commotion near the front. He looked up to see K. C. and Reeves at the door. *Shit! They're early!*

He wiped his hands on his jeans and smoothed out his T-shirt. He walked to the door, where people had gathered to greet them. He mustered his best salutation and stuck out his hand.

"Hi."

K. C. stepped forward and shook his hand. "St. John?"

I'm standing with a celebrity! "Yes. Come in." St. John looked around at the people gathered near him, looking at him, waiting for him to continue.

He froze.

K. C. picked up the slack. "We'll look around."

St. John nodded as K. C. and Reeves walked in and moved to the small raised platform set up in a corner of the store, the swarm of people around them impeding any further movement.

St. John looked out at the parking lot. He saw his mother fumbling with a tray. A large container of liquid sat on the ground. Two men, one African American, one white, offered to help her. One leaned down and lifted the large container of what he knew was lemonade.

He turned his attention back to his store. He needed another table.

He waved over his assistant. "Run next door and borrow a table. Don't come back until you have one."

People had gathered near K. C. and were peppering him with questions and requests for autographs. St. John held the door open for his mother and the two men. One carried a stack of small cups, the other the container of liquid.

"I'm so sorry!" his mother exclaimed. She looked over at K. C. "That's him! The TV guy!"

"Yes, Mom."

Sheridan and Des edged past her.

"Where do you want these?" Des asked.

"Um, over there, next to the books. We're getting another table."

Des rested the container on a box and Sheridan put the cups on top of it.

People didn't wait. A man grabbed a cup and helped himself while others lined up behind him.

Des and Sheridan moved to the back of the store near the venomous reptiles and out of sight.

Finally, St. John's assistant returned with a table and set up the refreshments.

St. John looked around at the people streaming into his store, worried about whether the ancient air-conditioning system would hold up. He'd jacked it up earlier and now wondered what *that* would cost him at the end of the month.

He turned and saw his friend Warren enter, and hurried over to him.

"Hey, man," Warren said.

"Glad you're here," St. John said hurriedly. He took in Warren's neat appearance, his dark Hawaiian shirt setting off his tan. Sunglasses were perched on top of his head.

"Do me a favor?" St. John pleaded. "Introduce K. C. for me? I need to make this look good."

"Sure! No problem."

"Great. Where's your girlfriend?" St. John asked.

"Eh…," Warren replied, waving off the question.

St. John patted Warren's arm with a dirty hand. "Thanks for coming. You're a lifesaver."

Since they were alone, Des and Sheridan took their time looking at St. John's venomous snakes, from the "Big Muddy" copperhead—a seemingly always-pissed-off southern Illinois reptile—to the not-sure-it-was-still-alive long-nosed viper. *Not an impressive assortment*, Sheridan thought, after scoping out the collection and wondering about the last snake.

"We'll have to ask him about provenance on these," Sheridan said.

"Yeah. I don't see any permits," Des added, looking around.

The two then stood silently in their cramped quarters with terrariums on one side and shelving on the other, the musky smell of reptiles palpable within the ill-ventilated area. Des looked around for something to sit on. Sheridan stuffed his hands in his pockets while they waited for the main event to begin.

"When do you want to talk to him?" Des asked, meaning K. C.

Sheridan thought about that. He had briefed Des about Isaac's phone call on the way to the store. He had also clued him in on Global Initiatives owning the trucking firm that had been found to be transporting king cobras. Was K. C. involved in any of that? Hard to know, he had thought at the time.

"Let's see how it plays out," Sheridan answered finally.

"Any word from Stone?" Des asked, changing the subject.

"He hasn't called back," Sheridan answered. Thinking of that, he took out his cell phone and called his work phone. He listened for awhile and then shook his head. Sheridan put his phone away. He perused a shelf at eye level, then picked up a jar of vitamins and began reading the ingredients.

"Ah…I wonder how she did that," Des said, as he caught a glimpse of Johnny and Adam entering the store.

"Did what?" Sheridan asked, not following.

"Johnny wasn't sure she could get Adam here. Yet, there they are." Des watched as the two were greeted by St. John and then by Warren.

Sheridan followed Des's gaze, but people had moved into his line of vision.

"He's filled out a bit," Des added, looking at Adam and then down at one of the snakes. "Johnny looks more relaxed. Let's see how well she plays this."

Sheridan went back to reading the label and then handed the jar to Des. "What do you think about these?"

Des looked at it for a moment and handed the jar back. "It's nothing. It's like engine additive."

K. C. had seen the Fish and Wildlife agents enter and, extracting himself from the group around him, walked to the back of the store. People smiled as he passed and some followed him. He turned a corner and came up behind Sheridan and Des.

"What a coincidence," K. C. said, as they turned to face him. "Why are you here?"

"To hear the talk," Des answered.

"You could have heard it this afternoon," K. C. replied.

"We were busy," Sheridan stated.

K. C. got to the point. "I'm not involved in your problem."

"We have more information since I last spoke to you," Sheridan started in, ignoring his comment. He placed the vitamins back on the shelf, carefully positioning the jar so the label was facing forward. He turned to K. C. and continued, "A source in Bangkok says kings are being shipped out from that city." Sheridan waited for a response but K. C. gave none. "Would you know anything about that? Who might be involved? And more importantly, why?"

K. C. shook his head. "I don't know anything about it. I can't even imagine the logistics of it. But the fact that they're leaving means you can find them. Right?"

"I don't know," Sheridan answered. "There's not much to go on."

K. C. folded his arms in front of him. The three men stood awkwardly, saying nothing, taking up all the space in the cramped aisle.

"It has to be good news that they're alive," K. C. said finally.

"We don't know that they're alive," Sheridan countered. "We know nothing except that they are no longer in Thailand."

"I see." K. C. paused. "Poachers won't kill king cobras. They're too valuable."

"To who?" Des asked.

K. C. gazed at Des for a long moment, then said, "You've said so yourself. To Thailand. How many are gone?"

"Enough to be noticed," Sheridan replied.

K. C. paused again and shrugged. "I don't know anything about it."

Johnny had watched K. C. walk to the back of the store. She looked around for Des and Sheridan, but didn't see either one. She kept looking for them as she listened to Adam tell Warren, in a much calmer manner now, how he would have bought his snakes and was in fact looking to add just those varieties to his collection, especially the king cobra.

Warren apologized, saying he did not think that Adam had the room to have them, especially the king, and how he had made a mistake getting rid of them.

Johnny caught a glimpse again of St. John, who looked absolutely distraught at having so many people in his store. *He should have washed his hair.*

Finally, she saw K. C. walking toward them. A man she didn't recognize was inching toward him through the crowd, hands in the air holding two cups. He gave one to K. C.

"Hey, I get to introduce the big man," Warren said, as he moved to the stage.

With little room to move about, Johnny stood planted in place alongside Adam and listened to Warren's introduction, then to K. C.'s talk that mirrored points made earlier at his show: the number of cobra varieties (twenty-three), the one with the dead-liest venom (the Indian), the largest (the king), the rarest (the Russian), and for all of them their declining habitats. He identi-fied them by their Latin names, and people in the store nodded as he moved through the list.

Johnny scanned the audience as he went on with his pres-entation. This crowd was much more civil, she decided. A few black-clad, tattoo-bearing young men were present. But mostly it was boys, many of whom clutched a copy of his best-selling book. Perhaps their being there was a promised stop after a day of shop-ping, she thought, taking in the number of women standing near the terrariums.

K. C. refrained from the thumping music and oration of his convention center spectacle, and he spoke almost exclusively to the boys, telling them how to safely handle a snake and that even nonvenomous ones can bite and inflict harm. He tried to con-vince them *not* to collect venomous varieties, a point he said often fell on deaf ears. Much to the audience's dismay, he would not be handling any cobras in the store due to the tight quarters and the unpredictability of the reptiles.

Adam draped an arm over Johnny's shoulder and inched closer, and she smiled slowly to herself as he did so, his moves affirming her attempt to be more attentive. Doing so had brought about a huge change in Adam's demeanor. She had become his ally, convincing him that if he wanted to be like K. C. he needed to become K. C., especially in his public persona, which ultimately led to them coming to the talk.

"I could be wrong, but don't those two look like they're *together*?" Sheridan asked, seeing Johnny and Adam for the first time. He and Des had moved closer to take in K. C.'s talk and were now in Johnny and Adam's line of sight.

Des looked at them, noting Adam's arm resting on Johnny's shoulder.

"Nah! She's just playing it up."

"You sure?" Sheridan asked.

Des glanced at them again, watching Johnny closely. "Yeah," he said finally.

The talk ended, and people clapped and cheered as K. C. moved once again through the throng to the table set up with books. The sea of boys turned in his direction. Packed in as they were, it was the only movement possible. Some were leaving the store, the sound of the bells on the door ringing with each opening, giving the group in the middle a bit more elbow room.

Des caught sight of Adam lightly touching Johnny's back, his hand lingering there as he led her out of the store. Considering Sheridan's question again, he offered another response. "Not so sure."

56

Hilton Baltimore
Sunday evening

"I think it went well," K. C. said, as he fixed himself a drink in his suite after the Exotic Reptiles talk. He sat down and put his feet up, his first opportunity to relax all day. "Maybe I can pop into a pet store every now and then, since soon we won't be traveling."

"I think you surprised the group with that announcement," Reeves said.

"Yeah, well, everyone retires eventually." He took a long drink and then added, "I still have the TV show. I don't need to put the snakes through this stress any longer."

"Florida is the base," Reeves added.

"Like always," K. C. answered. Thinking of something, he took out the business card with Chang's hotel room number on it that Reeves had given him earlier.

"You're going to see him?" Reeves asked.

"Yeah. He can tell me what happened to my Russian." He stared at the card for a moment before putting it back in his shirt pocket.

"Why are the feds around so much?" Reeves asked, finishing his Coke and getting up to get another.

"Because it's a snake show and I'm here. I'm sure they don't know that Chang has arrived."

Reeves plopped ice cubes in his glass and took a seat again across from his boss.

"You know, they never *proved* he had anything to do with that big case of theirs," K. C. continued. "They just went after him. Like they went after me. Not that I like the man," he said of Chang.

"You're an easy target," Reeves replied.

K. C. flashed back to that seminal event when U.S. Fish and Wildlife had implicated him as an accomplice in one of its largest wildlife cases ever. It was an international ring, originating in Asia, selling protected, exotic reptiles. Federal agents had descended on Florida, and soon after, news stations had parked on his doorstep. With accusations flying at him from all directions, he had hired Miami's finest law firm to help defend himself.

What the feds didn't know, couldn't know, was that Chang had been plying his trade for decades and had a growing clientele in the United States and elsewhere. Pet store owners, for example, liked nothing more than having the rarest, most protected species to offer their best customers. *That's* where Fish and Wildlife needed to focus its resources, he had thought at the time— and still thought—at people under the radar, and not at himself, whose every move was an open book.

"The feds said they know that kings are being shipped out of Bangkok," K. C. went on.

Reeves thought about that. "Why, do you suppose?"

"That's the million-dollar question," K. C. answered, draining his drink and putting the glass on a table next to him. "We know the most about king cobras of just about anybody on the planet. But we're being left out of this loop."

"You think Chang is involved in that?"

"Oh, yeah," K. C. answered. "And I'll be asking him about it."

* * *

Alexandria, Virginia

Sheridan turned the pages in the Sunday paper, pausing to read about highway construction starting in September. Jason reclined on the floor a few feet away from him watching the last innings of the Orioles' ball game.

"You know your uncle is coming tomorrow for dinner?" Sheridan asked, without looking over at him.

"Uh-huh."

Sheridan peered around the paper. Jason was immersed in the game so he went back to reading.

After several minutes Jason interrupted him.

"Dad?"

Sheridan glanced back at his son and then at the TV. A commercial was on, of a smiling couple cooking and laughing together, then embracing in what appeared to be a million-dollar kitchen.

"What's ED?" Jason asked.

Sheridan hesitated as he put the paper down. "Well…it means…erectile dysfunction. It's when a man—"

"Can't get it up?" Jason asked.

"Yes," Sheridan answered. *Eight going on twelve.*

The game returned and Jason turned back to the television.

That's it? Sheridan realized he had had his first "talk"—if he could even call it that.

Later, sitting outside on his deck, beer in hand, Sheridan glanced up at the night sky. It had cooled off one degree, he decided. Yet, hot as it was, it was good to be out here, alone with his thoughts before another work week began.

He thought about Johnny and how absolutely extraordinary it was that their lives had intersected again. He would work with Des to approach this topic carefully. And approach it they would, he decided.

Sheridan thought about Thailand, but struggled to keep his mind on it. Instead, Wyoming loomed front and center. Could he help them out there? he wondered. More importantly, was there even a position for him? How much money would he make?

And what if it didn't work out?

Wyoming was a small state. It wasn't like he could walk down the street and find another job. He didn't have that much saved. Most of what he had was in Jason's college fund.

Thankfully, I planned for that.

His thoughts drifted on.

Joanna. He wondered if she thought about him. They had simply come to an end. And he accepted that. Did she?

Jason. Could he convince Joanna that Jase needed to be with him? Permanently? He wouldn't know until he asked.

Vicki. Yes. She was the one.

He looked skyward again. A move to Wyoming would be a huge change. A new life. A promise kept.

And not at all unwelcome.

57

How could it hurt?

Johnny examined Adam's backside as he leaned over the Russian cobra's terrarium in her apartment. *Yet he seems more interested in the snakes than in me.*

"How 'bout another beer?" she asked.

He turned to look at her and smiled. "Sure."

Johnny walked into her kitchen, determined now to get even more information from him. On the way back to her apartment, they had stopped at a neighborhood pub for a few drinks. Adam had begun telling her more about himself, like his arrest for a "domestic incident," as he called it, when he had hit his girlfriend after she threatened to walk out on him. He admitted he had been out of control because she wasn't telling the truth about seeing someone else.

Johnny reached for two glasses, wondering about that, knowing that she could never trust him implicitly with all that he said.

She wanted to know about the FedEx package that Patrick didn't receive. Who sent it? And how did Adam know the sender?

Johnny poured two beers and glanced at her reflection in the microwave's door, spiking up her hair a bit as she did so. *It's not like he's hard on the eyes,* she decided, an expression she had heard her aunt say once, as she made up her mind about how to get him to continue with his personal story. She felt a knot in her stomach, and visualized Des telling her not to proceed.

But I *can* do it, she convinced herself, overriding emotions to the contrary. She picked up the glasses and went back into the room.

"Do you know how old the snakes are?" Adam asked, taking his drink from her.

"I think twenty years," Johnny replied, making that up since the zoo hadn't told her. "My father didn't keep records."

"But he kept you and your sister involved?" he asked.

"Yes. He thought it was important." She knew that part was true of her middle-school friend back in San Francisco.

"Come sit on the couch," she said suddenly.

They both sat down and Johnny inched closer to him.

Adam smiled at the maneuver. He put his arm on the back of the couch, encircling her. They stared at the terrariums in front of them for awhile without saying anything.

"I don't even know what kind of work you do," she said finally, resting a hand on his leg.

"I'm in between things right now," he answered, noting her move. "I do computer stuff."

"What kind?"

"Systems work," he answered. He put his beer on a side table and turned back to her. He put a finger under her chin and brought her lips close to his, and kissed her lightly.

"Nice," Johnny said.

He reached for her glass and put it next to his.

They embraced and continued kissing until Johnny felt she could make her next move.

"Let's get more comfortable," she said softly, leading him into the bedroom.

They lay silently in bed, the covers thrown back haphazardly, the sheets in disarray after their urgent lovemaking.

Johnny lay quietly on her side close to Adam, one leg draped over him. She felt sleepy, but struggled to stay awake.

"What's this tattoo?" Adam asked, lightly fingering a small mark on her hip.

"It's a Chinese character.

"Yeah, well, what does it mean?"

She hesitated, and then replied, "It means be true to yourself."

"Hmm." He rubbed the figure with his thumb. "I like that."

Adam waited until Johnny was asleep and then quietly got up. He dressed quickly and went into the kitchen. Methodically, he grabbed a thin hand towel from a rack and draped it over a glass. Slowly, he opened a drawer and found a rubber band, and put it over the rim, tightening the cloth.

Adam put the glass on a table and moved in front of the Russian cobra. He removed the terrarium's top and leaned it next to a bookcase, being careful not to make any noise. With expert precision he picked up the snake, holding the head with one hand and balancing its body with the other.

He placed the cobra's mouth on top of the cloth and pushed down.

Nothing.

He pressed harder, feeling resistance behind the snake's head.

Nothing again.

He turned the snake toward him and shook it to open its mouth. Instead, he felt the cobra trying to raise its hood under his fingertips.

"Come on!" he admonished quietly.

He tightened his fingers behind the head and the snake relented, opening wide. He brought the head toward his face, inches from his nose, and peered inside, the ghastly smell of reptile mouth almost unbearable.

"I thought so," he muttered, turning it sideways, realizing that the altered snake posed no danger. He stepped back to the terrarium, threw the cobra inside and quickly secured the lid.

Seeing Johnny's purse, he went over to it and rummaged around inside, finding her EPA badge. He stared at the image of the person he knew.

Looking further, he found a pocket and unzipped it, and pulled out her Fish and Wildlife badge. He looked closely at this Johnny with long straight hair, the photo taken several months earlier when she was a new Service employee.

He had known from the beginning that she wasn't who she said she was, and this confirmed it. And how had he known? Because he made his way in the world being able to read people, knowing who to trust and who not to, and more importantly, who he could take advantage of, singling out those who would move him forward. It wasn't that she had said anything that tipped him off. It was her hard-edged, punk-rock look that didn't work for him.

He held the badges up side by side, glancing at one and then the other. Two different names. Two different looks. Two different employers.

Too bad!

She could have done better keeping to her natural self, he decided.

Adam put Johnny's EPA badge back in her purse. He pocketed the other and left.

58

Vicki poured herself a glass of wine and then headed back through her box-strewn house to the second bedroom that served as her office. After dinner out with friends, and promises to call when she was back in town, she committed herself to packing up this one room.

Vicki set the wineglass next to her computer and sat down at her desk. She opened the middle drawer where she kept an odd assortment of personal and work-related things: lipstick, Post-it notes, pens, paper clips.

Her fingers closed around an envelope and she pulled it out. A stack of old photos. She opened it and saw a picture taken a decade ago during a going-away party at the office, of a woman moving on just like herself.

She glanced at her watch: 11:25 p.m.

Should she look at them now or peruse them later?

Curiosity got the better of her.

Vicki thumbed through the pictures and came upon one of herself and Sheridan, standing in front of a punch bowl. He smiled graciously at the camera. She was leaning toward him. She was in her mid-twenties and Sheridan had just moved to Washington.

Vicki held on to the photo, gazing at the younger version of herself. Back then, so much had been in the way for them. Yet sitting here now, leaving in three days, she wondered if their being together would ever happen.

She sighed. "I'm gonna have to trust the Universe on this one."

She kept going. There was a photo of herself with Marsh, now head of the Wyoming office, on one of their first assignments, somewhere in rural Virginia, helping that state's Fish and Wildlife team tag threatened turtles. She couldn't remember which ones at the moment.

Their working together again was a good move, she knew.

More photos. Daniel Stone was in one. She stopped and looked at him, dressed in vest and tie, holding a cup of coffee. She didn't know why Sheridan thought she'd been with him, a man so annoying—people's usual take on Stone once they got to know him—that she could barely think the thought.

She looked at more pictures, coming upon one of Egan. She picked it up and stared at him, smiling as she did so, handsome as ever in his strictly military, buzz-cut sort of way. In the picture, Egan was standing with their co-worker, Sandy, the one leaving for Minnesota Fish and Wildlife.

Here was a bit of personal history that would never be shared, when she and Egan had been together before Sheridan joined the staff. It had been one night, a time both later regretted. They'd made a pact never to tell anyone, a promise that, as far as she knew, from a man known for his honesty and integrity, still held.

Would she ever tell Sheridan about this encounter? She sat there for some time, thinking it through, and made her decision.

Vicki took one last look at the photo and then put all of them back in the envelope. She reached for a box and put the envelope in it, as well as the other contents from the drawer and framed photos of family members that lined the desktop. Holding one, of her parents, she thought about their dinner invitation for tomorrow night, and the next night with Sheridan, her last before leaving.

Thinking of Sheridan, she glanced at her phone, noting the time: 11:29 p.m.

Too late. If Jason were there she might wake him. Instead, she stood up and began packing books from a corner bookshelf.

59

Adam swiped the badge through security and heard the front door click open. Smiling to himself, he walked into the glass-enclosed lobby of the government building. He stopped in front of a board with listings of federal employers, then moved on to the elevators. All four were on the first floor, their doors open. He entered one, saw the floor he wanted, and pushed the button.

Exiting, Adam walked straight toward more glass doors, with the Fish and Wildlife name and logo prominently displayed on the front.

He stopped and peered inside, the place eerily lit by a few recessed lights above. Seeing no signs of life, he casually walked in. The air was warm, the air-conditioning on its lowest level.

The government finding ways to save money, he thought. *Like it could really do that.*

In front of him, filling a large open space, were cubicles with low-level partitions, with the names of employees displayed on the outside of each. To his left were offices—small, he thought—with window views.

He made his way through the sea of cubicles, looking for one in particular. When he found it, he entered, taking in Johnny's sparsely decorated office: a computer, a calendar, and some pens and pencils in a holder.

Not an office in use, he decided.

Adam moved to the desk and looked at a storage area above. He tried to open it.

Locked.

There's nothing here.

He walked out and went over to the offices near the windows, reading the names of these employees as he passed by. He stopped at one. The name Ray Desmond had a red X through it, replaced with simply "Des."

Odd.

He moved to the next: James Sheridan. The door was open so he went in, quickly scoping out what he could see in the dim light. A clean desktop except for a stack of files. More files filled the top of a credenza behind a chair. He turned on a lamp, then went around the desk and sat down. In front of him were a couple of framed photos, of a boy in a baseball uniform and one of a woman leaning against a tree, arms crossed in front of her. He picked up the photo of Vicki.

Nice.

Adam set it back down and leaned back, hoisting his feet up and then down on top of the files. He looked out the glass wall of the office, which afforded him a view of the hallway and the maze of cubicles.

Isn't this just something, being here in the land of Fish and Wildlife! And isn't it just amazing how right I was about Johnny.

He sat forward suddenly. *Time to get to work.*

Adam reached for one of the files on Sheridan's desk and looked at the tab. Nothing was written on it. He opened it and saw a strange-looking diagram, like a baseball diamond with large bases at the corners.

"Son of a bitch!" Adam stood up suddenly, the chair flying into the credenza behind him.

Inside first base was a list of names.

Including his own.

He stared at the page, taking it all in. He felt a drop of perspiration make its way down the back of his neck.

"Son of a bitch!" he exclaimed again.

Adam read the rest of Sheridan's diagram. He saw K. C.'s name and the words "Op Chameleon" and "missing cobras."

The drawing said everything about everything. He picked it up and walked quickly into the hallway, looking for something. Not seeing what he wanted, Adam hurried toward a corner office and entered.

60

Adam parked the car in a Disabled Only spot and walked into the hotel's brightly lit lobby, then to an open elevator. On the fourth floor he got out, quickened his steps to the end of the hallway, and knocked on a door.

"Hello, Adam," Chang said, hesitating briefly and then opening the door.

Adam entered and began explaining what he had found, but stopped abruptly when he saw K. C. standing in the middle of the room.

"Adam Hunter, this is K. C. Sawyer," Chang said, introducing the men.

K. C. stuck out his hand. *His name's familiar somehow*. He detected an undercurrent of irritation in Chang's voice, and came to the conclusion that this visit at this hour by this young man was unexpected.

Adam fidgeted, finally returning the gesture. "I was at your talk at Exotic Reptiles."

"Ah...sorry. There were a lot of people there," K. C. said, turning back to Chang. But the name finally registered: it was one that Reeves had given him of DC-area collectors.

"You were about to tell me why I'm not getting any more cobras."

"I can't spare them," Chang replied.

"What does that mean?" K. C. asked the man he'd known for twenty-five years, who could get any animal anywhere in the world for anyone who wanted one.

Chang didn't answer, turning to Adam instead. "Help yourself to a drink."

"No, I'm good," Adam replied.

K. C. watched Adam shift his weight from one foot to the other, then stuff his hands into his back pockets.

K. C. resumed the conversation. "Federal agents are asking about missing king cobras. Would you know anything about that?"

Chang shook his head.

"Whatever it is you're doing, it's bringing attention."

"What I *do* isn't against the law," Chang answered. "There is no law."

"They'll shut you down," K. C. responded quickly, his anger beginning to rise.

K. C. glanced at Adam, who had his eyes trained on Chang.

"What happened to my Russian?" K. C. asked abruptly.

"As I understand it, there was a mishap on the ship," Chang answered.

"And why did that happen? We set up a tight distribution. I didn't know the man who delivered the snakes."

"I'm not passing along any more snakes. You bring too much attention, like those agents you just mentioned." Chang added, "My business priorities have changed."

"How so?" K. C. asked. Then, he quickly countered, "The *point* we agreed upon is to *take* in moderation and *talk* about conservation."

"That's your line," Chang replied sarcastically, "'*take to save.*'"

K. C. ignored the comment, but Chang went on.

"I tried to contact you eight years ago," Chang said.

"I never wanted to be part of what you were doing," K. C. countered, referring to the international movement of reptiles that became known as Operation Chameleon. "You were taking too many. And again, there were people involved I didn't know."

K. C. turned to look at Adam.

"Adam's in the snake trade," Chang offered, changing the subject before K. C. could ask him anything else.

"How so?" K. C. queried.

"My father," Adam replied.

"His father was an associate of mine," Chang explained. "He worked in Customs on the West Coast. He allowed things to go through when it was necessary to do so." He paused, and then turned to Adam. "I believe he's still incarcerated."

Adam nodded in response. "But he passed along helpful information."

K. C. started putting two and two together. Adam appeared to be a new associate for Chang, involved in whatever his new business was. K. C. turned back to Chang to say something, but Chang interrupted him.

"Here's what you need to know: take care of the kings you have. They're going to be valuable."

"They've always been valuable," K. C. said.

"They will be in a way now that you can't even imagine," Chang added.

K. C. stared at the man in front of him before responding. "I'm not sure what that means." He waited for Chang to explain, but he didn't. The conversation seemingly was at an end. Without saying anything further, K. C. turned and left.

Chang watched him leave and then sat down on a couch. "It's for the best," he said finally. He motioned to a chair for Adam.

Instead, Adam remained where he was. He took out the folded piece of paper from his back pocket and handed it to Chang, who looked at it briefly.

"What's this?"

"I was at the Fish and Wildlife offices," Adam answered. "Someone I was seeing turned out to be an undercover agent."

Chang looked up at him. "How much did you say?"

"Nothing. But I got her badge and went into the office. I thought I could find out more. But instead, I found out how much they know about us."

Adam waited while Chang read through the players on the page, concentrating on the contents of the crudely drawn baseball diamond.

"How did they get your name?" Chang asked.

"I have snakes." Adam shrugged. "Johnny must have said something."

"Who's Johnny?"

"The woman I was seeing." Adam paused. "I haven't done anything." He thought of something else. "The FedEx shipment—"

"Yes, that went well, didn't it?" Chang retorted. "You should have received it."

"I couldn't! The box would have gone to the house, my mother's house. What if she'd opened it?"

Chang looked down at the page.

"This changes everything, doesn't it?" Adam inquired nervously.

Chang folded the paper and put it in a breast pocket. "Work for my client has already been set in motion. But yes, it does mean my visit here is about to end."

"I want to go with you," Adam blurted out.

Chang sat back. He waited some time before responding. "That's something I'll think about."

61

Johnny stirred and reached across her bed, feeling only empty space. She sat up, wide awake.

"Adam?"

Hearing nothing, Johnny called out again and then quickly got up. She went into her living room and saw her purse lying on its side.

"*Shit!*"

She rushed over to it. The zippered compartment where she kept her Fish and Wildlife badge was open. She knew Adam could get into the headquarters building with a swipe of her card.

Johnny grabbed her cell phone and called Des, waking him up.

"This is Des," he replied, coming out of a deep sleep, his normal greeting etched into his brain.

Johnny paused, afraid to say what had happened.

"Hello?" Des said.

"He's got my badge," she said, almost in a whisper.

"What are you talking about?" Des asked, recognizing the voice.

She paused again, and then proceeded to tell him about her evening.

"Does he have a key...to your place?" Des asked.

"No," she answered, glancing at her own set of keys lying on the table where she had put them.

"I'm coming over to get you."

"I thought I could get information from him," she added, by way of explanation.

"It sounds like he got it from you," Des replied. "I'll be right there. If he shows up, don't let him back in."

He closed his cell phone and turned slowly, careful not to wake Carole.

"You're bringing her here?" Carole asked, awake after all.

"For tonight," he said, getting up. "Until we figure out what to do."

He dressed quickly and came back to the bed. "I'll be about an hour." He leaned down and kissed his partner on the forehead.

Des grabbed his wallet and badge, and walked into the kitchen. He took his keys off a rack near the door, wondering how he would tell Sheridan this bit of bad news.

He had about six hours to figure that out.

62

"We appreciate it," Sheridan added, before hanging up with Vicki's father. He looked up at Des in his familiar place, leaning against the door jamb of his office, arms folded in front of him.

"Johnny can stay there as long as we need her to," Sheridan said, in regard to moving Johnny to Vicki's parents' home for an indefinite amount of time, until they figured out how to deal with Adam.

"Good," Des said.

"Take her there, if you would," he said abruptly, looking away from his partner.

"I'll do it now," Des replied.

Sheridan paused. When he started again irritation laced his words. "Security says Adam came in after eleven thirty p.m., from what was seen on the cameras." He hesitated. "She fucked up. We don't have the manpower..." He let the rest trail off.

"I know." Des stood up straight. "This was on my watch."

Sheridan nodded in agreement, but then backed off. Like many a rookie, Johnny had made decisions on her own that his partner had no knowledge of.

"I have no idea what he did here," Sheridan said. "Actually, we have no way to prove he was even *in* here."

"Well, he can't get *back* in," Des said, knowing that staffers had had their badges recoded and that a security guard would be posted in the lobby twenty-four/seven for the short term. "Do you want to question him?" Des asked.

Sheridan took his time before answering. He didn't want to tip his hand that the two of them were watching him and the rest of his group. And yet, coming into a federal office building… Adam had to know that the government would have cameras. It was either an amazingly stupid move or a brazen, in-your-face one.

Sheridan went with the latter. "Not yet. I want to look around first, see if anything is missing. Have Johnny do something while she's out there. Have her read Chameleon. And don't let her leave."

Des nodded in agreement. "I'll call you later," he said, and left.

Sheridan watched his partner disappear down the hallway. Johnny was proving to be one of their more challenging rookies, matched by no one else he could think of at the moment. He didn't understand her motivation, why someone with her intelligence was jeopardizing her career, as she surely was with this latest fiasco. Thinking more about this, Sheridan picked up the phone and called Vicki.

"How are you?" he asked, feeling some of his frustration melt away.

"I'm okay," she answered. "It echoes in here."

In the background, he heard the sound of packing tape being peeled off a roll.

Sheridan proceeded to fill her in on Johnny's latest mishap and the news that their rookie was staying at her parents' place for awhile.

"Can I ask a favor?" he went on.

"Sure."

"If you have time, will you talk to her? I'm trying to understand why she's doing what she's doing."

"I'll see what I can do," Vicki said.

"Great. Tell your parents I appreciate their help."

"They would do it for you," she answered. "Am I seeing you tomorrow?"

"Nothing will stop me from that," he reassured her. "Call me later."

"I will."

He closed his phone and sat for a moment. A profound sadness filled his being again at the thought of her leaving. There would be empty, unfulfilled days ahead, he knew. And before he could put his own move in motion to be with her, there was everything else that needed to fall into place: solving this case, talking with Joanna, selling his place, finding another job.

He turned to e-mail. He saw that he had a message from Daniel Stone and opened it, reading his former co-worker's brief response to how Maryland was dealing with the FedEx package that hadn't arrived at Patrick's apartment, which then set off the snake-in-the-van mess.

> Sheridan:
>
> The FBI has taken over the case. I'll have nothing more until they tell me something. BTW, cause of death of one Patrick Gonzales was respiratory failure from the bite of a cobra. Which one, not important. His snakes are with animal control here.
>
> Daniel

Sheridan sat back. He glanced at his watch: 9:32 a.m. What else would the morning hold?

He thought again about Adam, then reached for a file and took out his hastily scribbled diagram of his case. After awhile, he underlined Adam's name, included with the Beltway collectors on first base.

How to proceed?

He rubbed his hands over his face but soon sensed someone at his door.

"Were you here over the weekend?" Kim, the intern, asked.

Sheridan felt his stomach drop. "No. Why?"

"Mr. Egan's copier is on," she answered.

Sheridan rose and came around his desk. He knew Egan wasn't due back for another week.

"Did you touch anything in there?" he asked.

"No."

The two walked down the hallway to Egan's office.

"Did you notice if anything was missing?" Sheridan asked, entering the well-appointed office.

"I didn't see anything," Kim answered, "I just saw the machine on."

Kim remained standing near a small conference table as Sheridan came up behind Egan's chair. He looked down at the desktop, one week's worth of mail organized into neat piles. Sheridan took in the framed photos near the edge of the desk, one in particular of Egan and his family on their sailboat in Maine where, presumably, he still was. He turned to a credenza nearby and saw the fax/copier on top of it, the green light on.

He took out his cell phone and called the CSI unit down the hallway, starting in when co-worker Ron Grady answered.

"Ron, can you come down to Egan's office? I need a sweep on the copier and the phone"—he glanced at the desktop again—"and the desk." He waited until he heard an answer. "Great. Thanks." He turned to Kim. "He'll be here in a few minutes."

In short order, a balding, burly man who'd been with the CSI units of several government agencies hurried into Egan's office and joined Sheridan behind the desk.

"What we got?" he asked, opening a zippered pouch and putting on thin nitrile gloves.

"Hopefully prints, first on the power button," Sheridan answered, nodding toward the copier.

Ron took out a vial of white dusting powder and lightly sprinkled it over the button. "You think someone was in here?" he asked.

"Yeah," Sheridan responded.

Ron changed the subject. "You see that game last night?" he asked, meaning the Orioles' come-from-behind win over the visiting Mariners. He had done this procedure so many times it was a rote exercise for him.

"Yeah. Amazing." Sheridan watched as Ron took out a miniature brush, corresponding to the size of the power switch, and with a surgeon's precision dusted it, instantly getting part of a fingerprint.

"This isn't much," Ron said. He took a digital camera out of his pocket and, bending forward, photographed the print and then showed the image to Sheridan.

"It's something."

"I guess." Ron next took out a piece of cellophane tape and pressed it over the print, lifting it off the switch. Then he applied the print to a card.

Exhibit number one.

"What else?"

"The phone," Sheridan answered.

Ron reached first for a portable ultraviolet light and bent down, shining the light on the handset and numbers.

"Might be something here." He lightly dusted the handset, getting partial prints again, and then dusted several buttons. He got a full print off the number nine. He took photos, lifted the prints, and put each on a separate card. He wrote the time, date, place, and a brief description of each.

Sheridan took the card for number nine and looked at it. "This will work. Have Gil run it, will you?"

"Yep," Ron said, packing up and taking the cards with him.

"Kim," Sheridan said, "call accounting and have them get any numbers phoned from this office in the past forty-eight hours."

"Okay."

Before leaving, Sheridan took one last look around.

What was the person looking for?

More importantly, *what was copied?* He looked at the desktop again. Everything appeared as it should, neatly arranged like Egan would have it. He glanced again at the photo of his boss and then at a locked file drawer below. He pulled on the drawer where Egan kept confidential papers, including promotions and salary histories. The drawer didn't budge.

Whoever had been in here, Sheridan decided, knew that Egan was out of town or found the only copier that could be accessed without a code.

He continued thinking about that as he made his way back to his office, passing Eddie's cubicle. Eddie—the department's writer and American history buff—had come on board many years ago when teaching jobs were scarce. And had stayed, much to their good fortune.

Putting questions about the copier to the side for a moment, and remembering his conversation with Vicki's father, he stepped inside Eddie's cubicle. Sheridan stood in front of the desk until he looked up.

"What are you working on?" Sheridan asked.

"Reports for Egan."

"Do me a favor when you get a moment?" Sheridan asked.

Eddie waited for him to continue.

"Get me some history on large-scale taking."

"Large scale," Eddie repeated. "Along the lines of…what, Dave Hall?" he asked, referring to the legendary 1970s Fish and Wildlife undercover agent.

"Yes," Sheridan responded. "And earlier."

"What, exactly?"

Sheridan gave an exasperated reply. "*That* would answer it, wouldn't it?" He proceeded with details after seeing Eddie's puzzled expression.

"Look for a pattern, a place, a purpose—whatever you can find."

"Okay," Eddie replied. "Do you want me to repeat the Chameleon information?"

Sheridan confirmed that he did not. "On that Dave Hall stuff, give me as much as you can about numbers. And see if you can find anything about the taking of snakes."

"Got it," Eddie said.

63

Des pulled into Vicki's parents' circular driveway and then down a gravel road past the main house. Johnny sat silently next to him, as she had on the entirety of the trip.

It didn't matter that she didn't want to talk, he thought. She could listen. He had things to say. And they would be said.

Des saw the small outbuilding where Johnny would be staying. He pulled over and turned off the car.

"I'll go in and tell them we're here."

Johnny stared out the window at the McDermott's vast cultivated grounds. Resigned to her situation, she got out and opened the van's back door. She retrieved her bags and laptop, then walked across the grass and onto a path that led to the building.

She tried the door and it opened, so she walked in. Seeing what the place had to offer, she set her bags on the small bed and sat down.

"You're in already," Des said, entering not far behind. He walked over and handed her a key. He looked down at her, noticing her discouraged look.

"Johnny, this is for your safety. We want to watch Adam, but not with you around."

"I know."

"You can help us."

"You already know about Chameleon. You were there." She leaned back on her elbows and crossed her legs. She looked up at him briefly and then turned away.

He stood in front of her. "Sheridan wants you to look at the past case and compare it to the new one. And see if there are similarities."

She didn't say anything.

"We didn't cause your situation," he added.

Johnny looked down at the floor.

Des caught sight of her computer. "You can start any time."

When she still didn't respond, he moved around the small room, looking at Vicki's grandfather's oil paintings. He ambled into the tiny kitchen area and opened the refrigerator, and scoped out the small oven and microwave.

"Not bad," he said, looking back at her.

"It'll do." She got up, put her laptop on a table and turned it on.

He didn't know what she was thinking, but it appeared that she was ready to begin. Des looked out the window at the pond. *I think, in her situation, I would have been a bit more apologetic. Maybe this generation doesn't apologize*, he thought. *Or maybe the situation is so embarrassing the only response is silence.*

He turned to address her again. Johnny was leaning over her computer opening Web pages.

"Johnny…"

She glanced over at him.

Des grabbed a chair and went over to her. Turning the chair around, he sat down, arms over the back of it, and started in.

"Everyone in the Service has a story about how they screwed up, including me. And some day I'll tell you about it."

Johnny turned in her chair to face him.

Of course, it would not be *the* case, the one she could identify with, when he and Sheridan were tracking Leland Chang in San Francisco, knowing his involvement in Chameleon and his role in delivering dried animal parts from endangered species to Johnny's father.

"I'll preface it by saying this: you need to cultivate a healthy sense of skepticism in this field. In other words: guilty until proven innocent."

Johnny nodded in understanding.

Des looked at her, remembering the six-year-old who had been standing on the street corner with her mother when Chang killed her father right in front of them. He and Sheridan had gone to Johnny's father and asked for his help in cornering Chang. He refused. But Chang had caught on to their being there and, not knowing what Johnny's father would do, decided simply to kill him.

Des and Sheridan had kept the conversation with Johnny's father to themselves, never telling anyone at headquarters.

64

Sheridan opened the door. His portly stepbrother, in suit and tie, sans jacket, wiped perspiration from his forehead and stepped inside, a small black box tucked under his arm.

"Wow," Les said, noticing Sheridan's head. "You've still got hair!"

"Yeah, yeah," Sheridan answered, closing the door and giving his only sibling a hug. "How 'bout a beer?"

"Not soon enough!" He followed Sheridan into the kitchen. "It couldn't get any stickier," he said, about the Beltway's hot, humid evening.

"That's August for you," Sheridan responded. "We'll eat inside. What do you think?"

"Good call."

Sheridan poured a beer into a glass and handed it to him.

Les set the box on the kitchen table. "You don't have to be fancy," he said, meaning the formality of a glass. "Once a slob, always a slob." He loosened his tie and took a long drink. Finally, he nodded toward the box.

"Thought you'd be interested in these."

Sheridan looked at the box.

"Open it!" Les encouraged him.

Sheridan walked over to it and slid the lid off. He stared at the contents, and then looked at his stepbrother. "You still have them," he said reverentially of the odd-lot of 1950s baseball cards inside. "I can't believe it. Is there a Mantle in here?"

"Sure!" Les leafed through the collection and pulled it out. He handed it to Sheridan and took another long draw on his beer.

Sheridan took the card and looked at it in disbelief. It was a '56 Mantle. Not perfect. But not bad. Maybe a PSA 8. Instinctively, he put it up to his nose. Musty. Old.

Les laughed. "I think these will mean more to you than they will to Jason. But they're yours."

"I can't believe you still have them." Sheridan placed the card carefully on top of the pile and yelled out for his son. "Jase! C'mere a minute."

"That's not all," Les said. He pulled something out of his pocket. "Here's Jason's college fund." He handed Sheridan a card in a plastic case.

"Oh my God!" Sheridan exclaimed. He stared at the card in his hand, a '52 Mantle. But this was graded, near-mint PSA 9. About as perfect as they come. "Do you know what this is worth?" he asked, looking up.

"A year at a private school?" his stepbrother asked.

"More than that," Sheridan answered.

"It's yours."

"Are you sure?"

Les nodded, in a way that said, "You don't have to say more."

Jason came in and shook hands, a little awkwardly, with his step uncle, then looked through the box of cards.

"I'm stunned." Sheridan put the card on a shelf with his wineglasses. "Thank you."

His stepbrother shrugged in acknowledgment.

Sheridan changed the subject. "Why the suit?"

"Oh, I gave a talk," Les answered.

"On what?" Sheridan moved to the refrigerator and took out a beer for himself and another for his stepbrother.

Les plopped down in a chair, taking in Jason's concentration on the box of cards. "A buddy and I are doing research, how prices are set on commodities." He munched on a small carrot, dipping it twice in the ranch dressing, as Sheridan got hamburger out of the refrigerator.

"Like supply and demand?" Sheridan asked.

"Sort of. We're using the gem trade as a model. It's a billion-dollar industry, but under the radar screen as far as rules and regs. And not listed on a formal exchange."

Sheridan nodded as he talked.

"It's a wide-open market," Les continued. "So the question is: what sets the price when a large group—diamond brokers, for example—aren't factors?"

"What's the answer?" Sheridan asked immediately.

His stepbrother laughed. "I have no idea." He took a long drink of his beer and finished it. "People say the causes are ephemeral. But that's not good enough for the *dismal science*. Or the *dismal scientists*, like your brother here."

Sheridan stopped in the middle of making patties, then continued, smiling to himself. It was the first time Les had referred to him as his brother.

Les grabbed two more carrots and popped them in his mouth. "Anyway, we're hoping what we extrapolate can be applied broadly. Might be good to know."

"Hmm," Sheridan responded to his stepbrother's academic explanation.

Les laughed again. "You asked! So, what about you? What's going on in the world of *fish and feathers*?"

"Oh, the usual...the taking and the taking."

"You had a question about something."

"Yeah." Sheridan arranged the patties on a plate. "Let me put these on the grill first."

When he returned, Sheridan filled him in on his case, adding, "The king cobras are simply missing."

"That's the large snake?" Les asked.

"Yes. They're nowhere. It's like we're dealing with a vacuum."

"They have to be somewhere," Les stated, mirroring the words of Ashland's statistician. He finished off half of his third beer. "There's no vacuum in markets. Maybe in outer space."

There was a lull while Les seemed to be pondering something. "You're thinking someone took all these animals, cleared them out?"

"Well, it's a question I wanted to ask you."

Les thought it over and then shook his head. "No one person—not a Hunt brother with silver, for example—can own it all. It's not statistically possible." Les appeared to consider something else. "You can drive your competitors out of business, though. There are laws against it, but it happens."

Sheridan waited for him to continue.

"It's simple econ: pay a higher price for whatever it is you're buying," Les explained. "Buyers move markets because of the way they control them."

Sheridan thought about that. "But I don't even know if the *buying* has happened."

"Well, *something's* going on," Les replied.

They had dinner and caught up on non-work-related things. Sheridan confided in him about his interest in moving out West, but refrained from going into detail about Vicki. Les listened to Jason's description of his baseball team, saw his collection of cards, and heard about his favorite players.

"He sounds like you," Les said later, helping him clear the table.

"Yeah," Sheridan responded. "He's a good kid. Good to have around."

65

Vicki stood at the kitchen sink washing her hands, ready to make the drive back home. She looked out the window and saw a light on in the painting shed. Remembering Sheridan's request, she went out the back door and down the path to the building.

Vicki knocked on the door and soon heard movement inside.

"Hello?" Johnny called out.

"Johnny, it's me, Vicki."

She heard the door unlock and then it opened. Johnny stood there quietly.

"How are you?" Vicki asked.

Johnny shrugged. "Okay, I guess. Come in."

Johnny walked back to the chair in front of her computer and sat down. She tucked her legs under her and turned the chair to face Vicki.

Vicki pulled the old painting chair closer and sat down, the easel and picture of the oriole now packed safely in the trunk of her car. She crossed her legs and arms, feeling uncomfortable and not quite sure how to approach the topic Sheridan wanted her to discuss.

"So, how's it going?" Vicki asked.

"Okay. I'm doing research for Des and Sheridan."

"Yeah, I heard. Chameleon."

"Yeah."

"Are you finding anything?"

"Well, I just started. Both cases are about snakes. Not cobras with Chameleon, of course."

Vicki nodded, hoping she would continue.

She did. "I know I screwed up."

"Everybody does, Johnny. Sometimes it's big. Sometimes... not," Vicki said, trying to be reassuring.

"So you know about it."

Vicki uncrossed and crossed her legs again. "Well, it's a small office. You'll see that it becomes like family there."

Johnny didn't respond, but nodded in understanding.

Vicki decided to press on. "Was he...someone you were interested in?"

"Well...," Johnny said, and looked away. "I wanted to get information. And then I began to like him."

"I see." Vicki remained quiet, noting that Johnny was struggling with something, and fiddling with a ring on her finger.

"My father had a store in Chinatown, in San Francisco," Johnny began. "He served the immigrants where we lived. He... um...was killed by a man who brought Chinese products to his store." Johnny paused.

Vicki nodded. "Go on."

"The man...he was part of something in China that we only vaguely knew about. But he always delivered. My father didn't ask questions. My mother told me all of this later because I was six when he died."

Vicki nodded again.

"This man started asking for more money. He was...keeping my father hostage. Finally, my father stopped paying and the products stopped coming. One night...my father and the man had an argument on the street. My mother and I were waiting on the corner. The man took out a gun and shot my father."

"And you saw this?" Vicki asked.

Johnny nodded that she had.

"I'm sorry."

A pained look crossed Johnny's face before she continued. "I thought I could find him. Someday." Johnny paused, and then went on. "I did like him. Adam, that is."

Vicki got up and went over to her. "Sometimes these things happen," was all she could think to say, hugging her. It was an awkward gesture between them, but seemed to reassure Johnny.

"You're leaving soon," Johnny said.

"Yes."

"Will Sheridan go?"

Vicki paused. "Not right away. But soon, I hope."

Johnny changed the subject. "Des will be here tomorrow."

"I know he's been supportive of you."

"Yeah, even after all this..." Johnny trailed off. She turned to her computer. "I'll show you what I've been doing."

Johnny opened the Chameleon file on the Service's network. "I'm writing a report for Sheridan and Des, trying to come up with similarities—"

"Because of Thailand?" Vicki interrupted.

"Yes. We learned at Glynco that for some people, poaching is a career."

Vicki looked down at the computer screen as Johnny opened other files related to Chameleon.

"Hong Kong was where the Chameleon people came from, and we know one didn't go to jail. That person had always been involved in taking reptiles."

"Right," Vicki responded.

"So why not again?"

"I think Sheridan and Des are going down that very road," Vicki said.

"I know. I'm trying to answer *why*."

66

Baltimore Convention Center
Tuesday morning

K. C. slipped unseen into his exhibit on this, the last full day of the show, when attendance never matched the fury of the weekend's crowds. In the far reaches of the vast hall he heard vendors tearing down their displays, getting a head start on the trip home.

He passed the terrarium holding the king cobra and entered *All the World's Cobras*. He walked among his collection, cooled by the extra air-conditioning units he'd had placed early on.

It was here that he felt at peace, just as he did at home, with no one around but his prized snakes, many of which, he knew, would have been taken, killed, eaten, or worn as vestments by now in one culture or another.

He passed the monocled cobra terrarium and looked in on a snake prized in India, but still used in endless tourist shows everywhere in the country. He had three of these snakes, but they were getting harder to come by. He wondered if Chang had something to do with that.

K. C. walked on, passing the bulky brown and white Thai spitter, partially hidden behind its hide box. With its striking striped colors it was a mainstay in that country's zoos and exhibits, but not often seen outside of Thailand.

Thailand.

He moved on, thinking about Chang again. He had been involved with him for decades, but Chang had never seen the animals in the same light that he did. To Chang, the reptiles were a means to an end.

To him, they *were* the end, the sole reason for his one-man crusade.

He stopped in front of the African cobra. The snake moved slightly and then lay still. It was one of the oldest in his collection, received from Chang himself long before the feds started cracking down on collectors. This one had lived near the pyramids, he had been told, and had been taken from a passel of cobras living in the hidden crevices of the tombs.

He crouched down and took in its blunt snout and triangular head. He had a certain respect for this one, fast as it was. *Probably due to all that high heat.*

He continued to regard the seemingly comatose creature. *Am I fighting a losing battle, trying to save the world's cobras?*

He stood up and moved on, and came to the Russian. He was sure his snake had met an untimely end on that ship, beaten to death or crushed by people who didn't understand its value.

K. C. walked around the Russian's terrarium, taking in the most northern living cobra of all. He would have to do a better job of educating people about snakes, he decided, bending down to get a last look at the all-black reptile.

He would start by helping the feds find the missing cobras.

67

Hilton Baltimore
Tuesday morning

"Of course it's important! I'm betting a business on numbers!" Chang barked to his caller.

The conversation grew more annoying by the second. Chang pushed his unfinished breakfast to the side as he sat in his hotel room, his laptop in front of him.

"Why can't you give me exact figures?" Chang asked. "Get the numbers from Sumatra and call me back!"

He ended the call abruptly. He looked at the laptop's screen, every nook and cranny of Malaysia, Indonesia, China, etc.—and their king cobra numbers—revealed in his elaborate spreadsheet:

> Malaysia: 26,426
> Indonesia: 39,822
> China: 63,467
> Thailand: 40,073

He scrolled through the numbers, settling on Malaysia. Approximately 65 percent of the snakes in this country were now his.

He was thinking through the long process of getting the reptiles shipped from halfway around the world when his cell phone rang again. He answered, expecting a familiar voice giving him the information he had requested.

"Where are you?" a voice asked.

Chang hesitated, then recognized the caller, an associate connected with his latest venture and one of the two men he had met earlier in an airport bar. He was never one to precisely name his location, but finally he relented.

"I'm in DC. Maryland, actually," Chang said.

"So are we, and we're ready to meet." Before Chang could say anything, his caller continued. "We'll see you tomorrow afternoon at Capers. It's the lounge at Dulles. Be there at three p.m."

Chang heard a click and then closed his phone. He thought of the impending, unpleasant meeting with people he had grown to detest. Lately, they broke into their native German tongue when they didn't want him to understand what they were saying.

But he did understand. He made his living dealing with the world, after all. They were trying to undercut his fee for the work it took to catch and ship the snakes. He wouldn't let it happen.

Chang closed his laptop and sat silently.

Thinking.

There was more about the men that he disliked, which had nothing to do with money. He found them *overbearing*—even as he was going to make them rich; *unruly*—wanting it all when it wasn't possible to have it all; and, one in particular, as witnessed during their last meeting in another airport bar—*undisciplined*.

* * *

Washington, DC

Eddie unlocked the door to the archives in the basement of the Department of the Interior, although why it was locked was a mystery to him.

No one comes in here.

Anything deemed important was online.

Stepping inside, Eddie turned on the lights and closed the door behind him, taking in the musty smell of old books. Ahead of him on a shelf were neat files and bound reports of the Service's most recent years.

Eddie looked down at his list, written hastily while Sheridan had been talking to him. Apparently, whatever information Sheridan wanted was from earlier documents, the ones they never looked at.

Before coming down here he had gone back to reports from the 1960s—some were online—and read cases that referenced earlier cases about the large-scale taking of animals, and made notes about them. He would be checking twelve years of writings, hoping to shed light on Sheridan's investigation.

Eddie made his way deeper into the archives, literally to the front, where the first reports resided. He walked past stacks and stacks of material, and realized he hadn't been in here since ten years ago, when he and two interns had scanned the summaries most often referred to and put them on the department's internal database.

He touched one of the bindings for reports written in 1954, feeling the dust on his fingertip. He wondered who had prepared them and what Service investigations merited top billing inside. There was something about this work, this preparing of reports, he had decided long ago, that appealed to him, similar as it was to literature searches and his unfinished PhD dissertation on early twentieth century federal laws that helped shape American history.

Problem was, he had determined, it was the other way around: history shaped the laws.

He moved on and came to the end, to the earliest-bound handwritten reports. These were not as neatly organized as the ones near the door. Some lay on their sides, their peeling binding clearly visible. Alongside of them were boxes holding who-knew-what information with a date scribbled on the outside.

The first reports and box showed the year 1901, covering the initial year of Fish and Wildlife's existence. Other bound volumes and boxes continued through 1920 on the bottom shelf. Eddie started with year one, grabbing the dusty book. He looked at his notes and took books from 1908, 1913, and 1920. He'd start with these, he decided, taking the books to a table.

He sat down and arranged the books in front of him. Something pulled him toward 1908. It just so happened he knew something about those early years of the last century. The Indian Wars were over, but the frontier remained. Teddy Roosevelt presided over forty-six states in the USA. He knew other things as well: Most U.S. families toiled in agriculture. Most of the cities held the immigrants.

What did 1908 hold for animals? he wondered.

More importantly, had anything changed?

He reached for the worn, nubby leather cover and opened it.

68

"There was one call made from Egan's phone," Kim began, as Sheridan motioned her into his office. "We traced it to a cell phone, to a man by the name of Richard Chiu. The number originates in Hong Kong."

"Any address?" Sheridan asked.

"Only a post office in Hong Kong." She handed him a note with the number on it.

Sheridan looked at it. He wondered about calling it, and then picked up his desk phone. He put the receiver down abruptly and took out his cell phone instead. Sheridan punched in the numbers and waited.

The call went to voice mail.

Sheridan ended the call. "I'll do this later," he said. "Thanks."

"Sure," Kim said, and left.

Sheridan turned back to his computer, but was interrupted by his cell phone ringing. He stared at the phone and then picked it up. The number was the one he had just called. He let it ring. Would he leave a message?

Sheridan answered, but refrained from identifying himself. "Hello?"

The caller remained silent.

Sheridan waited. No one spoke, each trying to identify the other, he surmised.

Finally, he heard a click.

After a time, Sheridan put his phone down and sat thinking. He glanced at the number again on the sheet of paper, then picked up his phone again and speed-dialed Des.

"We got a number from a call made in Egan's office. Contact Jimmy," Sheridan requested. Jimmy was one of their Saturday morning basketball buddies and an agent at Immigration and Customs Enforcement—ICE—at Dulles International Airport. "See if he can find something on the name Richard Chiu from Hong Kong."

"I'll call him now," Des answered.

"Thanks."

Sheridan turned back to his computer. Suddenly, his cell phone rang again, startling him. He looked at the number and saw that it was Isaac in Germany.

"I've got more for you," Isaac began, after Sheridan had answered.

Sheridan sat back, cradling his phone. "Go ahead."

"This name may not be familiar to you in the States: All Feed." Isaac also said it in German. He was right; it meant nothing to Sheridan.

"It's a subsidiary of Nestle," Isaac continued. "Global Initiatives is buying boatloads of mice and rats from them."

Sheridan let that sink in for what seemed like a long time. "Really," he said finally.

"It's a name that keeps popping up," Isaac remarked.

"Where's the feed going?" Sheridan asked.

"We're looking into it."

"The snakes are in Germany, then," Sheridan pressed.

"It would appear so," Isaac replied. "As I said, we're looking around."

"Okay. Thanks," Sheridan said, ending the call.

He put his cell phone down and reached for his diagram. He added the name All Feed to the box at third base holding the grouping for Global Initiatives.

The box was getting full.

He stared at it for awhile, knowing the information was key to his case, but having nowhere to go with it. Not for the time being, anyway. Sheridan thought about Marsh and his problem in Wyoming. He reached for his work phone and called him.

When his former co-worker answered, Sheridan filled him in on what Vicki had told him about their eagle case, that perhaps someone was harboring them all.

"How did you arrive at that?" Sheridan asked.

"It was all that was left."

Sheridan glanced at his sheet.

"That doesn't mean we know any more than we did yesterday," Marsh added. "You know, we had a case out here about ten years ago involving the taking of eagles, many numbers of them. We thought it was for feathers, but no carcasses were ever found."

"I remember," Sheridan said.

"It's still unsolved." Marsh paused. "I still think it's about using a piece of the animal for something else."

Sheridan thought about that, a concept that divided takers from collectors. But in Fish and Wildlife's world, collectors *were* takers.

"Listen," Marsh said, changing the subject. "Vicki's coming. And we're happy to have her."

"I'm sure she can help you," Sheridan said, an even answer that disguised his uneven feelings about her move.

"Now...what about you?"

The question took him aback. "Working there?"

"Yes," Marsh answered. "There's plenty going on: wolves, bears, angry ranchers. Give it some thought."

It seems unreal.

"I will." He ended the call and sat back, stunned, elated. But abruptly his mood changed. No time to think about it. Instead, he concentrated on something else Marsh had said: *many numbers of them.*

He picked up his diagram again, sat back in his chair, and began going through the players on the page.

Sheridan started at first base with the Beltway collectors. He still didn't think they were suspects in international wildlife crimes. And yet, Adam was proving his mettle as a felon.

Sheridan moved to home plate and K. C. Of everyone on the page, he was the person who jumped out at him. Even his name was synonymous with the snake. Yet Sheridan's gut was telling him that K. C. had nothing to do with the current situation. He wasn't sure why, but something about the man had changed—softened, perhaps—since their last encounter. Age? Diminished interest? He didn't know.

Sheridan thought about a connection between Adam and K. C., but ruled it out. K. C. didn't seem to know Adam at Exotic Reptiles.

He came back to a familiar question: who *does* Adam know?

Sheridan moved to third base, the box holding information about Global Initiatives, Germany, and the trucking line. And now All Feed. Again, having information about Global Initiatives was imperative, obviously. He'd have to wait for Isaac on that.

Sheridan stopped at the box for Bangkok in the shortstop position. He glanced up at the clock and then back at the box. Reaching for his phone, he called the Ashland lab. Getting voice mail for Simpson the statistician, he left a message.

"Mel, if we have forty thousand king cobras in Thailand and approximately twenty-six thousand go missing," Sheridan said, "what's the *resource base* for regeneration? Call me on my cell," he added, leaving the number.

He heard a knock at his door and looked up to see Eddie.

"I've got that info you wanted from the archives."

"That was quick. Come in."

Eddie settled into a chair in front of Sheridan's desk. He crossed his legs and put his notes on his lap.

"I'll try to frame this for you," Eddie began, resting his elbows on the arms of the chair and spreading his hands out in front of him, "because, as you know, there were many, many takings over many, many years."

Sheridan nodded in agreement.

Eddie reached for his notes. "But when you're talking about numbers of animals—many numbers of them—"

That phrase again.

"*Nothing* compares to the *millions* of birds—passenger pigeons—taken in this country. By 1893"—he put one hand up again, as if swatting a fly—"gone. The buffalo: by 1810, it was gone from the Appalachians. By 1860, thirty to sixty million had been slaughtered on the prairie. And millions more on the Canadian prairie."

Eddie referred again to his notes as Sheridan waited.

"Way back," Eddie continued, "the beaver population. Millions and millions taken for their pelts."

"Right," Sheridan replied. "They came back, somehow."

"We stopped killing them," Eddie replied.

Sheridan nodded.

"You wanted big numbers," Eddie said, sensing that the information wasn't quite what Sheridan had in mind.

"Yes, they're big."

Eddie looked down at his notes again. "Something more contemporary; I went back to when the Lacey Act went into effect in 1900. In 1901," he explained, "forty-eight Illinois men were charged with illegally shipping more than twenty-two thousand birds *into* the state. Quail, grouse, ducks, for hunting. Same year, nine men were charged in New York with illegally trading and killing forty thousand game birds. The birds were put in cold storage."

These were numbers he could work with, Sheridan thought, numbers that a few men could be responsible for.

"Again, birds were a big thing," Eddie continued.

Sheridan nodded in agreement.

"The alligator cases: these are your closest reptile cases, other than Chameleon," he said, as an aside. "The animals were killed and taken to New York, then shipped to Europe and Asia. They made their way back into the U.S. as shoes, belts, purses, vests, whatever. An estimated thirteen million alligators were taken, or *ninety percent* of the population in Louisiana, over a twenty-year period, from 1938 to 1958."

Sheridan thought about that. He knew the number had been high. He'd forgotten the percentage.

"The biggest reptile taking in history was right here on our own shore," Eddie added.

Sheridan nodded again at that little-known fact.

Eddie went on. "Dave Hall's ivory cases. More than five *tons* of walrus ivory recovered in Alaska. One trafficker alone took ten thousand pounds a year in the late 1970s. By 1980, the price of ivory on the world market had gone from six dollars to forty dollars a pound." He looked up. "Not even Chameleon matches these."

"Right," Sheridan said.

"I wasn't clear on what you wanted as far as a pattern."

After a moment, Sheridan said, "So far, the only pattern that emerges is greed. Which we knew. But the numbers are huge."

Eddie handed him his notes. "I wrote it all down."

"Thanks," Sheridan said, taking the pages.

"You know," Eddie added, the conversation almost at an end, "something interesting happened in 1908."

"What's that?" Sheridan responded.

"A man in Florida had cobras. But not the volume you're looking for."

"Sounds like K. C."

"A fire destroyed everything," Eddie said, rising. "Miami was watching him because he had cobras."

Sheridan wondered about that. "Did you find anything else on it?"

"No. It was barely a mention in the state summaries."

"I see."

"You got a case?" Eddie asked, changing the subject.

"Yeah," Sheridan responded after a time, thinking about 1908 and Florida. "Somewhere."

69

Chantilly, Virginia
Early Tuesday afternoon

Jimmy Sloan wadded up his lunch bag and took aim for the trash bin across the room. Letting it fly, he banked the bag off the wall for a perfect three-point shot. A smile crossed his lips as ICE agents in the room nodded in his direction.

Sloan rose and bid good-bye to his co-workers. He walked into the hallway at Dulles International Airport to make his way back to work, work that included checking passport entries for Homeland Security, of which Immigration and Customs Enforcement, or ICE, was an integral part. He turned a corner behind the main concourse, took out his cell phone and saw a message from Des. He punched in a few numbers and listened to Des's request for a look-up on the name Richard Chiu.

Back at his desk in a cordoned-off area near international arrivals, Sloan logged on to his computer and entered the Customs database that held millions of U.S. and international passport numbers of individuals leaving and entering the United States. He entered the name Richard Chiu, a popular Chinese moniker. Instantly, the name filled the screen. He looked at a number in the upper right corner: 5,065. From a menu, he chose "travel within last six months."

About twenty names popped up.

"Okay," he said, to no one in particular. "Let's see what we got."

Sloan clicked on the first entry. A photo and particulars from the passport for an elderly man from Shenzhen, China, came up. He saw from the database that he came into the U.S. in April.

Sloan scrolled down. A contact phone number in the U.S. showed a Virginia area code.

He clicked on the number. A name—also Chiu—and an address in northern Virginia appeared. Sloan clicked on the link for the telephone number and heard it dial. With all identification for ICE blocked on caller ID, and the recipient unable to get anything from phone company dial-back numbers like *69, he never worried that the call could be traced. Unless, of course, he was calling another Department of Homeland Security number.

No one answered and there was no voice mail. Sometimes immigrants left messages on voice mail in their native tongue, a tip to ICE to make that very entry in their records.

Sloan knew it wasn't fair to make assumptions based on voice, but it was done all the time. New immigrants were always suspect. Those with heavy accents speaking English also were suspect. Someone with a foreign name but no accent was suspected˙ less, but that fact also was duly noted.

He clicked on a link to the three credit agencies and selected one of them: TransUnion. Two credit cards popped up for the contact. Sloan saw that balances were paid in full every month, not unusual for immigrants, he knew. He clicked on the Visa card and saw last month's activity. Often, ICE discerned the age of the person by what was bought. He scrolled through a short list of items—a department store jewelry item, an auto repair shop in Virginia, and a clothing store—but nothing that indicated gender or age. It was possible to go back several years on any credit card.

Sloan decided not to, and also decided not to look further at the contact's phone records, banking transactions, movement in or out of the country, or recent infractions, if there were any, which would include speeding tickets and arrests. Because it was so difficult to get information on foreigners, ICE made assumptions based on the contact's information.

Sloan decided that this contact and Richard Chiu himself didn't pose risks to the country. He backpedaled out of the credit agencies to his original page and opened files on Richard Chiu number two.

After several hours of research on fourteen more names, including four Americans and ten foreigners, Sloan took a break. He logged off the computer, as he was required to do even for a short time away, stood up and stretched, then walked into the men's room.

He knew that since 9/11 it was imperative for the government to view private information. But he was sure the public didn't know *how* much data were available for him to see. With recent ICE tie-ins to the major job-posting sites on the Web, resumes posted online gave valuable information about a person's movement and addresses over years of work history. With this data and a full viewing of the person's private information—and especially the ability of new software to sort it all by date—he could form a pretty good description of an individual that included movement, buying habits, credit history, home ownership, marital status, travel plans, restaurants visited, cars rented, and on and on. He had been part of a team doing this very search on the 9/11 hijackers. He had run a similar check on himself that brought up all his charges on credit cards over the last five years. That spooked him a bit, looking at the amount he had spent.

Even if someone used only cash, Sloan could see a large cash transaction at a bank and make assumptions based on that. Most Americans had bank accounts. In short, nothing was hidden.

Sloan looked at his watch. Getting this information for Des—especially if he checked all the contacts—could take the rest of the day.

He washed up, glanced at himself in the mirror, and made his way back to his station to begin a search on Richard Chiu number fifteen.

70

Arlington, Virginia
Tuesday evening

Sheridan sat at the bar at Hugo's ruminating on the figures Eddie had relayed to him earlier.

Forty thousand.

Ninety percent.

Sheridan thought about collectors he knew and a friend who had every card for every Yankee player from the mid-1950s to the present day, as well as doubles and triples of some. He thought about K. C., who had at least one of every cobra on the planet. And doubles and triples of some.

What category did these men fit into?

Try as he might, he couldn't put either one in the same category with *forty thousand* or *ninety percent*.

He was interrupted by his cell phone ringing. Answering it, he heard Ron Grady from the department's CSI unit apologize for being so late in getting back to him. Then, Grady filled him in on the fingerprints taken from Egan's office.

"The print matches a local guy, one Adam Hunter," Grady said. "His was the only print."

"I thought so. That definitely places him in our offices," Sheridan answered.

Grady didn't respond.

"He's the reason our badges were recoded," Sheridan added.

"Ah," Grady said.

"Listen," Sheridan said, thinking of something, "if you would, go back to Egan's office and dust for prints on the files on his desk. Then ask Kim to give you a file in my office. It has a diagram inside. Dust that for fingerprints, although I've compromised it already."

Grady said he would start on it first thing in the morning. Sheridan thanked him and ended the call. He set his phone down and took a long draw on his beer. Adam had copied something he deemed important. Sheridan was pretty sure that document was his diagram. Picking up his cell again, he made a quick call to Kim and left a voice mail, detailing to her what he'd just told Grady. He added that she shouldn't touch the diagram inside.

In the mirror behind the bar, he saw Des and Carole emerge from the restaurant, and waved them over. The three exchanged greetings, then Carole excused herself.

"I'm going to the ladies' room." Before leaving, she placed a hand on Sheridan's arm. "When Vicki's back, please bring her for dinner. Our schedules, as busy as we've been—"

"Don't apologize," Sheridan said quickly. "There wasn't time. We'll do it when she's here."

"Good," Carole replied.

"Meet you out front," Des said to Carole as she walked off. "How's it going?" he asked Sheridan, not taking a seat, electing to remain standing next to his partner instead.

"Okay," Sheridan answered, then repeated the information Eddie had told him earlier. "Those early takings…the numbers were huge."

"You're thinking that's what we've got?" Des asked.

"Yeah. It's what we've got." He thought for a moment. "But I don't know how." He quickly explained what Isaac had found. "Or why."

They lapsed into silence, both staring at the TV. The bar had begun to fill up and had gotten louder, as regulars greeted one another and took their usual seats. Stan turned up the volume for the end of the Nationals' game.

Sheridan watched the screen, but wasn't concentrating on the game. Instead, he thought about Carole's comment, genuine as it had been. The awkwardness he had perceived between the two women socializing for the first time since his divorce now seemed a notch less distressing.

"You and Carole," Sheridan said, as Des turned to him. "You thinking about getting married?"

Des hesitated before answering. "We don't talk about it."

"You've been together..." Sheridan let the rest trail off.

"Yeah. I'm not sure either of us wants marriage again."

"She's okay with that?" Sheridan asked.

Des shrugged. He seemed to be thinking it through. "We're in a good place."

Sheridan changed course. "I feel like I'm treading water."

"Vicki?"

"No. Work." He didn't elaborate on the phone call with Marsh. "I want to get back in the field."

"I know what you mean."

"I need the black and white," Sheridan added. Since it was a night for personal revelations, he continued. "How're you doing?"

Des shrugged again. "I'm okay. Work's okay. It's not field-work"—he shot Sheridan a glance—"but we're not getting any younger."

"Right, right."

"By the way," Des went on, "Jimmy got back to me on that name, Richard Chiu."

"Yeah?"

"One man came in via Kennedy from Paris. No flag," Des stated, referring to a U.S. government "tag" in a database that alerted authorities to infractions or other matters. "I've got him checking aliases."

"Good. Thanks," Sheridan said.

Des looked over Sheridan's shoulder and saw Carole waiting
for him. "I better run." He patted Sheridan on the back. "I'll see
you tomorrow."

Sheridan watched Des leave and then saw Curtis, the bar regular with disheveled hair and dirty glasses, hurrying in.

"Hey," he said, greeting Sheridan and taking the seat next to
him.

"Hi," Sheridan responded, the conversation with Des still on
his mind.

Curtis settled in. "Can I show you something?"

"Sure."

"Remember we were talking about baseball cards?" Curtis
asked.

"Yeah, I remember."

Curtis opened his briefcase and took out a worn envelope.
He reached in and pulled out a stack of old cards.

"These were my father's," he said, fanning them out on top
of the bar.

Sheridan saw a Milwaukee Braves catcher from the 1950s. He
picked up the cards and looked through them, taking his time.

"Wow, look at this," Sheridan said finally. He took two cocktail napkins from the bar and laid two cards on top of them.

Stan the bartender, wiping a glass, came over and joined
them.

"These aren't 'forgotten men,'" Sheridan said, referring to
the remark Curtis had made previously. He pointed at the first
card for a St. Louis Cardinal. "This is Ray Washburn. Minor fact
about this guy; he was the first Cardinal to pitch in the new Busch
Stadium. The '66 stadium. He also no-hit Willie Mays and the
Giants."

Sheridan nodded at the second card. "That's Ron Fairly. He
was good. But he was surrounded by greats. He's an announcer

now." Sheridan picked up the Fairly card and held it at an angle, looking at the gloss on the front. "This is in good shape."

He put the card back on the napkin and gently pushed both over to Curtis. "Go to PSAcard.com and join. Then get these graded. The others you can sell at card shows."

"Thanks!" Curtis exclaimed, gathering up his odd lot. "It's Jim, right?"

"Sheridan. People call me by my last name."

Curtis reached into his wallet and took out a business card. "In case you need anything."

"Food and Drug Administration," Sheridan said, reading it.

"Yeah. And I'd like to get out of *that* hellhole," Curtis said, putting his wallet away.

"Another disgruntled fed!" Stan said, listening to them. He plopped down two coasters. "Nationals won. I'll buy you both drinks."

71

Alexandria, Virginia
Wednesday morning

Sheridan leaned against the kitchen counter, nursing a cup of coffee. Vicki walked around him, opening empty drawers and cabinets, giving the once-over to the areas she had already packed. Everywhere, it seemed, filling every corner of the small kitchen, were boxes, taped shut and stacked high—save for one.

He put his coffee cup down and lightly touched Vicki's arm, drawing her to him. Her arms encircled him and he kissed the top of her head, smelling the scent of shampoo. Their last night together had been a simple one: pizza ordered in and some TV. And little talk of the event that was now upon them.

"I want to say to you what I've already said," Sheridan said. "This isn't good-bye for us."

She looked up at him and hesitated before answering. "I know."

She kissed his neck and left to attend to something in the dining room, preoccupied with others things, he surmised. He turned off the coffeemaker, washed the carafe, and set it on a burner on the stove.

Vicki came back into the kitchen with two suitcases.

"I'll take those," he said quickly. He slid the shoulder bag off her arm and grabbed the large duffle bag, and took both outside. He opened the trunk of her car and saw her easel and a carefully wrapped rectangular item on top of it.

Will she finish that painting before I get out there?

He placed the bags carefully around it and shut the trunk.

Vicki had stepped outside and was standing near the kitchen door, looking back in through a window. Then she turned and came up to him.

"My niece will be here in about an hour," she said.

He nodded in response.

"You don't have to wait."

The morning's agenda had already been talked through: the early start, the niece letting the real estate agent in, the call from the road later that morning.

And what about him? *Yes, what about me? This is awkward.*

She opened the car door and put her purse and coffee cup inside. Then she turned to face him. She put her arms around Sheridan's neck. "Think of this as the first leg of our journey," she said, smiling. "I'll scope out the territory, get us a place…" She hesitated. Then tears came.

He, too, felt a wave of sadness, along with all the important things he hadn't mentioned but hoped she knew. It was his moment to say something, but words failed him. Sheridan hugged her and blinked back his own tears. When would he feel her like this again?

"I'll miss you," he whispered.

"I know." She held him and then kissed him deeply. "I love you."

He looked down at her. "I love you, too."

Then he let her go and she got in the car. The window slid open and he bent down to her.

She touched his arm. "I'll call you later."

He kissed her again. "You keep me up-to-date about that case out there."

"I will."

She pulled out of the driveway and Sheridan watched as she drove off. At the corner, before turning, she waved back at him.

And then she was gone.

He dug his hands into his pockets. He stood there for a few minutes looking at the empty place in the road where her car had been. Sheridan thought about what he had told her earlier, that it wasn't good-bye.

He turned and went back inside the house, closing the door softly. The place wasn't the same, feeling void of its soul and he like an outsider. Sheridan made his way back toward the bedroom, noting faint outlines on the walls where framed pictures had been. Vicki had packed sporadically, a whole room here, a partial room there, and a few pictures everywhere. She would be back to finish. He knew that.

Sheridan stepped into the bathroom and saw a small envelope with his name on it on a towel near the sink. He opened it.

> Today is not how we end, it is how we begin.
> You can expect a call from me every day until we are together.
> I love you more than you will ever know.
> —V

He held the note, rereading it several times before putting it away. An emptiness washed over him as he stepped into the shower. All her personal items were gone from it, save for a bar of soap she'd left there for him. He smiled at her thoughtfulness, then showered quickly and got dressed. He packed up, taking shirts on hangers with him. He grabbed his coffee mug from the kitchen and left, locking the door behind him.

As he backed out of the driveway he took one last look at the house. Yes, he told himself as he drove away, it wasn't good-bye for them.

72

Arlington, Virginia
Wednesday morning

Kim followed Ron Grady out of Sheridan's office after show-ing him the file her boss wanted dusted for prints. Previously, they'd gone into Egan's office to get files there, all of which Grady now held in his gloved hands.

"Ever watch this being done?" Grady asked, as they entered the elevator. CSI's lab was on the third floor. He punched the number three.

"Only on TV," Kim replied.

"It's pretty cool. The procedure was developed by the Japanese. Lucky for us, they were willing to share it."

"What's it called?" Kim asked.

"Cyanoacrylate fuming. Know what that is?"

"No."

"Superglue," Grady replied.

They exited the elevator and walked to a door at the end of the hallway. Using his key, Grady opened it and the two stepped inside. He began opening cabinets and drawers for the necessary hardware and chemicals.

"We'll start with Sheridan's first, so you can get going," Grady said. He carefully took the top file and set it on top of a mesh screen, to avoid compromising any prints on the back cover. "I'm gonna speed this up a bit, to get through all of them," he said.

Moving quickly, Grady opened his fingerprint kit. "I'll dust the outside first and we'll get this in the machine," he added, nod-ding to a contraption in a corner of the room. "That thing burns superglue and the fumes adhere to the fingerprints. Or so we hope. I have little fans going inside to speed up the process."

He put on a surgical mask, then opened the file and looked at the diagram. "Wouldn't you know," he said in muffled voice, looking up at Kim, "that he'd bring it all back to baseball."

With tweezers, he carefully lifted Sheridan's diagram, drawn on an empty sheet torn from the back of an Oriole program and set it on another screen.

He noted the shine of the paper stock and looked up again at Kim. "Hmm. Might be easier to get prints from the folder first. We'll see." Grady took contrasting black magnetic dusting powder out of his bag.

"Here we go," he said, carefully sprinkling a film of dust over the folder's cover. He reached for his miniature bellows and carefully blew away the top dust. A conglomeration of prints remained.

"These are bunched together," he said. He reached for his camera and took close-ups of the folder. Then he turned it over and repeated the experiment on the back.

"There's a few here that are clean."

Moving to the diagram, he repeated the procedure. "Wow. This is even worse."

Kim followed him over to the machine and watched him suspend the folder and diagram inside. In the middle was what appeared to be a small heater.

"I'm going to put a couple of drops of cyanoacrylate in this container," he said, doing that and placing it on top of the heater. He turned a knob and closed the door to the airtight chamber.

"We'll see what develops," he said. "Tell Sheridan I'll have this for him soon."

* * *

At his desk, fiddling with a pen and staring into space, Sheridan waited for Des to finish a conversation with a co-worker in the hallway. The mixture of emotions that had engulfed him earlier was still with him. He glanced at the clock: 9:35 a.m. Vicki had been on the road three hours.

He sat back and crossed his arms. He knew that people would ask him about her, if she had gotten off all right, when she would get to Wyoming.

He needed to be able to answer them. And move on.

Des finished and walked in. "Vick get off all right?"

Sheridan looked up at him. "Yeah."

Des sat down in a chair across from Sheridan's desk and put his feet up on the edge, and proceeded to tell him about getting Johnny settled.

"What are we doing about Adam?" Sheridan asked.

"I'm keeping an eye on him," Des explained. "He lives with his mother. He's got a job now with a moving company. From what I can tell—and that's not much, without Johnny—there's nothing going on at the moment with him or anyone else in the Beltway group."

Sheridan then filled him in on Grady and his attempt to get prints off the diagram. "Kim said he'll have something soon, hopefully. How's Johnny doing?"

"I'm checking in on her later," Des answered.

Sheridan's cell phone rang. He looked at the number, hesitated, then looked back at Des.

Des smiled, then got up and left, closing the door behind him.

"Where are you?" Sheridan asked.

"Somewhere. Hard to tell," Vicki said. "Are you at work?"

"Yes."

"You know, I've got a lot of time. And I've been thinking about your case," Vicki said.

"Great. Like what?" he asked.

"Well, for starters, why would someone even *want* millions of king cobras?" she asked, half joking. "From what you've told me, collectors aren't the reason."

"Right."

"How do you know the Thai government isn't involved?" she asked.

His first response was to laugh. But then he thought about this "out of the box" revelation.

"Well—" he began, but was interrupted.

"I mean," Vicki continued, "Thailand knows the IUC will be all over their country next year doing counts. So maybe they're covering up by saying something now, even as they help the snakes disappear. Otherwise, they'll be asked about the low numbers."

"That will be years down the road," Sheridan said, playing devil's advocate, knowing how long it took agencies to compile their numbers. "And where's the gain? There's no selling that we know of."

"Yet," Vicki replied.

"Right."

"I'll keep thinking about it," she added.

"You do that, and call me later," he said, thanking her.

He sat at his desk for awhile thinking through Vicki's idea, but his instinct gave it no credence. And yet…

Nah!

He got up and walked out into the hallway. He turned to the right in time to see a familiar face coming toward him.

Oh, man.

He watched his ex-wife's gait quicken when she saw him.

"Rick's father," Joanna explained, coming up to him and adjusting a bag slung over one shoulder. "Sudden heart attack."

"Wow." It was all he could think to say. He noted people in the office staring at them.

"I'm taking the train to New York, but Jase is at his game." She held up an insulated lunch bag, a Baltimore Oriole prominently displayed on the front. "He'll need his extra inhaler," she said, handing it to him. "There's a sandwich in there, too. Can you keep him for several days?" she asked. "It's earlier than we'd planned."

"Of course."

Joanna looked at her watch. Sheridan took her by the elbow and led her back down the hallway, passing Des's office.

"Hello, Desmond," Joanna said as they passed.

Des looked up at the two of them walking by, but said nothing.

"Sorry about Rick's father," Sheridan said.

"It's not the first time."

They continued in silence until they reached the elevator.

He let the awkwardness drop away. "Tell Rick I'm sorry."

"I will."

Sheridan hesitated. "When you get back, I want to talk to you about something."

She turned to him, but he saw that she was preoccupied with her current situation.

"Not now," he said quickly.

"Go ahead," she responded.

Against his better judgment, he proceeded. "I want to take Jase with me. If I move."

She looked stunned. "Move where?"

"Wyoming," he answered.

"*Wyoming?*"

"Yes." He could tell by her expression that his request had come out of the blue. As he knew it would.

"What would he do there?" Joanna asked.

Sheridan paused and shrugged. "I imagine Wyoming things."

"How would I see him?"

"He can travel. He's old enough."

"Across two thousand miles?" Joanna asked.

"Seventeen hundred, actually." He saw the pained look on her face and tried to reassure her. "We can talk about this later."

Joanna didn't say anything.

"I just want you to think about it," Sheridan added. He pressed the elevator button and the door opened. Joanna stepped in. She held his gaze as the door closed.

He stood there for a few moments staring at the elevator, the Orioles bag dangling from his hand. For a moment, he flashed on a scene of them back in Washington State. They were on a day hike outside of Seattle. Jason, barely two, was in a carrier on his back. Joanna was in front, leading the way, and he was watching her walk, thinking how great she looked in a pair of jeans. Those were happier, unencumbered times, with job relocations and their slowly disintegrating marriage far in the future.

He turned and headed back toward his office.

73

Johnny sat at her computer finishing an e-mail to her mother, telling her that she was fine, that her work was exciting, and that she hoped to come for a visit in about a month. She refrained from any details about where she was now living.

The next e-mail, to her friend Stephanie, told a different story.

> *I'm in this crappy shed doing meaningless work on a case that was already solved. I'm sure you have more things going on in cargo.*
>
> *I thought I could get information, Steff. But I think Adam had me figured out from the beginning. Shows you how difficult it is being someone else.*
>
> *I'm working on* Operation Chameleon. *Remember that? F&W caught Chinese takers in Mexico who sold to collectors in the states. I'm supposed to look for similarities in the present case. So far I have nothing. Actually, I haven't looked, so I better go. Des is coming later. Write!*

Johnny sent the e-mail. She sat back and stared at her computer screen, thinking through the events of the last week. Where along the line had Adam suspected her? she wondered. She'd like to ask him one question: at what point was her cover not credible? She really wanted the answer to that.

She thought about Des and Sheridan, and how disappointed they must be in her. Yet here she was, still on the job. They were giving her a break.

Johnny logged on to the Services internal LEMIS database. She brought up the file on Chameleon and began reading Sheridan's summary of the case. Fish and Wildlife agents had partnered with members of INTERPOL's wildlife crimes unit to intercept shipments of Asian reptiles being shipped from Germany and the Netherlands to the states. The shipments came in through Miami International Airport. Prominent collector and television personality K. C. Sawyer had been arrested as an accomplice, but was later released when no evidence of his involvement was found.

The case hinged on Sheridan going undercover as a buyer and luring the primary suspects to Mexico City for a sale of endangered reptiles, mostly the seldom seen Boelen's and Timor pythons, green tree pythons, and the critically endangered radiated tortoise from Madagascar. On the black market, which consisted primarily of U.S. collectors and pet shops, the reptiles sold for fifteen thousand dollars to thirty thousand dollars. *Each.*

Johnny read the final paragraphs. Three men were arrested in the case. Leland Chang was the primary suspect, who took reptiles from throughout Asia. Arrested with him were two "couriers" with addresses in Hong Kong and San Francisco. She noted that Leland Chang also had an address in San Francisco.

Only the two couriers went to jail, convicted of money laundering, which brought the largest fine and longest jail time. Somehow, Mr. Chang had gotten away.

She scrolled down and for the first time saw photos of the men, which hadn't been in the brief case reports they had studied in school. First, there were the Hong Kong and San Francisco couriers, now in jail: Samuel Lee and Richard Liu. The third photo, of Leland Chang, stopped her cold. She stared into his eyes, recognizing in an instant who he was.

74

Chantilly, Virginia
Wednesday afternoon

Jimmy Sloan leaned back in his chair and yawned. He'd been in front of his computer for three hours, completing another request from Des to go back to the twenty people with the surname Chiu and do a search for aliases. He had just completed that task and had nothing to give Des. There were none.

He sat forward again and stared at his screen. Obviously, Des had a reason for a second request, something he would find out in due time, no doubt. One thing about their basketball group: they shared information, filling each other in on pending cases and new developments. It was data that might otherwise never be known to them, seeing as how government agencies kept their confidential information close to the chest.

Sloan continued staring at the screen. After several minutes, he reached for mouse and moved the cursor to the upper-right search box.

He deleted the name C-h-i-u and typed in C-h-e-w.

Would it be this easy?

The screen filled again with names. He looked at the number of them: 113. Sloan scrolled slowly down the page and then stopped. He clicked on a name that had been flagged and entered another database. He clicked on a link for aliases. Three names for Richard Chew—post office box Hong Kong—appeared in front of him: Richard Lin, James Chen, and Leland Chang.

Jimmy reached for his cell phone. "Des," he said, after the call went to voice mail, "I've got something for you on that name. You might say I 'chewed' on it a bit, if you catch my drift."

* * *

Arlington, Virginia

Sheridan looked up from his desk and saw Grady standing in the hallway, about to knock on his door. Sheridan motioned him in.

"I got two clear prints," Grady said. "Yours and Adam Hunter's."

"Somehow that's not a surprise."

Grady handed Sheridan his file. Sheridan opened it and stared at the diagram. "So this is what he copied." It was an odd feeling, knowing that Adam was now privy to his thinking.

"I didn't get anything but Egan's prints on the files from his office," Grady stated.

"I see. Thanks for doing this," Sheridan said, and the CSI veteran left.

Sheridan put the folder back on top of the others, noting a slight grayish tinge from the dusting. He turned off his computer and then the lights as he prepared to leave for the day.

"I've got Jason's game," Sheridan explained to Kim as he passed by her desk. "It's an early one."

He stopped in Des's office and told him what Grady had found.

"What do you want to do about him?" Des asked, meaning Adam.

"Let me think about it. I'll call you later," Sheridan answered.

He walked past Vicki's empty cubicle without looking in.

Sheridan sat away from the crowd, at the top of the stands, the newspaper he had taken from the car folded at his feet. Jason's was the visiting team, and from up here he could clearly see his son in left field, and be less of a bother if he got a phone call.

He would have to deal with Adam soon, since it was apparent that he knew something about Thailand. Yet he still was having a hard time placing Adam—a relative nobody—in the center of an international reptile case.

Sheridan looked at the scoreboard. It was the fourth inning, no score. Soon, he felt his phone vibrate. He glanced at the number, saw that it was the Ashland lab, and answered.

Mel Simpson, the statistician, got right to the point. "I've got an answer regarding that resource base."

"Great. Go ahead," Sheridan replied.

Simpson started in. "You know that we deal with relative probabilities when it comes to animal counts. It's not like we knock on a door and do a census."

"Right."

"We do, however, factor in life span, genetic diversity, geographic diversity, accidental killing, purposeful killing, taking, disease, environmental disruption, and destruction as factors. We estimate that a twelve percent loss occurs for these reasons alone. And some of the missing will be fecund, which will impact future counts."

"Right," Sheridan said again.

Simpson paused, seemingly for effect. "I won't bore you with stats. But based on your numbers, your king cobra will not regenerate. Not in Thailand."

The statements didn't register at first. And then they did: the impossible was possible.

"I see," Sheridan said. He wasn't sure what else to say. He thanked Simpson and ended the call.

Sheridan put his phone away and sat quietly, thinking. People were moving around him, but he didn't notice. He knew that a species' viability depended upon a key statistical number, a minimum base, to produce the next generation. If the population dipped below that number, in due time it disappeared.

Sheridan looked out at the field again, and then past it at a stand of trees.

For what purpose were they being taken, as he knew they were?

He heard a ball being hit below.

Exotic snake collectors were off the hook, there was no uptick in the skin trade, no sudden virus or environmental event...

He saw Jason looking to his left. The runner would get a double without much trouble.

Sheridan glanced at leaves fluttering in the breeze. The next batter came up, a big guy for his age. He watched the outfield move back.

First pitch: down the middle. And there it went, right over the center field wall. People stood up, cheering.

Sheridan, however, remained seated, lost in thought. He visualized the diagram on his desk, the players neatly boxed off in categories. He thought again about the conversation with Simpson, and his talk with his stepbrother, Les.

"Holy shit!"

Sheridan stood up suddenly, grabbing the discarded newspaper, the conversation with Les fresh in his mind. Ignoring people around him giving him odd looks, he turned to the business page and quickly scanned the listings for commodities: corn, soybeans, cattle. He looked at the list for "spot metals": copper, gold, palladium.

How did one track the commodities with no list and no exchange: fish roe, bat dung...*snake venom*?

Les's words came back to him: "*under the radar screen as far as rules and regs.*"

He imagined traders in Chicago bidding up futures contracts, yelling above everyone else to be heard.

"*A wide-open market*," Les had said.

His stepbrother, without realizing it, had told him everything. Sheridan took out his phone and called Kim at work.

"Kim!" Without pausing, he snapped a command. "Find the companies, research firms, *anybody* that processes snakes for venom, and get back to me. *Immediately*."

He closed his phone before she could respond and stared out beyond the field again.

The snakes would never hit the market, he realized. The physical evidence—skins, meat, wallets, purses—would never be there. Essentially, they were looking everywhere in the world.

For nothing.

The snakes were being *held*.

Only one thought came to mind: Asian medicinals.

But these snakes were leaving Asia.

He thought of something he'd read about venom used as a drug, its potency harnessed. It had been a footnote in one of their annual reports. Which one? When? He couldn't remember.

Sheridan reached for his wallet and fished around for the business card given to him by the bar regular at Hugo's. Finding it, he called Curtis Marks at work.

"Curtis? Sheridan here...from Hugo's...baseball cards?"

"Oh, yeah! How ya doing?" Curtis exclaimed.

"Great. I need to ask you some questions, if you have time."

"Sure."

"What do you know about snake venom?"

"Um...it's potent," Curtis answered. "It's used in drugs."

His hunch confirmed, Sheridan continued. "Which ones, do you know?"

"I'd have to get that information," he replied. "I know venom from the Fer de lance snake is used for dissolving blood clots.

And there's a measure of prothrombin time in cardiology, called Factor X, taken from the Russell's viper. Very effective," Curtis added.

"What do you know about cobra venom?" Sheridan asked.

Curtis thought for a moment. "Not much." He seemed to be considering the question. "I imagine, given its properties, that it helps with digestion…tremors…who knows?"

"How can I find out?" Sheridan said quickly, more questions popping up now than he could ask.

"I'll bet one of your Mickey Mantles there isn't much. But somebody might be doing a clinical study."

Sheridan wasn't sure where he was going.

"Do you know someone at a hospital that does clinical trials? Or someone on an Institutional Review Board, called an IRB?" Curtis asked.

"No," Sheridan responded.

"What you need is a protocol for doing a study using a particular substance for a particular disease or condition. That's proprietary information, but it has to be stated. The protocol will also give you a brief history of using the substance in other studies."

"I see," Sheridan said.

Curtis paused. "You could also find an FDA employee who would go into the files and read the 1572s."

"The what?"

Someone hit a line drive into left field. A runner on second was being waved around third. Sheridan glanced at Jason running after the ball, and strained to hear above the noise.

"It's a form that's required to be filled out on every clinical trial in the United States," Curtis went on. "It lists the title of the study and all the investigators at a specific institution."

"How many are there?"

"Studies?" Curtis asked. "Thousands."

Sheridan exhaled noisily, clearly out of his league. He couldn't think what else to ask.

"They're organized by phase, by region, by year," Curtis continued, picking up the slack.

Sheridan looked at the scoreboard. Jason's team was behind.

"A Phase I study," Curtis explained, "would be the smallest of the Phase I through III trials. It establishes dose and toxicity using a small number of subjects over a short period of time." He paused. "I would start there."

75

Chang didn't understand why the meeting needed to take place at all, seeing that they handled everything by cell phone and e-mail. Nonetheless, here he was, placating this difficult client once again at yet another airport bar, this time at Dulles International.

In today's world, buying a short-hop ticket to get into the airport bar was what was required, although doing so, at any time, was a risk to him. He refrained from telling them that, since they wouldn't care.

He glanced at his bar mates. No surprise to Chang, the one who had over-imbibed previously was intoxicated again. Chang watched as he leaned over his chair and clawed at a server, a nice-looking young woman with a tray who was passing by.

"Miss!"

She turned to look at him.

"Bring me an *empty* wineglass."

In due time, the noticeably irritated server came back with the glass and placed it in front of him. The man reached in his breast pocket and took out a vial of gold-colored fluid.

He opened it and poured the contents into the glass—a taster's serving—while people at the next table watched him. He held it up to the light.

"Look at the color…how clear. Thicker than water…lighter than syrup."

Chang watched him go on, out of control, drawing attention.

The man addressed Chang. "Do you know what this is worth?" he slurred.

Chang watched as he swirled the contents, then tilted the glass, staring at it as if analyzing a fine wine. "This is a hundred thousand dollars of pure venom, the venom from twenty *king* cobras, fined and filtered to crystal clarity!"

"That's enough," Chang said, keeping his voice low. The other man said nothing, amused by his partner's theatrics.

"The value's in the venom!" the man continued in a loud voice, unaware of the people seated at other tables watching him. "Sell the snake and the deal is done." He looked directly at Chang. "Sell the venom and it's an endless *stream*!"

With that, he tipped the glass upside down, the contents flowing like a river onto the burgundy-colored carpet.

Out of control! Chang thought. *People are staring. Luckily, they don't know what it is.*

Chang kept his composure. And his focus. The men at his table were laughing now, speaking in hushed German. And he understood them. They were talking about money. He saw people peering around seatmates to stare at the empty glass and the spot on the rug.

Just a little prank that no one here understands.

Chang thought back to the workers in the jungle, clearing a place for him to do business, collapsing from heat and humidity. He thought of the boys taking risks to obtain a snake. He thought of the long trek when transporting the cobras under secrecy to Germany.

He thought of the venom, invisible now on the floor, and the small amount each snake gave. He thought about the mentality of this man—and the waste.

Frankfurt, Germany
Late Wednesday night

The security guard looked at his watch. Something was not quite right with his dog again. The German shepherd emitted a low growl and then a whine. It lifted its nose in the air, then sniffed at the ground. And it was pulling forward on its leash, just as it did every night when they came to this spot—the end of the alley and the beginning of the garbage-strewn dirt field that divided two warehouses.

Beyond, taking up the entire block, was an old brick building, nothing more than a trash heap, with rusting metal drums lying about the perimeter. He looked up and saw worn, thick block letters that he knew spelled *Bäckerei*, now all but faded away.

The security guard gave slack to the leash and followed the dog across the dusty field. In this decrepit part of town not even grass grew in the open spaces.

He had never seen anyone at the old warehouse, until recently. Trucks came in late at night, his usual beat for his employer. Two men unloaded crates, then left: one in the truck, one in a car. He had never seen a light on inside.

Across the field now, he pulled the dog closer to his side. He walked to the area where he had seen the trucks come in and saw that it was a loading dock, with large garage doors and a smaller door off to the right.

The security guard walked up the short flight of stairs to the single door. The dog—at his ankles now—whined and growled as they proceeded. He tried the handle.

Locked.

He bent down and grasped the handle on one of the garage doors.

Locked.

He tried the other one.

It opened slightly.

He pulled harder and the door creaked upward. He aimed his flashlight inside. Rats scattered before him. The dog let out a high-pitched bark.

"Easy, easy."

The security guard walked in past stacked, collapsed cardboard boxes and more metal drums, less rusty than their counterparts outside. He entered a room and saw conveyer belts with baking equipment stacked haphazardly on them, and large ovens lining one wall. On the other wall were what he guessed were cooling racks, and near them stacks of metal pans.

More rats scattered and the dog strained again at its leash. The man shone his flashlight into the distance and saw a closed door, a purple light visible in the space beneath it.

He walked toward it, but suddenly was jerked back.

The dog refused to move.

"Come on!" He yanked the leash and the dog slowly inched forward.

He got to the door and stopped, his hand on the handle. He looked down. The purple light illuminated the tips of his shoes.

He opened the door. The dog whined and drew back.

The security guard pulled on the leash, but the dog resisted.

He let go and the dog disappeared behind him into the darkness, the leash trailing after it like a snake.

The security guard walked into the room alone.

He guessed he had entered what was once the bakery's garage for its trucks. But no trucks were in sight. Instead, filling every conceivable space were terrariums, each with an ultraviolet light shining above it.

He pointed the flashlight at them. Rows upon rows of them. He walked over to a terrarium against one wall on his right. About fifteen more rose above it.

The security guard looked inside.

Reptile eyes stared back from a huge snake lying within. He felt a cold chill go up his spine. He had never seen a snake so large.

The security guard shone his flashlight up and saw another. And another.

He walked the length of the wall and counted the terrariums: thirty the length of the wall and fifteen high. He did the math: 450 snakes on this wall alone.

He turned and looked into the room, and counted a hundred rows of terrariums from left to right. He walked forward and down a row, counting again. One hundred long. And fifteen terrariums high.

The security guard couldn't do this math without pen and paper.

He guessed there were tens of thousands.

77

Sheridan drove to the convention center with Jason at his side, released from his losing game. Thinking of something, he reached for his phone and took it off vibrate, just as Des was calling him.

"Here's what Jimmy found," Des began, and proceeded to tell him about the three aliases that had come up in his search. "I think we have a connection from Adam to Chang through the name Richard *Chew*, with a new spelling. Most likely Adam was calling Chang—Chew—from Egan's office—"

"We need to talk to Adam," Sheridan said, interrupting him.

"I think so, too," Des replied.

"He can enlighten us on the FedEx package, which most likely was arranged by Chang," Sheridan added. "Perhaps he also can tell us where Chang is." Sheridan then explained his conversation with Mel Simpson in Ashland, the conclusions he'd come to at Jason's game, as well as his talk with Curtis Marks at the FDA.

"We're talking about something huge," Sheridan said, thinking out loud. Des didn't respond, so he continued. "The dissolution of a species had to be part of the plan," he added, repeating what Simpson had told him about the king cobra's numbers.

"To do...what?" Des asked. "*Own* the animal?"

"Yes," Sheridan answered.

"For its venom," Des added, as a statement.

"Yes. Venom to make drugs."

Sheridan waited. Des seemed to be sifting through that piece of information.

"You're telling me an *entity* is stockpiling cobras to make drugs?" Des asked finally.

"Not just that."

Silence again, then Des said, "So no one *else* makes drugs."

"Now you're talking."

"What's the drug?" Des asked.

"That's the million-dollar question," Sheridan replied.

"If this is true, then this is...*something*," Des replied.

"I can't think of another instance in which snakes were taken solely for venom, can you?" Sheridan asked.

More silence before Des said, "No." Another pause. "Any animal taken in large numbers has been destroyed. That's been our model."

"This is different."

Des seemed to be letting that settle in. "You think Chang is behind this?"

"Yes."

"Do you know where he is?"

"I'm hoping to find out."

Sheridan drove into the convention center's loading area, where several semis took up coveted parking spots. Sheridan found an empty slot not far away and pulled in. He saw K. C.'s stoic sidekick, Reeves, giving instructions to workmen who were putting crates into a van. Sheridan kept his eye on him and was about to exit the car when his phone rang again.

"I found the places that process snakes," Kim began.

"Great," Sheridan replied. "Go ahead."

"They're in Europe and South America. Latoxan in France and Instituto Vital in Brazil are the biggest. They each have a large farm of snakes that they milk for venom. And they make antivenins."

Sheridan heard her turning pages.

"The big buyers of antivenin are governments. The Thai government buys quite a bit."

"I see," Sheridan said.

"And then there are the pharmaceutical companies in Europe. They buy raw venom for research. This is a big business, apparently. I couldn't find a lot of information. On their Web sites, the companies say they research venom, but don't say what the research is. I made a list of them for you."

"Great, Kim. Anything in the U.S.?"

"Merck processes U.S. rattlesnakes for polyvenins. They also make an antivenin for the eastern coral snake, *Micrurus fulvius*." She rattled off the Latin as if she used it every day. "That's all I could find right now."

"Excellent work," Sheridan said, and hung up. For a moment he remained where he was, sitting and staring into space as he thought through this new information.

"What?" Jason asked.

Sheridan turned to look at his son. "We have a break in the case."

"You mean with the snakes?" Jason asked.

Sheridan signaled for him to get out of the car. "Yeah. With the snakes."

They approached the huge loading dock and walked up the stairs. Sheridan saw Reeves glance over at them and then take out his cell phone.

Sheridan ignored him as they moved on through the maze of crates, boxes, and workmen in a hurry.

K. C. saw them first, walking toward him as he stood in the convention center's long center aisle near his exhibit. Sheridan closed the distance between them.

"Mr. Sheridan," K. C. said, as a greeting. He looked down at the young ballplayer at his side and smiled at him.

Sheridan started right in. "About the missing cobras."

K. C. folded his arms and waited for him to continue.

"We know they were taken and why. Try as I may, I can't link you to either of those pieces," Sheridan said.

"I should be flattered," K. C. responded.

Sheridan ignored the comment. "I think you can help us."

K. C. paused before responding. "Why don't you tell me what this is about?"

"The cobras are being taken for their venom," Sheridan replied. "There's only one person who can move that many reptiles." Sheridan saw that he had K. C.'s attention. "The venom is being used to make drugs."

"They'll be taken care of, then," K. C. answered.

"Not the ones in the wild. They've been taken in large enough numbers," Sheridan added, "to ensure that they don't recover."

"You're talking *very* large numbers, then," K. C. responded.

"Yes."

K. C. stared at him and then looked away. "Brilliant," he said finally.

"Obviously well planned," Sheridan added.

K. C. nodded in agreement. Sheridan watched K. C. glance down at Jason and then rest his hand on his son's shoulder.

"Where is Chang?" Sheridan asked.

"Try the Hilton," K. C. answered, without looking up at his longtime nemesis. "Remember that he uses a maze of aliases."

"So he's here?" Sheridan asked.

"Yes."

"Why?"

"He came to see me," K. C. replied. "Unrelated to what you're looking for."

Sheridan was aware of Jason, standing between them, looking up and glancing at each man as he spoke. For a moment, neither man said anything.

"I have something to say," Sheridan began. "I want to apolo-gize for what you went through during Chameleon. You had noth-ing to do with it."

The statement seemed to throw K. C. off guard. Instead of acknowledging Sheridan, he looked down and made eye contact again with Jason.

Sheridan's cell phone rang, interrupting them. He thought about not answering it, but reached for it and looked at the number. He glanced at K. C. and then touched the screen.

Curtis started right in. "Can you meet me at Hugo's in about an hour? I've got something for you."

78

Johnny opened the door and let Des inside. "I suppose Sheridan is still angry," she said, moving back to her computer before Des could say anything.

"He's a little upset," Des responded. "But he's got a lot going on." Looking around, he spotted a chair and brought it over to sit down across from her. "What have you been doing?"

"Research," she answered, glancing at her computer. "Just looking into Chameleon."

He nodded.

"Anything more on yours?" Johnny asked.

"Yeah. We have something finally." He sat forward, elbows on his knees. "We have a pretty good idea why the cobras are being taken."

She waited for him to continue.

"They're being taken for venom."

"Venom," she repeated. "For...drugs?"

Des nodded.

Johnny looked confused. "If the venom is for drugs, why are the snakes leaving Asia?"

Des thought about that, but didn't know what she meant. "Sheridan thinks a company is behind this."

"So, not Chinese drugs," Johnny said. "And not in Asia."

Des thought that through, too, recognizing that what meant one thing to him meant something else to her. "We don't have any of those pieces yet," he said finally. "The only connections we have are venom and drugs, and possibly a man by the name of Leland Chang."

"*Chang?*" she asked.

"Yes. The Chameleon Chang."

Johnny hesitated for what seemed like quite awhile to Des.

She couldn't possibly…

Johnny turned to her computer. "I've been reading Chameleon," she said finally, opening the report online. She scrolled down until she came to Leland Chang's photo. "Remember when I told you about my father?"

"Yes."

"He's the one who shot him," Johnny explained, pointing to Chang's photo. "He was the Chinese medicinal supplier to my father's store."

Des didn't say anything, looking for words that would not expose what he already knew.

"You know, Johnny…we knew about Chang," he said after a time, nodding toward the computer screen. Then he stopped. He knew they could never tell her.

She waited for him to continue.

His phone ringing saved him. He quickly added, "We knew the medicinals he was bringing in were from threatened species."

He sat up, checked the number, and answered. He looked at Johnny as he listened to Sheridan giving him instructions.

"Which Hilton?" Des asked, looking at Chang's photo on the monitor.

Johnny watched him, then turned to look at Chang's picture on her screen again.

"I'm leaving now." He put his phone in the pocket and stood up.

"We'll continue this later," he said, moving to the door. "I gotta run."

79

Arlington, Virginia
Wednesday afternoon

Sheridan maneuvered the SUV into traffic, keeping one hand on the steering wheel as he and Jason made their way to Hugo's. His other hand pressed his cell phone firmly against his ear.

"We have something very big," Isaac said.

"Great, Isaac, what?" he asked.

"We've found the snakes."

"*What?*"

"They're here. In Germany. Thousands and thousands of them," he added, and then filled him in on the night security guard's discovery. "I'll tell you, it's more than one person can comprehend. But they seem to be well taken care of. Someone knew what they were doing."

"I can't believe it," Sheridan said, glancing at Jason next to him, realizing that his case, finally, was about to be solved.

"There's more," Isaac said. "The police looked into trucking lines picking up containers over the past year from a rail yard here. Schauffmann Trucking has been picking them up on a regular basis, all going to—"

"The warehouse," Sheridan said.

"Right. The driver of the truck—or I should say, the man who was *supposed* to be driving the night a shipment was intercepted—gets his paycheck from Hasse Pharmaceuticals."

"The ED people?" Sheridan asked, looking again at Jason.

"Correct."

Sheridan turned off the highway and came to a stop behind a line of cars waiting at a red light. He visualized the boxes in the diagram on his desk.

Where to put Hasse Pharmaceuticals?

"Do you have any leads there on who took the snakes?" Sheridan asked.

"Not yet," Isaac replied.

"I may have that piece for you soon," Sheridan said.

80

Hilton Baltimore
Wednesday afternoon

Des walked into the hotel's lobby and up to the front desk. "Do you have a Leland Chang registered here?" he asked, taking out his badge and laying it on the counter.

The clerk took some time looking at it. "That says 'Fish and Wildlife.'"

"Read the bottom," Des replied.

The clerk looked at it again. "Law enforcement." The clerk eyed Des and then looked at his computer screen.

Des added, "I should tell you that he may not be registered under that name."

The clerk waited for him to continue.

"It could be another name," Des explained, taking out a piece of paper on which he had written Chang's aliases, the ones found by Jimmy Sloan.

"We have a lot of guests," the clerk replied. "I really will need a name." He returned to perusing his screen. "I'm not finding a Leland Chang."

Des pushed the piece of paper toward the clerk, who looked down at it.

"I'm gonna need a minute," he said, looking back at his computer.

Des waited while the clerk concentrated on his screen. After a few moments, he looked up at Des and shook his head.

"I'm not finding any of these people." The clerk thought for a moment. "When did he check in?"

Des hesitated. "Good question." He placed a quick call to Sheridan.

"Where are you?" Des asked.

"Just getting to Hugo's," his partner said. "I'll explain why later."

"When did Chang get here?" Des asked.

Sheridan paused before he responded. "I don't know. Earlier this week?"

"Monday," Des said to the clerk. He stepped away from the desk to ask Sheridan another question. "Are you sure he's here?"

"Yes."

"You're certain we can believe K. C.?"

"Yes."

"Why?"

"I can only speculate. He wasn't included in Chang's latest venture. I don't think he trusts him," Sheridan replied.

Des thought about that. "Okay. I'll call you later." He put his phone away and moved back to the desk, waiting again as the clerk concentrated on his screen. Finally, the man looked up from his computer and shook his head again to confirm nothing found.

"All right. Thanks." Des pocketed his badge and the piece of paper, and moved to a window where he could be alone to think.

He knew Jimmy would have been more than thorough, digging and finding names. There was no need to call him again. The only thing he could think of was that Chang had a new alias.

Like finding a needle in the proverbial haystack.

Des turned back to the front desk and saw a man standing there with his back to him, talking to the clerk. The man turned and Des locked eyes with none other than Leland Chang, who held his gaze momentarily before walking quickly to a stairwell.

Des took off after him, but stopped abruptly. Coming through the hotel's revolving front door was Johnny.

81

Late afternoon sunlight filtered in through the skylight at Hugo's, illuminating the long row of liquor bottles in front of the bar's mirror. Curtis was already seated when Sheridan arrived. He opened his briefcase and took out a piece of paper as Sheridan came up to him.

"I don't have to tell you how confidential this is," Curtis began.

Sheridan took the proffered page and looked down at bold letters that read: U.S. Food and Drug Administration. Form 1572.

"Miami General is doing a Phase I study using venom from *Ophiophagus hannah*."

"The king cobra," Sheridan said immediately.

Curtis nodded. "The title and the investigators' names are on there. And the company sponsoring the research."

Sheridan read down the page. "Hasse Pharmaceuticals."

Twice in one day.

"You asked about cobra venom, so I did some research," Curtis said, pushing up his glasses with his thumb. "There are two drugs that use it as a base: Cobroxin and Nyloxin. One blocks nerve transmission. The other is used for arthritis. It is clarified and refined first."

Sheridan stared at him without answering, the information beginning to register. "So, there are drugs on the market that use cobra venom."

"Yes."

"*King* cobra venom?"

Curtis thought for a moment. "No. These drugs are from other cobras. However, venom pharmacology is a growing field."

Sheridan didn't say anything, so Curtis added, "I found that venom is remarkably stable outside of the snake. But it's hard to replicate in a lab." He emphasized his last point. "*You need the real thing.*"

Sheridan nodded in understanding, all of it now "clarified and refined."

"You got something going on?" Curtis asked.

"Yeah," Sheridan responded. "We're aware that snakes are being taken for venom. And you just confirmed why." He skimmed the FDA form again and passed it back to Curtis. "You said the important information is in the protocol."

Curtis nodded. "Do you have a budget for travel?"

"Yes."

"Do you want me to help you?"

"Yes," Sheridan answered again, without hesitating.

"Good. I'll call you from the road."

82

Hilton Baltimore
Wednesday afternoon

"What are you doing here?" Des asked Johnny as she entered the lobby. "Never mind," he added quickly. "Come with me." He hurried her toward the front desk.

"Who was that?" Des demanded.

The clerk looked up without responding.

Des reached for his badge again, but the clerk held up his hand. "His name is Raymond Chou."

"*Raymond Chou.* Does he have a car?" Des asked.

The clerk looked at his screen. "Yes."

"Give me the model and license number."

The man looked back at his screen. "It's a tan Camry, license B-A four-two-seven-six."

Des made a mental note of the number and he and Johnny took off for the door. Outside, they hurried toward Des's car as the Camry came up the ramp from the hotel's underground parking and zoomed past them. It ignored a stop sign and sped into traffic.

But Johnny had caught Chang's eye when he turned to look at them, the second time in her life she had seen him face-to-face.

"How will we get him? And what will you get him on?" she asked as she got in next to Des, her stomach churning as she did so.

"Everything. Chameleon, CITES, Lacey. And endangering a protected species," Des added, turning the car toward the exit and accelerating after Chang, "by sending it through the mail."

"You have proof of that?" Johnny asked in amazement.

Des looked at her as if she were crazy. "Of course not!"

Des picked up his phone and called Randy Pruitt, another Saturday morning basketball buddy and a Maryland police officer.

"Randy! Des here. I need an APB on a tan Camry, license B-A four-two-seven-six. It's heading east on ninety-five." Des listened while Pruitt explained something. "Great. Thanks."

He put his phone down and glanced at Johnny. He saw that she was waiting for him to continue. "I'm calling in my *chits*. Know what those are?"

"Favors."

"Correct. Making contacts is the most important thing you'll do in this business," Des said, without explaining further.

He headed onto the ramp for I-495. After driving some distance, he turned to Johnny.

"Get on the phone and check flights out of town."

"Which airport?" Johnny asked, reaching for her phone.

Des thought about that: three airports, hundreds of possibilities. He was matching wits again with the man who had outsmarted them before.

They were closest to Baltimore.

"How familiar are you with BWI?" he asked.

"Somewhat," Johnny answered. "If I can get a flight to San Francisco, I use it."

"What airline?"

"United."

"Start there," Des said. "Check times and see who else flies to the West Coast." He thought again about what Chang might do.

Just impossible to know.

He gave Johnny a look that said this was a lost cause. "Give it your best shot."

Chang sped into traffic and fell in line behind a white minivan making its way toward the Maryland suburbs. He stayed behind it and thought about his next move, which he knew he would need to make quickly. After ten minutes the van moved into the right lane and exited, and Chang followed. The two vehicles proceeded down a busy highway past big-box retailers and car lots, in an area of Maryland he had never been to. Ahead he saw a Toyota dealership, its lot filled with new cars and trucks. He split away from the minivan and moved into the left lane, then turned off the highway. Chang proceeded about a hundred yards and turned right into the back of the Toyota car lot, and drove into an area of used vehicles for sale.

He got out, leaving the keys inside. Close by was a field that bordered the back of the car dealership. Chang walked toward it and, without hesitating, disappeared into a maze of corn.

83

K. C. watched the last of his terrariums being packed up and moved onto carts for the short trip to the loading dock, the conversation—an apology, really—fresh in his mind. He'd been dumbfounded to hear the words.

Of course, he knew it wasn't the U.S. government apologizing. But it was close enough. In many ways, he and Sheridan had ended up on the same page. And after all these years.

K. C. glanced back at the terrariums. Only the Russian cobra remained, waiting for its ride back to the National Zoo.

I should have pressed Reeves about getting the Russian back first.

He got out of the way as workmen came by and began tearing down his exhibit. Behind them he saw a young man he recognized coming toward him, a person he had seen only once before, at the hotel.

"Where's Chang?" Adam asked, ignoring pleasantries as he walked up to K. C.

"Haven't seen him." K. C. kept his attention on the workmen who now were taking up carpeting near the Russian cobra's terrarium. With nothing left of the exhibit, the snake seemed unnaturally exposed in the convention center's wide-open space.

Adam moved into K. C.'s line of sight. "I can't find him and he's not answering his phone."

"Then he's gone," K. C. replied, taking in Adam's agitated look. Seeing that he had an opportunity to inquire about a relationship with a man they both knew well, he continued. "You seem to have a lot on the ball," K. C. said. "So, why this? You could choose to do anything."

Adam fidgeted. K. C. wasn't sure he'd answer, but finally he did.

"Money. The reason anyone goes to work every day."

K. C. eyed the young man carefully. "Let me give you a tip: find another line of work while you can salvage your reputation."

Adam stopped fidgeting.

"Chang will never be someone you can trust," K. C. added.

"You did."

"Early on. But everything's changed. He'll never get away with what I think he's doing. But then, I don't know what he's doing. Do you?" K. C. inquired.

"He's in a business that will never end," Adam answered.

K. C. waited, hoping he would add more to that statement. But Adam didn't elaborate, and he didn't want to tip his hand about how much he himself already knew.

"Chang's model is based on greed," K. C. explained. "There's nothing wrong with taking snakes for collections. I believe that's what will save them in the end. But he's in another realm. You can walk away from this."

"No way."

K. C. shook his head. The conversation was at an end. He moved away to help workmen who were securing the remaining terrariums.

"We're gonna move these to the truck," one of the workmen said, looking up at him. All twenty-two snakes were crated and ready to go.

"Think I'll go with you," K. C. answered. He took out his phone and admonished Reeves to get the Russian cobra back where it belonged.

Then, without looking back, K. C. followed the men as they made their way down the center aisle of the hall. People waved at him as he passed and he returned the gesture. A young worker fell in line next to him and asked for an autograph. K. C. obliged, slowing down to scribble his name.

He resumed his pace and looked out across the floor as more exhibits came down and the convention center reclaimed its space. K. C. thought about how many shows he had been to over the years. He thought about his trip home and getting his cobras there safely, always his first concern.

He thought about Reeves, a friend who would always be with him, and Chang, a man who had once been so necessary to him. Chang's knowledge of his world, especially Asia, was why he had stayed with him. Chang knew where the snakes were, the boys who caught them, and the middlemen who sold them. He knew markets, and spoke six languages and who knew how many dialects. But Chang went beyond dishonesty, beyond morality even. K. C. wasn't sure how to come to terms with his absolute disregard for people and, for that matter, animals.

K. C. looked behind him and saw Adam standing where he had left him, hands in pockets, staring back at him.

The workmen turned toward the loading dock and K. C. stayed with them. Thinking of something, he pulled Sheridan's business card out of his breast pocket. He stared at it, thinking again about their earlier encounter and the others they had had over the years.

He had been right to inform Sheridan of Chang's whereabouts. Now he'd add another.

He reached for his cell phone. On Sheridan's voice mail, K. C. said: "I highly doubt that you will find Mr. Chang. But there is someone who can help you. His name is Adam Hunter. He's here at the convention center. Threaten him with Lacey and I'll bet you'll get the information you need."

84

"I'm trying to find a tan Camry," Des said, as he took the call from Sheridan. "It's Chang's rental." Then he proceeded to fill him in on events of the last thirty minutes.

Des glanced at Johnny. Conveniently—or maybe not—he hadn't informed his partner about her being with him. "I asked Randy to put out an APB. Randy will call if Chang's left the car anywhere. That is, if they find it. Where are you?" Des asked, changing the subject.

"Just leaving Hugo's," Sheridan said. "Remember that guy with the baseball cards?"

"Yeah."

"He's proving to be very helpful." Sheridan went on. "This will interest you: I just picked up a call from K. C.."

"No way!"

"Adam is at the convention center. Can you go there?"

Des looked over at Johnny again. "Yes. I'll head there now."

"Good."

Des pulled into a strip mall, turned around, and then sped back into traffic. "One thing, if you can look into it," Des suggested before ending the call. "Chang didn't have time to pack."

* * *

Chang wiped perspiration from his forehead and looked at his watch. He had been walking for ten minutes and had reached the end of the field. In front of him lay undeveloped land, and beyond that, about half a mile away, he saw boxcars rolling by on a slow-moving train. Chang quickened his pace over the uneven terrain. As he did so, a corn snake near his foot quickly moved out of his way.

Chang involuntarily lifted his leg. "Shit! Goddamn snake!"

He sped up and got to the tracks, and ran after the train making its way west. He jumped inside the only open car and quickly surmised, from the equipment inside, that it was being used as storage for the railroad.

Chang moved to the side, away from the door, then slid down into a crouched position with his back against the wall, and stayed that way as the train picked up speed.

He knew that now, for the second time in his life, he would be starting over.

85

Startled, the research administrator looked up from her desk. "Yes?"

The man in her doorway held up his badge, the FDA emblem clearly visible.

"I'm sorry," Curtis began, walking into her office. "We have reason to believe that the investigators' lists on some of your 1572s are incomplete. I need to see protocols for clinical trials, informed consent forms, minutes of IRB meetings"—he glanced at his watch—"from February first to August first of this year. This audit will be quick. I promise."

Stunned, the research administrator picked up her phone.

In no time, a harried man, whom Curtis believed was the director, joined them.

"This is ridiculous," the director said. "The FDA was here just five months ago."

"I completely understand," Curtis responded. "But some of your paperwork has been filed *since* that time, yes?" Curtis nodded as he asked the question.

The research administrator nodded in agreement.

Curtis placed his hand on his heart. "I'm sure this is nothing."

He sat behind a desk in an empty office as staff members from Miami General's Clinical Research Unit unloaded file drawers and placed bulging folders in front of him.

"Any Phase I studies?" Curtis asked.

"Just a few." A research associate took out three folders and placed them in a separate pile next to the others.

Curtis looked up at the young associate and smiled. "Thank you."

When she had left, he quickly read the tabs on the files, found the one he wanted, and opened it. He saw the title page of the protocol, with CONFIDENTIAL stamped in bold red letters across the front.

He turned the pages and started scanning with a scanning pen the formal protocol name: Phase I Pilot Study to Determine Maximum Tolerable Dose (MTD) of CT1-a as Initial Therapy in Viral Infections.

"Hmm," Curtis murmured. He kept reading, coming finally to the rationale for the study.

> *This study seeks to define MTD of CT1-a, a protein from Ophiophagus Hannah (OH) venom, in patients with central nervous system (CNS) viral infections, and will further explore CT1-a as first-line therapy in the setting of all viral diseases.*

"Wow." He read on.

> *OH venom has been shown to be a potent and consistently reliable antiviral agent in mouse and canine models, and in early human trials. Published reports by Juris et al. in 2000 showed long-acting, protective effects to neuroglial cells in patients with CNS viral infections.*

Protective. Curtis sat back. *How can a poison confer protection?*

He turned the page. He knew the question had to be answered. He just had to find it.

And there it was:

Repeating studies by Juris et al., based on unpublished reports by Reicker, we have demonstrated OH toxin's specificity in interfering with RNA viral replication in vivo.

Well, that's huge, he thought.

This agent also exhibited protective effects in previously established central nervous system viral disorders. Amyotrophic Lateral Sclerosis, for example, was tested in our OH-824 clinical trial. While the OH protein did not restore movement in animal models with advanced ALS, symptoms did not worsen over a five-year period in which models were treated. All study models are alive today. We have identified CT1-a from the OH snake as the primary protein responsible for the venom's protective effects. Further studies will explore the CT1-a protein as the basis for a viral vaccine.

"Wow," Curtis said again.

So, a natural protein. Were the investigators trying to establish that the venom conferred protected against *all* viral disorders? *All* of them? AIDS, hepatitis, herpes? If that were the case... He tried to read between the lines.

Did the protection last?

It appeared so. He'd done research on cobras and their venoms since talking with Sheridan. He'd learned that the king cobra unleashed all its venom in a single bite, depositing seven milliliters, or 0.2 fluid ounces, of toxin into tissue. It was a wallop that killed an elephant or twenty human beings. So few people lived that no research *in vivo* of the venom's long-term effects had ever been done.

Until now, apparently.

Curtis sat back. If one manipulated the amount of toxin injected—something the snake couldn't do, but a clinical researcher could—then one could gradually measure progress, and the right dose, with the subject still alive. *Precisely what a Phase I study would reveal.*

He turned more pages, seeing a brief history of snake venom as a therapeutic agent, as well as information on various cobra neurotoxins.

The protocol wasn't a pilot study, he surmised. It was a patent application.

It was a gold mine.

Before settling back to read the document in its entirety, Curtis took out his cell phone and called Sheridan, leaving a message.

"This is Curtis, in Miami. I've got something for you," he said, "and it's huge."

86

Sheridan—a hastily obtained search warrant in hand—stood behind the manager of the Hilton Baltimore as he opened the door to Chang's room. The manager stepped aside and Sheridan walked in. He saw that the room had not yet been cleaned. A breakfast tray sat on a table. The bed was still unmade.

Sheridan walked into the bathroom and saw Chang's shaving kit on the counter. He touched a neatly hung towel on a rack and felt dampness.

He returned to the main room and went to a dresser. On top was a China Airlines envelope. He picked it up, opened it and saw tickets originating in Hong Kong to DC. A return flight was booked two days from now.

Sheridan pocketed the ticket and began opening drawers. Most were empty. One had underwear in it. He rummaged through it until his fingers caught on something—several things, actually—and he pulled them all out. Four passports, one each for Richard Chew, Richard Lin, James Chen, and Raymond Chou. All men from Hong Kong. All with the same photo.

Sheridan pocketed these as well, then went to a closet and opened the door as the hotel manager stood by. Clothes hung on hangers. On the floor he saw a computer case. Sheridan bent down to pick it up, and took it to a table and opened it.

* * *

"Why did we turn around?" Johnny asked for the second time.

Des glanced over at his seatmate. Johnny held his gaze, her cell phone suspended in one hand as she waited for his answer. She had made seven or eight calls to airlines, each one giving progressively less information than the last.

"We're down a dead end. You know that, don't you?" he said finally.

"No," she answered. "I'm not sure about that."

Des hesitated, then picked up his phone and called his buddy who had put out the APB. "Randy, do you have anything yet?" Des asked. He looked at Johnny and shook his head. "Okay. Thanks." He put his phone down and stared at the road in front of him. Finally, he glanced at her again. "What?" he asked.

"Where are we going," Johnny began, "*and* do you want me to continue calling the airlines? *And*, why am I just doing busywork for you and Sheridan? *And*, why aren't we following Chang?"

Des saw a look of determination he was beginning to associate with their young rookie, albeit a stumbling young rookie of late. He sat up straight. "Let me answer your last question first. There is nothing we can do about Chang. Sheridan will get a search warrant for his hotel room and Randy is searching the roads. And we are on our way to pick up Adam."

"Adam!"

"Did you know he was working with Chang?"

"No!"

Des watched her in silence. He could only imagine what she thought of her *amour* now.

"Are you sure about this?" she asked finally.

Des nodded that he was. "Sheridan got a call from K. C. We don't know yet how K. C. knows what he knows. But we need to question Adam. Hopefully, he'll come with us. If he's smart he'll come willingly."

"You're sure?" Johnny asked again.

"I don't know anything for sure. All I'm going to do is ask him questions," Des answered. "We have a lot of unanswered questions."

Johnny stared at the road. "Do I have to ride in the same car with him?"

"It would appear that way," Des answered sarcastically. He nodded toward her phone. "You can stop calling the airlines. Chang won't risk getting cornered in an airport."

They drove on in silence for a short time, then Des continued.

"I want to answer your other question. You're not doing busywork. Making phone calls is something we do routinely, so get used to it. And, we always look to past cases to help us with current ones. As it turns out, there *is* a connection between Chameleon and what we're involved in now. And that connection is Chang."

Des looked over at her. She stared back at him, waiting for him to continue.

"We'll do everything we can to find him." He glanced at her again. "For everything he's done."

87

Arlington, Virginia
Wednesday afternoon

Sheridan sat with Lindsay, the department's computer expert, as he turned on Chang's computer and perused the files.

"I'll have to work a bit to get into e-mail," Lindsay explained, going through places on the hard drive Sheridan didn't know existed. "It doesn't appear that he's hidden anything. Looks like what he's got the most of are Excel files."

One in particular, titled simply Numbers, caught Sheridan's eye.

"Open that one," he said, and Lindsay did. Then he moved the laptop closer to Sheridan and rose, leaving him to examine the spreadsheet alone.

Sheridan looked closely at the screen and began scrolling down the page. He saw that each cell was filled with a number ranging into the thousands. To the left, in the first column, were the names of countries, and below them, he presumed, were locales within the countries, most of which he'd never heard of.

But some of the numbers looked familiar. Finally, after several moments and putting two and two together, he recognized what he was looking at: counts for the world's king cobras, from tiny corners of Sumatra, Java, Sulawesi, Thailand, China. Everywhere they lived.

Thousands upon thousands of them.

Would the numbers jibe with the tally in the warehouse? He was sure they would. He also was sure the data had been compiled from the IUC Web site. In an era of transparency, the agency posted its figures to help wildlife groups worldwide keep tabs on animal populations.

He stared at the screen.

How did he do it? Corner a species, that is.

Of course, it had been done before: alligators, seals, carrier pigeons. Their numbers had ranged into the millions. One day they were here. And then, seemingly overnight, they were not.

He scrolled up and down the page, losing track of where he was in the world. Finally, he realized he was witnessing a modern-day case of a past-century crime. But this taking—Chang's taking—was different. In Chang's business model the animals lived. There was some consolation in that, Sheridan thought, but not much. In Chang's world, the animals lost their souls.

88

Des pulled into a parking space and turned off the motor. "Do you have Adam's cell phone number?" he asked Johnny.

"Yes."

"Give it to me and I'll call it." Then he thought about that and changed his mind. "You call him."

"*Why?*"

"Because he might answer."

"What am I supposed to say if he does?"

"Tell him you want to talk."

"About what? And where?"

"The 'what' isn't important. Did you go out with him to dinner, or anyplace?"

"Yes."

"Say you'll meet him at that place."

Johnny hesitated for a moment, staring back at him, saying nothing. Then she bent down to get her purse and pulled out her cell phone. She went into Contacts and pressed a number.

Johnny waited, listening. After a time she shook her head.

"Well, it was a long shot." Des opened the door. "This may be another long shot," he added. "Wait here. *Don't go anywhere.*"

They searched every corner of the vast hall, Des and the contingent of security people at his disposal, but they had come up empty. There was simply no way to find Adam. Of course, Des had had an inkling of that, too. After an hour scoping out the premises, he thanked the staff for its help and returned to his car.

As he approached, he saw Johnny leaning against the side of it, arms crossed in front of her. He walked up to her, his expression saying what he didn't have to verbalize.

"We can try to find him in other ways," he stated. "We'll question his mother, search his cell phone records, contact his employer. He motioned for her to get back in the car. "Let's go."

* * *

Sheridan positioned Chang's computer on his desk, anxious to check the many numbers again against the IUC database. He was comparing files when his cell phone rang. He looked at the screen and recognized the international number.

"We are about to witness an amazing press conference," Isaac said. "You will be seeing some of it, I am sure, on your news."

"Oh, yeah?" Sheridan inquired.

Isaac went on. "Because of its 'egregious infraction against the world'—those were the actual words used by our court—Hasse Pharmaceuticals will be forced to open its research files. I'll let you know what's reported. But I can tell you now, the warehouse snakes most assuredly will play a role."

"No doubt about that. I have information for you as well," Sheridan responded. He explained what he'd found on Chang's computer that implicated him as an accomplice in the German crime. "The numbers jibe with the IUC database," Sheridan added. "I'm sending it to you. It's information you'll want to have. We're working on opening the e-mails."

"That's good news, Sheridan. I should tell you that Hasse is making those available on this end as well."

Sheridan ended the call and returned to searching through the database. His cell phone rang again and, seeing Des's number, he took the call.

"We've come up cold," Des said, concerning his search to find Adam. "There's just no sign of him."

"What do you mean, *we?*" Sheridan asked.

After a pause, Des said, "I have Johnny with me."

It wasn't what Sheridan expected and he didn't understand. "*Why?*"

"She left Vicki's and followed me. We were talking about Chang when you called."

Sheridan felt his stomach turn. "What, exactly?" he asked.

Another pause. "I'll ask and you answer."

"All right."

"Did you say anything to her about our—"

"No."

"She doesn't know that we ever talked to her father?"

"That is correct."

He felt a sense of relief. "I don't think we should say anything to her now about that."

"You are right."

"Are you coming back to the office?" Sheridan asked.

"Tomorrow. Early."

"You can say more now," Sheridan added.

"Okay, yes!" Des exclaimed. "Do you want me to tell Randy to put out an APB nationwide?"

"Not yet," Sheridan answered. "Let's check some other avenues first."

"All right," Des said. "Think I'll stop by Adam's mother's place, see if she can help."

"Good call. I'll see you later." Sheridan closed his phone and put it aside. He sat back, thinking. He would not be confronting the players in his disturbing dream after all—not now, anyway—especially that little girl who was standing on a street corner in San Francisco the day her father was shot. He knew that one way they could make amends in the short term would be to ratchet up their apprehension of Chang and in the process put more than one mind at ease.

But regarding Adam, he had questions that only she could answer.

89

Maryland suburbs
Early Wednesday evening

Des pulled into Adam's mother's driveway. A late-model Ford Taurus sat in front of twin doors to a two-story garage.

"This is a nice house," Johnny said, taking in the Cape Cod-style home.

"You've never been here?" Des asked.

"No."

"He's probably got a nice mother," Des added, opening the door and leaving Johnny sitting by herself again. He walked up to the front door, rang the bell and waited.

Finally, the door opened and a middle-aged woman stared back at him. "Yes?"

"You are Mrs. Hunter?" Des asked.

"Yes. Can I help you?"

"We're trying to find Adam. To ask him some questions."

"Are you with the police?"

"Sort of. I'm a wildlife officer."

Des heard her intake of breath, saw her hand involuntarily reach up to her mouth.

"He…he's not here. I don't know where he is. I *really* don't," she added.

Des realized that in such circumstances he got more by simply saying nothing. He reached into his back pocket, took out his wallet, and held up his badge.

"Oh! They're in the garage," she blurted out.

"Can we see them?" Des asked.

"Yes, of course. He took such good care of them. They weren't harmed in *any* way," she added. "I'll meet you in back," she said, closing the door.

He turned and motioned to Johnny to join him. She did, falling in step with him.

"We may have gotten more than we bargained for," Des said.

They walked the length of the driveway and joined Adam's mother near a side door to the garage.

"I'm sure it's open." She turned the handle. "He won't go to jail, will he?"

The three walked inside and Des recognized the unmistakable smell of reptiles.

"He lives up there," Adam's mother said, pointing above. "That's where his snakes are."

"Does he have permits for them?" Des asked.

"I…I don't know."

"We'll have to check them out," Des said.

"Of course. I'll leave you alone." She regarded Johnny. "Are you a police officer?"

"Yes."

"You're so young."

Johnny smiled, but didn't reply.

"I'll…go now. I don't like snakes," Adam's mother said.

"Can we ask you a few more questions?" Des asked.

"Yes."

"When was the last time you saw your son?"

"Yesterday morning. I saw him leave for work. But he hasn't been back." She looked at Des and said, "You know young men…"

"Did he have a bag, a suitcase with him?" Des asked.

"No. He would tell me if he was leaving. He wouldn't go away and just leave the snakes," she said. "I didn't want them in the house. You understand."

Johnny nodded, then decided to jump in and help Des. "Mrs. Hunter, we want to ask Adam questions about a person he knows."

"A friend?" she asked.

"In a way," Johnny answered.

"I don't know what to tell you," she replied. "I haven't seen him."

"Okay," Johnny said.

When Adam's mother left, they climbed the stairs to the loft. "Remember, by law we can't do a search," Des reminded Johnny. "We're only *looking* at the snakes." He asked again, "You were never here?"

"No!" she answered immediately.

They took in the cramped living quarters, the air conditioners humming in the windows. Des walked by a desk and saw an open cell phone bill on top. He sneezed and several pages fell to the floor. He bent down and coughed. The top page slid away, revealing phone numbers called.

Des rubbed his nose. "Snake dander." He scanned the page. "Johnny, write these down," he said, rattling off a series of numbers.

90

Sheridan looked up from his desk and saw Johnny standing in his doorway.

"Come in," he said. "And close the door."

She did as she was told and sat down without looking at him. Before he could say anything, she started in. "We checked rental car agencies again, and this time we found something."

"Oh?"

"A Toyota dealership found a stray car on its lot. An employee saw that it was a rental and called the agency. It was rented to a Raymond Chou, and Des says that's Chang."

"He's on foot, then," Sheridan said. "He could be anywhere."

She nodded.

"What we'll do now, Johnny, is contact the state police. They'll work with their ports and transportation lines. In a week, if nothing turns up, we'll contact the FBI."

"That may be too late," she said.

"It may be."

Neither said anything. But before Sheridan could begin, Johnny preempted him again.

"I know I shouldn't have trusted Adam."

Sheridan nodded and looked down at his desktop.

"I don't know how or when he suspected me, but he did."

Sheridan nodded a second time.

"I'm sorry," she added. "It won't happen again. That is, if I still have a job."

Sheridan started to answer, but Des opened the door.

"Can I come in?"

"Sure," Sheridan responded, glad to have company during what had become an uncomfortable conversation. He sat back as Des took a seat next to Johnny.

"We were…just talking," Sheridan said to Des, without further explanation. He looked at Johnny and saw a subdued if not depressed young woman.

"Des didn't go into his ocelot story with you?" Sheridan said suddenly, addressing her.

"No," Johnny replied.

"Why don't you?" Sheridan prodded.

Des wondered why this was coming up now, but then sensed he had missed something in their conversation.

"Okay." Des sat forward, elbows on his knees. "Here's the screwup I promised I'd tell you about. I was on a case, undercover, years ago. I had just gotten out of the army, in Texas. I had been an MP, so the Texas wildlife group hired me. The case had to do with guys in the service suspected of catching endangered ocelots—when they could find them—and getting them into the world market via Mexico. The army got involved when Texas Wildlife complained to them. My new employer suspected several Army men, including my former roommate, Marcus. You can see why Texas wanted me involved."

Johnny nodded.

"Except that I wanted to prove them wrong. About my friend." Des paused for effect. "This was a person I knew. We went through basic together. I knew his family." Des sat back and crossed his legs. "But I had turned a blind eye to what essentially was in front of me all the time, primarily his telling me about growing up in the South poaching animals. Anyway, we set up a sting at the border, selling to Mexican nationals. They wanted the cats alive. This is a beautiful animal—"

"Yes," Johnny agreed.

"And they wanted the kittens, especially. I was in charge but not part of the sale, obviously. Texas kept insisting that my old roommate was involved. I thought I knew better. I hinted to Marcus in the broadest way possible about an about-to-commence sting of a very endangered animal. We put it in motion, and of course nothing happened." Des paused, noting Johnny's rapt attention.

"What *did* happen?" she asked.

"Texas suspected me."

Johnny's eyes widened.

"Certainly, from their perspective, I was involved. Marcus could only have learned about the sting from me."

"So...," Johnny said.

"I vehemently denied any role. I offered to take a lie-detector test and passed. Two, actually. Stepping up like that puts you in good stead."

Johnny diverted her eyes for a moment.

"I went to Marcus and told him my new career was on the line. What I thought about the man I knew proved true. He went to the authorities and fessed up, naming his role but not that of the others. In exchange, he got a dishonorable discharge. I haven't seen him since."

"So he was a good guy," Johnny said.

"He had *some* moral underpinnings." Des paused again, and then continued. "But people who get into poaching learn it early and do it often. And you know why."

"Money," Johnny responded.

"*Big* money," Des emphasized.

There was a brief silence, and then Johnny asked, "So, what happened to you?"

"I stayed with Texas for awhile. They were giving me a break. But I didn't think people there trusted me. Then my wife at the time wanted to move back to DC, so…here I am." He thought of something else. "Was this case brought up at Glynco?"

Johnny indicated that it hadn't been.

"Too small, probably," Des said. "The point is, I knew Marcus and would have bet my life on his character. Can you say that about Adam?"

Johnny looked at the floor, suddenly on the spot again. "No," she answered softly.

There was a knock at Sheridan's door. Before responding, he turned to Johnny. "You're going to be fine. And yes, you still have a job." Then he got up and went to the door.

"Someone is here to see you," Kim said. "His name is Curtis Marks."

91

Arlington, Virginia
Thursday morning

"Nice office," Curtis said, coming from behind Kim and walking past her into Sheridan's tight quarters. "It's about as big as mine."

"I got your message," Sheridan said, by way of a greeting. He introduced Johnny and Des, and Curtis extended his hand to shake theirs.

Sheridan asked, "You've found something we can use?"

"In a big way," Curtis replied, putting his briefcase on Sheridan's credenza. "I saw the news in the airport about the cobras in the warehouse. It's all related, isn't it? The research I found, the snakes in Germany."

"As far as we know, yes," Sheridan answered.

Curtis nodded in understanding, then opened his briefcase and took out a thick document. He handed it to Sheridan. "For reading in your spare time."

Sheridan took it and read the title page, with the word CONFIDENTIAL stamped across the front of it.

"Do you want the science behind all of this?" Curtis asked suddenly, crossing his arms in front of him. He leaned against the edge of Sheridan's desk, and appeared to Sheridan a bit smug and full of himself, but ready to proceed.

"That would be helpful," Sheridan answered, putting the document aside. He turned back to his visitor. "Any coffee for you, or a Coke, before we begin?"

"No, I'm fine."

Sheridan held up his hand. He turned to Kim. "Have Lindsay and Eddie come in. And you, too," he added.

Once all were gathered, Curtis began distilling the research he had read in Miami, as well as more on his own.

"It's not just cobras," Curtis said, referring to the investigation he'd become involved in with them. "It's the whole field of venoms, from bees, scorpions, sea snakes—they're all used therapeutically. It's a research field that's exploding. And a lot of it isn't new."

He repositioned himself, now half sitting on the edge of Sheridan's desk.

"Back in 1908, two scientists began looking at cobra venom's use as a medicinal. One had done previous research on the venom of the eastern coral snake, which, as I'm sure you know, is related to the cobra. They set up a lab in Florida to look at the possibility of using venom for diseases in which tremors, stiff gait, anything of a neurological basis, were significant issues." Curtis looked around the room and thought he should explain. "Cobra venom is a neurotoxin. It paralyzes nerves. You can see that I'm talking about something like Parkinson's disease, which at the time was considered simply a part of aging."

Eddie, the department writer, interrupted. "That lab in Florida, 1908—*that's* what I came across in the old report!" He looked at Sheridan and saw him nodding in recognition. "How did you find information about this?"

Curtis pushed up his glasses. "Because the researchers wrote an article that was never published. However, it was referenced quite often in the protocol I read in Miami." He pointed to the document he'd given Sheridan. Curtis paused. "Just because something goes unpublished doesn't mean it goes unnoticed. Their research laid the foundation for the eventual studies that the March of Dimes funded."

A stunned silence enveloped the room.

"I'll explain," Curtis said. "Over the years, other scientists saw what snake venom could do. In the 1950s, researchers started looking at cobra venom for treatment of a particular virus: polio. They postulated that cobra venom interfered with the replication of the virus, meaning that the disease could be stopped."

"How did they know that?" Eddie asked.

"They couldn't have known *how* at the time. They only presumed. But they know now," Curtis answered.

"Who was doing the research?" Sheridan asked.

"A contemporary of that guy on TV, K. C.," Curtis answered. "His name is William Haast, at the Miami Serpentarium."

"Oh, yeah," Sheridan replied, thinking of the other well-known venomous snake collector.

"And a professor friend of his, Murray Sanders, at the University of Miami. Their research had enough weight behind it that the March of Dimes funded it. But when the polio vaccine was developed, their study died on the vine. But not really. The professor had seen how effective cobra venom had been in dismantling a virus, although nothing was yet understood at the molecular level. He moved on to another neurological disease: ALS—Lou Gehrig's disease. Over two decades, Sanders started injecting ALS patients with cobra venom. And guess what?"

He looked around the room as people waited for him to continue. "Their disease stopped. Sanders started proclaiming cobra venom a cure for ALS. But then the FDA stepped in."

Curtis hesitated. He shook his head and crossed his arms before continuing. "We're in the late 1970s now. The FDA wanted regulated clinical trials set up, so they set them up. But they were short-duration studies that didn't follow Sanders's own trials. The FDA studies showed no gain, so people stopped taking the venom. Later, Sanders went back—now we're in the early 1980s—and compared people who had continued *his* venom treatment against those who hadn't, and then compared *both* to a baseline survival time of forty-two months."

Curtis explained, "The accepted, expected time from first diagnosis of ALS to death is forty-two months. Here's what Sanders found: Those who had taken cobra venom but stopped survived sixty-two months. Those who continued the venom treatment survived seventy-seven months. And longer." Curtis let the figures settle in before he went on. "Pretty amazing, from a natural toxin against a deadly disease."

He turned suddenly to Johnny. "But then, the Chinese had known all about cobra venom for centuries, using it for arthritis and cancer."

Startled, Johnny looked up and nodded in agreement.

"And in India it was used for epilepsy," Curtis added, "for *thousands* of years."

"Hang on a sec," Lindsay interrupted. "How did the original patients get cobra venom when the FDA had intervened?"

"You can get venom anywhere," Curtis answered, pushing up his glasses again. "People sell venom. Was it against the law that Sanders injected people with venom? Not really. ALS is a deadly disease with no known cure. Was he wrong in proclaiming venom a cure for ALS? *Possibly*."

Curtis turned to Eddie. "Back to your question: venom knocks out a virus's RNA. Researchers had known for some time that venom is an analgesic and has *antiviral* properties. The reason is the RNA factor. But here's the point I want to make. What was found early on is that cobra venom is active against *particular* viruses. What was found recently, by Hasse Pharmaceuticals in Germany, is that *king* cobra venom is active against *all* of them. The venom from this snake, given in doses yet to be established, *protects* the body from the deadly effects of viruses."

Silence engulfed the room. Curtis repositioned himself and waited, it seemed, for questions. "Do you see where this is headed, and why this snake is so valuable?"

Eddie offered, "I would imagine a vaccine."

"Yes," Curtis answered.

"A cure for cancer," Des added.

"Possibly," Curtis replied.

The sound of Sheridan's desk phone ringing startled everyone. Sheridan answered, and the assembled group watched him and waited. Finally, after speaking to his caller for a few moments, Sheridan put the call on speaker mode.

"Go ahead, Isaac," Sheridan said.

"I wanted you to know that Hasse Pharmaceuticals is taking full responsibility for everything that's happened with the cobras," Isaac began. "Its president went on TV this afternoon and told the country about its drug research and the procurement of snakes. Two executives also talked to investigators about their dealings with a Leland Chang, so your computer information will help implicate him, Sheridan, as do all the e-mails on this end."

He went on, "Essentially, our court found Hasse guilty of CITES violations and then added its own fines, for the following reasons: Hasse took what it needed, but it also took enough so that no one else would have access to a natural resource. It's *that* point—the willful taking, harboring, endangering, *monopolizing* leading to *destroying* a species in the wild—that riled the court. And like your U.S. system, monopolizing a commodity is what landed Hasse the stiffest sentence."

"What will happen to the snakes?" Sheridan asked.

"Those details are being worked out. It appears that Hasse will pay the IUC and nations individually to put the snakes back where they belong," Isaac answered, "although they'll never know which ones belong where. I imagine the public relations firm

Hasse hires to tidy up the damage will cost them even more. The PR fallout has been significant, with front-page headlines and TV coverage everywhere. They've had to answer to angry shareholders and pissed-off animal rights groups, which you know can be quite militant in Europe."

"So, essentially the IUC will work to reverse what Chang put in motion," Sheridan said.

"Exactly," Isaac said. "Do you want to know *why* Hasse took all those king cobras?"

Sheridan glanced at Curtis. "We've already been briefed on that."

"Absolutely amazing, isn't it, that this could happen in today's world?" Isaac asked.

Sheridan thought about it. "Isaac, you know better than that."

92

Somewhere in the Pacific Ocean
One week later

The ship rocked rhythmically on the ocean's waves. Thankfully, no one was vomiting. They had been at sea three days. Four more to go. This trek was not at all what he had in mind, heading back to Hong Kong in a forty-foot container. All he had worked for—all that money—lost. All he had now was his freedom.

Chang tried to convince himself that that was enough.

He leaned back against the side of the metal container, feeling its coolness, and perused his onboard mates as best he could in the darkness. All were men, seven of them were going back home. Not the usual route for stowaways. But sometimes it was necessary to go back. They all had their own stories. He didn't want to hear any of them.

Chang studied the silhouettes across from him and tried to pick out Adam's. Why had he allowed him to come? Because Adam had youth on his side and was willing to do anything. Chang could overlook his many limitations, which he chalked up to age and inexperience. More importantly, with the snake business over—and, he was sure, the German pharmaceutical company taking the fallout—he would need another hand when he took on his next venture. It was another large job for a client he had known briefly in the past, a wealthy man who specifically mentioned his interest in American eagles. Having an American involved was nothing short of perfect.

Chang smelled something foul. The man next to him had fallen asleep and was leaning toward him. He pushed him violently and the man woke up. Chang said something and he moved away.

Chang swatted at a fly somewhere in front of him. Formerly well groomed, he looked down at his clothing. His pants were stained and torn from getting in and out of train cars after a week on the run. He fingered a hole in the sleeve of his Brooks Brothers white Egyptian cotton dress shirt. He tried not to think about how long he had been wearing his one pair of socks.

Chang scratched at his scraggly beard and pushed away the hair that fell around his face. Four more days in this container, and it will only get worse, he reminded himself.

He repositioned himself and thought through what would come next. He—they—would disembark after the container was taken off the ship and placed in the holding yard. Hopefully, they could get out before it was put on a train or truck. He had experience with just such a situation. It was how he had escaped what the U.S. referred to as Operation Chameleon. Chang imagined the men around him had thought through their next moves as well.

He decided he would help none of them.

93

"So we're done with this?" Egan asked, pausing but not looking up.

"To the best of our knowledge, yes," Sheridan replied.

Egan, newly back from his Maine vacation, closed the cover of the report and put it to one side. Finally, he looked up at his deputies. Sheridan sat in his usual seat in front of his desk. Des leaned against the door frame. Neither had spoken while Egan read the summary accompanying the eight-page report about the case they now referred to as Op King Cobra.

"This was one of the largest takings of a natural resource in history," Sheridan stated. "The only thing that matches it in modern times is Dave Hall's alligator case."

"Germany is working with the IUC to disperse the snakes," Des added.

"Thailand will be appeased," Egan said.

Sheridan nodded in agreement. "It's a guesstimate, of course, how many each country should get. But Thailand will receive the bulk of them."

"Speaking of that," Egan interjected, "the State Department is doing a photo op when the secretary's there tomorrow."

"Of course," Sheridan replied. He'd learned long ago how politicians stepped forward when the outcome was a positive one.

Egan paused for a moment. "So Chang was here and now he's gone."

Des and Sheridan both nodded in agreement.

"We have his prints when he came through Dulles," Des said.

"Which we didn't have before," Sheridan added.

"I don't think he'll risk coming back," Des surmised.

"Wasn't his name flagged?" Egan asked.

"Yes," Des answered, "but not the alias on the passport he used to enter this time."

Egan paused again. "What about the logistics around all of this? How'd Chang do it?"

Sheridan shook his head in amazement. "You know, Simpson finally explained it to me," he said, referring to the Fish and Wildlife's statistician at the Ashland Forensics Laboratory. "In essence, Chang used the IUC database to get counts of king cobras, and then figured out mathematically how to take enough in each country to drop the resource base. He had a plan to corner the market and kill a native species at the same time, so that the only king cobras alive would be in a research lab. *One* research lab."

"He must have had help," Egan said.

"I would imagine so," Des said.

"So, we won't know if the resource base has recovered for several years," Egan added.

"Right," Sheridan replied. "He had five years to put his plan in motion, if he started right after the last IUC count. Then factor in another year for the figures to be made public."

"What about the company behind all this? Egan asked. "What's happening with that?"

"As part of the court order, Hasse had to open its files," Sheridan explained. "Instead of one company with a research discovery, there might be five companies now."

"Hopefully, balance will be put back in play," Des said. "Boys in Asia can catch the snakes and the labs can buy them in the markets without disrupting the species. But we're back to square one on this," he added, changing the subject. "We need a federal law creating an international database of people who buy and trade exotic animals."

Egan looked at his two deputies in disbelief. "You know as well as I do that cases like this involve no laws and no treaties. We can put any law we want in place and nothing will change," he added.

"I'd like to think that this case might start moving things in the right direction," Sheridan replied.

Egan chose not to answer. He glanced at his watch and addressed Sheridan. "Thanks for all of your work on this. Let's move on to CoP Eighteen," he said, referring to the international meeting coming up. But then he thought of something else. "Why was Chang *here?*"

Sheridan looked at Des before answering. "We can only speculate that he was here to see K. C."

"And you found no involvement by K. C.?"

"No, we didn't," Sheridan answered. "We do know that Chang was acquainted with one of the Beltway collectors. That was information given to us by K. C." Sheridan nodded toward the report. "It's all in there."

Egan nodded. "And the rookie?"

There was a slight pause before Des answered. "She was a help. And she'll be fine."

"Good." Egan turned in his chair to leave. Before doing so, he addressed both of them again. "You did a great job on a difficult assignment. And no one will congratulate you more than I will."

The meeting finished, Egan got up and left.

Des looked over at his partner. "That's because no one will congratulate us *at all!*"

* * *

Back at his desk, Sheridan began reading through the eight or so e-mails that had come in over the course of the last forty-five minutes. He saw one from his stepbrother and opened it:

> Jim: *Amazing story about the snakes! I'm in DC again in October. I'll call you.*

Sheridan smiled. He would need to tell his stepbrother how he had helped him solve the case. He continued on. He saw an e-mail from Vicki and opened it immediately:

> *Marsh mentioned his talk with you. This could be perfect for us. Are you interested?*

Des popped in and Sheridan looked up at him.

"What are you doing this weekend?" Des asked.

Sheridan knew that he and Carole were trying their best to make sure he remained busy since Vicki's departure. It must show, he surmised, how much he missed her.

Sheridan sat back in his chair. "Well, we're going to the Orioles' game tomorrow." He shrugged. "Pretty open, actually."

"Come for a barbecue Sunday?" Des asked.

"Sure."

"Around three o'clock."

"Okay."

"Bring Jason."

"Great."

Des left and Sheridan went back to work, opening news briefs and reading through meeting minutes. He saw an e-mail from Isaac at INTERPOL and opened it.

> *I'm afraid I have bad news about David Shelton. His body and that of a former Bangkok police officer were found in a river. More will come of this, I'm sure. I'll be in London for the funeral.*

Isaac's message was a complete shock. Sheridan had forgotten to ask about David's whereabouts. He sat back and thought of the few times he had had contact with him. "A good man," he said, to no one in particular. Perhaps Hasse would be implicated in his death? That seemed unreal. Or was it, given all that had happened already?

He read the last of Isaac's e-mail:

> *Don't know what you've seen in the American press about the cobras. It was big news here. Germany knew it had a public relations event and took full advantage of it. Here's a photo.*

Sheridan opened the attachment, and to his amazement saw men, women, kids, people in wheelchairs—the line extending for blocks in the old warehouse district—waiting for a chance to see 151,992 king cobras. The sheer number hard to comprehend.

Would that happen here? he asked himself. Would people be that interested?

Probably so, he decided.

94

Camden Yards
Saturday afternoon

Sheridan sat in the stands with Jason watching the Orioles
soundly defeating the visiting White Sox, a meaningless game for
the home team, with their last-place standing and a playoff spot
out of the question. Across from them, the sun cast a late-after-
noon glow on some empty seats.

Sheridan sipped his beer as Jason sat quietly, his mitt at the
ready, waiting for a wayward foul ball. He ran his hand through
his son's hair, then looked back at the players on the field, their
eyes focused on the batter, waiting for something to happen.

He thought about Vicki's e-mail, the double entendre clear as
day: *Are you interested?*

He knew his opportunity to start fresh in the West and
be with her was at hand, a time that might never come again.
Sheridan stretched his legs over the empty seat in front of him.
There was no more thinking about it, he reasoned. He had made
up his mind. He took out his cell phone and called her.

"What are you doing?" Sheridan asked, after she answered.

"I'm standing naked in the bedroom," she replied.

He shifted in his seat and glanced at Jason. "Tell me more."

"I'm walking toward the shower. I'm a bit sweaty."

"Hmm," he said.

"I've been out exploring the grounds that this nice house sits
on," she added.

"Sounds good." He heard water running in the background.

"I've been tracking some birds, a ferruginous hawk and a cinnamon teal. I took pictures and I'm going to paint them."

"Great."

"I know you'd love the wide openness out here," she added.

He heard the sound of water getting louder.

"Tell me what *you're* doing," Vicki said.

"We're at a game," he said. "The Orioles will win, but will go nowhere with it."

"What would you *like* to be doing?" she asked.

Sheridan glanced again at Jason, who had his mitt up near his face, covering his nose.

He didn't have to think about how to answer that. Instead, he asked about her painting.

"Have you finished the oriole?"

"No. It's still packed."

"I want to watch you finish it," he said. "I want to watch you paint."

"You're coming, then?" she asked.

He laughed. Another double entendre. She was good at this.

"Yes." He heard a scream.

Jason heard it, too. "Dad, what's wrong with Vicki?"

"Nothing, nothing," he said to Jason, putting his arm around him. Then, to Vicki, "I'll call you later and we can talk. In detail."

* * *

Warren Anderson, former Beltway collector and newly separated from his short-term relationship with his girlfriend, finished moving boxes into his new place. He kicked lighter ones overflowing with sheets and towels into a bedroom. Back in the living room, he carefully picked up two terrariums, each with a small snake inside, and placed them on a rack in a corner.

He heard his cell phone ring and scrambled to find it, brushing aside crumpled newspaper on a tabletop.

"Warren here," he answered. "Hey, man. How's it going?"

He unpacked plates while he listened to his caller.

"I expect it at any moment," Warren answered.

The doorbell in his apartment rang. Warren rushed to the window and looked outside.

"It's here! I'll call you back," he said, and flipped the phone closed.

Warren ran down the stairs and opened the door. A FedEx delivery person handed him a package and he signed for it. Then, holding the box a good distance away from him, he climbed the stairs back to his apartment.

Back in the game!

End Notes

Many resources exist for information about U.S. wildlife laws and international treaties developed to protect exotic species. A good starting point is the U.S. Department of the Interior's Fish and Wildlife Service Web site, especially the Service's history and online annual reports.

Here is a list of books, medical journals, and Web sites consulted during the writing of this book.

Books

Dolin, Eric Jay. *Fur, Fortune and Empire: The Epic History of the Fur Trade in America*. New York: W. W. Norton & Company, 2010.

Goddard, Ken. *Prey*. New York: Tor Books, 1992.

Goddard, Ken. *Wildfire*. New York: Forge Publishing, 1994.

Green, Alan, and the Center for Public Integrity. *Animal Underworld: Inside America's Black Market for Rare and Exotic Species*. New York: Public Affairs, 1999.

Grosz, Terry. *For Love of Wilderness: The Journal of a U.S. Game Management Agent*. Boulder, Colorado: Johnson Books, 2000.

Grosz, Terry. *No Safe Refuge: Man as Predator in the World of Wildlife*. Boulder, Colorado: Johnson Books, 2003.

Grosz, Terry. *The Thin Green Line: Outwitting Poachers, Smugglers & Market Hunters*. Boulder, Colorado: Johnson Books, 2004.

Grosz, Terry. *Wildlife Wars*. Boulder, Colorado: Johnson Books, 1999.

Reisner, Marc. *Game Wars: The Undercover Pursuit of Wildlife Poachers*. London: Martin Secker & Warburg, Ltd., 1991.

Rinella, Steven. *American Buffalo: In Search of a Lost Icon*. New York: Spiegel & Grau, 2008.

Scully, Matthew. *Dominion: The Power of Man, the Suffering of Animals, and the Call to Mercy*. New York: St. Martin's Press, 2002.

Medical Journals

Chippaux J. P., V. Williams, and J. White. "Snake Venom Variability: Methods of Study, Results and Interpretation." *Toxicon* 29, 11 (1991): 1279–303.

Daltry, J. C., W. Wuster, and R. S. Thorpe. "Diet and Snake Venom Evolution." *Nature* 379 (1996): 537–40.

Frazer, T. R. "The Rendering of Animals Immune Against the Venom of the Cobra and Other Serpents and the Antidotal Properties of the Blood Serum of Immunized Animals." *Br Med J* 1 (1895): 1309–12.

Gold, B. S., R. C. Dart, and R. A. Barish. "Bites of Venomous Snakes." *N Engl J Med* 347 (2002): 347–56.

Gomes, A., S. Bhattacharya, M. Chakraborty, et al. "Anti-arthritic Activity of Indian Monocellate Cobra (Naja Kaouthia) Venom on Adjuvant Induced Arthritis." *Toxicon* 55, 2–3 (2010): 670–73.

Grasset, E. "The Cobra Neurotoxin; Pharmacology and Clinical Applications in the Treatment of Pain." *Med Hyg* (Geneve) 10, 212 (1952): 55–58.

Hills, R. G., and W. M. Firor. "The Use of More Potent Cobra Venom for Intractable Pain." *Am Surg* 18, 9 (1952): 875–79.

Hinman, C. L., R. Stevens-Truss, C. Schwarz, and R. A. Hudson. "Sequence Determinants of Modified Cobra Venom Neurotoxin Which Induce Immune Resistance to Experimental Allergic Encephalomyelitis: Molecular Mechanisms for Immunologic Action." *Immunopharmacol Immunotoxicol* 21, 3 (1999): 483–506.

Kordis, D., and F. Gubensek. "Adaptive Evolution of Animal Toxin Multigene Families." *Gene* 261 (2000): 43–52.

Lamb, G. "On the Serum Therapeutics of Cases of Snake Bite." *Lancet* ii (1904): 1273–77.

Lentz, T. C., and M. Wilson. "Neurotoxin-binding Site on the Acetylcholine Receptor." *Int Rev Neurobiol* 29 (1988): 117–60.

Li, X. B., M. J. Chen, D. Q. Lei, et al. "Bioactivities of Nerve Growth Factor from Chinese Cobra Venom." *J Nat Toxins* 8, 3 (1999): 359–62.

Liang, Y. X., L. P. Han, W. J. Jiang, and S. J. Zhao. "Isolation and Pharmacological Properties of Analgesic Fraction from Venom of Naja Naja Atra." *Zhong Yao Cai* 32, 7 (2009): 1022–25.

Lin, S. R., S. H. Chi, L. S. Chang, et al. "Chemical Modification of Cationic Residues in Toxin A from King Cobra (Ophiophagus Hannah) Venom." *J Protein Chem* 15 (1996): 95–101.

Looareesuwan, S., C. Viravan, and D. A. Warrell. "Factors Contributing to Fatal Snake Bite in the Tropics: Analysis of 46 Cases in Thailand." *Trans R Soc Trop Med Hyg* 82 (1988): 930–34.

Macht, D. I. "Experimental and Clinical Study of Cobra Venom as an Analgesic." *Proc Natl Acad Sci USA* 22, 1 (1936): 61–71.

Martin, B. M., B. A. Chibber, and A. Maelicke. "The Sites of Neurotoxicity in A-Cobratoxin." *J Biol Chem* 258, 14 (1983): 8714–22.

Miller, K. D., G. G. Miller, M. Sanders, and O. Fellowes. "Inhibition of Virus-Induced Plaque Formation by Atoxic Derivatives of Purified Cobra Neurotoxins." *Biochem Biophys Acta* 496 (1977): 192–96.

Modahl, C. M., R. Doley, and R. M. Kini. "Venom Analysis of Long-Term Captive Pakistan Cobra (Naja Naja) Populations." *Toxicon* 55, 2–3 (2010): 612–18.

Mohamed, A., P. F. Reid, L. Raymond, and T. Dufan. "Amelioration of Acute and Relapsing Stages of the Experimental Allergic Encephalomyelitis by Cobra Toxins." *Biomed Sci Instrum* 42 (2006): 399–404.

Mundy, H. R., S. J. Jones, J. C. Hobart, et al. "A Randomized Controlled Trial of Modified Cobratoxin in Adrenomyeloneuropathy." *Neurology* 61 (2003): 528–30.

Neri, P., L. Bracci, M. Rustici, and A. Santucci. "Sequence Homology Between HIV Gp120, Rabies Virus Glycoprotein, and Snake Venom Neurotoxins. Is the Nicotinic Acetylcholine Receptor an HIV Receptor?" *Arch Virol* 114 (1990): 265–69.

Reid, P. F. "Alpha-Cobratoxin as a Possible Therapy for Multiple Sclerosis: A Review of the Literature Leading to Its Development of This Application." *Crit Rev Immunol* 27, 4 (2007): 291–302.

Rivera, V. M., M. Grabois, W. Deaton, et al. "Modified Snake Venom in Amyotrophic Lateral Sclerosis." *Arch Neurol* 37 (1979): 201–03.

Sabin, A. B. "Behavior of Chimpanzee Avirulent Poliomyelitis Viruses in Experimentally Infected Human Volunteers." *Am J Med Sci* 230, 1 (1955): 1–8.

Salk, J. E. "Studies in Human Subjects on Active Immunization Against Poliomyelitis. I. A Preliminary Report of Experiments in Progress." *JAMA* 151, 13 (1953): 1081–98.

Sanders, M., and O. N. Fellowes. "Use of Detoxified Snake Neurotoxin as a Partial Treatment for Amyotrophic Lateral Sclerosis." *Cancer Cytol* 15 (1975): 26–30.

Sanders, M., M. G. Soret, and B. Akin. "Neurotoxoid Interference with Two Human Strains of Poliomyelitis in Rhesus Monkeys." *Ann NY Acad Sci* 58 (1953): 1–12.

Sanders, M., M. G. Soret, and B. Akin. "Naja Flava Neurotoxoid Interference Late in Experimental Poliomyelitis." *J Path Bact* 68 (1954): 1267.

Sanders, M., M. G. Soret, B. A. Akin, and L. Roizin. "Neurotoxoid Interference in Macacus Rhesus Infected Intramuscularly with Poliovirus." *Science* 127 (1958): 594–96.

Tyler, H. R. "Double-blind Study of Modified Neurotoxin in Motor Neuron Disease." *Neurology* 29 (1979): 77–81.

Westhoff, G., M. Boetig, H. Bleckmann, and B. A. Young. "Target Tracking During Venom 'Spitting' By Cobras." *J Exp Biol* 213 (2010): 1797–802.

Zhang, H. L., R. Han, Z. X. Chen, et al. "Analgesic Effects of Receptin, a Chemically Modified Cobratoxin from Thailand Cobra Venom." *Neurosci Bull* 22, 5 (2006): 267–73.

Web Sites

http://www.cites.org – Convention on International Trade in Endangered Species of Wild Fauna and Flora (CITES)

http://www3.imperial.ac.uk/cpb/research/patterns-andprocesses/gpdd – Global Population Dynamics Database (GPDD)

http://www.interpol.int/ – International Criminal Police Organization (INTERPOL)

http://www.iunc.org – International Union for the Conservation of Nature (IUNC) http://www.fws.gov/ – U.S. Fish & Wildlife Service (USFWS)

http://www.oie.int/wahis/public.php?page=home   –   World Animal Health Information Database (WAHID)

http://www.worldwildlife.org – World Wildlife Fund (WWF)